CW01080733

Alex Halpern is just 16 years old
he attends Rochester Indepe:
parents, two younger brothers ᴀɴᴅ ... ᴠᴇ., — , _
always been a big fan of the horror genre and therefore chose this
for 'House of Wolves', his first novel.

Part of the original idea of 'House of Wolves' was inspired by
ideas originating from other horror stories and various activities
and experiences he has encountered. A lot of his inspiration also
comes from music which he enjoys, of which often the lyrics, style
and themes have triggered ideas for future work.

As well as being interested by writing as a hobby, Alex also enjoys
reading, acting and directing in his free time, and plans to take that
into a career position in the future.

Alex's preferred literature to read is social commentary, as well as
other genres of fiction including fantasy and science fiction. Alex's
favourite authors include Christopher Ransom, Stephen King,
Dan Brown and John Steinbeck, because of their creativity,
atmosphere within their work, and their themes which they create
and evolve throughout the progression their intriguing stories.

In the future, Alex plans to write many more novels and expand
into a variety of genres, although horror is his personal favourite.
This year he is entering sixth form to participate in his A Level
studies.

He would like to thank Tim Hirst, Louise McDonald, Robert
Hammond, and Edward Smyth for making all this happen.
Alex would also like to thank every last one of his family and
friends who have supported him during the planning and writing
of the novel, and continue to inspire him every day to carry on
and do more.

HOUSE OF WOLVES

ALEX HALPERN

House of Wolves
Alex Halpern

First Published in the UK in December 2010 by Hirst Publishing

Hirst Publishing, Suite 285 Andover House, George Yard,
Andover, Hants, SP10 1PB

ISBN 978-1-907959-19-6

Cover Design by Robert Hammond

Printed and bound by Good News Digital Books

Paper stock used is natural, recyclable and made from wood grown in
sustainable forests. The manufacturing processes conform to
environmental regulations.

www.hirstbooks.com

"It is not through any other emotion which flows within our blood that the soul of our character may change. However, through the wake of rage within the mind, that is when the monster shall arise and take effect upon all those around them."

Introduction

Fear. One simple emotion that dominates all human thoughts. It is the presence of something so powerful it is too disturbing to even look back upon. Many events like this have happened to any archetypical human being that this is no longer countable. When a surfer comes face to face with a shark, when a small child comes face to face with a spider which seems so enormous to their size, when a man or women must face their greatest fears and shut out all other thoughts around them, these are their most terrifying ordeals.

Many have fallen prey to these foes, because that is what they want us to feel, to tremble and cower at the shock and horror of what they are imposing.

Yet for those who have fought back, this is a different matter entirely. To conquer and dominate what has partly possessed their own mind is a new level of bravery and a struggle to win back their sanity. This is a tale of one such story, when the Barrow family decided to stray from the path of Dilas Forest, eager to discover more, only to become trapped in their darkest nightmare. Whilst trying to survive the night they encountered a series of terrifying forms; wolves, death, insanity; but worst of all, they encountered something monstrous, dwelling in the forest, emerging under the moonlight, and never giving rest.

This is their story.

Chapter 1:   Return Beyond Shadow

The door opened quietly, dim rays of sunlight spilling in from the world outside. The room was dark and musty, as the sinister figure entered the space. The area was almost completely empty apart from one large steel desk in the centre with a light shining down upon it. Behind the table facing the door, was another eerie, sinister figure, covered in darkness with only small parts of his plain clothing revealed in the light.

The door closed shut slowly and quietly behind the first individual, leaving them both in the dim light of the lamp, isolated and blocked out from the rest of the world. Steadily and easily, the first figure came slowly from the door towards the chair facing the other form on the opposite side. He pulled out the chair and sat down gradually, slightly nervous to face the other, who was hidden in the dimness.

"I'm sorry I'm late," he said gently, laying out a list of files across the table. His voice was smooth and calm. "How are you feeling today?" He opened up one of the files and removed a recorder from within. Placing it on the table softly, he looked back up at the silent figure who sat before him.

The voiceless stature ignored his question, and did not open its mouth in reply.

The first man breathed out a long, drawn breath, as if trying to settle down into the situation. He picked up the small recorder and held it out before the spine-chilling silhouette.

"Are you ready to answer any questions yet?" he asked kindly.

There was a long, awkward silence in which the tension between the two characters grew thicker and thicker. The first man was waiting patiently and rather anxiously for the other being's response. Silence echoed throughout the room, like the wind it swept through and haunted the eerie, secluded chamber.

Finally, after a few long minutes, the silent figure answered back gravely.

"All I remember was the blood and the anger."

The reporter clicked on the recorder as fast as he could when he heard this news. Yet he almost jumped back in surprise from this horrible response.

"I'm sorry sir?" he held the microphone back slightly to respond to the question, only to raise it back up again once more, waiting for a reply.

Once more, a sinister silence followed.

"Why have you called me here today, Mr Wilson?" the concealed form asked suspiciously.

The reporter hesitated nervously, the sweat upon his brow beginning to show.

"Well, sir, I was wondering if, well maybe, if you're up to it, if you could explain your story. I am a researcher and an investigator. Not one of your usual paparazzi members." He smiled at the edges of his mouth weakly. Mr Wilson was a kind man, and respected those whom he interviewed.

"Very well," replied the dark shape opposite him on the table after a moment's pause. "It is starting to come back to me, that night of horrors, only to be followed by a day of bloody revenge. This was a nightmare we all stepped into, and couldn't seem to break out of. I'd do anything to erase the past and change the future, but this is fate. And we can't stop it."

Mr Wilson watched curiously. He could not see the figure's face, since it was covered behind the veil of darkness around the desk beyond the ray of light hanging from above. He held the microphone outwards, greedy for that precious material that is knowledge. Suddenly, a hand reached out from the shadow curtain and rested upon the small desk before him. Mr Wilson tried not to grimace in

9

repulse as he looked down at the foul, disturbing sight, his pulse beginning to race faster.

The hand was twisted and deformed. Two fingers were missing and the rest of the arm was thankfully covered up by his sleeves. Wilson was now becoming extremely nervous as he sat in his now not so comfortable chair. Whatever this person had been through, it must have been agony beyond all others.

The ominous voice spoke once more. "However. There is one thing that you must understand before I tell you my story."

The investigator paused in surprise unexpectedly. "Why, yes. Of course." He waited patiently for a reply.

The usual pause spread out across the room, creating a merge of tension and trepidation. Finally, the figure responded.

"By telling you this information, I will have condemned you."

"But, what do you mean?" Wilson answered in surprise, not quite understanding what the strange man had meant.

"They know. They always know. They will find out, and they will come for you."

"I'm sorry? Who's they?" he wondered curiously.

"Them. What we encountered that night amongst the trees and darkness." He breathed out a long sigh which rasped and wheezed. "They will come for you Mr Wilson. They will find you and they will kill you."

Wilson was quite taken aback by this odd remark. He still didn't understand what was going on. Yet that was his job, to find out. Kind and believing as he was, Wilson was not a man who listened to too many ghost stories.

"Well. I'm sorry to disappoint Sir, but I am not really one to believe any of that kind of business, I'm afraid…"

"Listen to me!" shouted the figure at the top of his lungs, lunging forward in his seat and slamming his fists down heavily upon the table. That was when Mr Wilson saw the horror behind the mask of shadows, as the strange shape that was sitting before him passed into the ray of light hanging from the ceiling. He almost screamed in shock as he saw the traumatising face of whom he was interviewing.

It was a young man, who looked around the age of twenty. His face was brutally battered and scarred all over, with severe cuts which carved deep into his skin. His hair was washed and cleaned as if it had been prepared for the interview, unlike the rest of his face. On the right hand side of his jaw, a huge chunk seemed to have been carved out, revealing swollen gums, layered flesh and fading white teeth beneath. His eyes were wide and bloodshot with anger and fear. This poor victim must have been through so much to end up in this terrible position.

Wilson gulped in alarm and continued fearfully again. "Okay, I'm sorry. Please carry on." He was almost shaking with terror, trying desperately to hide his revolt.

The young, deformed man sat slowly back into his seat, and breathed out another one of his long, rasping breaths. "When you called me for this interview Mr Wilson, I was eager to share my story with you. Hoping that you would understand the true monstrosity of which I went through to bring this news to you today. You are the first to hear me speak of this." He stood up slowly from his chair, twisted, injured hands hanging by his sides, and walked slowly over to the wall behind him. His grey shirt and casual blue jeans caught fragments of light as he passed. He stood there for a moment, bowing his head and sighed. "Yet you may also be the last. Due to certain circumstances I will most likely not be explaining this story to any others."

Wilson felt rather taken aback, yet also proud inside that he had managed to arrange this. He also felt a wave of dread tremble down his spine.

"So when I choose to explain this, Mr Wilson, I suggest that you should listen closely." He turned to face the tubby,

11

keen man sitting there at the desk. His jaw wound glinted in the dim light, creating an eerie, haunting effect upon him.

"Of course sir," replied the blonde reporter in awe of the character's bravery and determination. "That's why I've come here. To hear your fascinating story and discover more."

There was a short pause, as the dark man stood there thinking. "Very well. I shall tell you my story."

Wilson was more excited now. He was about to uncover a rare piece of news which had never been heard before. This was going to be the longest night of his life. He picked up the tape recorder once more and prepared himself for the what-may-be intriguing story.

The tall, dark haired young man remained standing. He looked to the ground, thinking hard to himself, remembering it all as it flooded back.

"My name is Max Barrow," he said confidently yet sternly to Mr Wilson. "Exactly one year ago, I entered a world of terror, and remembered why humans were once afraid of the darkness."

Chapter 2: The Monster Inside

Jason stubbed out the cigarette into the ash tray on his large, wooden desk. He breathed out a huge breath of air as smoke gushed from his mouth placidly like a waterfall. He coughed, looking down at the local newspaper. The room was dark and dim, with only a desk-side lamp to light up the surroundings. Several objects lay sprawled across Jason's desk. A collection of the local weekly newspapers from the past month, an old rusty telephone wired up to a nearby socket in the cracked dry wall, an ashtray filled with at least a dozen old cigarettes and a mysterious photo album bound in dirty black leather. He hardly ever looked inside it. Only when a certain article would appear in the newspapers then he would turn the ancient rotting pages and add to its contents.

Jason sighed as he turned the newspaper over to read the disturbing front page headline. *Group of friends missing in Dilas Forest.* He closed his eyes briefly in shock and disappointment, before slowly reaching down into his black leather jacket pocket and pulling out another packet of cigarettes. Rolling his eyes, he pulled one out and lit it with his lighter from on the old, wooden counter. He puffed smoke from his mouth, seeping upwards like a snake into the air this time. His eyes scanned the page down and down, reading further and further into the article's depth.

Last week a group of students from north Cambridgeshire were reported missing by local friends and family. They were known to have departed on a hiking trip in the woodland and country area between Cambridge and Peterborough. Jason choked on his cigarette, as it came tumbling out of his mouth and burnt in a crisp pile on the floor. The article was right. It was Dilas Forest where they had disappeared. He continued to read on. *The group consisted of four students from Cambridge University, all bright*

13

academics studying in different subjects. The group of friends were reported to have discussed their route to their families before their departure. Becky Swindell, Jack Carner, Bradley Farlon and Elizabeth Winchester were planning to follow the country roads through towards south Peterborough using their developed map reading skills. Jason began to scan the page faster and faster. His eyes were darting from left to right like a bullet. *Searches will be conducted as soon as the local police have gathered enough information to start.* Jason's eyes widened. A sudden pulse of nervousness rushed through his body. What if they came here? What if the whole operation itself was shut down? This was not possible. Without the guards of Dilas Forest, the country would not be safe. For what they were hiding was far beyond the world of spoken tongue. It was a much darker matter which had to be concealed, for the fate of all those close to them and more.

"What is it this time?"

Jason spun around in his chair so fast he almost toppled over backwards in surprise. Markus, a tall dark-skinned sinister man with jet black uniform strode through the nearby door and into the musty, smoke-filled office. He pulled out a lighter from his leather belt and snatched one of Jason's cigarettes from the table. With the lighter in his hand and lighting the cigarette, he spoke sternly to Jason.

"So tell me who went missing this time? Another group of scientists?" He stared down at Jason, his big, dark brown, glaring eyes were unnerving and intimidating. A huge scar lay gashed across his left eye, although no one knew the reasons how he got it. Jason coughed and switched back to the newspaper. Recoiling from the shock of Markus' sudden entrance, he replied "No, this time it was a group of students from Cambridge. Becky Swindell, Jack Carner, Bradley Farlon and Elizabeth Winchester. They went missing a couple of days ago, apparently here. The police are gonna start searching soon though." He looked back up at Markus, waiting for a response.

14

Markus removed the cigarette from his mouth with two fingers and breathed out a long wave of smoke.

"Well that makes a difference." His voice was cold and icy. He had always given Jason the creeps, ever since Jason had first joined the organisation two years ago. "I'm getting sick of hearing the same old news of geologists and inexperienced scientists going missing in these woods." He chuckled cruelly, putting the cigarette back into his mouth again and sucking at the warm tobacco smoke from within. "And they don't even have a clue." His grin was twisted. "They come and go in their numbers: the scientists studying the environment, the families on their holidays, and the students on their excursions. And yet there is always one. One group which doesn't listen. We tell them to leave once the siren sounds and they just carry on. They're like flies Jason. Like bugs with no common sense."

He turned back to Jason once more, who was staring up at Markus with unease in his bright green eyes. Markus smirked and looked back outside the dusty window.

Beyond the cracked and filthy window, beyond the dimly lit office and the grim outpost itself, lay Dilas Forest. A place the very few who knew its disturbing secret chose to stay well away from, many who feared it and many who were concerned by the very mystery surrounding it. No one but those deeply involved knew this monstrous secret, and no one else would ever discover it. A sense of evil hung over it. Through the sea of trees and never ending undergrowth it breathed. Many who entered its depths would feel this unnerving sense. Yet many who ventured too far would never return.

There it lay in the middle of the vast countryside, a mass of green and brown covered with the scent of mystery and death. Darkness leapt out from the undergrowth beneath and a mist of fresh morning anxiety flowed through the tree tops. It was like the whole forest itself was alive and breathing monstrously, waiting in hunger and patience.

Markus surveyed it closely, watching every detail and turning rapidly at everything that moved. He was the oldest and toughest of all the guards who ran the borders of Dilas Forest, they were the ones who watched over the operation. It was their job to make sure that everything around the woodland ran efficiently, to make sure that when the borders were closed no one got in... and no one got out.

Markus looked back down at Jason slowly.

"How long will it take before this news story will be well known amongst the public?" he asked coldly. Jason quickly looked back down at the make and the date on the newspaper.

"Quite a while I should think," he replied scanning the main text. "It's only a small newspaper company; it'll probably be quite a while before the general public starts to really worry."

Markus walked over to where Jason was sitting back in his chair at the desk and snatched the newspaper from him. His eyes darting from side to side faster than a rattlesnake's attack, he looked up and whispered uncannily.

"Hmmm. The police aren't going to be finding anything soon." He looked down at Jason, who was trying hard to not stare back up at him sheepishly. "For what's found in the forest stays in the forest." He smiled evilly, grinning from the corners of his mouth; he turned away from the young guard towards the door. "You've got another one to add to the collection." Jason nodded seriously, and, turning his back to Markus began to reach across the old wooden desk towards the mysterious black photo album.

Chapter 3:   The Barrow Family

"Come on! It's going to be great, people!" exclaimed Adrian loudly behind the steering wheel. He looked back behind him in the mirror towards the rest of the Barrow family who just about managed to fit inside the large MPV car.

"Yeah, but you say this every time we go somewhere, and it always turns out for the worst," moaned Max from the seat next to him. He watched uninterestedly out of the window, as civilisation slowly disappeared into nothingness around them. He slumped his head on the window and groaned quietly as towns turned to villages, villages turned to hamlets, those then turned to bare landscape. On and on the Barrow family drove, into the ever green countryside of Cambridgeshire. Watching the world go past him, Max thought of all the good things which he could be doing right now. He could have stayed in his flat in London and partied with friends until Sunday morning. But no, instead he to come here, on a pointless expedition holiday weekend with his family.

Behind him in the old car, littered with wrappers, sat the rest of his family. Eve, his step mum, gently trying not to wake his younger step-sister Sarah who was sprawled fast asleep on her lap. Lauren, her long brown-blonde hair all over the back seat as she had just sat in the car texting throughout the entire two hour journey so far. Sophie, his other younger sister, who was only fourteen, was listening to her iPod on full volume; and yet still refused to turn it down even after countless times of Eve telling her off for it. There was Sean, his younger brother, who had been fiddling with an old Rubiks cube ever since he had found it up amongst the clutter in the attic at home. Finally, there was Adrian, his dad. His thick brown moustache was noticeable from a mile

17

away, which made him look a little like something of an old school rocker. His dark sunglasses were tinted as the sun's light bounced back off them. This was the Barrow family, in all its glory. There were fun ones, exciting ones, strange ones, and dull ones. Together, they completed the family.

Max straightened his glasses and sighed out deeply. The trip had been long and aggravating with much frustration. There had been tantrums, throwing up on the side of the road, even getting lost several times. He barely even knew where they were heading towards.

"Speaking of which," he turned to ask his dad driving next to him, "where are we going anyway?"

"Dilas Forest," he replied proudly. "It's an apparently beautiful area of woodland not too far from here. Supposedly run by the local wildlife organisation. We might see falcons and wolves, and maybe even bears if we're lucky."

Eve looked up suddenly at Adrian.

"Bears?!" she cried out shocked. "Adrian, you didn't mention any of this before we came here!"

"Relax Sweetheart, it's going to be fine. Trust me," he responded casually. "Besides, the chance of seeing a bear is extremely rare anyway."

The large old car drove on through the countryside. They swerved round a huge bend to reveal a sign coming up a few hundred metres away from them which read *Dilas Country Park – 20km*.

Sean looked up from his game.

"This place is a park?"

"Well, kind of," replied Adrian, "It's more of a vast woodland area which travellers and tourists use to explore and wander around. I've heard it's a great experience."

"Oh yeah?" Lauren looked up, speaking for the first time since they set off. "And just where did you hear that dad?!" she asked angrily.

"The pub," Adrian answered, relaxed.

"That's the pub dad! Those guys in there are old drunks. You can't trust a word they say! For all we know this place might be a run down old dump! It might be just a field for crying out loud!"

"She's got a point dad," added Sean.

Adrian was speechless; he set his eyes on the road and focused ahead. "Well, we're almost there. So then we'll see what it's really like."

"Trust me, this place is gonna be a lame," grumbled Lauren quietly to Sophie, who didn't hear a word because of her iPod music being so loud.

"Sorry?" jumped Sophie, realising that she was being spoken to. Lauren rolled her eyes and stared out the window at the passing trees.

Sophie finally removed her earpiece.

"Are we there yet?"

Adrian looked up into the mirror irritably. "We'll be there when I say we're there."

Sophie looked dumbstruck. "Sorry for asking," she moaned sarcastically.

A sign flew past their window as they sped onwards, which read *Dilas Country Park – 10km.*

Adrian sighed and said to his family, "Look I'm sorry alright. It's just, I thought this would be a great weekend. I mean, Max, I managed to get you all the way back from London to come with us. I know you could have stayed with friends and you too Lauren. But I mean, this could be a really good family adventure. Uniting the Barrows once again, you know. I didn't mean to cause any chaos, it's just we haven't gone on a decent family trip in ages, and I thought, well, now's our chance." He sighed once again deeply in sorrow and frustration, focusing on the long country road before them.

Everyone was staring at him with different expressions. Lauren frowned at him slightly. Eve smiled at the corners of her mouth, Sarah still fast asleep on her lap. Sean looked away awkwardly out the window. Sophie just stared at him blankly. Max thought to himself for a moment and then turned slowly to face his dad.

"Its okay dad. Don't worry. We're really sorry too." Adrian began to curve a smile on his lips. "You try too hard sometimes, but that's a good thing. This is gonna be a great trip and everyone knows it really."

His father smiled happily back. "Thank you son. Thank you."

The blue car drove on ahead, round corners and bends, trees and bushes increasingly growing on either side and gradually building up into what was a forest. As the light from the sun was slowly blotted out from the trees surrounding them, a shade of bright green engulfed the car itself. The path began to grow rougher, stones and branches lay increasingly scattered in the middle of the road. *Welcome to hell* thought Lauren to herself.

The forest began to close in around them like a giant green monster, consuming the car whole, before suddenly a huge sign appeared out of nowhere in the trees. It lay visible and clear on one side of the road, its writing was big and bold in dirty white fading letters... *Welcome to Dilas Country Park.*

Chapter 4:   They're Coming

The cabin was cold and grim. It always was and it always would be. Even with the bright sunlight glaring in from outside the room still lay sinister and haunting. Shadows skulked up the walls like spiders and the scent of abhorrence crawled out from the nooks and crannies. The antiquity of the outpost was obvious from its interior. Most of the lights were either broken or destroyed. They had been for so long that not even Zack could remember when they had died. An old rusty radio lay on a shelf in one corner, it had only been used once back in 2007 for some strange reason. A collection of magazines collecting dust were piled high on the shelf below, one of which Jason was reading, leaning against a radiator by a window nearby.

Markus stood on the other side of the room smoking his eighteenth cigarette today. This made his voice sound croaky and sour. He was a strange man, whom both Zack and Jason were afraid of. His disturbing scar was enough to stare at for days. When Zack had first been recruited, he was working with Markus and two other guards named Argus and Craig. They weren't scared by the man in the slightest, since they had been working with him for so long. Even by now Zack wasn't as nervous of him as he once was when he first joined the organisation. Jason however was still frightened of the tall, eerie guard. He joined a few weeks after Argus and Craig were both taken one night. The thought still made Zack shudder to this day. Now there were only three of them at the outpost. Jason Grey, Markus Wild and himself, Zack Caleb. Sitting around in the dark, dingy cabin, waiting for their time to take action and announce the warning to the visitors that so many had ignored in the past.

A flash of light caught his eye from outside. Zack moved forward in his seat and looked out of the dusty broken window to see what it was. It was a large blue MPV car pulling out from the woodland entrance road into the bright clearing of parking spaces. Already filling up the other spaces were other cars and vehicles, camper vans and big trucks, tourists and visitors from across the country, gradually emerging from beyond. Zack looked out upon the crowd, which was gradually increasing in number by the minute. They were old, young, fat and thin, tall and short, a good mixture of a crowd.

"They've arrived," he announced quietly to Markus and Jason. With that, Jason slowly closed his magazine and returned it to the pile on the shelf next to him. Zack turned around and looked out of the window behind him to see the emerging crowd. He sighed loudly in preparation. "Okay. Are you ready guys?"

Markus stepped closer towards the window to get a better look, stumping out his cigarette upon the slowly collapsing window sill as he did so. His eyes squinted as he looked out upon the unsuspecting crowd. This was merely another day's work ahead of them. By 10:00 am they would arrive, by 8:00 pm... at least most of them would leave.

"Well lads," he projected to Jason and Zack who looked back up at him, "once again let's show this crowd that we're serious... and let's hope that they take our warning this time." He groaned quietly.

Jason and Zack nodded, their eyes filled with nerve, which was increasingly showing. They turned to look back out of the window at the seemingly happy crowd. A painful feeling grew in Jason's gut once more, this happened every time they were to announce this. Zack almost felt the same, except by now he was well used to this. Markus merely stared out at them. He had been working in this operation for so long now that his heart was filled with nothing but hatred and lies. In appearance and within, he was a dark and twisted human being, and everyone he knew thought the same thing. His breath was cold and icy as he uttered his last question before facing the contented crowd.

"So who do you think it will be this time?"

Chapter 5:   Never Stray From the Path

Wheels skidded upon the ground and dirt flew back into the air as the large Barrow family car drove sharply round a bend and entered a huge clearing from the trees, which was the parking area for visitors to Dilas Country Park. The sharp light reflected off the shiny surface and glimmered as they entered. Sophie and Sean looked out and surveyed the scene as the big car drove around and prepared to park in a suitable shady space within the large clearing. Already there were a lot of other people parking their cars and emerging into the daylight. Sean thought to himself for a moment, *how many people usually come here?* It only lasted a moment, before the large vehicle swung round and halted in a nearby slot.

The door to the blue Toyota opened sharply and from within, the right foot of Adrian Barrow emerged and set foot upon the dusty earth beneath. A split second later the whole of him emerged into the mid autumn fresh air. He breathed in the morning scent and felt the morning sunlight brush energetically against his fifty one year old skin. His thick moustache tickled against his upper lip in the light breeze flowing. This was what he was born for, adventure. All his life he had grown up confronting the face of thrill, the scent of escapade calling him forward. And yet here he was now, taking his unenthusiastic family on a holiday they would never forget. He was welcoming them into their world, where a true Barrow belonged.

A moment later Max got out of the other side and walked round to stand beside him.

"Well this looks... fun," he said casually, looking ahead at what lay before them. Roughly a hundred yards away from them were a pair of enormous barbed wired gates with fences either side of them which ran for as far as the eye could see before entering the cover of the trees and undergrowth. A few other civilians were already making their way towards them, excitement written on their faces. One group were a troupe of youths who looked roughly around Max's age, yet he had never met them before in his life. They were tall and muscular, wearing green and brown camouflage uniforms with the symbol of the Royal Marines on each of their chests, all walking swiftly towards the shut gates on the other side of the clearing. Another group consisted of two women and a man, the two women persistently trying to drag the man out of the car, who clearly did not wish to be here. One group were a family from what appeared to be Liverpool. Three young boys all wore football t-shirts of Liverpool FC, whilst speaking with their parents in strong accents. At the gates ahead stood three tall, stern looking guards, all dressed in black uniform with serious and sour faces. There they stood, watching and waiting.

"Everyone else is getting a move on," Max turned to his dad, "surely we should too."

There was a brief pause before Adrian finally answered, "Yeah, let's get going."

They both strode around to the other side of the car where all the others were gradually climbing out of the vehicle slowly. Lauren stood several feet away texting, whilst Eve was helping Sarah to her feet. She had just woken up, so therefore would not be in the best of moods. Max walked over to her and knelt down beside her to talk to her in a comforting voice.

"Hi, you okay?"

"Yeah," she yawned tiredly. "Are we there yet?"

Max smiled warmly and almost chuckled with laughter.

"Yeah, we're there." He looked up and around. "Come on. Let's find your mum and get going." He beamed tenderly. He stood up slowly and walked around to the boot of the car where Adrian and Sean were unloading the rucksacks rapidly.

"Here Max, heads!" came Sean's voice suddenly as he suddenly tossed a bag to Max, who swiftly caught it in his hands and hauled it over his back. He then carried on to Adrian, who looked up and talked to him whilst removing something from the car.

"Well, its 10:00 now, by my best estimate, we should be out of there by around five-ish."

Max looked around suspiciously, staring over at the three uncanny men at the gates, a sense of evil wavering over them.

"I don't know dad. Maybe there's something fishy going on around here. I mean those guards don't look like the friendliest of chaps, do they?"

Adrian looked around at the three sinister looking men and smiled.

"Well, maybe they're not having the best of days. And besides..." He looked up at Max, "I'm not going to let a bunch of guys in black uniforms ruin my day. No one messes with me," he joked, grinning.

Max smiled back from the humour for a second. He looked down and thought to himself for a moment. *You know, maybe he's right. You're too cautious Max! Chill out. It's going to be great. Don't worry.*

Meanwhile, whilst all the commotion was going on beside the car, Sophie was several feet away, peering into the windows of other nearby transports. She pressed her hands and face against the window of an old truck. It was rusty and dirty on the outside, bird droppings littered the bonnet and windshield and the whole vehicle itself seemed like it hadn't been touched for a very long time. Sophie peered in nosily. The inside was old and rugged, its seats dusty and the leather withering like dead flowers in a vase. This whole car seemed completely abandoned. Sophie ran around and peered in the occupant of the next space along. Again, the same empty car, abandoned and what seemed to be discarded. She ran across the pathway and stared into another, deserted and derelict vehicle. Half the parking lot seemed to be like a ghost town. Neglected and collecting dust.

"Dad?" she called across the parking ground to their own car.

"Sophie, come away from there immediately!" shouted Eve from the other side of the car park whilst picking up her bag. Sophie quickly looked back at the old, deserted car and then hurried back over to her busy family.

"Sophie, you know you shouldn't be nosing around into other people's property," said her father annoyed.

"But dad!" she pleaded back eagerly, looking up at him. "I don't think these are anyone's cars. They're old and abandoned. No one seems to have used them for long, long time."

Adrian looked up and around the clearing. It was true, half the cars here were collecting dust. This was very mysterious. "Well, maybe they've all parked their old vehicles here and got new ones elsewhere." He looked down at his daughter and smiled. She smiled ever so slightly back, her eyes fearful and grave. Why were so many other trucks and cars just left deserted here? Where they really just old cars which people had dumped here? She would have liked to believe it, yet her thoughts had the tiniest tinge of doubt still left.

"Hey Soph," Sean said as he wandered over to her and stood beside her, "here's your bag." He passed it over to her. She accepted it, yet her eyes never left the vast collection of disused cars. "Look I know you're worried about all this." He gestured over to the array. "But you just have to accept it. Dad's right. These things just happen every now and again, people dump their unwanted cars in the nearest place available, it makes life so much easier." He paused momentarily. "Just relax. It's going to be fine."

Sophie frowned slightly and looked across to her brother. "I don't know Sean. I mean, what if people haven't just abandoned their cars here. This place is in the middle of nowhere, right? The nearest sign of civilisation was when we stopped back at that service station about half an hour ago. There's bound to be somewhere else where people dispose of their waste."

She stopped and turned to face the tall green borderline which was the trees and start of Dilas Forest. "Look at the place. It's got the creeps written all over it. Those guards don't look too happy to be around. I mean maybe these people, the owners of these cars went missing in Dilas Forest. I'm not making any references or definite ideas, it's just that feeling you know? When you don't feel quite right all of a sudden. Like when you feel a sense of..." She paused and shrugged her shoulders. "Never mind..."

Sean looked at the tall, wired gates roughly one hundred metres away, the barbed wire above them like a snake of needles. He thought, concerned for what Sophie had just said.

"I don't know sis," he replied. "I'm sure you don't like this place, but you just got to admit it's OK. Nothing's wrong. Besides, dad wouldn't have taken us here if he knew it wasn't safe."

Sophie looked back at her brother with scepticism. "Sean. Dad spends all his Friday evenings in the pub. He hears a lot of things."

Sean shrugged. "Well, I don't know." He sighed. "I guess we'll just have to wait and see." He wandered over to Adrian and the rest of the family who were about to head on. Sophie looked down at the ground in thought for a moment. Thinking, and yet also trying to calm herself down.

"Hey Soph! Come on, we're going!" called out her dad from several feet away. She quickly snapped back to reality, threw away the horrific thought, smiled and grabbed her bag to join the others.

Adrian was fast paced and eager to get going. Eve hurriedly tried to keep up behind, holding Sarah's hand safely. Max, Sean and Sophie followed shortly, whilst

28

Lauren slowly dragged her feet behind. Her face was a picture of boredom and disinterest. Her smile earlier on in the day had slowly been drooping lower and lower towards her chin. She was hot, tired and definitely did not want to be here. She had been dragged along in a boring two hour car journey with her little step-sister Sarah throwing tantrums, her step mum Eve always telling her what to do, and her other sister Sophie listening to her iPod loudly. Her rucksack was heavy, mostly with make-up and other pointless accessories. You could see the regret on her face from a mile away. This was her dad's heaven, and her hell.

The Barrow family gradually assembled outside the gates where a fair amount of other visitors had already gathered and were waiting to be let into the forest. Standing before the sharp silver entrance were three tall, serious looking men in black uniforms and their hands were behind their backs smartly. These men were not to be messed with.

One of them, who appeared to be the leader was dark skinned with a gaping scar which ran across his left eye. Another was much younger; he looked roughly nineteen, the same as Max, with dark hair. The final one looked roughly around twenty seven: he wore a dark black cap which covered most of his face. Nonetheless, all three of them were sinister figures. Suddenly one of the men in front with the scar on his face took a step forward and began to address the crowd.

"Good morning, ladies and gentlemen," said Markus in his deep and hoarse voice. The whole group fell quiet all of a sudden. The tone of the man's voice was enough to create silence in the air. "I trust you all had a safe trip." He looked around at the crowd, his beady eyes passing rapidly from one human to another. Sean could not take his eyes off him, as he was terrified of the tall, eerie man. "First of all, I would like to welcome you all to Dilas Country Park, opened on the twenty first of January 2006 to all the public. Now I am very much aware of your eagerness…" with that

29

he turned to look at Jason standing behind him for a moment, then quickly turned back to the audience once more, "... to carry on forth into the woods. But, I am afraid however, that there are some important guidelines which we must run through beforehand, for the importance of your safety." On that note Lauren rolled her eyes in boredom. *Great.* She thought. *Just great. More stupid rules to follow. Thanks dad!* Next to her stood Sophie. She did not like or trust the man at all. His smile was cruel and twisted, which linked to the very tip of the horrible scar across his eye.

"We thank you for all of your patience during this short time," continued Markus. "The first rule is no littering of any kind what so ever. We are devoted to keeping the natural environment safe and healthy as it is a law of the government, thank you very much. The second, is that you must keep to the paths. Dilas Forest is a very large and vast area of land and is extremely easy to get lost in should you choose to stray from the selected routes. There have been several cases of this in the past, so please, for your sakes, keep to the selected footpaths. And finally, the last rule before we are allowed to set you free for your own expedition is to leave at approximately eight o'clock at the latest, when the siren is heard."

With that the entire crowd started whispering and murmuring amongst each other, as Markus hesitated, thinking. Everyone was wondering and asking questions to one another as to what this mysterious siren might be. "The siren is a loud and thunderous sound which can be heard from all sides of the forest from the footpaths. It is unmistakable, and everyone should be able to hear it instantly from anywhere in the surrounding region. We ask you when you hear this alarm, to immediately start making your way back to this checkpoint and leave the woodland section. Roughly fifteen minutes after the siren will be rung the gates will be shut for the night."

Sophie looked directly at Lauren and Sean each standing either side of her. "Siren? What's going on?"

"Fifteen minutes?" whispered Max to his father quietly. "But how are we supposed to get back to the entrance point in that time? Especially if we're right on the other side of the forest?"

Adrian looked stern and deep in thought. Sarah looked up at Eve, who gave her a comforting hug for reassurance. Max stood and stared at Markus, the two briefly met eye contact for a moment as he stared back, frowning, his eyes cold and haunting. What was going on inside that man's head, Max wondered. A man of many sinister words may seem just about reliable on the outside, but a more monstrous demon within. Lauren looked back at Sophie and agitatedly said. "What is this, some kind of a joke?!"

Sophie didn't reply, she was deep in thought, along with her elder brother Max and her father Adrian. They were confused, wondering, misunderstanding the reason behind it all.

"Excuse me," an elderly woman with pure white hair and a gentle voice said. Her clothing was new and professional, as she was clearly healthy for her age. "What is this Siren for?"

Markus' head snapped to face her, his eyes bearing his thoughts. His eyes quivered and looked uneasy for a second. Silence fell suddenly upon the group, every eye watching Markus, as his eyes darted back and forth, across all ages of the travellers before him. Max watched him promptly, waiting for a slip up and a chance to notice that there really was something mysterious going on. Sophie was eager too, her eyes unflinching, waiting for a response. Waiting, as more than a dozen eyes watched impatiently.

"I am afraid that is for confidential reasons only, and I nor any of my colleagues are not permitted to admit that," replied Markus eventually. "The important thing is that it is to keep the forest in good shape and to ensure that visitors are able to wander amongst the forest at a steady pace and for safety reasons."

Eve nodded approvingly, she didn't particularly want to dwell on this matter. Adrian smiled slightly and looked down at Sophie. "You'll see," he said comfortingly, "everything's going to be fine. They wouldn't just send us in if they knew anything was going to go wrong."

Sophie hesitated for a moment and then smiled vaguely. She knew he was probably right, yet in her mind she felt an unease that most likely wouldn't die out. Max however, wasn't convinced. The guard may have fooled everyone else, yet he was not persuaded. He continued to stare at the tall man in dark black uniform, as the guard smiled and nodded at various people in the group. "Dad, I don't think we should do this," he lent over and whispered in his dad's ear.

"Now, don't be silly son," Adrian defied back, turning to face him. "You just have to face it. There is nothing going on in Dilas Forest. The only reason they have that siren is a way of telling people that it is time to leave for the day. I know Sophie wasn't too happy about this just a moment ago, but she just needed some reassurance to get her going. You're a grown man now, Max. There's no more monsters hiding beneath the bed, no more nightmares chasing after you. This is the real world. Reality. You've got to learn to deal with these things. You can't keep running forever or chasing them, you've just got to go out there and face it. Eve and I have taken you all on this trip to be a weekend to remember, not one to dread. Now come on, let's go." He smiled at Max, who just smiled uncomfortably back.

With a positive outlook beginning to rise up, he responded warmly back to his father, "OK."

There was a loud creaking and cranking sound, as every head turned to see the huge iron gates being pulled open by Zack and Markus. The mesh of bars and wires slowly disappeared to reveal the mysterious woodland path beyond. A shade of dark green filled the space beneath the trees, with tiny areas of light darting from gaps amongst the canopy. Everyone stared outwards into the unknown for a moment's hesitation. This was the entrance to Dilas Country Park. None of the group of visitors knew what lay beyond: to many, including the Barrow family, this was a new adventure. A chance to explore and learn more. Only the disturbing thoughts which ran through the minds of Markus, Zack and Jason could really understand the threatening truth behind Dilas Forest.

"You are now free to travel through at your own pace," declared Markus to the troupe. "Just please remember those rules which I warned you all about." He looked around, as if expecting for someone to speak back, but they never did. "We wish you all a very pleasant day." He turned around and looked sternly at Zack and Jason. They knew what they had to do, as did he.

The first set of travellers headed off, this was the group of cadets in their green and brown camouflage uniform. They walked off into the woodland wilderness with their heads held high. No one knew what on Earth they were up to. The next group also set off. This time, a group of five friends including the elderly woman. They soon disappeared round a bend in the path and out of sight.

Adrian turned to his family, who all stood in a semi-circle watching him. They were like soldiers, silent and waiting on his command. "Well team." He addressed them. "This is it. Time to rock 'n' roll. Eve do you have the map?" She nodded, confirming. "OK then. We are ready to set sail."

And with that, he swivelled around on his heels and headed for the open gates. Sean and Sophie looked at each other, shrugged and followed him in suit. Eve picked up Sarah by the waist and sat her on her shoulders. Sarah didn't really care what was going on. She just sat there on her mother's shoulders and watched as butterflies and dandelion seeds floated by in the air almost magically. Lauren began to follow them, but then stopped and then turned round once more. "Are you coming Max?" she asked, groaning subtly under her breath to herself.

Max just stood and stared, his eyes were a mixture between squinting and frowning, as he looked out upon the borderline of trees of Dilas Forest. Even after his father's kind words of wisdom, the sudden urge of suspicion had never left. If anything it had only grown in magnitude. This was where they had been taken rather than a beach of luxury and lavishness, they had come to woodland, the cold feel of the soil and the hard trunks of trees. Max pondered, wondering, thinking. His nerves were not taking over, getting the better of him, fear was not an option. It was his doubt which rooted him to the spot, concealed in a suspicion which could not appear to be moved. He was sure that the guards were hiding something, something abnormal and mysterious. He tried not to think about it and to pull away from the thought, but no, the tension was merely dragging him in further.

"Max? Are you OK?" asked Lauren once more, a little confused. Max suddenly awoke from his daydream and contemplation, and snapped back to real world around him.

"Yeah, sure. Let's go." He smiled to his sister and the two of them headed onwards towards the beginning of the long, winding path. As they reached the entrance Max slowed down. He could feel the unnerving gaze of the guards boring into the back of his skull. He could sense their twisted thoughts. He managed to shake off those ideas however and carried on. He sighed deeply, took a deep breath and stepped forward onto the soft soil and earth, into Dilas Forest itself. He looked up at the trees, like snakes and serpents where their branches twisted and turned, like claws where their roots dug deep into the ground. He bit his lip, his eyes determined and looking straight ahead. Maybe his dad was right. Maybe the guards were right and there wasn't anything suspicious going on after all. He smiled and carried on up the path to catch up with Lauren and the rest of his family, the anxiety in his heart fading to be filled with a feeling of contentment inside.

Little did he know of the horrors waiting, hungry, amongst the darkness ahead.

Chapter 6:   The Sound Of Terror

The midday sunlight was warm and refreshing. Its dazzling rays spilling through the canopies down into the vivid green forest floor beneath. Leaves slowly fell from their branches, seasonal nature spiralling down like helicopters to join the many thousands in the soil and earth. The ants and the worms wriggled vigorously beneath them, craving the moist underbelly of the dirt. A maze of trees and bushes swarmed throughout the entire area, making the path almost impossible to see. The cold iron gates had disappeared behind them a long time ago. The eerie guards left behind in the wilderness at the entrance to this new world. It was beautiful. The sunlight shining through the leaves leaving a glimmering green glow about the air.

Sean trawled through the roots and the terrain, the rough dirt clawing at his boots like creatures dragging him down deep into the earth. His rucksack was heavy and weighing him down like a slave. Unlike his sister Lauren, he had filled his with items of which he needed, such as spare food, a compass and a survival bag. The sun's powerful light was bearing down upon him, making him sweat and thirst for water. He stopped abruptly, kneeled down and quickly removed a water flask from his bag pocket. It was light and stimulating, its cool stream flowing down his throat was soothing and calm. He removed the flask and breathed heavily, panting because of the severe heat of the day.

All of a sudden, Max appeared behind him and said down to him, "Hi man, are you alright?"

Sean looked up at him surprised and answered back, "Yeah, sure, thanks. Just stopping for something to drink."

"I see, okay," responded Max. "We best keep moving though. Don't want to fall behind."

"No, we won't. Trust me. I even brought a compass and a map to tell us where we are going," responded Sean casually.

"Wow, you're prepared. How come? When I talked to dad over the phone he said that this was a new place he had just discovered."

"Well," replied Sean, "I got it off an online internet map source book. It had displays of everywhere on it. If we ever go on holiday again to somewhere like this I am using that site," he declared triumphantly. "But anyway, as I was saying. I got a hold of this map which shows a rough detail of the surrounding area. See, look." He passed the small, gridded map over to Max, who looked at it, confused at first.

"But this has hardly anything on it," he exclaimed uncertainly. "The only things which show are the scale and a huge gaping circle in the middle."

He passed it back over to Sean, who took it back hastily, correcting his brother. "Yeah, that's because this is it. Dilas Forest is only really one big track, linking around in a circle. I reckon dad only chose this place because of the adventure and to get us up on our feet again."

Max smirked slightly. "Ah, good old dad. Have you shown him this yet?"

"Nah," replied Sean, "He wouldn't want it anyway, since he is more into discovering and finding his own way about places."

"Yeah, that's him alright." Max chuckled.

"But hey. I found this really weird thing on the edge of the map. Take a look." Sean pointed to a certain area on the corner of the map, and Max looked over his shoulder inquisitively.

On the very edge of the area shaded of Dilas Forest was what appeared to be several small buildings clumped together, of which looked like a small village.

"What's that?" asked Max curiously.

37

"I don't know," replied Sean, "it looks like some kind of tiny hamlet. But it can't be since there is no record or mention of it at all. Or at least not from what I've heard." He looked up, puzzled, at his older brother.

Max frowned in interest. "Hmmm, that is odd." His tone was quiet and thoughtful.

Suddenly, a loud voice called from several trees away, "Hey, Sean! Max! Hurry Up! We almost lost you guys, you're so slow."

Max and Sean looked up surprised. It was Adrian. His voice was slightly muffled from the distance behind the trees and undergrowth. Sean quickly knelt down and hurriedly put the map back into the bag, as Max walked past him to join the others. Sean shoved the creased piece of paper into his bag and swung it over his shoulder as he stood up. He turned around and started heading off towards the others.

Suddenly, a loud crack snapped from behind him. Sean spun around rapidly, only to face an empty pathway. He looked around, expecting to see something, another tourist maybe or some kind of animal, but no, nothing. His eyes darted through the trees into the swarm of green, searching for any signs of movement. The canopy and wildlife lay silent, quiet as the grave. The whole scene was haunting and ghostly. Disturbingly quiet. He squinted for a moment, staring into what felt like oblivion. Gazing through as the merge of plant life turned to green and nothingness.

All of a sudden, his eyes stopped sharp on one particular point. Staring through the trees and the bushes, his gaze fixed upon one particular point which had caught his eye. Squinting and peering closer to try and make out the entity, his eyes opened wide in horror as he realised what it was.

With terror filling his eyes, he fell backwards into a pile of mud in shock. Covered in dirt and grime, almost throwing up from what he had just seen, he stared terrified as he could not take his eyes off of the disturbing sight. With

38

sheer nerve, he managed to tear his eyes away from the horrific thing and fled down the pathway and through the trees towards the rest of his family, who were sitting a short distance away, stopped for a rest. As he ran, sweat dripping from his forehead, tears swelling in his eye sockets, Eve looked up from feeding Sarah and jumped up at the sight of Sean's terrified face.

"Huh!" she exclaimed suddenly, "Sean! Oh My God! Sean! What happened?!"

Sean could not speak as he reached the rest point. He curved over forward, panting and wheezing like a tired dog. With that, the rest of the family looked up dramatically and rushed towards the young boy.

"Sean! Sean, look at me!" said Adrian loudly so that Sean could hear above his gasping. "Tell me. What happened?"

Lauren stared down open mouthed at the traumatised Sean. Sophie held her hands over her mouth in shock. Max could not believe his eyes. He had been with his younger brother just seconds ago. Something terrorising had just happened immediately after their discussion. Something wasn't right here. He knew it. The urge of suspicion swiftly rose inside him like a knife stabbing at its prey. Something sinister was happening in this forest. Now he had Sean as a witness, he felt a disturbing feeling crawl through his stomach and up the back of his rigid spine.

Sarah started crying, her weeping almost covering the sound of Sean's wheezing entirely. However, everyone was now staring directly at Sean, desperate to find out what had just happened.

"Sean! Listen to me!" said Adrian loudly once more, "what happened?! It's okay, you're with us now. You're safe."

Sean was now curled up on the floor in tears, sweat and mud, his step mum dearly trying hard to comfort him. With parched lips and in a horrified tone, he said. "Back there! Through the trees. I saw something. Something horrible!" He burst out crying into his hands.

"It's alright son!" comforted Adrian. "It's okay. You're safe now. You're with us. Now please, tell us what you saw. We need to know; otherwise, we can't do anything about it."

Sean felt sick. A heavy weight had just dropped to his stomach. Plucking up the courage, he shared his horrific news to the family. "Between the trees... there was a corpse. Its insides were everywhere!"

With that the rest of the family lurched back in horror. Disgusted by the observation, Adrian nodded and continued to listen intimately. "I don't want to talk about it," Sean choked and spluttered amongst the tears and mucus.

Eve quickly knelt down and covered Sarah' ears. Lauren's mouth lay wide open in repulsion and horror. Sophie was about to be sick. Max gritted his teeth to bear the news. Adrian swallowed nervously and said to Sean once more. "Son? I know you're not alright, but please can you show me where you saw this?"

"Adrian no! He can't!" interrupted Eve angrily.

"We need to know Eve!" shouted Adrian back. He addressed the rest of the Barrows. "Okay. Everyone else stay here. Sean and I are going to go back a few steps and see what this is all about."

He did not even look back at his petrified family as he stood up, put his arm around Sean and helped him up. "Okay son. Everything's going to be okay. Now, are you alright to go back and show me?"

"Of course he's not bloody alright! He's just seen a body!" interrupted Lauren, enraged. "How do you think he feels dad!?"

"No, no." Sean muttered quietly back. "I'll go."

Adrian nodded appreciatively. He gave Sean a big hug once more. "It's okay. You're with us now. Everything is alright."

With that, Sean slowly stood up and walked over to the pathway to continue back up to where he had first seen the mutilated corpse. Adrian walking beside him as they set off at a steady pace. The rest of the Barrow family just looked on and thought in confusion. *What had just happened? Did Sean really just see a body? Why were they even going back there?* Everyone was shocked and perplexed. No-one knew what was going on.

"I don't like this." Sophie worriedly mentioned. "This place is giving me the creeps already."

"Yeah, same here," Lauren commented back. "No doubt dad's going to make us carry on further." She was severely irritated.

"Now look everyone," Eve said calmly, trying to soothe the others. "Your father is going with Sean to see what really happened. Everything is going to be okay I'm sure."

"What really happened?" Lauren retaliated back. "What really happened?! Do you not believe Sean?! Do think that this was all made up?!" She was on the brink of shouting now.

"No," replied Eve steadily, yet slightly worried. "I'm just saying that today is an extremely hot day, and it wouldn't be any surprise if the heat was finally getting to Sean. Maybe he fell behind a bit, got a little lost and confused and the heat must have caused him to hallucinate in some way."

There was a brief pause, in which Sophie and Lauren took in this thought. "It has happened many times before, and I would not be surprised if that were the same in this case. He's only fifteen. He must have imagined something, surprisingly."

Lauren thought carefully. She said quietly under her breath sarcastically. "Mmm, because fifteen year olds do dream up bloody corpses don't they?" She rolled her eyes and turned to talk to Sophie next to her.

Meanwhile, on the other side of a clump of trees and undergrowth, Sean was showing Adrian where he had first seen this horrific sight. He climbed up a mound of dirt, next to where he had fallen into the pit of mud, and looked around for the exact place where he had seen it, his eyes

41

scanning through the sea of thick brown trunks, searching for that specific one. He shook very slightly as he searched, trembling with fear. Suddenly his eyes met upon the one place where he had seen the body, only to find a surprise waiting for them.

The disfigured body which had been tied to the tree had disappeared. Everything about it was gone. There were no blood stains, no remnants, nothing. Just a blank, plain old tree which was left in its place. He stared at it in confusion, wondering what had happened.

"Go on son. Where was it?" asked his father kindly and patiently.

Sean was bewildered. "It was right there, I'm sure of it." He pointed towards the selected tree trunk, his voice still quivering slightly in astonishment.

Adrian stared back at the tree. *What on Earth was he talking about?* "Sean, I think maybe the heat has been getting to you a little. Here, take off your jacket..."

"I'm fine!" he interrupted abruptly. "I'm sure it was there." The tears in his eyes were cleared now, in disbelief that it had just vanished.

Adrian looked down at him over his shoulder and talked with sympathy, yet slight frustration. "Sean, look. I know it's a hot day and I know none of you really want to be here, but please here me out. This is going to be worth it. Maybe the heat has just got to you. It's happened before hasn't it? When we were on holiday in Spain, remember? You're covered in mud, maybe you just fell over and panicked. Now, it wouldn't do any harm in giving you some medicine. Eve's got some in her bag, we'll get it when we get back to the others. And hey," he looked back at Sean has he turned. "It's okay. Nothing was there." He said reassuringly.

Sean did not look at him once. Instead he continued to stare into the eerie wilderness of trees. He was sure it was right here, definitely. So why had it disappeared?

Adrian disappeared off round the corner to join the others, whilst Sean stayed in utter puzzlement. He lowered his head eventually, thinking to himself. Maybe he had just dreamed this up due to the heat. Maybe his mind was playing tricks on him like last time. It was a very hot day after all. He looked back up at the trunk once more just to check that it still wasn't there, and it wasn't. Sean looked down to the rough forest floor pathway in relief. He breathed in and out slowly a few times for reassurance, then cleared his head and ran off to join the rest of his family.

On the other side of the undergrowth, Adrian lifted his heavy backpack from the ground and hauled it over his strong shoulder.

"Adrian, is he alright?" asked Eve affectionately.

"Yeah, he's fine." He paused for a moment and looked thoughtfully down to the ground. "He just needs some water. Maybe some stress relieving wouldn't be so bad either." He suddenly withdrew a small bottle of water from his blue jacket pocket, the midday sunlight glinting off his dark sunglasses. The gigantic shapes of trees old and young towering over them, their shadows covering the ground like a swarm of rats, spreading as the glowing sun changed position in the sky over the day.

Adrian walked over to Sean, who had just come around the corner, his tears had now dried away and his face was clean and fresh like nothing had ever happened. He handed the bottle of water over to him smiling. "There you go son. Are you okay now?" he asked reassuringly.

"Yeah," he replied positively. "Yeah I'm fine. Thanks." He smiled politely back at his dad, who acknowledged the answer and then turned to the rest of his family to keep on going. Sean stayed put for a moment, and looked around at the warm surroundings. He stared up into the trees and the clouds, the sunlight seeping through like bullet holes in a wall. He felt relaxed now. He must have dreamed it all: it must have been the colossal heat affecting him. He trusted his father for everything, and so far his dad had never let him down, and he doubted that he ever would.

Sean breathed out, refreshing his lungs from the hot day. He hauled his backpack over his shoulder and walked slowly towards the other Barrows gathered in the small clearing.

Adrian stood facing his family in a semi-circle position. He stood upright and addressed them confidently and securely. "Okay everyone. First of all well done to all of you for making it this far. You've done extremely well to put up with this, especially with the hot weather conditions today." His voice was serious, as he said like a general in the army. "Especially well done to our little Sarah." He smiled happily and placed a hand on his daughter's shoulder beside him. "I think you would agree she has been a very brave girl all day." He laughed jokingly, as the rest of the family did so shortly after. "Sean is fine, by the way. I've given him some water and he'll be well and kicking shortly." He nodded at Sean who had just joined them, who nodded back and looked downwards timidly. Lauren felt sympathy for him and put her arm around him kindly. Although she was incredibly spoilt and often exasperating, she did look out for her younger siblings with care and affection. Adrian continued, "The plan is, we'll keep on going in this direction for now, following the pathway until we reach another clearing, then we'll stop and have a break for lunch. After that, we'll find an area which we can wander freely from the path, and see what we can discover elsewhere."

Max looked up sharply at Adrian, a look of astonishment crawled over his face rapidly. "Dad, we can't stray from the path! Are you mad?!"

Adrian paused for a moment and looked down, contemplating. He then looked up with a more serious face and walked slowly over to Max, who waited, wondering what was going on. Adrian came about a foot from Max's face and said more quietly to him. "Son, when we said over the phone in your flat, and you agreed to come with us…"

44

"After you never shut up about coming here," interrupted Max irritated.

Adrian frowned slightly and looked deeply into his eyes, then continued to speak. "I said that we were going on an adventure. And to me an adventure is all about straying from the known. You can't just keep one routine the whole day long and suffer from boredom under the sun. A real adventurer has no limits. And that's what makes them extraordinary and unique. We are human beings because we can make choices of our own; we won't just sit in the darkness and be told what to do. I know the guards told us not to stray from the path, and I know you're all anxious about this whole siren business, whatever that's about. But honestly, if there really was any danger, then they wouldn't let us go on. Many people, when they see a forest they see an obstacle course, a challenge they have to make it through, a fortress they have to breach. But no. I see a new world, full of excitement and admiration, a chance to break free from the ordinary and explore. That is what your grandfather, may he rest in peace, told me. He was a man of many adventures, and that is what he passed on greatly to me." He stopped shortly, his frown turned to a look of sincerity. "And that is what I intend to pass, this amazing gift, onto you."

Max took a long moment to think about this, as he stared back deeply into his father's eyes. A cold, unbearable father and son tension had forged itself into existence. They stared at one another as Max thought gravely. *Is dad really serious? Is he really going to risk our safety and chance of getting out by nightfall for the sake of just exploring?*

Right now he was thinking for the sake of the rest of his family, of little Sarah, brave Sean, irritable Lauren, inquisitive Sophie, even Eve who he barely knew well he thought of and cared for.

The tension was growing steadily, as silence flowed around them. "Guys?" asked Eve quietly, trying not to cause

45

any anger. The sun bore down sharply upon them. The day was streaming by. Finally, Max made his decision.

He opened his mouth efficiently and uttered two syllables. "Okay."

The Barrows all turned to face him with surprise on their face. They all knew Max was a very cautious character, and always thought twice before accepting something. He trusted his dad dearly, even though there was the odd moment of tension when they disagreed.

Adrian nodded and smiled thankfully, patting his eldest on the shoulder a couple of times. "I knew you wouldn't let me down." He then turned around to pick up his bag.

"Dad, are you sure you know what you're doing?" asked Sophie cautiously. "I don't want to end up like what happened back in Turkey, when we got lost on the hillside."

Adrian didn't even look back at her, yet he answered whilst packing up. "Relax honey. Have I ever let you down?"

"Err, yes!" she replied aggravated. "Like I just said!"

Her father turned to face her almost laughing because of her tone. "That was in the past Sophie. And I'm sorry. But you've got to live with adventure. Even getting lost is a part of the excitement. It's part of your survival skills. And besides, we won't get lost. When we hear the siren, we'll just go back the way we came. Simple as that." He smiled, satisfied, turning to face her. "Now we better get a move on. It's gone twelve already, and if we don't start picking up the pace a little, we're going to run out of time fast. So let's go people." And with that he nodded to the troupe and set off. Everyone else just looked blankly at each other for a moment. Then Eve followed shortly after, still holding Sarah's little hand. Sophie and Lauren turned to follow the beaten pathway also, their backpacks rustling with all sorts of equipment and unnecessary items. Now it was just Max and Sean left, facing each other in the, what was, family circle.

Max sighed and held out his arm pointing towards the exit of the clearing. "After you," he gestured kindly.

Sean looked slightly nervous and a little sick. "Thanks," he muttered quietly and hurriedly, before vanishing behind the bush cover and around the corner.

Max was about to follow, when he stopped suddenly, dead in his tracks. He looked around, high in the trees, high into the sunlight which almost blinded him by its sheer power. There was little cover, yet enough to look upwards into the tree canopies, the mass sea of green leaves swarming at the top of giant bark trunks. Max looked deeply, frowning. He could not see anything, yet he was sure that something was here. Something strange that shouldn't be. He could not feel it's presence near him, yet he could feel its wake surrounding the forest. Sean could not have just dreamed up that horrific vision, even if he was the only one who saw it. This was not a safe place, and if he could convince his father to lead them away from the woods then that would make him feel much better and safer inside. He looked around for one last time before setting off round the corner towards the Barrow family's chosen route, and in a flash he vanished.

Little did he know, that the exact place where he had been staring up into the tree cover, something had been staring back.

Chapter 7: Try to Survive

The sun bore down overhead, the giant celestial sphere spinning approximately one hundred and fifty million kilometres from the Earth, its heat tearing away at the moist soil, even from such a colossal distance. The brown, dusty gravel was hot from the immense heat boring down upon it. Small dust clouds were gathering and forming in the early summer air. The gates to Dilas Forest lay wide open, allowing a cool, fresh breeze to come gushing through at regular paces. The border between the car park and the woodland was easily distinguishable. The line which turned from dusty sand to soft earth and soil changed rapidly, across the line of which the long, metal fence ran, never-ending until it reached the cover of the tall menacing green trees and vanished within.

Markus, Jason and Zack were all inside the small office outpost, smoking, drinking and waiting for the day to pass slowly and grimly. The rest of the outside world was quiet. Birds sung from the tree tops, twigs and branches rustled as rodents and other small animals darted swiftly between them. Every one of the visitors had entered and disappeared into the forest a few hours ago. Now there was no-one left in sight... except for a lone figure that emerged suddenly from within the tree line.

His feet dragged weakly across the dry ground, blood seeping out from his worn down shoes, revealing blood-spattered wounds in his skin. His clothes were ragged and torn, splattered with dirt, grime, ash and blood, which covered him all the way from his shoulders to the tips of his shoes. His hands were gnarled and broken, his fingers twisted out of place and seeping with pus, one missing from each hand. He limped on one leg, the other so badly wounded he could not use it. His dark hair was foul and missing in many areas. His face was scarred, bruised,

48

battered and bleeding. One eye faced upwards, the other straight ahead, a look of fear and sheer horror engaged what was left of his face. He wheezed long and hard as his lungs swelled inflamed and savaged. His crooked mouth bore teeth, broken and bloody. His whole body and form was a twisted wreck, like a living corpse wandering the earth.

The guards in the outpost were too occupied in a game of cards to see the disturbingly injured man limping across towards the road and exit to Dilas Country Park. Around the corner he crawled, and in a flash, he was out of sight.

Four hours later, the weak, young man lay upon a clean, light blue hospital bed. The doctors and kindly nurses of the hospital had cleaned, bandaged and helped his wounds with care and sensitivity, and were now attending patients elsewhere. The ward around him was completely empty, and as quiet as the grave itself. The walls were pallid and dull yet peaceful at the same time. The ward itself was completely lifeless, apart from the machines and beds which were used to deal with the patients as they came and left. It was like one simple man had entered a void of machines and a wasteland of bleakness.

The twenty two year old was lying there silently, watching the world flash past him in a blur of white noise and colours. He wheezed in and out of the tube linking his mouth to a nearby oxygen supply, his breathing flow slowly getting better, minute by minute. He stared upwards at the clear blue ceiling. Everything that had happened over the last week was racing through his mind in lightning speed. He couldn't get it out of his head. It was like voices were talking to him, whispering damned and long forgotten words, the horrors of the night chasing after him, reaching out and grabbing at his very soul. He just had to try to survive the terrors that he believed were still crawling after him from his horrific past.

All of a sudden, a dark, silhouetted shape loomed over him. He jumped inside and gulped in fright, his heart monitor racing on the screen beside his bed. His eyes rolled in the chaos and confusion. He was breathing heavily, his breaths turning to wheezing once more from anxiety.

The black shape bent down closer. It felt like it was one of them, one of those things chasing after him and had finally found him. Closer and closer it came. It was a foot away from him; he could feel its breath brushing against his fragile skin. He closed his eyes tightly in terror. He could feel it opening its demonic maw and about to tear a chunk from him, when suddenly, a voice said, kindly, and in a gentle manner.

"It's okay my friend. Nothing can hurt you now."

Slowly but surely, the young, severely injured man opened his eyes. To his disbelief, he looked up and saw a friendly, nice looking man leaning down over him, a slight smile across his face, of relief and worry. The heavy weight of anxiety which was rising high within the dying man's stomach suddenly dropped to nothingness. It was okay. He was safe now.

"My name is Detective Scott Walkins. I am an officer in the local police force of north Cambridgeshire," he greeted once more in a soothing, comforting voice. The injured man knew this figure was no enemy, due to his tone and to his expression. "I understand, young man, that you were involved in a horrific incident within Dilas Country Park. Now, if it is alright with you, if you are feeling up to it... I would like to ask you a few questions, Mr Carner."

Chapter 8:   Spreading the Seed

Max slumped himself down suddenly upon a nearby log. His bag was exhausting, dragging him downwards and downwards for the past few hours. He was strong, but as the late summer heat gradually got to him more and more, its effects started to take place. He unzipped a small pocket in his large, heavy bag, and quickly withdrew a plastic water flask from within. It was cool and refreshing, as he felt its soothing flow pass its way down his neck and towards his insides. Max gasped at the air after his long swig from the bottle. He was breathing deeply from the heat of the hot summer's day, which was scorching down upon his, and all of his family's, backs. Lauren sighed and sat down next to him on the dead fallen tree. She was also tired, drained already from the hike inwards, further and further into the forest. She too drank rapidly from her own pink flask. Max looked at her and smiled. "Wow, you were thirsty!" he laughed slightly.

She finished her drink and smiled back at him sarcastically. "Look who's talking. So were you."

His smile dropped slightly, in a joking manner. "Yeah, well." He grinned again.

The rest of the Barrows were all nearby, in the small clearing of undergrowth of which the path had led them. Sarah was talking enthusiastically to her dad, who was chatting happily back, yet also trying to feed her at the same time. Sean was kneeling down next to them, chewing hungrily upon a crunchy chocolate bar. Sophie was talking to her step mum, Eve, whilst removing lunches from their backpacks. Flies and other insects buzzed and began to swarm within the air above them all. One landed on Max's shoulder, of which he quickly swatted away with his right hand. Lauren looked really annoyed.

51

"Arrgghh! This is so irritating!" she moaned and spat. She speedily withdrew a bug repellent from within her backpack and sprayed a cluster of flies, inches away from her face. "Why won't these things ever go away?!"

"Chill out Loz," said Adrian who was dealing with the infestation quite calmly. "This is a forest. You're just going to have to get used to them. It's their natural environment. Besides, its summer. They love human sweat."

"I was expecting bugs!" she shouted back angrily. "Just not whole bloody swarms of them!"

"Now you watch your language young lady!" interrupted Eve, trying gently to calm her down.

"Uuurrghh! I'm Sorry!" she said, stressed, but slightly more relaxed.

"That's okay," said Sarah back, her voice as sweet and tender as an angel. She was the most lovable out of all of the Barrow family by a long way, merely because of her age and her innocence.

"Have we done something, to make them act like this? I mean, when was the last time we were literally attacked by swarms of flies and other pesky bugs?" asked Sophie surprised.

"They want our lunch. Hungry little things are after that," responded Adrian quietly to the others. His voice was not raised or angry, he just said casually.

"Do you think it would be better if we moved somewhere else to eat?" suggested Eve.

"Nah, forget about it," he answered back. "Wherever we move there's always going to be bugs coming at us."

From the corner of the group, Lauren mouthed the word *Great!* sarcastically to herself in annoyance. Max simply dismissed this comment and continued tucking into his sandwich, which he had woken up this morning at his dad's house at six am just to make, and finish packing up. He didn't care about the irritating and exasperating insects bothering everyone. He merely carried on. Nothing would stand in the way of him and his lunch.

The rest of the world seemed to wash over them. They were like tiny ants in the woodland microcosm, hidden away in a shade of green and brown, leaves and branches camouflaging them from the outside planet. They were completely surrounded by it all, their own hibernation to face on their own.

Sean had hardly spoken anything since his supposed encounter. Everyone believed that he had shaken it off a long time ago, yet the sullen look on his face made it easy to believe that he hadn't. Whilst everyone was talking eagerly amongst each other, Max spared a quick moment of his time to walk over and sit beside him to talk to him quietly.

"Hi man, how are you feeling? Any better?" he asked cautiously.

"Yeah, I think so," he answered back slowly and furtively. "I just think, well, I know, I must have hallucinated what I saw. But, you know, you just get that feeling of, you know, what if it wasn't the heat getting to me."

Max looked up and around into the wilderness of Dilas Forest surrounding the clearing. "Yeah, I know what you mean," he muttered quietly back. "I get that all the time back in Uni, when you don't understand. It's natural, don't worry. Everyone gets it. Trust me, we are not a lunatic family. When it's a hot, long day your mind does start to play tricks on you. Especially since we haven't had a summer like this in a long, long time." He looked at Sean, who was knelt down beside him, who looked back, his face slightly better now from the short comforting. He smiled slightly, yet inside he still felt the dreadful urge that was crawling through his insides.

"Thanks," he said kindly, trying to keep his older brother happy with his expression on the outside. Nothing could shake off what he had seen earlier on. It may have been a hallucination, yet not even the greatest of modern day cures, psychological or not, could take away his pain inside at the moment.

Several feet away, sitting down on the rotting, dead tree which Max was also once on, was Lauren. There she sat, chewing on a really badly made sandwich which she had thrown together at the last second before leaving. She stared around her into the unknown wilderness of trees and the vast sea of green and brown which surrounded the clearing. Blazing sunlight seeped down through the gaps in the tree canopy. She turned her head to look behind her. None of the others were facing in this direction at all. Her eyes wandered through the trees and the undergrowth. Past thick barked trunks and tall twisting plants. All seemed quiet and lifeless in her sight, except for suddenly, when her eyes met upon one particular point.

Ahead of her, her eyes appeared to have been caught by something, and as she stared on through the leaves and the branches, her heart missed several beats as she noticed that something was staring back.

She froze in shock for a moment, as she then tried to see what it was. She squinted, her vision narrowing down to this one point. Staring nervously through the trees, beneath the dark area of undergrowth several hundred yards away, she saw a pair of eyes, staring eerily back at her. Her heart beat began to rise rapidly; it was straining like a dog on a leash in horror. She was becoming more and more scared by the second. The eyes continued to stare back. Even though they were a long distance away, she could still see their brightness, their glare, their hate.

Suddenly, Adrian shouted to her from across the small clearing from where he was sitting. "Hey Lauren, are you alright?"

She turned her head rapidly to face him and the others who were all staring at her confused. "Yeah, sure. Just... looking around," she replied quickly, smiling to reassure them.

"Okay," said Adrian quietly. "When you're all ready then we'll get going again." He smiled to the group and then turned swiftly to collect his rucksack. Max and Sophie began to tidy their leftovers away into their rucksacks. Eve tried to pack Sarah's away, whilst also trying to keep her under control, since she was constantly picking up random objects off the forest floor and attempting to eat them. Sean got up more slowly; he was still shaken by the day's earlier event. He had hardly touched his lunch, merely tearing off scraps from the edges and chewing them with fear still plaguing his mind. Yet he knew that what he had seen wasn't real. He was fifteen and was old enough to understand the pressure of heat on a young human's mind on a day like this.

Lauren also packed her food away more slowly than the others. Not through anxiety however, it was through suspicion. She folded the top of her backpack over and gradually cautiously turned to face the spot where she had seen the beady pair of eyes before. She squinted as her eyes met the spot. But instead of seeing the terrifying pair of eyes once more, she was faced with nothing. Instead, she stared once again into the dark, lifeless undergrowth metres away. She began to relax a little, still curious of what those distant eyes where. *It must have been a badger or a fox.* She thought to herself. *They're natural in woods like these.* Her pulse began to slow right down as she continued staring into the trees and greenery, making sure to the very last moment that nothing was there.

"Lauren, are you coming or what?" came a sudden voice from behind her. With that she leapt out of her skin and almost screamed, as she tuned around to see her older brother's friendly face looking at her sceptically. Everyone else had vanished on ahead, leaving only the two of them left in the small clearing space.

"You made me jump there." She exhaled, sighing and breathing heavily in shock and relief.

"Oh, I'm sorry," Max responded back, calmly. "Everyone else has gone on ahead. I just came back to see whether you were OK."

"Yeah, I'm fine," she said, relieved. "Thanks."

"No problem." He beamed kindly. "Come on. Let's go."

Lauren stood up at normal speed now, lifting her backpack high and bringing it down upon her shoulders. She didn't even look back once as she followed her brother into the swarm of trees through which the path led. Lauren confidently believed that the eyes which met hers in the darkness must have belonged to some form of wild animal which was native to this habitat. Yet inside, she really hoped that she was right.

Chapter 9: With Claws of Blood and Steel

Brittle twigs crumbled into the earth as hard boots crashed down upon them like giants dominating a microscopic world. The realm of rotting branches and wild plant life was becoming increasingly irritating as Sophie Barrow had just about had enough. The late afternoon sun was hot and unsettling, the insects leeching off her sweat and weakness. The day was slowly turning into a complete disaster in its own twisted, eerie way. First, all the cars outside the forest seemed suspiciously like they had been abandoned for weeks, even months. Then Sean had supposedly seen some kind of body a few hours ago. And finally, just about half an hour ago, her older sister Lauren was acting rather mysteriously, like she was worried, or had just seen something frightening. This was all leading towards disaster; she could feel it within her bones. Something horrible was going to happen. What might happen next? Was some form of monster just going to come rushing out from behind a nearby tree? Sophie was not normally one to mull over and reflect over something like this, but this was starting to become extremely worrying. Her brother Sean was fifteen and yet he was still reduced to tears by something which only he had seen. And yet her father was blind to all of this. Soon enough, he would lead them from the path on his own little adventure course, and possibly lead them to the worst part of it all.

Sean followed her close behind, sweat also beginning to drip from his warm forehead. His bag was heavy as he had packed more than enough for a day's hike through the woodland. He reached his arm back towards his backpack, stretching until his hand grasped hold of a cool, damp water flask. He removed it rapidly and drunk hurriedly. The heat and effort of the day was really taking its toll upon him. Like a flaming dragon, it breathed fire and scorching energy down upon the Barrows as they walked steadily along the narrow forest path, trees and undergrowth closing in on them from all sides like they were alive and ready to attack.

Adrian led the way. He was a born leader. Even since he was a child, he had been exploring and discovering his way to greater aspects. From the age of eighteen months he had been walking happily on two feet. When he was four he was top of the class in his old nursery school. When he was eleven he passed his SATS with all Level fives. When he was sixteen he had mastered the Duke of Edinburgh Gold Award Expedition and every subject in school along the lines of Hiking and Travel. He succeeded with ten GCSEs, the majority resulting as A's and A Stars. Upon reaching eighteen he passed into Oxford University and left with a Distinction. When he reached twenty nine, he married Christina Simpson and had four children, Max, Lauren, Sophie and Sean. At the age of forty five he divorced his wife and married again to Eve Fallon, who then later gave birth to another daughter, Sarah. At fifty one, he was sitting in a local pub wondering how to deal with it all.

But that was why they were here, in Dilas Forest, to learn how to put up with these stereotypical childhood problems of complaining and moaning. By the end of today, they would leave the woods as a much happier family together. His four eldest children did not think too much of his more recent wife, so therefore they would learn to appreciate her company more through this. And that was final.

Adrian ducked beneath a branch as the wind swung it creakingly towards him. He held it up kindly as Sophie ducked under it also, holding it out to her brother behind her. Adrian turned slowly to his left, to see another smaller, rugged pathway leading out from beneath a clump of small trees. It quickly turned around a corner, and led on mysteriously into the unknown. He looked back once more at the much wider path which lay straight ahead of them.

The other visitors would have disappeared on up ahead a long time ago. Adrian debated, looking at the alternative pathway to their side, as the rest of the family began to gather up behind their frozen leader.

"What is it honey? Why have we stopped?" asked Eve from a few heads back.

Adrian didn't answer. He was deep in though, thinking wisely about the two possible directions which they could take. Little did he know that whichever path they took would decide their impending fate.

The rest of the family were staring at him, confused. "Dad? Are you alright?" asked Sophie, looking up at him in surprise.

Adrian's eyes darted from left to right like cogs whirring within a machine. This was it, time to decide where the real adventure would begin. His pupils focused once more on the path to their left, which led away from the eroded main path route way and off into the heart of the woods. His mouth opened steadily, concern and excitement filling his mind, and said two syllables. "Okay."

Max, Lauren, Eve, Sarah, Sean and Sophie all stared at Adrian in utter perplexity. "I'm sorry?" asked Max, bemused. "What's going on?"

His father turned around swiftly to address the onlookers. "Right, folks. This is where the tables turn."

"What do you mean?" asked Lauren surprised.

"What I mean, is that from here, we are no longer going to follow the main path which we were told to. From now on, we are going to stray elsewhere, where we can discover our own route from here onwards."

Everyone just stared and ogled at him like he was some kind of lunatic.

"Don't even think about it!" said Max sharply from the back. "We're not…"

"Oh yes Max," interrupted Adrian. "From now on we're leaving the public path and making our own way through Dilas Forest."

"Adrian dear, I don't think that this is a very good idea," said Eve, trying to stay calm.

"But come on, sweetheart. It's going to be much better than sticking to this boring old route. I mean, what have we seen so far? Bushes, trees, lots and lots of flies." His tone was of annoyance and lust for wanting to venture outwards. "I'm talking about waterfalls, natural sculptures, real wildlife, that sort of thing. If you want to go for the real thing, you've got to fight for it."

"Yeah, but..!" said out a frustrated Lauren. "We're not actually going to see these things because you're going to get us lost again, as you always do!"

Adrian stood there, paused for a moment. His aggravation was low yet his patience was weakening. "Lauren, Lauren, Lauren. That's all part of the adventure involved. Even if we do get stuck a little off course, we will find a way to repair this mistake. In scouting, the guys and girls would be prepared for this challenge. And since none of you were interested in scouting then I thought you might as well have some form of experience."

"I didn't mind doing it," added Max quietly from the very back of the troupe.

"Yes well that was when you were eleven Max, and this wasn't so much of a problem back then."

Max nodded slightly, understanding. Sean however did not. "So you're going to drag us way off from the path, and try and get us to become more daring with our lives."

Adrian nodded. "Yes, that's exactly right. You guys are all young and Eve and I only want the best from you..."

"Eve?! What as she got to do with it? She didn't raise us or anything!" Lauren burst out.

Eve looked down at the ground sadly, trying to ignore that remark.

60

"That is not the kind of language I expect to hear from you Lauren!" Adrian was becoming really irritated by now with his children's behaviour and attitude towards the journey so far. Tensions were running high by now. "Now you will all love Eve just as much as she loves you." There was a silence in which every one of the group felt their own kind of annoyance and frustration deep inside. "Now, as I was saying. It is just coming up to five o'clock now. Therefore if we split off here, we can easily make our way back to the entrance for around eight o'clock. Just before we have to leave. Therefore all is accomplished. And hopefully you will appreciate things more from then on. Learn to value the wonders of nature and what it has to offer. Especially you, Lauren." Lauren sighed and rolled her eyes blatantly.

At that moment, a large dragonfly hovered closely towards her face. With all her anger loaded up, she punched the dragonfly out of the air with what seemed like a fistful of steel. The blue insect fell to the floor with a surge of speed. Sophie was staring at her with disbelief. Lauren turned to stare back at her, eyebrows curved with fury. "I hate bugs."

By now, the family had spread out and was now facing Adrian in a form of semi-circle. Sarah didn't have a clue what was going on, yet she held tightly to her mother and sucked her thumb gently. Max stood out to address Adrian in irritation. "Dad, what's the point? Why are we doing this? Straying from the path has no real means of training us. It's just causing more chaos!"

"Now son, we've had this conversation before..." retaliated Adrian calmly.

"I know!" interrupted Max sharply with anger. "But this is the real thing! I was hoping that you'd change your mind over the hours we've been wandering through this sea of trees, but no! You haven't changed your mind one bit."

His father sighed, trying desperately to find the right words to calm his nineteen year old son down. "Look Max.

61

I've watched you since you were born. I've seen you grow from baby, to toddler, to child, to teenager, to man. And you've changed your attitude and personality so many times. I've seen you set your mind to so many great things in the past. You all have." He looked around slowly at all the other Barrow children, who were listening in. "Now I'm simply asking you to turn your mind to this one thing, and in about three hours, it will all be over. Thinking of others before yourselves is a very important matter. And you're the next generation of Barrows. This is something you can pass on to your children and speak of your adventures. This could be the first. Yet it could also be the last if you wish to dismiss it completely. Just think about it when we go on. I am your guide, and someday you will be one too towards your family. Everyone finds their own separate path. And someday you will find yours. And that is going to start now." And with that, he turned around swiftly to face the rough, dirt trodden path and started to head off down it, into the wilderness and oblivion.

Max seemed gobsmacked for a moment. The very extraordinary speech from his father had left them all hanging, except for the fact that he didn't even wait for a reply was particularly peculiar. Lauren sighed and looked up around at Sophie to speak grumpily. "Okay. I take it we're going then."

Sophie didn't respond at first. A moments silence echoed as she stared after Adrian who was trekking off into the wilderness of trees. "We can't just leave him wandering alone," she eventually replied quietly. "Better go before we lose him altogether." With that, she breathed deeply in and out, and stepped over the dividing line into the void of green and brown. Lauren shortly followed after her.

Max looked across to see Sean standing there, looking rather nervous. "Sean, we have to go on. Dad's made his choice stubbornly and we can't refuse it. I'm sorry," he said caringly to his younger brother.

Sean looked up at him and managed to tweak the tiniest glimpse of a smile onto his face. He looked out at the three figures slowly disappearing into the distance and the cover of trees and undergrowth. They were growing smaller and smaller as the distance increased. He had a dark, uneasy feeling deep down inside. It was like the forest was calling them closer, deeper and deeper, corrupting them disturbingly. It was like it was alive and was leading them towards a terrible, grave fate. It had already gotten to Adrian, who was clearly one of the strongest members of the group. Sean thought to himself. How long was it going to be before it reached everyone else? "I'm still nervous about everything that dad's doing. I just know something horrible is going to happen. I can feel it coming."

There was a short moment of silence, but the tension made it feel like it lasted forever, before Max said back. "I know. Me too."

Sarah seemed her usual toddler self, confused, bored and not really caring about anything that was going on around her. "Mummy?" she asked her mother whilst holding her hand.

"Yes sweetheart. I know, lets go," replied Eve, as she kissed her three year old daughter on the forehead and started following on too. "Are you coming guys?" she asked politely. Looking back as she passed them.

"Yeah we're coming," answered Max, awakening from being lost in thought. "Just give us a moment. We'll be right behind you."

"OK," she nodded, turning towards the large open hole in the surrounding barrier of branches to join the others.

Max waited for a moment until Eve was almost completely out of sight, before turning back to Sean once more, speaking quietly. "Alright. I know this place doesn't seem very hospitable, but we've just got to stay calm for now. I know that something isn't right here, and you can feel it too."

Sean gulped and started breathing heavily again in panic. "Yeah. I'm really scared Max. What I saw earlier, it can't have just been me."

"Okay, calm down. It's alright. Dad, Eve and Sarah can't see it, but I know we can. I haven't seen anything yet, but from the suspicion which I think is rising here, others can feel something wrong is here too."

"Really?" Sean asked curiously in surprise. "Like who?"

"Well. When we first arrived at the entrance and were unloading, Sophie seemed very disturbed by the fact that most of the other cars around seemed completely abandoned. Also, when we stopped for lunch a while ago we were all packed up and ready to leave, except for Lauren, who seemed to be rather frightened and confused by something which she might have seen. I told her it must have been some kind of animal, which it probably was. I knew it most likely was some form of wildlife on the outside, but on the inside I still felt some form of suspicion linking on to Sophie's comments earlier on. And with what you believed to have seen earlier as well, something sinister seems to be going on right beneath our noses, unfurling bit by bit. But we just can't see what it is." Max looked up and around at the forest surrounding them. The branches snaked and winded like twisting arms reaching out for them, blowing gently in the late summer wind. The vast tree canopies above seemed like swarms of insects trying to block out the sun from all below on the forest floor. The place almost felt like it was haunted, that something was screaming at them that was hidden from sight. Yet the more Max thought about it, the more he became afraid.

"I don't like this place at all. I'm beginning to sound like Lauren but this is the only place I've visited in years that I've really wanted to…" Sean paused fearfully for a moment. "… Get away from."

Max was silent. He thought hard to himself. "I know we're scared but we have to keep following the others. It's our only way of getting out and it's what we've got to do. Dad may not see it, and there is no way of making him see." He breathed heavily outwards, scared and frustrated. "I don't know what to do."

"But your nineteen Max! You've got to have some kind of plan to convince the others."

Max almost chuckled quietly at the small joke, but now was not the time. Right now he was worried and bewildered. "Ok, for now just keep calm, act natural and think to yourself that it's only your mind playing tricks on you. We'll see if something sinister is really happening later. But for now just stay calm and under control. Be brave Sean. Now come on. We've got to catch up with the others. And hey…" He put both his arms on his brother's shoulders and said firmly to him. "Just think to yourself. By the time we leave this place we'll know that it was all in our heads." He nodded caringly as Sean nodded back at him. Max stood up fully, checked his buckles were still clutching the bag to his back and looked at Sean once more. Three syllables were spoken to end the ominous conversation. "After you." He held out his left arm, which pointed towards the off-road pathway formed from where others had barged their way through it.

Sean looked over at him, smiled ever so slightly and walked off onto the rough track, a look of nervousness imprinted upon his teenage face. Max turned around once more to look over the surrounding woodland. The darkness leaping out from the shadows like it was ambushing prey. His heart was worried and his brain confused beyond belief. For one of the first times in his life, Max was actually worried for Sean and the rest of his family. He turned slowly to continue onto the path, still thinking about the eerie past events of the day so far. Something was out there. Watching. Waiting.

The water ran rapidly and swiftly off the ledge into the deep chasm of the pool below. The clean mixture of blue and crystal clear colour stood out amongst the surrounding forest and the moss-covered rock which it sloped off. The whole scene seemed almost surreal, compared to the surrounding world which was a jungle of insects and heat. This was the candle in the darkness, the oasis in the desert.

Adrian stepped out from behind a clump of trees and bushes to witness the flowing waterfall in all of its glory. He smiled to himself with pride, happy with what he had found. The fine water droplets dazzled and twinkled in the late afternoon sunlight. This was what adventure was made for.

"You see. If we had stayed to the path then we wouldn't have seen any of this kind of excitement," he beamed excitedly. "This is what we really came here for," he said smiling to himself.

Sophie ducked beneath a branch and breathed out in relief as she stood beside her father, who was looking up at the high ledge above, and occasionally following the odd branch or cluster of leaves which would fall from the stream above into the rocky pool below, which they were standing next to. "Wow. That's quite impressive," she remarked, not too amazed because of her exhaustion.

Adrian could see she was out of breath. "Oh come on. It wasn't that far." He commented jokingly.

"Well, if you've got what you've got in my bag, then surely you'd feel the same," she exclaimed almost angrily. "I'm flippin' fourteen. You're big and old and strong."

"Alright, chill out dear. I'm only joking," he replied casually, almost laughing. "And besides, I'm not old, I'm fifty one." he chuckled as his daughter laughed back. Adrian lifted her bag off from her back as she undid the strap and buckles. "Crikey Soph!" he exclaimed in surprise. "What have you got in here?!" He lifted the bag up with one hand, yet still felt the heavy weight bearing down on him like a ton of bricks. "You only needed to bring your lunch, a couple of bottles of water and extra clothes in case it rained."

"Yeah, well." She looked up at the massive waterfall towering over her just a few metres away. "I have my reasons." She smiled to herself.

Max was several yards away, on the other side of the pool, washing his face rapidly in the refreshing water which splashed onto his sweating, overheated face. It made him feel so much better, a cool, uplifting shield of liquid swallowing his head into its new refreshing world. Cold droplets of water fell like raindrops onto the edges of his pure white t-shirt. He breathed in and out slowly, taking in all the breeze of the passing wind as it swooped down into one of the many small clearings in Dilas Forest. He smiled slightly in relief, as for a very short moment, all of his thoughts and worries seemed to wash away. This was what the heat was doing to him and to his family. It was extremely irritating and exasperating, causing heads to spin and minds to collapse. In areas closer to the equator of the Earth, the deserts were hot enough to kill. But this was the summer in England however, and the heat wasn't quite as deadly yet.

Max sighed, relaxing. He stood up and sat down on a rock facing away from the pool, towards the rest of his family, who were scattered across the small clearing, each with a different situation and subject in mind. Adrian and Sophie were arguing jokingly about the contents of her rucksack. Eve was sat down on a nearby rock, showing Sarah her reflection as she ogled at it in awe, whilst also trying to stop her from falling in. Lauren and Sean were sat down on their backpacks in the centre of the clearing, Lauren fussing with her make-up like she did back at home, whilst Sean was looking away, rather nervously into the surrounding trees, peering into the distance for any sign of life. This was not good. He was worrying. Max knew deep inside that their connection of thoughts from earlier had still not passed. He had tried to forget about it over the past hour hiking into the wilderness, with only Adrian as their guide.

Max was nineteen. He was old enough to forget about problems like these. However Sean was not. He was only fifteen, and was still a young teenager in a huge open world. Max could sense his fear, his nervousness, his alarm. Max looked up and around at the dark green forest which they had just walked through. It was quiet. Too quiet. He could sense Sean's fear growing and could tell that his younger brother was scared. He was about to walk over casually and try to calm his younger brother down quietly, when suddenly Lauren put her make-up back in the bag and turned to talk to Sean.

Max straightened his black glasses and looked over at the pair of them chatting. Sean now seemed to calm down a little from his expression. Max didn't know what they were talking about, since he could not hear their conversation from this distance, yet he hoped inside that his sister was not talking to Sean about the surrounding woodland itself.

Max removed his glasses from his face to clean them from the dirt and grime which had gathered upon them over the past several hours in the forest. He dipped them shallowly into the water-filled pit behind him. Taking his glasses out, he looked into the calm, clear liquid and saw his reflection staring back. He was fully grown, tall and slightly muscular beneath his clothing. His dark hair was short as the highest tips blew in the air as the wind whispered and swept throughout the land. He was an adult now. He had passed the days when he was a frightened kid, afraid of monsters beneath the bed. Yet despite his confidence and his fearlessness, the kid inside still cried out from deep within. He could see it in his eyes, and feel it writhing within his veins. But he mustn't show fear. He was an inspiration to Sean and to Sarah and all those who looked up to him. He had to show them that he was not scared.

He tried to calm himself, looking deeply into the bottom of the pool to try and drown his dark thoughts. Yet all he could see was his reflection. He could see in the reflection the waterfall, gloriously running off the top of the ledge above into the pool into which he was looking. He saw trees above on the ledge and plants growing on the face of the small cliff, their leaves shaking slightly in the summer breeze. All seemed peaceful and quiet in nature's playground.

Suddenly, in Max's view of reflection, something moved in the background. He looked up dramatically, almost dropping his glasses into the water below. He hurriedly placed them back upon his face and looked around rapidly into the trees and bushes on the top of the cliff ledge above, searching for something which he had seen flash from out of the corner of his eye. Yet nothing was there. The trees and undergrowth above seemed at peace once more. Max swore he had seen something move. He breathed out again, trying to relax. It must have been a rabbit or a fox or some other kind of wild animal. He was becoming paranoid, as it was really starting to show by now.

"Max? Are you alright?" came a suspicious voice from behind him. Max spun around in his seat to see Adrian and Sophie both staring at him from a short distance away. Sophie looked sceptical, most likely wondering what on earth was going on. However, his father seemed more concerned.

"Yeah, sure, I'm fine. Thanks," replied Max calmly. He looked around once more to see if anything was there for the final time, only to greet the silence above once again.

Adrian and Sophie turned around once again to continue their comical, ridiculous argument. Each convinced that their reason was in the right; each refusing to back down. "Fine!" cried out Sophie. "Alright, alright. I won't take the extra make-up removers next time."

69

Her father began to laugh humorously. "There's a good girl."

Sophie was sulking jokingly, as she sat down upon a nearby rock and started foraging through the mindless clutter in her bag for her drink.

Adrian turned around to face an opposite direction to which everyone else in the group was facing. His cheerful face began to drop slightly. Then lower, and lower, until a few moments later his expression was the most serious and concerned it had ever been. He breathed out fearfully, short stops broke here and there in his strung out sigh. He was worried. Not about what the others were secretly nervous about, but something else, something dark and disturbing which only he knew about. Soon enough however, he would have to show the rest of his innocent family what was really going on, for everyone's sake. Adrian slowly reached into his pocket and withdrew a small photo. It was dusty and old, yet this image reached deep into Adrian's soul, and drew out the anxiety from the shadows. He stared deeply into the photograph, thinking to himself of what he should do. What he could do. But it was hopeless. He turned around slowly to check if any of his family were watching, and then quickly folded the photograph back to how it was and slipped it deep down into his pocket. He breathed out long and hard once more, trying to calm himself down. Bravely, Adrian put a smile upon his face once more and then turned to talk to his daughter again.

Meanwhile, from several yards away, Max had been watching his father, his back turned and mysteriously staring down at an unknown object which Max could not see from where he was sitting. He was not a nosy man but still found it very bewildering, what his father was doing. There were no secrets he could possibly be hiding, no sinister happenings which could be going on. Max looked down at the floor, he picked up a small stone from the many hundreds scattered around the clearing. Looking at it for a second, he tossed it up into the air, caught it, and started fiddling around with it in his wet, clean hands.

Suddenly an alarmed gasp came from the front of the clearing near the woods. Max looked up in fright hurriedly, he dropped the stone rapidly as he saw a shocking sight staring back at them. Adrian and Sophie turned around also at the sound and were completely stunned by what they saw, their jaws gaping open in utter disbelief. Eve had to close her hand to Sarah's mouth to stop her from screaming. Lauren was the one who had gasped and had seen the sight first. She sat there on a rock almost traumatised along with Sean. The two of them were closest to the tree line, and could see the terrifying form the clearest.

From just within the borderline of the trees, standing beneath a cluster of dead and withering branches, stood a monstrous, snarling wolf. Its hair was rough, a mixture of white and grey, yet withering and thin as if it was hungry and unclean. Its teeth bore out like knives, yellow and sharp as they were. There it stood, like a monstrous guardian angel, staring. Its whole form was chilling to the bone. Its eyes were red and bulging like blood, thin black pupil slits stared into the eyes of those closest, and that was Sean.

"Okay," said Adrian quietly and stuttering slightly in terror, trying to keep everyone calm and not to alert the animal. "Nobody move. If we panic then we will only aggravate it more. Everyone just try and stay calm, stay still, and it will go away."

It wasn't that everyone wasn't trying to remain calm; it was the fact that everyone else was completely terrified of the creature. Sean was breathing heavily. He didn't know what to do. He was only metres away from those monstrous teeth and claws. Saliva drooled down from the wolf's wide mouth. It looked like it was about to pounce and attack at any moment.

Lauren sat next to her brother. "Sean. It's alright. Don't panic. Everything's going to be okay." Her lips were barely

71

moving, as she did not wish to attract attention and was almost equally as petrified as he was.

Sean nodded very slightly, his lips trembling with fear as the beast watched him, hunger screaming in its eyes. Sean didn't know if he could take it any more. It was like staring into the face of oblivion. All of the madness and the terror loaded up inside of that beast. He was waiting for it, praying deep inside his head that it would go away. He kept on breathing heavily, terrified. Everyone was staring at the wolf, goose bumps rising as hairs tilted on the backs of their necks. For the first time today, the Barrows were feeling the real power of the word 'fear'.

All of a sudden, the wolf struck. It leapt high into the air from its perch and landed sharply a few feet from where Sean and Lauren were sitting. Lauren screamed. The wolf was snarling; a low, deep growl erupted from the back of its throat. Sean was frozen in fear as the wolf suddenly ran towards him and leapt, its mouth gaping open, revealing a huge maw of teeth and fangs. It leaped through the air, soaring towards him, and crunched down hard onto Sean's leg. He screamed deafeningly in pain just as Lauren beside him screamed in terror and fright. Max jumped to his feet, as several feet away, Adrian also jumped up to help his son. The wolf was biting hard and ferociously onto Sean's leg. It was flaying his leg from side to side trying to tear it off as Sean screamed in pain as he tried to hold back for dear life. Max ran as fast as he could towards the attack, bending down and grabbing a huge fallen branch from the ground as he dashed to save his brother. The wolf was still holding on and biting hard as it wrenched viciously at the lower half of Sean's leg. Max came running up to the position of the terrorising wolf. Raising the dead branch high into the air, he built up all his strength, and smashed the object down swiftly and hard upon the wolf's head. The blow seemed immense and unreal to Max for a moment. The wolf seemed almost dazed for a second as its grip loosened slightly and Sean tried to break free. But this was not to last, as the monstrous mammal snapped out of its split-second trance and strengthened it's bite as it tore deeper into Sean's leg. Sean screamed over and over again, his cries echoing out into the late afternoon air. Max lifted his weapon into the air again and crashed the blow down upon the savage animal's thick skull. Still the animal wouldn't let go. It was desperate, hungry beyond belief to take such a blowing like this one, yet it just wouldn't let go.

This was when the unexpected came. Max had brought the club down upon the animal with such might and to no effect. Adrian was holding onto Sean tightly with all of his strength. "Hold on son! Just keep holding on!" he screamed loudly, sweat and fear pounding down upon him. He knew he could not hold on for much longer.

That was when the fight increased to the next level.

For a moment, Adrian thought about this hard, but then the situation was forcing him to take desperate measures. Screaming his lungs out, he let go of his son and jumped onto the wolf. Suddenly, the creature miraculously let go of Sean's leg. It lumbered around, desperately trying to shake the angry Adrian from its back. He raised his fist high, clenching it with the strength of an ox, and brought it down like a hammer upon the wolf's head. The beast collapsed suddenly, causing Adrian to fly off and roll across the floor several metres away. Everyone was in shock. Sophie was clutching her mouth in terror. Eve was on the verge of tears, desperately trying to stop Sarah from seeing the monster before them. Slowly, with everyone's eyes upon it, the wolf got up and wandered dazedly away at a quickened pace, off into the darkness of the surrounding woodland.

Everyone stared after it in disbelief until the last tail hair had disappeared around the corner. Lauren was terrified out of mind, her expression like she had been scarred deep inside. Eve held Sarah tightly and rushed over to her stepson who was lying wounded on the floor. Sean was wheezing heavily, choking and spluttering frequently.

"Sean!" cried Adrian lifting himself up off the floor and hurrying over to help his son. "Oh my God! It's okay. Stay calm. Everything is going to be alright. Just keep breathing gently!" He looked down at the severe bite marks on Sean's leg. It was very badly wounded. Blood was pouring slowly from the many tiny cuts in teeth marks above his heel. Lauren gasped with shock from seeing the wound, her eyes fixed upon the horrific sight.

"Mummy, what was that?" asked Sarah in shock loudly. She had not seen the huge animal itself, yet only heard the struggle from her young innocent ears.

"A wolf?!" remarked Sophie. "But what was that doing here? Wolves are extinct in England!"

"Well, this place was only opened to the public in January a few years back," said Adrian hurriedly in stress and panic. He had whipped out a strip of bandage from his backpack and was now tying it hurriedly around the leg of a distressed Sean, along with adding several strong doses of treatment onto it too. "Maybe a lot of its more ancient wildlife has survived and is still around today, hence the wolf."

"But wolves normally hunt in packs!" Sophie came rushing over to help the others. "This one was all on its own. Why?"

"I don't know Soph! I just don't know!" Adrian's voice was stressed. He was nervous, worried and concerned over so many problems now.

Max was kneeling down a few feet away, thinking to himself, trying to calm down the stress and panic that was engulfing his body. *Wolves always hunt in packs, then why was this one alone?* He thought to himself. A growing concern was developing in his mind. Something he mustn't tell Sean for fear of dragging him into further unease. The poor boy had been through so much today so far.

Something must have killed the others off.

74

It was almost impossible for a lone wolf to attack a pack of another species on its own. Unless it was extremely aggressive and hungry, which wasn't usual in woods like these. This was extremely abnormal, and was one more to add to the vast amount of panic which was spreading like a disease throughout the family.

Max looked over towards the others, who had bandaged Sean's leg and were now helping to lift him up and rest him upon a nearby boulder. "We need to get him to hospital Adrian!" he heard Eve exclaim. "That wound is serious. It could get worse by the minute. The sooner we find the path and get out of here, the better."

Everyone was spreading out and doing different jobs, packing rucksacks away and preparing to move out. "But what if it's still out there?" he heard Lauren speak.

Adrian hurriedly removed his mobile phone from within his pocket and dialled 999 as fast as he could. He lifted the device to his ear in a flash, biting down upon his lip as he uttered the words *Come on! Come on!* under his breath. A long second past before finally the phone responded with a loud beep. Adrian removed the phone from his ear and stared horrified down at the screen, which read boldly 'Signal Unavailable'.

"Damn it!" he shouted, throwing his phone at the dirt aggressively. "There's no signal! We can't reach any help at this rate."

Everyone was staring at him, confused and shocked, unknowing what they could do. "We'll have to find our own way back. Get back to the entrance and dial 999 from the outpost," responded Eve eventually. "But what if the thing comes back?"

"It was injured. It will probably wander off into the wilderness and rest for a while. It won't bother us any longer," replied Adrian, a million things on his mind at once.

Max stood up slowly, his legs weak from the attack. He looked up, breathed a deep breath in, and was about to walk over and help the others, when he noticed something tiny out of the corner of his eye. He stopped dead in his tracks, and turned slowly to face the small unknown object. Gradually his eyes adjusted to see what it was. As he noticed, he was surprised to see what this entity was doing here. It must have been something that his dad must have dropped when he rolled from the wolf's back. Lying in the dirt and the uneven earth was a photograph. Max walked over to it slowly, apprehensively. His eyes squinting to see what it was as he knelt down and picked up the tiny picture. Max looked deep into the heart of the photograph, to see a pair of contented eyes looking back at him. The photograph was a picture of a middle aged man, around the age of his father. He was bald, with a broad smile written upon his face. The background displayed what looked like a pub, its glowing lights and many beer glasses left finished along the bar. The main focus of the photo however was the man in the picture. *Who was he? And what was this photo doing here?* This wasn't a coincidence. Something mysterious was going on, and he was going to find out why.

Max turned to face his father who had just helped, along with Eve, Sean onto a nearby rock, who was still wincing in pain from the bite wound, groaning through gritted teeth and watering eyes. He frowned curiously and asked a simple question to Adrian. "Dad? Who's this?"

Adrian looked up and saw the horrible, unexpected sight of his son holding up the photograph towards him. His heart missed several beats as he dropped the water flask he was holding and was frozen in thought and worry. He had been found out, the profound secret behind through which he had really dragged them all into this new nightmare for.

There was a long pause in which everyone else gradually adjusted their eyesight to realise what the surprising image contained. Six pairs of eyes all staring directly at Adrian, waiting, concerned and astounded for him to reveal what this photo meant. Adrian was incredibly nervous now. Sweat was dripping slowly and exasperatingly down from his forehead. He opened his mouth to speak, and to enter the chaos. "Okay guys. I'm going to be honest here." He said truthfully, gulping regrettably.

"What do you mean?" retaliated Eve apprehensively. "Adrian, who is this man?" She was becoming extremely worried now, as was everyone else.

"I know, I know." He replied, breathing heavily with fear and frustration. "I know I haven't explained everything, but I will…"

"You will?!" interrupted Lauren furiously. "Dad, you've been hiding something from us and we have a right to know!"

Adrian paused, a thousand thoughts all spiralling around in his mind at once. "Look Lauren, everyone… I only wish it was that simple." He paused a second time. "I should have told you a long time ago, but that would have only worried you more."

Every one of all ages, young and old were staring at him, as the silence grew and tensions were raised.

"There's nothing wrong with this place. I lead you here so that we could have a good time, like I said. It's just that, there is, well… something else which I myself came here for."

"Go on!" added Sophie through gritted teeth.

Adrian sighed long and hard. "Several months ago my good friend, Matthew Tarron went missing." A long moment of silence rung out like a wave around the group as all were lost in a mixture shock and confusion. "When the police were looking for evidence of how he had disappeared, they could find nothing. However a few weeks afterwards, I discovered something more, behind it all… a piece of evidence."

"And then?" asked Eve, more curious now, yet still cross and agitated.

Adrian continued. "I arrived home from work early one day, and so I thought I would try and find anything more within the Tarron house. Since I was a very good friend of his, he gave me a set of keys to his house beforehand for any emergencies." He paused and took a deep sigh out. "Anyway. Once I was in his house, I was searching his bedroom and discovered something rather peculiar in a hidden chest of draws which I accidentally discovered. A small booklet filled with all sorts of material all leading to one thing."

"Yes, and then what did they all lead to?" asked Sean, who was leaning up against the rock, speaking with difficulty because of his wound.

"You just keep resting Sean," responded his father gently, before returning to his narrative. "What was in the booklet, were collections of newspaper articles, ancient photographs, and other sinister references."

"To what dad?!" asked Sophie, on the verge of shouting. "What did they lead to?!"

Adrian was completely blown back by the sudden comment. He stood there, with what felt like the whole world watching him in disbelief. He had been dreading this moment for so long. "Here." He said that one syllable quietly. "This place. Dilas Forest. Every object, every bit of paper, every scribbled drawing led to these woods."

The entire troupe was astonished. Scared, quiet, and feeling suddenly much colder.

"That's partly why I'm here." He looked almost as if he was about to cry with fear. "I've got to find him. He knew something that we didn't. Something he wasn't telling the rest of us at work. It was like he was on a mission of some kind. Here in Dilas Forest."

Sarah was becoming very anxious, and was holding on tightly to her mother's warm jacket. Eve hugged her closer, holding the back of Sarah's coat for comfort. She was becoming angry now, and very scared. "And you brought us into the middle of this!" she remarked aggressively towards her husband. "You knew about this sinister place a long time ago, and yet you still came here, with your whole family along with you!"

"Eve, please. I am positive that Mathew did not disappear in here. I came here to find out any more possible evidence towards the case with the police. They didn't seem to listen to me for some strange reason. It took me a very long time to think about this. For the past few weeks I have been very nervous in deciding whether to take all of you or not," replied Adrian in response. "But then in the end I was sure that everything would be safe. All the love which you guys bring along everywhere we go is always the best kind of comfort. Sure, it may not be the nicest of love." He thought back to when Lauren was her usual dramatic self, and Sophie who didn't care for anything. "But you're still my family. Besides..." His expression changed. "First of all, I stand by my word that you need the exercise and the experience of trekking amongst the wildlife and the great outdoors. And secondly..." He suddenly looked more solemn and serious, not taking any interruptions or other points. "Mr Tarron is most likely in another area in Britain, or probably got lost and is still living in here somewhere, okay?"

This last comment relaxed Eve and Sarah a little. Knowing deep inside that nothing was seriously wrong by means of the supernatural. Max, Lauren, Sophie and Sean however, were not convinced. "I still can't believe you did this dad," growled Lauren, looking at him in disapproval. "Sure you did drag us along to help find your friend, but Sean is hurt. We know now that there are wolves out there. Sean really needs to get to a hospital straight away," she said caringly.

"I agree. His leg is badly wounded," commented Sophie. "The sooner we get out of here the better."

"Yes. We should get packed up and leave immediately," agreed Eve. She then turned around in her seat and continued to pack the rest of her equipment away rapidly. The rest followed shortly after, with Sophie packing Sean's bag away whilst he lay there rested against a rock wincing at his severe leg bite wound.

Adrian stood there for a moment, thinking to himself. Why had he done this? He had put his family at a risk and gotten his son injured because of it. This was a mistake coming here. His dear friend may have gone missing, yet his family were much closer, and much more important. His son needed to get to a hospital before his wound became infected and became even worse. He looked up again and snapped back to reality. He must help his family. Their cause came first, and not his.

He walked over to Sean and stood above him, looking down. "Son, are you okay? How do you feel?" he asked kindly.

"How do you think I feel?!" Sean replied irritated. "My leg, it hurts so much!" he moaned angrily.

"Sshh." He hushed him gently and soothingly. "You just stay here and rest. Some of us are going to get help, you understand?"

"Okay," he answered slowly.

Adrian stood up fully, and walked over to address Max and Lauren. "You two. We're going to get help."

"But what about everyone else?" asked Lauren surprised.

"They're going to stay here, whilst the three of us go and search for the entrance point. We'll get assistance and aid for Sean from the guards there."

Eve looked up in surprise and shock. "Are you suggesting that the rest of us stay here?"

Adrian looked down at his wife, sitting on the rock. "Look sweetheart, that animal was alone and injured. There is a very minimal chance that it will come back, okay?" He tried his hardest to find a route around the mass of sudden panic echoing throughout the clearing which they were currently positioned in.

Eve listened closely to the supporting words of her husband, but was still nervous and worried for the rest of the family. "But what if it does? What if that minimal chance actually happens and it returns with greater numbers?"

Adrian looked up and around thoughtfully. "Wolves usually attack in packs. Why would this one be all by itself?" He thought hard, speaking aloud, but tried to push the concerning thought out his head, and focus on dealing with the greater problems at hand. "Look, that won't happen." He returned to look down at Eve. "But just in case the worst comes to hand." He walked over to the place where Max had attacked the huge beast and picked up the branch, blood stains still splattered on the edges. "Here." He handed it to his anxious wife. "I'm a pacifist, but if danger comes to present itself then there is always a last resort."

Eve stared back at him in horror. Her husband had just handed her a possible weapon. She was not a woman of violence either, yet she dreaded the thought of actually coming into contact with that creature again. "We shouldn't split up honey, it's all going to lead to disaster."

"Look I know sweetheart." Adrian's expression was more serious and grave than ever before. "But it's the only way. Sean's leg is badly injured and he can't walk. You, Sarah and Sophie should stay here with Sean and make sure he is okay. I will take Max and Lauren out to the starting area to try and get help…"

"Don't!"

"…Look darling, just listen to me. Everything's going to be alright. Its only going to be a short while of waiting here calmly and then help will arrive and take Sean to hospital."

Eve was scared and filled with apprehension. She paused, shaking slightly and finally managed to open her mouth to speak. "Okay."

Adrian nodded in understanding. He then stood up and turned swiftly on his heels to face Max and Lauren waiting behind him, ready to leave. "Right then. Are you two ready?"

They nodded, worried, but ready to help their brother in need.

Their father nodded back. "Okay then. Let's go." He turned and picked up a small bag from the ground and hauled it over his shoulder. Walking on, he picked up his photograph which lay tattered on the mixture of gravel, grass and rock which was the floor of the forest clearing. Adrian turned to face his family, who were once again in the position of staring at him, looking up to him as a leader and a guide. He looked back at them, his eyes passing each member as they lapped the eye level of the Barrows. "The time is now 7:46pm. Since we have all been travelling in a circular route it will only take a very short time to reach the entrance point, don't worry. We will soon return with help, trust me." He looked down at his son, lying there with pain so sharp, yet he still looked up to his father with pride amongst the irritation. "Sean. You're going to be just fine." He smiled kindly. He cared for his family so much, yet now he had to leave them in two pieces, for the better, in hope of finding help. This was how it must be done, this was a part of human nature itself.

Chapter 10:   The Sirens

The once bright, undying sun which shone high in the late summer's sky, was now dying and gradually sinking lower and lower into the dim twilight. As the sun was slowly setting, a new world seemed to emerge from beneath. Rodents, reptiles and other small animals would emerge to take advantage of the human-less environment.

The whole of Dilas Forest seemed quiet and surreal. Except for three backpackers lost in the wilderness, as night was approaching fast.

"This isn't right," exclaimed Max. "We've been travelling through dirt and undergrowth for almost fifteen minutes. I'm sure we came from another route which linked back to the path!" He was annoyed, frustrated, and livid. If their selfish father hadn't driven them off course and dragged them into finding his missing evidence, they would not be in this mess. Now they were searching through the endless mass of trees and plants to try and find an exit out of the never-ending woodlands.

"We're gonna keep on going!" shouted Adrian back. "The whole path leads into one big circuit which then leads back to the entrance point. You see?" He too was irritated, both by his stupidity and by his lack of concentration to the task which was at hand. He kept on thinking back to his son, lying there, wounded and injured with the rest of his family. He couldn't let them down. He wouldn't let them down.

"Look! Think straight guys. Does anyone have a compass or some other form of tracking equipment on them?" asked Lauren helpfully. Unlike most times, she was fully focused and knew what she was doing. It was her fear which compelled her, as the twilight of the forest began to close in around them, she did not want to be stuck in here all night.

"Yeah, sure. Here." Max reached one of the tiny side pockets of his bag and pulled out a small, simple compass. He handed it over to his sister, who looked at it thoughtfully for a moment.

"Okay," she said after a short pause. "Do you remember what direction we came in from?"

There was a brief moment of silence until Adrian finally answered back. "Yeah, south."

"Good," she continued, "well, look up. You see those stars there pointing in a row of three?" She indicated upwards to three faint stars in the mostly dark night sky. The other two nodded in agreement. "That's Orion's Belt. They point to the North Star. If I'm correct then... aha!" she exclaimed as her eyes followed the line until she set them upon a bright star in the distance. "There we go. Brightest star in the sky." She began to speak quieter, as if thinking to herself, concentrating, looking between her compass and the stars in the sky. "If we line that up... and if that's right, then." No-one could understand entirely what she was saying, as Max and Adrian only picked up half the words she was mentioning, looking briefly at one another in amazement. "And there you have it! We need to go in that direction!" she declared proudly, pointing her arm to their right.

"Well done Lauren. I'm impressed," said Adrian surprised. "Wherever did you learn that?"

"Hmm." She smiled contently. "I know my astronomy when the worse comes to the worst."

Max smiled too. Finally they had found a possible exit route out of the haunting surroundings.

Suddenly, a faint beeping noise buzzed from beneath his sleeve. He looked surprised for a moment, jumping subtly, then pulled back his jacket sleeve to reveal his old watch strapped to his arm. His astonishment reduced as he realised what it was. His pulse then raced in shock as he realised what was going to happen.

"Guys!" he spun around rapidly to face the others, lifting up his arm to show them his watch. The happy, satisfied smiles on their faces dropped like a weight, as they too realised what was about to happen. All three of them looked in horror at the watch, which buzzed and read very clearly, eight pm.

A distant memory suddenly flashed back into Adrian's mind. Several hours earlier, when they had all been waiting outside the entrance gate whilst the guard was giving his briefing. *"... Leave at approximately eight pm at the latest, when the siren is heard."* The thoughts were whirring inside his head so fast he could barely think of anything else. *"...Roughly fifteen minutes after the siren will be rung; the gates will be shut for the night! ... Night! ... Night!"* That last word kept ringing inside of his head over and over again. Like a nightmare, a dark memory twisting and turning into oblivion. With a terrified thought in mind, he said in shock, eyes wide open. "We're not going to make it."

The other two turned to stare at him. Max put away his watch slowly, thinking in horror of what was to come. Lauren stared back. It was cold, dark, and things were about to get a lot worse.

Suddenly, the curse they had all been waiting for arrived. It started off as a quiet ringing, which slowly evolved and grew louder and louder, until eventually, an ear-splitting siren was burning its way through the air.

The three of them looked at each other once more in panic as the siren boomed around them. With terror racing through their minds, they ran.

A few kilometres away, Sean lay quietly against the same old rock which he had been lying against for the past long, draining thirteen minutes, after which Adrian had left to find help with Max and Lauren. The pain from his bitten leg had now almost completely died and only a tiny tingling sensation remained. He leant his head back and sighed.

Looking up at the sky, he saw the twilight closing in. A horrible thought occurred for a moment, as he realised that dark would come swiftly. He tried bravely to shake the dreadful thought out of his mind.

Up in the dim sky, he saw three stars, Orion's Belt. Following the line further, his eyes met with the brightest star in the sky, the North Star. Sean was not particularly good at astronomy, but he knew the basics of most facts in that subject. He lay there silently in the twilight, staring up into the vast evening sky. It seemed so lonely, this enormous realm of atmosphere and space above them which seemed to tower over them with such magnitude and power. With several stars already beginning to show, night was fast approaching, and he hoped deep inside that his father and the others would return soon.

Suddenly, a strange noise seemed to appear. Everyone looked up to where the sound was coming from immediately. They were scared, confused, worried out of their minds. Far away in the distance, starting off very quiet, it gradually grew louder and louder. Until eventually it was a deafening merge of noise and fury. It soon became clear what it was, as everyone realised with a bolt of panic. It was the siren.

"We have to leave now!" exclaimed Sophie immediately. Her pulse was pounding faster than ever before.

"We can't!" replied Eve, trying desperately to remain calm. "We have to wait here. Don't worry. The others will soon be back with help before you know it." She tried hard to put on a soothing smile, but it was no use. She too was terrified to the bone. She looked down at the ground, breathing heavily in and out, and trying to stay calm as much as possible.

"Mummy, I'm scared," whimpered Sarah quietly. "I know honey. It's alright. Just relax. Everything's going to be just fine." She held her young daughter close to her in her warm arms. Hugging her and rocking slightly from side to side, she tried to calm Sarah down. "Sssh. There, there."

"It's the siren!" cried out Sean from his position a few feet away. He stood up hurriedly, turning to face the others and pointed to the place where the nerve-racking noise was coming from, his leg burning with a singe of pain as he rose. "They'll be closing the gate soon. We have to hurry and leave!" He was almost bouncing on the ends of his toes with fear, before wincing in pain from his wounded leg.

"Sean, sit down immediately," commanded Eve. "You'll hurt your leg again. You need to rest it."

"Its fine!" He was almost on the verge of shouting. "But we really need to go! The others will be fine. They'll escape and find help. We should at least start to get a move on out of here!" He was warning the other three severely. In his eyes, trepidation could be seen in his soul.

"You can't go anywhere with that leg, Mister," she replied stubbornly, not listening to a word Sean was saying, and trying to hear herself over the ear-splitting siren. "The best thing to do would be to sit here and wait for your father and siblings to return."

Meanwhile, Sophie was desperately trying to shut out this conversation from her thoughts. The idea of being trapped in Dilas Forest overnight was a terrifying one. She looked around her. The sky was almost completely dark now, with more and more stars emerging by the moment. She looked out into the edge of the clearing where the gravel met the trees and undergrowth. The wilderness of the night was cold and eerie. It was like something was waiting there, patrolling the clearing, waiting for the right time to strike.

All of a sudden, a rustling came from within a clump of nearby bushes. Her head snapped around to the area where this occurred, only nothing was there. Silence covered the area, in mystery and suspense. Sophie breathed in and out slowly, trying to calm herself down. It must have been a fox or some other small rodent, she told herself over and over again.

"This is not going to work Sean! There's no point even trying!" said Eve aggravated. She was getting more annoyed by with every passing minute from Sean's desperation to leave. Confusion, irritation and fear were the three emotions flooding through her mind at the moment. And they were not a good combination.

"At least give it a go. For all we know I might be right. Maybe dad will change his mind and want us to find our own way back to the path," begged Sean persistently. "Please Eve!" Ever since his supposed 'vision' earlier on in the day he had known that something really sinister was going on all along. From one thing leading up to another the fear had grown and webbed out like a jigsaw puzzle. Now it was all coming together fast, and Sean was now desperate to get as far away from the forest as he could.

There was a long, eerie silence. A silence in which the call of the surrounding darkness seemed to lurch out at them in the large, vulnerable clearing, with nothing but the droning siren wailing in the background. Everyone was feeling the height of their anxiety at the moment. Everyone was slowly turning insane from the pressure. No-one was comfortable.

The siren suddenly stopped abruptly, leaving the monstrous darkness and silence to become even more intimidating.

"Fine." Eve eventually consented. "We'll see what your father has to say about this." She reached into her pocket frustrated, and pulled out a small phone. The time, three minutes past eight, flashed briefly as she unlocked the keypad.

Sean was satisfied, but his smugness over winning the argument was mostly drowned out by the pure stench of his concern.

Eve dialled a number onto her mobile as fast as she could. Her hands almost trembling with worry. To her astonishment and uttermost relief the screen read in bold writing 'Signal Connected'. She did not know what it was but something must have triggered a connection between the phones. Breathing out nervously, she held up the old Nokia to her ear, and waited.

Branches snapped, leaves collided, all kinds of nature's creations were smashing Adrian in the face as he ran and ran. Closely behind him followed Lauren and Max. They had been running constantly in this direction for the past few minutes and with no sign of the path. Adrian knew that they had to keep on going, it was their only choice. Sooner or later they were bound to find the path; he could sense it in his blood. As he fled, venturing further and further, ghostly tall trees flashed past him like shadows moving and twisting amongst the darkness. Night was now upon them, and they were extremely limited with time.

Suddenly, another small ringing noise appeared quietly in the distance. *Not again!* He thought to himself irritably. He tried to ignore the noise for a moment, before suddenly realising that the distant ringing sound was coming from within his jacket pocket. Adrian halted in his tracks unexpectedly, causing Max and Lauren to almost crash into him headlong.

Adrian frowned in curiosity. He slowly reached his right hand down and unzipped his main pocket.

"What's that?" asked Max, surprised and out of breath.

Adrian ignored him and continued inwards to reach for the noise. As he did so, he grasped hold of a small vibrating object and the ringing grew louder. He finally pulled the object out of his pocket completely to reveal his ringing phone. The whole electronic itself was alive and buzzing with a recorded song playing. The tiny screen was lit up and the words 'Incoming Call – Eve' were displayed boldly.

Adrian began to worry for a moment. Why was Eve calling so soon? Was there trouble? Had something happened to Sean, or to any of them?

89

He pressed the answer button and held the small electronic device to his ear hurriedly. "Eve?" he asked down the line.

"Honey, are you alright?" his wife questioned from the other side.

"Yeah." He paused quickly for a breather, since he was still panting from the major sprint which they had just undertaken. "We're all fine here. Just stay calm, I'm sure there's just a little while more to go." He looked up and around at the great, looming shadows of the trees in the surrounding wilderness. Not a single clue towards the path lay in sight. There was no question about it. They were well and truly lost.

"Have you found the path again?" asked Eve enthusiastically, hoping for a positive response.

There was a long pause as Adrian thought hard about what to say. He turned around to face Max and Lauren, waiting for some kind of ideas from them. Lauren was silently mouthing the word "No!" Whilst Max was mouthing the word "Yes!" This was no help at all, but yet he did not want to scare or disappoint his wife at all. He breathed in, extremely nervous about what he was about to do, and replied back "Yes."

Lauren rolled her eyes in irritation at what Adrian had just done. Max nodded in respect. He did not want to frighten the others either by saying that they were lost. Lauren however, wanted to tell the straight out truth. She thought it would make them all more aware of what they could do.

"Okay," came the reply. "Everything's good here. Except for the fact that, Sean, whose leg seems to be getting better by the minute…"

"Oh fantastic!" exclaimed Adrian, happy at this fact, but still anxious to move along.

"Adrian, Sean wants to know if we should start moving. At least get a head start on escaping this awful place," continued Eve. She was a calm person, and always tried to stay relaxed in the darkest of situations.

"Well…" he started to run again, trying to catch up with time, for soon they would be well and truly trapped for the night. As he ran, with his son and daughter in close pursuit, he thought hard about what the rest of his family should do. His mind was spinning rapidly, with a million things going through it at once. He ran faster, the panting starting up again. "Eve… I think you should… stay there and wait for us to… return… we'll keep you posted."

"Honey, are you alright? You sound wheezy," she asked concerned.

"Yeah," he was breathing heavily now. "Yeah I'm fine. You just stay safe babe. We'll be back to get you, I promise."

"Okay." she replied anxiously. "Take care sweetie."

"I love you!" Adrian hung up the phone immediately. He began to run faster, with Lauren and Max swiftly on his heels. They had to find the path and reach the entrance. He couldn't let the rest of them down. On and on he ran. Through branches which lashed at him in the face, and roots which caused him to stumble and trip. Yet still he carried on. "Come on guys. We've got to keep going." He called back to the others behind him.

"Uuurrgghh!" moaned Lauren tiredly.

Adrian was looking out for signals, messages or clues which would help them to find the path, anything would do.

Suddenly, his eyes fell upon a large, old, withering tree, and stopped sharply as he recognised it immediately by its curving posture. This was where they had first strayed from the path. This was where he had had the long, exhausting argument with Max before they disappeared into the wild. "Okay everyone, it's here somewhere. Look out for tracks and dirt trodden areas for the path.

The three of them gradually began to fan out, spreading out across the whole area. Searching, hard, for where the path was. "I'm sure it was here!" fired Adrian insistently. "I remember. It was around here." He paused for a moment and stopped dead in his tracks.

91

Lauren looked around saw her father standing there mysteriously. "What's wrong dad?" she asked curiously.

Adrian continued after a short moment of silence. "Something's changed. I can feel it. Something wasn't here before."

Max, who was several metres away, searching, heard this and looked up, curious like his sister too.

"The path was definitely here, I remember leaving at this point." Adrian looked down at the sea of green fern plants which lay gathered around all the nearby trees, swarming at his feet. The ground itself was not visible at all. A terrifying thought suddenly burst into Adrian's mind. "Someone's moved things around."

Lauren looked at him quite shocked, assuming he was joking. "No dad, please don't, your scaring me," she tried to chuckle and shake off the matter, but it was too no good.

"Sorry." He responded politely. "It's just…" He looked up and around at the vast number of green bushy plants which now covered the forest floor. "I just swear it wasn't like this before."

Lauren was getting very nervous by now. She didn't like what her father was suggesting. But none of this could be real. Surely the forest couldn't have just moved, surely they must be in the wrong place. "Well, we're probably in the wrong place," she suggested, trying to stay calm under so much pressure.

Max, who was quite a distance away by now, started to return closer to the area where Lauren and Adrian were standing. "Come on dad. You wanted to leave the path in the first place; surely you must remember where it is."

Adrian frowned in concentration, thinking hard to himself. "No. it was definitely here," he muttered in concentration, looking around all the time.

The whole atmosphere of the area was becoming more and more eerie by the minute. Tall, dark trees loomed over their heads like ghosts looking down upon them. The sky was now completely dark, with the moon shining high and several stars twinkling against the mass of green and dark blue. Far in the distance, between the trees, a faint, natural mist seemed to be growing. Wolves could be heard howling. Tiny animals scuttled around amongst the undergrowth. The scene was very dim and uncanny.

Max looked down and checked his watch once more. His eyes glowed with shock as he held it up to show the other two. "It's ten past eight! They'll be closing the gate in five minutes!"

The others both looked up dramatically and saw the digital time on Max's watch. Their mouth dropped in fright, and only one thought managed to break through the fear, run.

"Okay. I have an idea," said Max, directing. "The two of you head that way." He pointed over to an angle to the side of them. "And I'll go this way." He then nodded over to the long stretch of dark shapes and shadows behind him.

"Max, we have to stay together! If we all get lost then..." Adrian began to speak.

"No!" Max almost shouted back angrily. "It's the only way. I'll have my mobile on, so if there's anything wrong, or you've found the right path, call me straight away. Okay?"

The other two nodded slowly in response, stunned by Max's sudden attitude, but they knew that it was most likely the best way to reach the outside world. There was another long moment of silence, in which Adrian thought hard, wondering what they could possibly do. "Fine." he agreed at last. Max you head that way. Are you sure you'll be alright on your own?"

"Yeah. I'll be fine. Trust me." he replied, positively putting on a brave face, but scared deep inside. "Let's go." And with that, he turned swiftly on his heels and disappeared off ahead, into the darkness of Dilas Forest.

Adrian and Lauren were left there stunned for a moment. This was not like Max. He was in general just a normal, unperturbed young adult. But something had clicked inside of him. Something made him realise that this was a much more serious situation, something which they didn't know.

Adrian turned to his daughter. "Are you alright?" he asked hurriedly.

"Yeah." She never took her eyes away, as she watched Max jog further and further away into the mass of trees. "Just a bit nervous that's all." She looked at her father and smiled, trying to make him feel calm also.

"Look, it's okay to be scared. Even I'm a little nervous right now," soothed Adrian, putting his hands on her shoulders comfortingly. "But you've just got stay calm and set your mind to what we've got to do. Think of it like a challenge, something which we've been set to try and work out. It probably won't work, but it's worth a try."

Lauren smiled slightly at her father's stupidity. He came out with some of the oddest things sometimes, but it made her that little bit happier. "Come on dad. We better get going." The two of them turned around promptly, and continued to walk onwards in the way which Max had suggested. It was a long dark path ahead into the shadows of the wilderness before them, a dark and treacherous road to the other side. But with each other, they were ready for it.

"Well, I spoke to your father Sean," said Eve sternly. "And he said that we should wait here for help and further news. It doesn't matter what the state of your leg is, you never know the pain might suddenly come searing back and it hurt again. They have found the path again, so help will be on its way shortly." She was very anxious. The fear could be sensed in her voice and all the others knew it, for they were scared too and did not want to be trapped in this place of all fears for the remainder of the night. "And as I am the eldest member here, it is with apprehension that I will take charge."

"Alright!" Sean had pretty much had enough. He was sick of his step-mothers smugness, even amongst her anxiety.

He knew she was simply trying to help, but she had been like this ever since his father had married. "I've had it! You're not our mother Eve. You may be Sarah's but you're not ours! Okay. Got that straight?!"

Eve was quite taken aback by this rude and aggressive remark. "How dare you speak to me like that! Your father and I love each other very much and you should understand very well by now that I have taken full charge as the female figure head of the family. You're being very aggressive Sean and I don't like that one bit."

"Oh I'm the aggressive one, am I?" he fired back, irritated.

Sophie looked away in disgust of the argument. She knew better than to get involved. Everything was turning into chaos at the moment. Around half an hour ago, this clearing was happy and filled with so much life and laughter. Now, ever since the wolf attack on Sean's leg and the ringing of the siren, things had gone from bad to worse. Fear had broken out. The stench of it reeked and hung over the Barrow family. Now the clearing seemed dark and ghostly. The waterfall fell down sharply in the background, its tiny particles in each drop crashing down into the water upon rock and stone. The trees shook eerily in the cold wind. Sophie sunk down low against a rock and curled her jacket around herself tighter. The moon shone high in the sky, tiny distant stars twinkling like eyes watching down upon them. She looked back at the sharp cliff edge from which the water was falling down from. She could see the trees and undergrowth which grew wild and unattended and the top, like it was all going to fall down and erupt into a merge of anarchy and blood. There was no question about her feelings. At night, Dilas Forest was a completely different world.

Suddenly, she heard a faint shuffling sound in the background. She turned her head rapidly to see what it was. Her eyes came face to face with the same bush of which she believed there was some form of animal in before. Once again, the huge combination of plants shook for a moment, and then stopped. Was there a family of rabbits living there or something? Slowly, Sophie stood up and started to edge her way towards the undergrowth in curiosity. She was careful and silent as she stepped, gradually getting closer and closer to it. Her relatives, Sean and Eve didn't even notice her walking away as they were locked tightly in their argument. Sarah however, who was sitting quietly on a rock beside her mother looked up and saw her step sister approaching the hedge.

"Sophie?" she asked sweetly. "Where are you going?"

Sophie ignored her. Right now her mind was fixed and haunted by this huge rustling plant before her. She was inches away from it; her nose could almost touch the leaves. Silently and vigilantly, she leaned in slowly to hear what was going on. Her breathing became heavier in the wake of her anxiety. And to her horror, she heard breathing coming back.

Chapter 11:   What Are They?

The towering cover of the woodland trees began to clear gradually, as Officer Scott Walkins drove his old saloon car into the parking bay of Dilas Forest. The night was cold and dark around him, and for a moment, this small vehicle felt like a form of safe haven to him. Normally he listened to the radio loudly in the car, but this time he had it turned off completely. This was an investigation he was going to get to the bottom of, tonight.

As he drove in, and the trees parted to form a clearing, he noticed several other cars, sitting there, dusty and rusting with age. It wasn't difficult to tell that they had been there for a very long time. One of them looked unaffected by dirt or grime. It was a large blue Toyota MPV which looked like it had been parked fairly recently. This was very sinister, and Walkins already felt uncomfortable by this ghostly scene.

He drove over and parked his car cautiously, away from the large cluster of old, decaying cars. Slowly and quietly, Walkins turned off the engine and removed the keys from his car. He opened the door and stepped out carefully, trying desperately not to make a noise.

As he exited his small, old vehicle, a gust of cold air blasted into his unprotected face. It was a harsh night ahead. Fear and dread flowed in the wind. Walkins stood up, and shut the door behind him. He took a deep breath in, trying to relax and asses the situation. It had been a long time since he had undertaken a mission like this before his leaving. Now, all alone, with only himself to trust, ex-officer Scott Walkins was ready for anything. He took another deep breath in and out, letting the call of his old senses take control, and locked the car behind him.

Reaching into the interior pocket of his jacket, Walkins removed a small silver handgun. It had been a long time

97

since he had used one of these. It was not for attacking, but for mere defence. It also helped to retrieve vital information with a weapon at hand.

Thinking hard about his next moves constantly, Scott looked around at the surveying scene. It was dark, so not much could be seen. At the far end of the car park, lay a huge steel fence which ran as far as the eye could see along the border of the main forest where the trees became heavier in number. In the middle was a gate, presumably the entrance to the forest path, shut and locked tight together. Roughly one hundred yards from there was a small bunker, old and falling apart from the outside with weathering. This was where he would go. There were lights on inside, therefore there were bound to be people still around inside. He checked his watch beneath his leather jacket, which read clearly in digital numbers, 8:16 pm. Walkins looked up once more. His mission was set, his new task was at hand. It was time to return to the old days, and find out the dark information that was his job.

The large, glowing yellow light swayed on the ceiling in the wind. It lit up most of the old, decaying room, except for the darkest corners in the shadows. In the centre of the room lay a large, old wooden desk. Around it sat three men in dark uniform and combat clothing, playing poker on the desk before them, their cards sprawled all over the surface in untidy piles and sections. Jason looked down at his deck nervously. He was never good at bluffing yet this time he had a winning set. Looking up at Zack and Markus who sat opposite him at different angles, he could see their faces, tight with concentration. He knew Markus took games like this way too seriously. Finally it was Jason's turn to play his cards right. He put on a brave face, withdrew his three cards from his hand, and placed them down on the table triumphantly. "Triple aces," he declared proudly.

Zack looked up at him surprised. "Oh no way man!" He sighed in disappointment, and took a drink from a bottle of whiskey beside him.

Scott burst through the door and into the front room. All was quiet, too quiet. The room was almost completely empty, except for a book shelf in the corner, and a huge desk in the centre of the room. Walkins held his gun high, pointing ahead, as he cautiously entered the room. He swivelled around the corner, expecting someone to jump out upon him, but no, nothing. Scott looked around suspiciously. There was another door on the other side of the office, presumably leading through to other rooms in the outpost.

His eyes narrowed as he continued to walk on slowly into the office. Little light assisted him, there was only illumination from two small lamps on either side of the room. Suddenly, a huge gust of wind blew in from one of the open windows and swept a few pieces of paper from the desk. Scott Walkins stood tall however, and continued to pass through the room, searching for some means of life.

As he passed by the desk, something small and dark suddenly managed to grab the corner of his eye. Gradually, he looked over his shoulder to see, on the desk where the paper had blown away, a small, black, leather bound book. Scott peered closer to see clear enough that it was a photograph album, sinister and mysterious. Letting curiosity take over him, Scott lowered his gun slightly and turned to look down upon the black book. Resting his gun upon the old desk, he slowly opened the photo album to see what was inside. What he was greeted with produced pure shock and anger it its mightiest degree.

The black photo album's contents were filled not with photographs, but with old and new newspaper extracts. Scott saw newspaper companies from all over the country, ones he recognised and some he didn't. All of the articles

99

displayed on every page, all bore the same theme and resemblance horrifically. Scott clenched his teeth, as he read quickly through one of the many articles. 'Matthew Tarron, forty five, Goes Missing.' Scott read on in horror about this one particular man, who had reportedly gone missing several months ago. No-one had known where he had been to or where he had disappeared, only that a few selected friends believed that he had ventured forth on an expedition one weekend.

How mysterious. Scott soon realised that all of these articles either mentioned previous civilians who had disappeared within these woods, or strange peculiar sightings within the borders of Dilas National Park. Scott began to read through another article, which portrayed a rather strange picture of shadowy shapes moving in between the trees. This was a dark, dangerous matter, one which only he could sort out now. Scott Walkins slammed the black book shut in disgust, picked up his weapon once more, and continued on walking towards the next door in the dusty filth covered outpost.

Markus stared deep into Jason's eyes, and Jason could smell the pressure of which his colleague was focusing on him. Trying hard to shake the nerve off him, Jason grabbed the whiskey bottle and took a deep refreshing gulp.

"No-one move!" came a sudden cry from behind.

Jason leapt out of his skin, and dropped the Jack Daniels bottle with a crash. Broken glass and alcohol sprayed all over the floor. In shock and surprise, Jason slowly turned his head around nervously with his hands in the air.

As he looked around cautiously, he saw a short man, with a shaven head and a stern expression pointing a gun around at the three patrol guards in the dimly lit room. "Everyone up against the wall, now!" he shouted once more in anger. The gun beckoned threateningly towards the wall.

Zack was also surprised. Not being that much older than Jason himself, the young Asian man was severely startled,

100

and began to head towards the cold walls tensely. Markus however, was nowhere near as scared as his fellow comrades. The tall, dark man had dealt with tight, threatening situations like this many times before, and was therefore, well prepared to deal with the next one.

The three of them stood up against the wall waiting, there faces lit up eerily by the hanging light in the centre of the room. The man with the gun then stood back, the gun still pointing at the three of them in turn, thinking about how to address the situation.

Zack looked at Markus out of the corner of his eye for a plan, but Markus merely stared ahead, and followed the pacing intruder.

Finally, Walkins turned to face the mysterious trio of guards.

"Right," he said fiercely, moving the aim of the gun from one head to another without removing his defensive position. "I want no funny business, understand?! We're going to get to the bottom of this. None of you are going anywhere until I'm finished here. Got that?!"

Markus, Jason and Zack all nodded at different paces. Jason's was rapid with anxiousness; Markus' was slow and understanding; whilst Zack was somewhere lost in-between.

"Okay. Earlier on today I visited a young man dying in hospital. His wounds were brutal and traumatising. When I attempted to speak to the wounded civilian, the only thing he could mention was of something which he encountered in Dilas Forest, something which I am going to find out about now!" He stared at them darkly, his face lit up at different sides by shades of light and shadow, making him look like some form of cruel villain.

Jason thought deep inside his head, scared, his blood chilled. Yet despite his certain fear, Jason managed just, to keep a straight and concerning face. The other two watched the ex policeman closely.

"He was found by a passer by with life threatening and disturbing injuries all over his body. Luckily he survived, and when I visited him in his hospital ward, with machinery keeping him alive, he told me of his past experiences... And what he had just been through!"

Markus looked sternly across at the nervous yet angry Walkins, watching his every movement, his eyes, his position, his lips moving. Markus knew what was coming; he just had to think hard about what to do.

Walkins approached Zack, coming inches from his face. "After this terrifying story, I explored some more research into this matter."

Zack was extremely nervous and uncomfortable by now. Yet he couldn't show fear in the slightest. Fear led to weakness. Weakness led to downfall.

"A week ago the young man and his friends came here to this very place on a holiday expedition, Dilas Country Park." Walkins then turned on Jason, who was also trying to hide the anxiety. "Earlier on today, this poor young man returned, and is now lying in a hospital bed dying!" His eyes loomed into Jason's angrily. When Scott Walkins was doing his job, he became a completely different being. "That is why..." he gripped his hand tightly around his weapon in hand, "I am arresting you all for the assault and attempted murder of Jack Carner..."

But before Walkins could finish his sentence, something unexpected and sinister happened. He heard a noise and turned his head slowly and furiously towards the end of the line. It was there, where one tall, dark skinned man stood there laughing. Walkins rounded on him immediately. "You're laughing?!" he fired aggressively, anger building up inside his frustrated body. He raised the gun high to the man's head, but yet still he kept on laughing. "You sick freak! Why did you do this! A man is now lying in hospital dying because of you!"

"You really don't know, do you?" chuckled Markus back.

102

Walkins suddenly became even more intolerable and angry. "What don't I know?! Tell me!" he shouted.

Markus was unaffected by this threat. It wasn't the first time he had stared down the barrel of a gun. "You think it's us. So oblivious to what's going on, everyone is." He smiled cruelly.

Walkins looked over at Zack and Jason, not taking his gun away from Markus' head, both of whom looked extremely nervous. It wasn't difficult to tell that they were hiding something. He looked back at the suspect before him. "Okay. What is going on? I can tell that you're hiding something," he said, lowering his tone to try and get through to him. "I can smell it in you." He shot a dirty look over to Zack and Jason, who looked at each other for a second fearfully.

There was a long pause, in which Markus looked down at the ground. Walkins was waiting for a reply, his heart rate pounding and getting faster second by second. Finally, Markus answered back. "You don't know who they are, do you?" he said eerily and suspiciously.

Walkins was quite taken aback by this odd remark. "What the... who's they?" he asked slowly.

"They come for those who are left behind, those who cannot leave."

"I said, who are they?" responded Walkins, his heartbeat increasing in fear and anger. Sweat was beginning to pour down from his forehead. His blood was boiling, his voice was rising.

"They'll come for you next. They'll find out that you know. They'll find you, and they will kill you..."

"Who the hell are they?!" shouted Walkins. He lunged forward and grabbed Markus by the scruff of the neck. At that moment, Jason and Zack began to hurry forward to help their comrade. "Don't move!" Walkins bellowed at them, raising the gun to them for a moment, as they halted suddenly in shock, before he returned to pointing the small silver hand gun at their supposed leader. "I'm going to ask you one last time. Who are they? What is going on inside Dilas Forest?" He looked fiercely down the aiming position on the gun.

Markus paused and took a deep breath in. everyone in the room was now staring at him. "Are you really going to shoot me?"

"Yes, I will! If you don't give me answers now!" came the aggressive reply from the ex-policeman.

"Fine then. Go ahead, shoot me... Scott! I'll tell you what's happening. But when you find out... You're gonna want to run... really really fast!"

Scott Walkins ran outside as fast as he could. The door flung open rapidly as he burst out into the cold night air, slamming into the wall on the edge of its hinges. Summer nights were usually warm, but this one was cold, dark and sinister. Scott quickly withdrew his keys and ran to his car at once, on the other side of the parking clearing. What he had just heard had traumatised him a thousand times over. The news of what lay beyond those borders was beyond fear, beyond imagination. With a severe warning, Markus had told Scott of what had really happened to Jack Carner. That was after the very last syllable had been spoken, the middle aged ex-cop had fled the gate outpost. He needed to find help immediately, he would drive as fast as he could to the nearest police station and contact more help from there. There were dark occurrences happening beyond those trees. Something lurked in the darkness of the woods that was far beyond normal.

Walkins was also in shock from other news in the cabin. He had realised that the guard who he had hated and been the most aggressive towards, the one who was the leader in the group of untrustworthy, evil onlookers, was none other than his old college friend Markus Wild. The two of them were good friends at the security training facility which they had trained at. Markus was a good friend of Scott's once. At training they were great companions who always looked out for one another. That was until the very last day of their many years together, when Scott passed his final test to become a real police member, and Markus didn't quite make the shot. Markus was devastated, and never said to Scott again. Scott had almost completely forgotten what his old lost friend even looked like it had been so long.

The crack of a stone against the rest of the dust and dirt brought Mr Walkins spiralling back to reality.

He choked and spluttered as he sprinted like a bolt of lightning, wheezing in exhaustion, towards his car. Suddenly, a cry was heard in the distance. Scott spun around, only to be greeted by a wall of thick trees beyond the large closed gates. The cry was heard again, causing Scott to jump up in shock. Only for him to sink in relief as he realised that it was only the cry of a distant wolf. He fled onwards towards his car.

As he ran further and further away from the outpost, the forest itself seemed to erupt with noise around him. Animals were scurrying away in the bushes, hoots of owls and calls of other birds and beasts of the night could be heard, he could almost hear voices, of something monstrous calling his name. It was like something was haunting him, like Dilas Forest itself was aware of his intruding presence.

Finally, Scott Walkins reached his car. In the blink of an eye he unlocked the old vehicle with a short loud 'bleep'. He hurried inside and slammed the door shut behind him. Foraging with his keys, he muttered frustrated, "Come on, come on!" Eventually he found the right key and jammed it into the starting switch to turn on the engine. With a huge sigh of relief, the familiar sound of the engine starting appeared. Scott gripped the steering wheel tightly, waiting to be able to drive hurriedly away from this terrifying place.

Clunk.

Scott looked up suddenly in shock as he leapt out of his skin. A sudden noise had just emerged from the roof of his car.

Clunk.

It happened again. Scott was breathing fast in fear and horror. Had something just landed on the roof? Was it a large bird? A fox? Human-sized? Whatever it was, it was big judging by the size of the crash. Scott stared up at the interior roof of his car, frightened, and not knowing what was on the outside.

Clunk! Clunk! Clunk!

This thing, was walking across the roof of his car. Scott breathed in deeply, trying to stay calm and asses the situation. He had been trained a long time ago to deal with unexpected problems. Yet this was the first time in many years where he was actually scared. Slowly but nervously, he withdrew his pistol once more from his pocket, as the clunking upon the roof gradually became louder and louder.

Cautiously, and slowly with fear, he turned to face the window, gun in hand, bullets loaded, ready to fire.

Suddenly, the clanking stopped. All was left quiet; the birds outside had stopped shrieking, the wolves had stopped howling. All that Scott could hear was the ghostly wind and the breathing of the surrounding forest. As quiet as a mouse, carefully and gradually, he came closer to the window. He could see the border outpost in the background. The lights were out and the whole clearing was as ghostly and quiet as the grave itself. It was so quiet. Scott could even hear his own nervous breathing, condensation flowing from his mouth because of the sheer cold around him. The mysterious noise from the roof had suddenly ceased, leaving the world in suspense and mystery.

Scott was now gripping the handle of his weapon so hard, it was beginning to hurt. Condensation was starting to form on the window since he was so near. All was quiet and sinister. Scott stared out the window, waiting for something to happen.

Suddenly, the window smashed into pieces. And a dark, monstrous shape lunged into the car.

Chapter 12:   When Shadows Become Reality

Max had been walking along in this direction for quite some time now, his eyes constantly fixed upon the ground, searching for any sign of what could represent the path or route of any kind. The cold was beginning to get to him, as he wrapped his warm jacket around him tightly to keep the heat in. There was a cry as a small bat swooped down, inches from his face. Max flinched in surprise and dodged out of the way, staring back after it as it swept away into the growing darkness. This was unexpected, but a small bat was the least of his problems. Right now, Max had to find a way out, and fast. The night had arrived, and already the shadows seemed as if they were clawing out and closing in on him.

It had been approximately six minutes since he had departed from Adrian and Lauren. He could imagine the two of them alone together in the wild, trying to work together and figure things out. He had done a good thing, since he could not leave either of them on their own, so he had ventured forth on his own instead.

On and on he went. His feet were beginning to grow tired and his mind was ravaged by fear, guilt and concern. He almost felt sick of it all, and just wished for an exit out of this dreadful world of trees. But he had to keep going. He had family members counting on him, and he wouldn't let them down.

Suddenly, a flash of movement in the shadows caught the very corner of his eye. He whipped his head around just in time to see a dark sinister shape disappear behind a tree a few hundred yards away. Max blinked in astonishment. Had he really just seen what he thought he had just seen? A mysterious silhouette dash rapidly past him? He must have imagined it, he must have. All of his fears were coming

108

back. The past memories of earlier on that day flashed back to him, of when he said quietly to Sean about their concern over the whole place. There was something about it which they didn't quite like, and all of that was coming together now.

He kept on walking, trying to pretend that he had seen nothing. Thoughts kept on popping up into his mind as he walked on into the wilderness. Was this all in his imagination? Or was something really sinister actually going on within these woods? Whatever was happening, he did not want to be the one to find out the truth.

As he walked, his pace slowly became quicker and quicker with worry, as more curious things seemed to occur. Shadows began to flash past and appear from out of the corners of his eyes, darting and disappearing among the trees. He couldn't take it anymore. *It's all in your head Max! It's all in your head!* He reassured himself in his mind over and over again.

He snapped around suddenly, twisting his whole body to see if anything was really there. But no, not a thing in sight except mindless swarms of trees and undergrowth. Max turned and kept on going in the direction he was heading. It was like something was haunting him, chasing him, waiting for something. A horrific feeling was growing in his gut, as he picked up the pace once more and walked fast through the plants and roots which sprawled across his feet as he moved. Dead ahead, he stared, and tried to shut out everything distracting around him. The night was chilling and deceiving, and Max did not want to mess with anything too unnecessary.

Suddenly, he felt the ground unexpectedly give way, and Max was plunged into a world of darkness beneath.

"Aaarrgghh!" he cried as he fell rapidly and smacked his head sharply against the earth below. Cautiously and slowly he stood up. He winced painfully, rubbing his head and trying to focus his mind back to reality. He looked around, but could only see darkness in the huge hole which he had just fallen into. Max looked up above him to see a blanket of tree canopies with occasional gaps where stars and the night sky could be seen shining through.

He lowered his head and looked ahead into the sheet of black. Below him was a small pile of dead plants and dirt where he had fallen through. Max breathed in and out extremely nervously. It was okay. It was just a ditch he had dropped into accidentally, now to find a way out.

All of a sudden, a breath of air quivered in the wind from out of the shadows. Max's heart missed a beat. He looked deep into the darkness, trying to identify some kind of life within. *It must be a fox or a badger.* He thought to himself reassuringly. Max reached into his pocket and pulled out his torch, expecting to see some kind of animal when he turned it on. Only instead, he almost screamed.

Chapter 13: Memories Twisted To Annotations

Lauren was rushing and trying to keep up with the fast pace of her father ahead. She followed him as he was almost bursting into a run. They swept through bushes and between trees, ducking and edging. Every now and again an unsuspecting branch would suddenly appear and slash at her, making her wince as it left a cut across her face or body. This could be ignored however, as Lauren had to really focus on the task of finding some form of path ahead of her. She felt dejected inside, as she had a horrendous feeling that the gates had already been shut for the night, and locked with no way of getting out. Still, her father and herself had to find a way of escaping and rescue their family from the dark claws of the night and its horrors. More wolves would appear, maybe even bears, birds of prey from the isolated regions of the forest, terrifying as it sounded. *There must be a way out* she thought silently to herself. Sooner or later, something would happen.

Adrian suddenly stopped in front of her, as she tried to stop too, almost colliding into him once more. "Could you please stop suddenly stopping in front of me?!" she exclaimed irritably. "I'm going to crash into you one day."

He laughed quietly back, amused by her irritation. "Sorry. It's just funny when you complain a lot." He paused to look back at her annoyed expression. "Not that I get enough of that anyway."

Lauren raised one eyebrow at her dad. "Says the person who's always dragging us off to unexpected places and getting us into trouble." She was actually getting serious now, her blood beginning to boil. "Especially this time! You even dragged us into finding your friend, and now we're trapped. Here, in the bog-end of the world!"

111

Adrian paused, biting his lip, thinking of some form of comeback to his own daughter. "Now, look Lauren. I thought we all agreed that we'd move on from this. My friend was very dear to me, but I know that my family is more important. Now let's all move on, and try and find our way out."

"No dad!" she replied viscously. "I don't think anyone's going to forget about what you did. We are now trapped here. That's right. The siren went off about fifteen minutes ago, meaning the gates will have easily shut by now, and we're nowhere near the original path. I mean I know this place is beautiful during the daylight hours, but not when it's cold, dark and you're lost amongst the wilderness. It's like it could drive you mad after a while. Just face it dad, we're lost."

Adrian didn't answer back for a moment. He merely thought to himself, about all of the things which he had done. *What have I done? I've condemned my family to misery for the night. Sarah will be crying, the pain in Sean's leg will return, poor Sophie will be disappointed. I've left Eve to care for them all on her own. I've sent my eldest son off into the wilderness. I don't understand. I thought I was doing something right. My family would enjoy the day, with the forest's natural beauty and splendour. It's a wonderful place. But now I've taken it too far. But enough complaining. The past is the past, and now I need to get my family out of this situation.* He finally looked up to face his daughter. He had to act now, before it was really too late. "Look sweetheart I'm sorry. I'm so sorry."

She looked back at him, her aggravated expression seemed to soften, as she tried to forgive him.

"We've been through so much today," he smiled slightly, as if assessing the situation as just an experience. "But now I need you to do the best thing a daughter can in these situations, and that's to stay calm, alright. For a moment I want you to forget about everything bad that's happened, and just focus on what we need to do." He smiled warmly at her. "Can you do that for your old dad?"

She nodded sympathetically, and rushed forward to embrace her dad in a kind, welcoming hug. With arms around each other tightly, the rest of the dark world seemed to vanish for a mere moment. With each other by their sides, they felt safe.

Suddenly, Lauren looked up from her father's shoulder and looked over behind him. As her eyes fixed upon one thing, her vision seemed to focus more and more upon it. This was curious and strange. She let go of Adrian's hug and stepped backwards, never taking her eyes off of what she had seen.

"What is it?" asked her father. "What's wrong?" he followed her line of sight around until his eyes met upon this mysterious thing. He then squinted in confusion as he wondered what it was.

Several metres away, lying in a small ditch between two clumps of undergrowth, lay a sinister, dirty, object. Neither of them had any idea of what it could be. They looked at each other in wonder, and slowly, together, began to walk cautiously over to where the eerie form was.

Closer and closer they got, their breaths becoming faster and faster slowly as they neared the unknown shape. They were now almost a couple of metres away from it. The whole world seemed to disappear strangely as their minds were focused upon this one thing.

Suddenly, Lauren gasped in shock as she realised what the object was, Adrian followed shortly after as he too realised what this thing was.

They knew it. The two of them recognised it by the same minor details and the general form of the shape. They looked over in astonishment, knowing what it was. It was the wolf that had appeared earlier in the clearing and had attacked Sean. The same wolf which Max had beaten and Adrian had wrestled to the ground.

113

Lauren blinked, checking if this was actually the same beast, yet it was. It bore the same dent where Max had clobbered it over the head with the branch, the same rough dirty fur, the same eyes, cold and merciless. Only this time, it was dead. Flies hovered and buzzed around it, and its eyes and body were lifeless and covered in filth and grime. Mud splattered up the sides of its body from where it had fallen.

Adrian stepped backwards for a moment and turned around to pick up a stick from the floor. He then returned and prodded the animal once.

"Yeah. It's dead," he confirmed reassuringly.

Lauren just stared at it for a moment. "Are you sure?"

Adrian took a step back and stood beside her. "Yeah, I'm sure."

The flies buzzed and hovered around it rapidly, gradually gathering in their thousands and growing increasingly louder. It was not a pleasant sight at all.

Adrian began to bend down slowly, squinting his eyes in the darkness, trying to spot the tiniest details which could lead to further clues concerning the cause of the animal's death. He picked up the stick, crouching down so that he was inches from the wolf carcass. The smell was unbearable, but still he wanted to know more. Curious, he knelt down closer, and prodded the stick into the side of the body. Heaving with might, he used the end of the stick to upturn the wolf onto its back. The sight was horrendous.

Lauren jumped back repulsed, as did her father, almost falling back into the splattering mud. He dropped the stick suddenly, blood stained upon the very tip. It rolled off into the bushes with force, leaving a tiny trail of wolf blood behind in its wake. The two of them stared in confusion, horror and shock at the large dead beast before them. There it lay on its back, infested with flies and maggots, blood and dirt sprawled all over it. On its stomach it had a series of sinister, grotesque slash marks and tears. It was like another

114

animal of brute force had torn into the belly of the wolf, leaving behind its ugly remains.

Lauren stood there shocked, her hands covering her mouth, with nails digging into her skin with fright. Adrian however looked more confused than afraid. He had seen many unnerving things in his lifetime, and this horrific sight wasn't the worst. Yet he stood there, next to his terrified daughter, in thought. *Something's really not right here.* He turned quickly to face the other direction, thinking. "Lauren?" he said to her heavily, "are you alright?"

Lauren could not take her eyes off the enormous wound in the wolf's belly. "Yeah," she said slowly, her voice quivering. "Dad, what happened to that wolf?" She tried to face her dad, but wherever she looked her eyes were automatically drawn back to the disgusting sight. She was not used to these kinds of experiences, she knew her way out of many situations, but none at all like this.

"It's alright," he turned slowly to face the corpse once more, "it's just a part of nature." He uttered those words meaningfully, yet something still strained inside of him, a thought which he just couldn't shake away. He looked at his daughter. "But something's not right here. Not at all."

"What? What is it? What's not right?!" she urged back.

Adrian paused for a moment. He wondered whether he should tell his daughter or not. But no, she had to know the truth; he could not hold it in any longer. "Those wound marks," he pointed to the dead animal. Lauren nodded nervously back. "They're too obscure and extreme to be the work of another animal." Another pause followed. Lauren was looking more and more scared at her father. "Something else has done that. No other wolf or bear or bird could have done that. Something else killed that wolf."

"Well, maybe it was just the blow to the head which Max dealt it earlier," she said hurriedly, trying to shrug off the sinister thoughts. "Maybe the injury from Max's club

115

wounded it so badly that it stumbled off into the forest and died here…"

"We're not getting ideas here, Lauren. Do not overreact about this matter," interrupted Adrian, trying to pacify her again. He did not know what to do at all.

"…The insects and other scavengers must have fed off it from there."

She was scared. Adrian could see it in her eyes. Smell her fear. He took a deep breath in, and tried to calm his panicking seventeen year old daughter down into a calmer state. "Listen, sweetheart. Look at me." He looked deep into her eyes, calmingly and soothing, putting his hands on her shoulders. "Everything is going to be alright. I promise. We all just need to relax. Now, for a moment, I want you just to forget about everything that has happened so far." She nodded understandingly, this was actually working. "For just one moment, I want you to calm of the night take you away."

Chapter 14: Annotations Twisted To Meaning

Max lifted the torch up slowly, his heart racing, his pulse pounding. Gradually, he focused the unnatural light upon the other side of the large hole, and saw a sight that would tear out the minds of most.

About three metres away, lying on the dirt floor, covered in filth and a sickening smell, was a corpse. Max recoiled in shock and disgust, he leapt backwards into the path of moonlight shining down into the hole. He looked back at the body lying before him. Its clothes were familiar and recognisable, as it was easily a tourist or hiker. Its feet were mangled and blood-drenched, as was the rest of its mutilated body. Its chest was torn apart, with dark red, bloody flesh revealing sharp, blood-stained ribs. Max wanted to edge away further but he couldn't. He dared not look around for fear of what else may be hidden amongst the darkness of the pit. He shone the torch light over the scale of the corpse, looking upon, terrified, at the traumatising sight. Then, with a sudden bolt and surge of horror, Max saw the body's face.

Like the rest of the carcass, it was blood-stained and savaged. Its eyes popped out at obscene angles and its mouth was gaping open, bleeding like the jaw had been ripped apart. Scars and scratches bore across the person's face, as long brown hair, now stained red and black flowed across its face. He could see clearly that it was a woman.

The torch light followed down the body until it reached a mysterious white object lying about a foot from the dead woman's feet. Max didn't move a muscle nearer because of the pure extent of his fear inside. Instead, with difficulty, he tried to look closer, squinting amongst the light and the darkness, to see what the odd thing seemed to be.

Realising what it was, he tried to peer closer. It was an ID card, a pass for a club or building. Closer and closer he strained, searching for the name of this ruined body.

Eventually, he found it, at the top of the small white card, in small bold writing, which read, 'Becky Swindell'. Max had not a clue who this person was, yet still he remained terrified and concerned. He could hold his nerve no longer, and with the fear building up for too long within his heart, he took off. Turning rapidly on his heels, he started scrambling mindlessly upwards into the glowing moonlight. Grains of dirt and earth crumbled and fell onto his face as Max tried to scramble up the sides of the vast hole of which he had fallen into. It must have been a cavern, a large subterranean pit beneath the surface of the forest. What he had seen could only be a small part of it.

Max couldn't think right now, all he cared about was escaping from the nightmare that lay below, barely feet away. Higher and higher he reached, trying to grab hold of something, anything. Yet the harder he tried, the more he struggled. He was desperate to get out of the hole. What he had just seen was traumatising enough to put any man into shock. He was not weak minded however, he could go on. Yet fear and terror still filled his insides, as he scrambled around in the hole, trying with all his might to climb out and flee.

He lunged out and grabbed hold of a dead branch, yet slipped and fell back down again. Once more he tried, again and again. Nothing happened. He could see the moon from out of the top of his eye. It focused down upon him. It seemed almost like it was laughing at him, watching him in his misery and desperation, watching with glee and sending the cold to make things even worse. Max was becoming frustrated now. He was cold, tired, aggravated, and most of all, terrified. Building up all of his strength within him, trying once more, he jumped up and grasped hold of a nearby root sticking out of the ground. He could not see it,

118

since his head level was below the height of the pit, yet he assumed it was safe, and held on tighter. Holding on forcefully, he pulled with all of his might. Another hand burst from the darkness into the moonlight and the forest's surface. He pressed the other hand down too, and stretched with all of his muscle in his arms. Closer and closer he got, he could feel the cold wind brushing lightly against his face. With one final pull, he was out.

Suddenly, as Max was almost completely out of the hole, something down in the darkness of the cavern, brushed against the side of his leg. Like a cat he recoiled and fell back into a nearby formation of plants. Crawling out and standing up again, he hurried over to the hole in which he had fallen, and looked down into the darkness of the pit once more. He could see nothing. Nothing, except the eerie darkness and the rotting stench of the corpse. He knew deep down inside that he hadn't imagined that. What had just happened was very true and real. There was no doubt about it. Something very wrong and sinister was happening in Dilas Forest. He had no idea what it was, yet even now it was disturbing enough.

Max looked up into the bright moonlight once more. For the first time today he was glad to see the huge open space around him, eerie as it was. Whilst he was trapped in the pit he felt as if the world was closing in around him. It was horrible, like something was coming in to feed upon him.

He looked straight ahead and breathed out relaxing. He felt the calmness of the cool wind blowing against him through the tightly packed trees. He closed his eyes for a moment, trying to figure things out where he was and what he was doing. Slowly and steadily, he opened them. The rest of Dilas Forest slowly came back into focus, the shadow of night lying across the whole area. The obscurity was immense, and Max struggled to see through the trees to any sign of hope ahead. He lifted up his sleeve and drew back to section of his jacket to reveal his watch. With panic in mind, he observed gloomily as the watch struck 8:27pm. The gates had shut long ago. There was no way out of it now, they had to find the entrance immediately, or risk being trapped in the spooky and haunting woodland which surrounded them for the rest of the night.

Max looked ahead, focusing, thinking. He stared through the trees once more. Nothing but blackness stared back, the shadows of the many trees merging into one. Gradually, his vision cleared, and he could eventually just make out the outline of the tree silhouettes. He breathed in and out, haunted. Sight was one of the most valuable senses in a situation like this, and he was glad to have it on his side, weak as it may be.

Max let his confidence rise up again, still traumatised and shocked by his encounter in the gaping hole, and started running again, his pace increasing by the second. Twigs and leaves crunched and crumbled beneath his feet. The world seemed to rush by quicker all of a sudden. His pace increased, as his steps hastened.

Suddenly, he brought everything to a sudden halt, when he saw something, a large shadow amongst the mass of trees ahead, several hundred yards away, standing there, staring back at him.

Max stood there for a moment, his heart missing beats rapidly. He was scared deep down to the bone, his pulse racing and pounding once more as it had done a thousand times before, today. He could see the figure ahead. He could not recognise its shape, but he knew there was something there, waiting. He didn't know what to do. Was it a breed of animal, was it one of the guards who had come searching for them since they were missing? He couldn't tell. There were several long moments of tension as Max stood there rooted, watching the sinister figure; and, as the mysterious shape stood there, Max had an incredibly nervous feeling, it was watching him back.

Suddenly, after a long moment of hesitation, something happened. The shape was moving. Max could not see exactly what it was doing because of the flood of darkness, yet he knew that the eerie silhouette was moving in some way. Max stood there for a moment longer, wondering what on earth was going on. He suddenly felt a terrifying bolt of fear and panic, as he realised that the dark shape was running... at him.

Chapter 15:   The Thing from The Darkness

Sophie began to slowly edge back with fear, as the breathing from the undergrowth gradually became louder and louder. It was too noisy to be an animal, too wheezing to be a human. It was a horrible, droning sound which echoed ever so slightly throughout the surrounding area, drifting against the leaves on the trees, and the flow of the water rushing downwards.

Sean and Eve suddenly stopped their argument, as both of them slowly turned their heads in disbelief at the sound of the ghostly breathing nearby. Sean's mouth dropped when he saw his sister cautiously moving away from one of the many bushes surrounding them. He could hear the breathing, and see the undergrowth rustling faintly. There was no doubt about it, something was in that hedge. He agreed with Sophie's thoughts. It was not an animal, yet it could not be anything else. There were no humans nearby at all. *What is that?* he thought curiously and nervously.

Gently, he stood up and walked quietly over to where Sophie was edging backwards in fear.

"Sean, Sophie. Come back here now," called Eve worriedly. She too could hear the unnatural breathing noise, and shared similar thoughts to the others. "Both of you. Stay away from there!"

The two siblings ignored her however. They were more curious and worried as to what could be lurking in the undergrowth before them. "What do think it is?" asked Sean, alarm seeping from his breath as cold condensation poured forth into the night air.

There was a moment's pause, before Sophie finally answered. "I don't know." The two of them stood there, peering in slowly as to try and make some sort of suggestion as to what this thing could be. It wasn't the wind; it was too monstrous to be that for sure.

"Would the two of you please come back here this instant?!" Eve almost erupted.

Sophie and Sean finally listened to her, and moved away faster towards the other two family members. As her step-son and step-daughter came towards her, Eve did not take her eyes away from the undergrowth where the rustling was seen and heard. "It's just a fox, don't worry. They're very common around these regions." She tried to put on a brave smile, but it failed miserably. It was easy to tell that she was doing her best to try and calm the others down, when she herself feared for the worst.

"What if it's that wolf again?" asked Sophie nervously. "What if it's come back, in anger? Or hunger?!"

Sean threw her an anxious look. The least thing he wanted was to cross paths with that monstrous beast again. He knelt down and picked up Sarah, holding her tightly, yet refusing to sit down. The pain in his leg was burning steadily, but he was too scared to realise that now.

All of their belongings were already packed and ready for take off should the urge arise. They were ready to go. The clearing did not feel safe anymore, the breathing and rustling was becoming unnerving and disturbing. Sophie had her hand on her rucksack, as did Eve. Slowly she stood up and put it over her back.

All was quiet. The breathing stopped, the rustling halted, the wind died down, the distant animals were silent all of a sudden. Not a single sound escaped into the open. Instead, a silence was left that could drive even the bravest mad. "Mummy?" whispered Sarah almost silently. All was quiet, too quiet.

Suddenly, without warning, from out of the darkness, leapt a monstrous, dark, looming shape. It jumped from out of the undergrowth where the breathing was heard and growled horrifically at the unsuspecting group. Sophie and

Sean screamed at the top of their lungs, echoing around the surrounding trees and bouncing back towards them. The moving shadow walked slowly over towards them, none of it visible from the immense darkness that covered the forest. It growled and snarled, hissed and groaned, as it lumbered towards Eve, who stood there, petrified in shock and pure terror. She couldn't move, her legs were rooted to the spot where she was standing, and she watched in mind-numbing terror as the unknown thing, walked towards her.

Sean could not stop screaming. He finally came to his senses. Clutching Sarah tightly to him, he turned on his heels and fled into the obscurity of the surrounding trees, carrying his younger step-sister with him. Sophie followed in pursuit, her fear driving her away from the scene and into the blackness of the night mindlessly. It was too dark to see clearly, as Sophie tried desperately to follow her fleeing brother. She ran on, terrified, off into the woods.

Only Eve remained. Her insides were screaming with terror yet no sound escaped her gentle lips. She was petrified beyond imagination, as the creature was now towering over her. A huge, monstrous shadow stood before her. It was so close now; she could feel its breath brushing against her cold face. She could smell the stench, a disgusting, horrific stench of flesh and blood. Only when it came inches from her face did she see its own.

It wasn't human. It couldn't be human. For what stood before her was a monster of unimaginable terror. Its face was covered with scars and stitches, which twisted its face into a demonic mess. Its ears were bent and deformed like bats, pointed with chunks missing from them. Its jaw was crooked and wrenched, like something had smashed into it heavily. Its teeth were sharp and feral, like knives and blood-stained blades. But what was most terrifying were its eyes. They were dark and yet they glowed and glinted in the moonlight, evil and bloodthirsty as they stared deep into hers.

124

It snarled brutally, revealing a jaw full of dirty, rotting teeth, and spit and saliva dripped from its gaping maw. Suddenly, it moved closer to Eve, and grabbed hold of her head. Eve let out one last final scream of terror from her mouth, as the creature closed inwards, and crushed her skull with its monstrous strength.

Chapter 16: Into the Maw

Far, far away, through the ocean of trees and the sea of undergrowth, Adrian heard screams. He looked up dramatically, and knew, with a horrible feeling, that it was his family.

Lauren turned around rapidly at the horrific noise, as she knew too that something back in the clearing was terribly wrong. Her heart was pounding and her stomach lurched deep inside. *Oh no! That's them! Something's happened!* She thought extremely worried.

Adrian stood there in shock for a moment. Lauren could only see the back of his head, his thick hair staring back at her. He was agitated, nervous and feared for his family. *Eve. Sean. Sophie. Sarah.* Their names were ringing inside his head, over and over again. He had to help them, he knew he had to. He was preparing to run as fast as he possibly could. This was serious now. Something had happened back where the rest of his family were stationed, something horrific and terrifying was going on and he had no idea what it could be. He gritted his teeth in terror, and turned around to face his startled, horrified daughter.

"Come on!"

And with that, the two of them were off, racing back through the wilderness where they had just strayed before. The nightmare was coming back. As the branches lashed out and swiped against their fragile faces, Adrian could only think of one thing, his family. *Come on, come on!* He thought anxiously over and over again. He began to wheeze, exhausted from running so fast in fear.

Lauren followed him quickly in pursuit. She too feared the same terror as her father did. Her thoughts were dark and petrified. *Please be okay! Please!* She begged inside her mind. She did not have too much time for her step-mother, but this time she actually cared. The screams that were heard were no doubt those of her younger siblings. She could see their faces, cold, alone, scared, terrified. Something terrible had just happened, and she was going to find out what, immediately. The two of them ran on, through the darkness and the shades of night, the pain from the nature which slashed at them no longer mattered, the only thing that mattered now was finding their family again.

Suddenly, Adrian stopped sharply, with Lauren almost crashing into him once more.

"Urrgghh! Could you please stop doing that!" she said loudly in anger.

"Ssshhh!" he responded back quietly and seriously. His eyes stared dead ahead, cold and fearful.

"What is it?" she whispered back, curiously. Her question was suddenly answered when she saw what Adrian was staring silently at. She almost screamed in terror at the sight, before Adrian lashed his hand around her and covered her mouth with his palm. Not once did he take his terrified eyes off the thing before them.

Several metres away, where the trees seemed to divide into a small clearing of plants and undergrowth, in a small area where all was clear but dirt and soil, a small, ugly creature crouched. It was small and skinny, with sharp ribs which stuck out of pale grey skin. Its body was lined with deep gashes and brutal scars. One of its ears was missing, and its monstrous eyes were evil and livid. In its hands it held a small bone, from which it crouched there feeding off the meat like some kind of wild animal. This was no animal however; it was far too horrific and disturbing to be a wild breed of animal. Bloodstained teeth crunched hard around the rotting bone, as it fed savagely upon its food.

Adrian was beginning to shake and quiver, the drops of sweat falling from his forehead were increasing more and more. As he held his hand firmly over Lauren's mouth to prevent her from screaming, he watched in terror as the

127

monstrous beast fed. It had not noticed them yet. With one ear missing, its hearing must be less sensitive.

Slowly, and cautiously, Adrian turned his head and mouthed silently to Lauren. 'Quietly, move that way.' He pointed his hand slightly to the right, which led back into the huge cluster of tall trees. Lauren nodded, still shaking. She removed Adrian's hand from her mouth slowly, yet kept it shut with difficulty to keep herself from crying out. She lifted her left leg, and turned to move out.

She was silent, as quiet as a mouse as she moved stealthily. Adrian stayed behind for a moment, waiting for the right time which would be safe to move. For a moment, Adrian was spellbound. He stood there as silent as the grave, wondering in curiosity and fear, what that creature was. It definitely wasn't human; it was far too monstrous and alien to be that. *What is that thing?!* He thought sternly. Silence surrounded them, except for the crunching of teeth on bone. The world seemed surreal and imaginary; like something out of a nightmare.

'Dad!' Lauren mouthed to her father desperately. She had by now reached a point where it was alright to flee again, deep into the heart of the tree cover and out of the peculiar monsters' sight. Adrian looked around slowly to see her progress, and saw her frantic signals to come.

For the second time in this moment of terror, Adrian took his eyes off the strange beast ahead. He looked towards his daughter waiting to his right, worried out of her mind. Cautiously, he stepped, aware of his every move. He tried hard not to look back at the odd being, knowing his mind must stay focused on the path ahead.

Suddenly, he put his foot down, and unexpectedly, a stick snapped loudly beneath his feet. He looked up rapidly, to see the creature, its eyes insane and monstrous, glaring back at him. Lauren gasped in shock as she saw that the beast had noticed them. Adrian was petrified, as the monster stared at him for a long, disturbing moment. His mouth hung open, his skin white with horror. The pale, scarred thing before them snarled a long, droning growl. Lauren could only watch in terror as the creature snarled and stared lividly at her father.

Finally, Adrian managed to look around slowly and fearfully at his terrified daughter. He opened his mouth, watching the creature crawl slowly towards him, and shouted out loud.

"Run!"

With that the monster leapt through the air, sharp claws spitting forth from its hands, it writhed and growled as it pounced towards Lauren and Adrian. But it was too late. Adrian had already moved rapidly out of the way, and was fleeing deep into the shadow of the woods. The creature let out a monstrous, bloodthirsty roar into the cold night air. Its howl echoed around the entire forest, through the twisting maze of trees and into the dark, misty sky. Even as Adrian and Lauren sprinted through the trees and the shadowy wilderness, they could still hear the being's savage roar in the distance.

"What was that thing?!" cried Lauren towards her dad, running closely beside her.

"I don't know!" he shouted back. "I really don't know." He looked back for a split second whilst darting between the trees. "But, it's coming after us! Keep going!"

Lauren was wheezing loudly, her heart racing both from fear and adrenaline rushing through her. She too looked back for a split second, just in time to see a dark, grey shape chasing after them through the darkness, she could see the creature's glistening eyes under the moonlight. It's evil, glowing eyes.

Faster and faster they sprinted. Adrian had no real sense of direction except to find his family, and get away from that thing behind them. He flashed back his head. It was getting closer. Lauren breathed heavily, gasping for precious air as she ran as fast as she could. Trees and shadows flashed past her in the blink of an eye. She felt cold inside, like she was running into oblivion. They were alone, in a cold, isolated world, being chased, and terrified. There was nowhere to run, nowhere to hide, no one to save them.

Suddenly, Adrian tripped over a root which lay sticking out of the ground, and came flying through the air to come crashing down upon the hard forest floor.

"Dad!" cried Lauren and halted sharply to help him.

"No!" he shouted back at her, rolling over to try and stand up slowly, his back hurt from the fall. "Run Lauren, run!"

"No dad. I'm not leaving you..." she defied, hurriedly.

"I said RUN!" he shouted back aggressively.

Lauren didn't know what to do. Her mind was spinning with a million things at once. She took one last look at her father, who stared angrily back at her, and ran, on into the darkness of Dilas Forest.

Adrian was weak. The sharp and sudden fall had almost broken his back from the force. Desperately, he tried to crawl away to safety. A loud slam was heard from behind. Adrian stopped silently. It was here.

The crunching of footsteps against brittle leaves and twigs was sharp and left a horrible sound. Adrian turned his head steadily, to see a thin grey foot standing inches from his face, bones stuck out and scars and scabs made the thing look like some kind of ghostly being.

A firm hand grabbed him by back of the neck suddenly, and turned him over fiercely. Adrian winced as a bolt of pain rushed through his injured back. He looked up, to stare face to face with the creature. Its ugly, monstrous face stared down at him, a broken nose, sharp blood-stained teeth and eyes which would slice deep into the bravest of souls. For the first time in his life, Adrian was petrified with terror.

"Wwwwhat are you?" he asked, stuttering nervously.

The monster didn't reply. Instead, it snarled a cruel, twisted growl, revealing a maw of sharp canines and jagged teeth. The rags which it wore were tattered, torn and filthy, as they hung down low over Adrian's body. It was the eyes, however, that scared Adrian the most. There was something about them, something about the way they turned and stared, large black pupils and bloodshot edges. They revealed the being's soul, evil and bloodthirsty.

The monster raised a filthy, blood covered hand into the air. Adrian gasped in panic, as the creature brought its sharp feral claws down rapidly, and tore out his throat.

Chapter 17: The Voices

Max watched in confusion as the dark shape moved slowly and with agility through the twisting and winding maze of trees towards him. It was like a spider, the way it moved agilely. The night was too dark, as Max couldn't quite make out what this thing was. Was it one of the guards who had come to rescue them? Was it a wolf or a bear? He could not tell. Max wanted to call out to it, but he dared not. A deep dark feeling inside told him not too.

The mysterious shadow was about thirteen rows of trees in front of him, and Max was still frozen with worry and seriously concerned about what to do. Only when it was a few trees ahead of him, was when Max realised something. Whatever this was, it wasn't going to stop. It was coming for him. He began to recognise its shape, its form and appearance. It wasn't one of the guards, no; it was too hulking to be one of the guards. It wasn't a wolf or a bear, no, it was too tall and differently shaped to be one of them. Right now, Max knew that this thing was hostile, and coming straight for him.

He turned hurriedly on his heels and sprinted as fast as he could, desperate to get away from whatever was chasing him. Through branches and leaves, bushes and darkness, he fled. Nature began to scratch at him once again. The sharp edges of sticks and nettles were stinging against his face and his hands. But he didn't care about that right now; all he wanted was to get as far away as he possibly could from the thing behind him.

He looked back for a split second to see if it was still pursuing him. He saw that the thing really was. It wore a cloak, long and dark, flowing in the night, its material disgusting with dirt and filth. On it's hands, gloves were visible, with the tips of the fingers missing, revealing long,

132

spindly hands with sharp, unclean nails. The rest of its body was lined with rags and other unattended grimy materials and items. Max couldn't see it's face from the shadow which was covered beneath it's hood. He tried hard not to think about what was beneath the sinister cloak, the thought was too disturbing to be real.

He thought to himself as he ran panting through the woods. *Wait a minute! This is all a big prank. A group of stupid kids are putting this on just to scare us. And I bet those guards are the ones who organised it!* His fear suddenly turned from anxiety to anger. He was frustrated and mad. As he ran on, he knelt down momentarily, with the hooded prankster still on his tail, and picked up a section of a thick branch which lay fallen on the forest floor. He gritted his teeth in fury, his nerves building. With all his might, Max stopped suddenly and swung the branch round as fast as he could, hard into the face of his pursuer.

There was a loud crack, as the large stick collided with the hooded villain. It flew back into the air, to slump down to the floor, not moving. Max gripped his branch tighter in his hands, the ends bearing a few tiny streaks upon them. He clenched his fists, the bark beneath beginning to crumble. He looked down at the unknown figure lying before him, several metres away. It's body lying motionless on the floor. Slowly, Max stepped closer, his heart pounding even though he was sure this was all a joke. He could see it lying there through the darkness, unmoving, silent.

A thought suddenly clicked in Max's head, as he bent his arm back towards his back pocket of his rucksack and pulled out a torch from within. He flicked the light on hurriedly, and pointed it back at what lay before him. Instead, to his horror, the body had vanished. He jumped out of his skin in shock. This was unnatural, this was terrifying, this was disturbing. The aggravating thought of a big prank gradually began to disappear from his mind. Everything that was happening in Dilas Forest that day was leading from bad to worse, a chain of extraordinary, unspeakable events. First, the mysterious abandoned cars outside, the guards being so menacing, the corpse which Sean had supposedly seen, the corpse which he had seen, the figure which had just been chasing him through the trees and had now vanished. Max's pulse was racing; sweat was falling from his forehead, not from the heat, but through fear this time. He gripped the branch end tighter within his grasp. There was something horrific and monstrous going on within the borders of Dilas Forest, something murderous and foul which lurked among the shadows. At first he had his doubts, as did everyone else who simply believed Dilas Forest was a nature reserve. Now he was certain. There was evil here, in the trees, in the air, beneath the ground. They were all in a nest, a trap. Chased, followed, hunted. The path which had mysteriously disappeared earlier, it was all set up, someone had changed it. Someone, or something.

"Max," a sudden whisper flared from behind him.

Max spun around rapidly, his torch lit up, his weapon in the air, ready to hit, to kill, if anything came near him. But nothing was there, nothing but trees and blackness.

"Max," it came again, from behind him.

He swivelled around in the opposite direction, his torch lighting up where the voice had come from, yet still, nothing was shown. It was circling him, whatever it was. He was scared deep down to his core. He tried to convince himself that this was all still one big prank. "Right, come on. This isn't funny anymore!" he called out into the shadows.

"Max!" The voice was more aggressive now, yet still maintaining its whispering tone. It was eerie, chilling, haunting. If its goal was to try and scare him it was well and truly succeeding.

Max raised his blood-splattered club into the air with both hands threateningly. "That's it. If you don't quit this and come out after three, there'll be trouble!" he shouted, shrouded in fear, yet still he stood tall. "One..!"

"Max," the voice echoed spookily once more.

"Two..!" he gritted his teeth bravely.

"Max. Max. Max!" the ghostly voice called again and again. It was moving, around in circles, circling him like a shark. It was haunting him, moving agilely through the tree cover and the darkness beyond sight. He didn't know if there was one or more of them, it was too hard to tell.

Max tried to ignore the voices as much as possible. His torch kept moving as he did, light flashing in all directions at once, alert and attentive. *It's all a joke! It's all just one big joke!* he whimpered inside his head. "This is my last warning!" he shouted out bitterly once more. "If I get to three..." He was moving around as he spoke, trying to stay facing the same direction as the voice was all the time. Every second, the club ready and threatening in his hands.

Suddenly, the voice appeared behind him, only this time, it spoke out loud, and fiercely. "Max!" it growled.

Max couldn't take it anymore. He ran as fast as he could into the opposite direction of the chilling voice which circled him. He ran and ran, sprinting into the darkness, his torch lighting up the route ahead, as he darted past trees and undergrowth. Roots stuck out from the earth, branches came dramatically out of nothingness, yet Max managed to dodge them all. He was agile, running like a wolf. It was panic which drove him, and moved him faster. He did not look back. He wouldn't look back, for fear of the sight which followed. *What was that thing?!* He asked himself over and over again in his head. The vision of the unconscious figure lying there unflinching on the ground, vanishing when he turned back to look at it kept on appearing inside his thoughts. The thought agitated him, as he tried hard to ignore it.

He wasn't a man who believed in monsters anymore, but this was terrifying him. Something was actually here, in

135

Dilas Forest. Everything seemed to suddenly come together; everything suddenly seemed to come alive and claw out towards him.

Chapter 18:   Next in Line

Sean lay there quietly in the huge bush, watching, waiting. Next to him, Sarah sat, confused and dazed by what was going on.

"Where's Mummy?" she demanded.

"Sshhh!" Sean replied immediately. "Mummy's just fine Sarah. She's just… gone away for a few moments," he lied sadly and unnerved. They had been hiding there for the past few minutes, hoping dearly that someone would rush past and save them. His mind kept spinning back to the encounter in the clearing, the thought of the dark shape that had suddenly leapt out of the darkness. *What was that thing?* He thought to himself, shaking with fear. His lips were trembling and the rest of his body was almost going into a complete breakdown. He knew something had been wrong all along. Ever since they had first stepped foot in Dilas Country Park. He had felt a sinister, evil edge in the air. He had tried to ignore it many times during the day, and just tried to get along with enjoying a good day out with the family, but no. Their world had been mercilessly plunged into chaos. All along, he had known that there had been some kind of unnatural movement within the forest borders, even since when they had all first entered the place. There he crouched now, with his younger step-sister beside him, alone, cold, hungry, afraid.

He looked up and around, fearing that whatever that monster was, it would come back, searching for them. Sean wiped the tears bravely from his eyes. He tried to see further, yet all he could see was darkness. Fear blinded him, his pulse raced and his blood churned so much that he himself could not see a thing outside of their hiding place. He could barely see his hand before his face.

Sarah grabbed hold of his coat tightly, as he felt her fear back. He hugged her warmly.

"There… there," he stuttered. "Ev… everything is going to b…b…be okay," he droned off on the last syllable, gritting his teeth; and constantly looking over his shoulder and hers. He was relentlessly alert, always was, and always would be.

Suddenly, the crashing of collapsing undergrowth was heard in the distance. Sean jumped out of his skin and held his hand over Sarah's mouth to stop her from screaming. He peered out of a hole in the hedges, and tried hard to see what was coming. A horrific thought suddenly emerged inside of him. This was it, whatever the dreadful creature was which had appeared in the clearing, it was coming for them.

He hugged Sarah tightly to him, attempting to cover her eyes and ears. Despite his own fears, he was desperate that she didn't know what was approaching. Slowly but surely, the thing loomed closer and closer towards them. It grew in size and stature, as it lumbered from out of the trees. From a tiny distant shape, it emerged through the mass of tree trunks into a hulking beast. Closer and closer it came. Until eventually, it was standing right in front of the very bush where the two of them were hiding.

Sean was terrified to the bone. He could hear it breathing, heavily and eerily. It was almost a kind of wheeze, as its lungs thrust back and forward desperately. It was so tall, that from where Sean was hiding, he could not see its face. Instead, dimness and darkness completely covered the whole of its body. There it stood, towering and menacing. All he could see was a huge black shape standing there, about three metres away.

Suddenly, the face of the figure collided with the moonlight. What Sean saw petrified him beyond belief. The being's face was mutated and twisted, its lower jaw stuck out and its entire face was covered in scars and gashes. Its eyes glinted and shimmered under the bright moonlight. Like jewels they twinkled, yet evil filled them. They looked normal, just like a human, yet these eyes were the most monstrous and cruel that Sean had ever seen. It looked around, squinting like an animal, searching for any signs of life. This creature could not be human, it wasn't human. No, it was too twisted and deformed to be human. He had no idea what this creature was. All he knew, was that it was hostile, dangerous and unsympathetic. It had not seen them yet, hiding in the undergrowth beneath it, and he prayed that it wouldn't.

A sudden noise resonated in the distance, like a fox or a rabbit which had scuttled away into the plants. The creature looked up sharply, and bore its teeth in hunger. It looked around into the darkness of the night, and all around the area, before taking off at a fast pace, through the sea of trees, and into the blackness once more.

Sean breathed a huge sigh of relief. He was almost panting since he had been holding his breath in for so long. It all came out like a gust of wind. He let go of Sarah apologetically.

"Are you alright?" he asked quietly and caringly.

Sarah looked stunned, shocked and confused. "Sean?" she asked scared after a moment's hesitation. "What was that?" She looked as if she was about to burst into tears.

Sean felt much more concerned all of a sudden. She had seen it. She had found out. *What have I done?!* He thought to himself inside his head fearfully. *If I had just left her in Sophie's charge she would have been...*

A sudden, horrific thought clicked inside his mind. Sophie. Max. Lauren. Dad. Eve. He felt like he was going to be sick. His family were out there, somewhere in the darkness with that thing. *They could be in danger!* He was really starting to panic. But what could he do? If they left their hiding position they would be exposed to that thing. But he couldn't just stay there and hear his family scream around him. Sean had absolutely no idea at all what to do.

"Okay Sarah," he said quietly to his step-sister sitting shaking beside him. She looked back at him, tears beginning to fill her eyes. She was scared, and he could see that. Yet Sean didn't know what to do. He thought hard about what to say to her. What could he say to her?

All was quiet in the dim, gloomy darkness of Dilas Forest that night. The sound of owls hooting could be heard in the distance. Wolves howled and leaves rustled in the ghostly wind. Sean sat there miserably in the undergrowth beside his step-sister, staring up into the eerie moonlight.

Suddenly, the ground behind them creaked. Sean spun around in horror, just as a huge, dark shape lurched out of the darkness behind them. Sean struggled in pain and panic as it caught him within its grasp. The last thing he remembered, was Sarah screaming.

Chapter 19:   The War Will Begin

Sophie was fleeing mindlessly into the woods. The clearing and the screams of her family were echoing around inside her head, even after they had long disappeared. She jumped neatly over a large root sticking out of the ground to avoid falling over. The dark green tree and plant life seemed to rush past her faster than the speed of sound as she sprinted, fear driving her deep into the heart of Dilas Forest.

Sophie was disorientated, she had no idea what-so-ever where she was or where she was heading towards. She had tried to follow her brother and step-sister as they fled hurriedly into the trees when that thing attacked. She was hoping that she was close on their tail, but the darkness which blinded her vision was too powerful, and she had no idea what she was stumbling into.

Her mind suddenly clicked back to that thing in the clearing, that dark shadow which had lunged from the undergrowth and menaced the group. The thought haunted her beneath her cold skin, as it spun around over and over again inside her head, that vision of it towering towards them. She knew that Sean and Sarah had escaped, but what about Eve? She was extremely worried for all of them. Lost, alone, and fleeing further and further into the forest, Sophie desperately needed someone to be with her.

She didn't know what that creature was. *Was it human? No, it couldn't be human.* Sophie knew too well that whatever it was, it was too monstrous to be human. *It can't be a few kids playing a stupid prank on us. No, this is too serious to be a prank.* She was starting to cough and splutter as her breath began to run out from running so fast, as she entered oxygen debt. *But what could it be?!* She had never seen its face, since the darkness was too strong and blinding. She never saw what had happened to Eve, when she was too frozen with terror

141

to move or escape. Sophie was petrified. Abruptly, she halted in her tracks.

Sophie looked all around her rapidly, hurriedly making sure that it was not following her. Thankfully, all she could see where the intimidating shadows of the trees around her, nothing else was there. Sophie looked skywards and saw a huge tree trunk towering over her like a giant. An excellent idea suddenly fell into place inside her head. Turning slowly as the plan evolved, she grabbed hold of the trunk with both hands; she gripped both legs onto it hard, and began to climb hastily upwards into the branches, grabbing hold of whatever she could to reach a good height.

Up and up she climbed, high into the cage of branches which enclosed her next to the thick trunk safely. She hoped deep down inside that the creatures couldn't climb, and that she would be well and truly safe up here.

She breathed a long sigh of relief, letting all of her energy sink out of her head. She felt very slightly calmer, the memories of the past day's events haunting her constantly. She looked up into the grim moonlit sky. She could tell by the sheer blackness that it was well into the night. The moonlight shone down into the depths of the woods, a mesmerising glow overriding its ghostly appearance. Sophie looked down into the wilderness below. She looked out and around at the dark forest floor below, searching for any sign of movement or life. But no, nothing was there. Dilas Forest was completely still and unmoving. It was quiet, disturbingly quiet. She was not too high, meaning that she could escape easily if she suddenly needed to. She thought for a second about switching her torch on to search further, and to see if she could find her brother, or any other member of her family. But then she remembered, that thing was out there, in the darkness of the world below. If she activated the torch then that monster would know where she was. A sudden thought jolted within her mind. *Were there more of them?* Sophie had no idea what they were or how

142

many of them there were. All she knew was that that there were monsters out there. Something was hostile, and hunting them.

A twig snapped behind her. Like a flash she snapped around, swivelling her entire body in the blink of an eye, in shock. Her pulsed raced for a moment, before dying down as she just caught out of the corner of her eye, a squirrel crawling away into the branches. She sighed once more in relief, closing her eyes in release.

A twig snapped once more. Knowing it was another squirrel, she opened her eyes slowly and steadily. Her eyes bolted open rapidly when she saw what was actually there. Crouched amongst the maze of branches behind her, was not a squirrel, nor any other natural forest animal. A long, spindly hand reached through the web of sticks and branches to try and grab Sophie rapidly. She jumped out of her skin in fright, almost falling out of the tree itself. She backed away, crawling desperately away from the thing that was trying to get her. She tried to scream in terror, yet no sound emerged from the sheer amount of fear which had enveloped itself around her. Closer and closer it stalked like a cat. But this was no cat, it was an indescribable sight.

Creeping through the branches of the tree towards her, was a creature. It had black feminine hair which flowed long and wild, matted and dirty around it. Its skin was rotting and withered, scarred with dirt, grime, and disease. Long nails erupted from thin, gangling fingers. Its teeth were all over its mouth, sticking out at all different angles and areas. It was cloaked in ragged robes, pieces of patchwork and material which once could have been fine clothing. Its eyes were filled with hate and rage, burning anger and evil glared out at Sophie's terrified face along with a murderous hunger.

Suddenly, it crawled beneath a branch, as Sophie was edging backwards, and lunged. A handful of claws sliced out into the cold night air, trying to tear away at its prey. Sophie jumped back in shock; and with terror, fell through the branch with her weight. Down and down she fell. Branches lashed out and struck her in the face. She smashed through leaves and branches, screaming at the top of her lungs. A sound had finally come out; only this time no-one could save her.

She rocketed downwards and crashed into the ground heavily. She lay there for a moment, silent, on the edge of unconsciousness. The high fall should have killed her, but no, she was still alive, and breathing. She stared upwards, her back feeling like it had been broken a thousand times. Her eyes were squinting as she was in so much pain. Her vision was blurred and unfocused. Yet through the blur and haze of barely being able to see anything, she could see something, one thing, looming out amongst oblivion. She soon realised with dread, that it was the monstrous creature in the tree crawling down the thick trunk after her. She wheezed a breath of air, desperately trying to grab precious oxygen into her lungs. She could barely breathe. It was like a heavy weight was blocking her from getting up. She knew she had to move before that thing reached her. Yet somehow she couldn't move at all. She hadn't broken any bones otherwise she would have felt the pain. She lifted her arm up and slammed it heavily back down upon the ground to try and lift herself upwards. She was only fourteen, yet she tried with all of the strength that remained within her. She pressed another arm against the ground, and began pushing the rest of her body upwards. She tried to open her eyes more; vision was the most important thing in this situation. Her face burned from the stinging cuts which had grazed her cheeks. Sophie was desperate to get away: she couldn't let that monster get to her. There was no time to think about it, no time to wonder what on earth that being was, all she wanted to do now was to escape and get as far away as possible from it. She craved her family, lost and alone amongst the wilderness. She had no idea where they were, or even what had happened to them. The creature in the tree was not the one which they had encountered back in the clearing. No, this one was new. She knew now, she was certain. There was more than one of those beings, whatever they were.

Sophie looked upwards to see where the creature was. But to sheer surprise it had disappeared. Looking around, there was not a single sight of it amongst the branches. Her vision was clearing now, she had re-awoken into reality. She could see better, smell the scent which flowed in the wind. There was no rustling above, no movement to give away its position.

A sudden crash echoed to her side. She gulped and tried to hold her screams, as she knew very well, that the monster was coming towards her. From the corner of her eye, Sophie could see that it was approaching. Rugged shoes against damp earth. The dark night air departed, as the creature emerged from within. Sophie was already sitting up, her thorax half upright; her lower half still sprawled out on the floor. She did not move, not even a single muscle as the female being arrived, and stood over her menacingly.

Sophie sat there, and slowly, moved her head sideways to see the creature. Its face was wicked and cruel, snarling, revealing a maw of sharp teeth. This was not human; its features were way beyond that. She began to shake in fear, as the creature towered closer and closer. Sophie could almost feel the monster's icy cold breath emerging from the darkness of the night, and touching her warm body. It was spine chilling, disturbing and eerie. Sophie tried not to move. It was going to kill her, she knew it. All she could do for now was sit there, whilst the thing stood over her, and studied her curiously.

She had to move, fast. As the creature above her snarled a cruel, monstrous roar, Sophie tried desperately to think of a plan. Her mind was baffled, spinning in circles in the chaos. She tried desperately not to look up at the thing closing

145

down on her, and let it snarl and growl at her for longer. There was nothing she could do. Nowhere to run, nowhere to hide. It was going to find her, she knew it. Wherever Sophie ran, it was going to find her. She gritted her teeth. There was only one thing she could do. Her head felt better now. Her eyes had adjusted to the darkness. Fear was wrapped around her mind, but she tried with all her strength to push it away. She had to do it, now.

Sophie pushed herself upwards, straining her hands as she lifted her body into the air. With speed and accuracy, she swung her legs around into the air, and smashed them heavily into the legs of the thing staring down over her. A bolt of pain suddenly rushed through her leg as she winced loudly. The creature flew into the air and came crashing down a moment later. Sophie seized that moment, and ran. She leapt rapidly to her feet whilst the creature lay there on the floor in shock, slowly scrambling to get up. Sophie ran, on and on, sprinting off into the forest. The darkness parted around her as she ran desperately. Her eyes had adjusted, and she was awake, alive, fleeing. She did not look back once, for fear of seeing that creature chasing after her. That was a horrible vision. The thing she least expected today, which hadn't even crossed her mind, was to be fleeing into the darkness, holding her screams in, whilst being chased by something horrific.

She tried desperately to not look back, the vision or even the thought of that monster rising up and chasing after her was disturbing. It would slow her down, she had to keep going. There was plenty of undergrowth surrounding her. There wasn't even a real path guiding her. She merely ran helplessly into blindness. Bravely, Sophie swallowed her fear, and decided to take a chance.

She looked over to her side where a huge range of thick plants was fast approaching. Sophie stared at the upcoming target as she ran, and lunged forward, diving headfirst into the bush. She rolled over mindlessly before smacking into a tree. Sophie collapsed to the floor, dizzy. Once more her mind was whirling hazily, and she had no idea where she was. The blood was rushing around her head. She fell back to the floor, the back of her head battered by too many disasters today. She spun around to kneeling on the spot, hidden away amongst the plant life.

Nothing was there. Sophie felt a huge sigh of relief flow out from within her. Tired, stressed and afraid, she realised that whatever it was, she had knocked it down, and it was not coming after her. Sophie sat back, letting the cold night air wrap around her. She didn't care, for now, she was safe. The forest seemed quiet around her. The sound of crickets and wolves had died down. The sinister edge was rising, not a sound emerged. All was silent, except for a distant noise which was slowly getting louder and louder. Sophie listened intently, wondering what that sound could be. It seemed as if the whole forest was afraid of the monstrous creatures, every form of life hiding silently in its wake.

She held her breath in, and leaned right back up against the tree trunk, when she realised that it was the faint sound of footsteps, getting closer and closer. She couldn't see anything, yet she knew that something was definitely coming. *It's that thing!* she thought nervously inside her head. *It's coming for me!* Quietly she remained on the spot, not moving a single muscle in her body, not a single nerve twitching or shivering.

Suddenly, it came. Rushing around the corner to halt immediately, and stare around into the surrounding area. Sophie could see it through the gaps in the leaves, its bloodthirsty eyes scanning the trees in search of her. Sophie was very afraid. It knew she was here, she could sense it.

Its nose stuck upwards, sniffing and hunting for its victim. Sophie knew it was going to find her.

She was almost lost for thought. *What is that thing?* She had no idea, as she stared unflinching out at it. The creature moved around cautiously; its body curving like a snake when it turned to look, its numerous amounts of scars and injuries glinting as they flashed beneath the grim moonlight. It looked female, with its long, dirty flowing hair. When its teeth were revealed horrifically blood stains flashed within its maw. This creature was searching for her, it knew she was here; all Sophie had to do now, was to stay very, very quiet.

The monster's eyes were evil and cruel as they scanned the surrounding area. They were bloodshot, disturbed, like something had warped them into another form. This was unnatural. It couldn't be happening. Sophie couldn't hold her breath in for much longer, she was dying to breathe. The creature looked around once more, before dismissing the area, and disappearing on ahead into the trees.

Sophie's eyes followed it as it disappeared off into the wilderness. Only when it was completely out of sight did she remove her hand from her mouth and let air enter her lungs. She was almost wheezing with holding her breath in for that long. Her eyes were watering. She didn't know what to do. Her family were out there, alone amongst the darkness. She had seen the terror, and realised that this was only going to evolve into a long fight for survival. Putting all of her surviving strength together, she stood up. A merge of anger, hatred, fear and unease was flowing through her. She looked around, trying to see if there were any more of those creatures coming after her. She didn't know if there was one or a million. All she knew was that she had to save her family.

She picked up a large dead branch which lay by her feet. Feeling its rough bark scrape against her hands, she held it tight. It was a weapon, to fight back, to defend herself and others from those things.

She looked around for what could be a path. Her eyes squinted to see through the darkness. The creature had disappeared down that way, and only her hate was going to chase after it. Her fear however would keep her well and truly away. The pain inside of her felt like a raging war. The war had begun, and felt like it was never going to end.

Chapter 20:   For Those That Survive

She was going to scream, she couldn't hold on any longer. As Lauren Barrow ran terrified through the darkness of the night, her fears seemed to lunge out at her from all angles, as if the forest was playing cruel, deceitful tricks upon her very mind. She halted and turned around suddenly, tears beginning to fall from her eyes. She looked behind to see if her father was there, but he wasn't. He wasn't following her trail, he hadn't caught up, he might have not even survived.

Lauren blinked, confused entirely with what was going on. She didn't understand. Did she just imagine that creature back in the clearing? Were her eyes playing tricks on her in the darkness? She couldn't tell. All she could remember was a cold, mysterious monster staring deep into her father's eyes, and fleeing whilst it chased savagely after them. She kept on looking back, determined that it was all just a bad vision. But no, her father was not coming, he was not behind, he was not coming to save her this time.

Quickly, scared and cold, Lauren turned around and began to run cautiously on ahead. She didn't know what to do. What was that thing? Was it some new breed of animal native to this region of the forest? Was it some foolish teenager playing a prank? No, this creature was definitely not human.

Lauren looked up into the trees, searching around to see if that thing had followed her, and was stalking her amongst the branches above. Yet the shadows were too dark, and despite her eyes adjusting to it, Lauren could not see a thing. A wolf howled in the distance, as Lauren spun around in fright. Her pulse was racing; goose bumps were appearing on her skin, her eyes bursting out of their sockets. For one of the first times in her seventeen year old life, Lauren was very, very afraid. The most terrified and unnerved she had ever been.

A thought flashed into her racing head. She had to keep moving. She had to find the rest of her family and save them. Her mind flashed to an image of Max wandering lost and alone amongst the darkness, afraid and being chased by that creature. The same applied to all the others. She had no idea what was happening right now back in the clearing. Had they left? Were they still there? She was blind to all communication and the rest of the world.

Another sudden thought clicked within her mind. Were there more of those things? Out there, haunting amongst the darkness? Lauren shuddered at the thought and quickly rushed over to one of the many areas of undergrowth, and crawled into it to hide. She hurriedly pulled out her mobile phone from within her pocket and opened her address book within it. *Come on! Come on! Come on!* she thought frustrated, as she scanned down, until the highlighted box which read 'Eve' appeared. She had no idea what had happened back in the clearing. All she had heard were screams and cries.

She pressed the call button and held the phone to her ear intently, waiting for at least some form of response. The phone kept on ringing, again and again. *Please pick up!* She dared not say that out loud for fear that creature may be near by. She then slammed the mobile shut a moment later, when all she could her was the droning tone of Eve's answer machine.

Lauren wiped the tears from her eyes. Someone had to pick up, they just had to. She flicked her phone open again, and scanned down the phonebook list until she finally found 'Dad'. She called again and again, waiting for an answer, but no, there was no reply. Her father always answered the phone. Maybe her dad had actually fallen to that thing. She tried desperately to shake the thought out of her mind. But however hard she tried it just wouldn't go away. The pain and the anger were rising. Her dad had just been killed by this monster, whatever it was. She was scared, alone, cold, and in the dark, and most disturbing of all, she was becoming enraged. She slammed her phone shut after many constant tries. She tried to ring her brothers, her sister, but still, no reply. She placed her phone back into her pocket, and looked around through the leaves of the hedge. Making sure that nothing was there, waiting intently for her to appear. No, nothing was there, nothing but the shadows of trees, and the encircling darkness. Her breathing grew heavier in fear as she stood up out of the undergrowth. Constantly looking around, she began to run, through the trees and the dirt. Over roots she jumped and under branches she ducked. This forest was against her now, and it was her job to stay alive and to find her family, before that thing did.

She looked all around her, up into the sky and the moonlit canopy as she ran, feeling its cold embrace and cruelty as the moon shone down. She ducked under a branch and continued to sprint onwards. Suddenly, a huge dark shape fell from the tree in front of her. Lauren halted suddenly having leapt out of her skin in fright and let out a long terrified gasp. The black shadow fell from the branches above, and landed curled up in a heap before her feet. Lauren screamed, yet nothing escaped her lips. She was startled, terrified, petrified. She couldn't breathe. All she could do was stand and watch, as the dark shape writhed and churned only a few feet away from her. She could not see its face, yet Lauren knew what it was. It was one of those creatures, it had come for her again. Her mouth gawped open in shock. She wanted to run, but no strength could save her now. Her skin was as cold as ice, as she knew any moment now; the thing coiled up on the floor would rise up and come for her.

Lauren looked down at it in horror, and suddenly wondered. It didn't look anything like the other encounter with her father. The thought of her dad lying dead on the

152

floor made her want to cry and be sick, and she tried hard to shut it out of her mind. But what was this new thing? It was not moving except for tiny flinches and tremors on its body every moment or two. It was really strange, and Lauren didn't quite know what to do. At first she wondered whether the thing lying on the floor before her feet wasn't actually one of those things. But then she remembered to stay sharp and alert, and backed a few steps away in caution.

The shape did nothing; it merely stayed there, flinching and silent. What was it? Lauren didn't know whether to take a step closer to it, or back away further. Lauren was left speechless and concerned. Suddenly, it moved. Lauren stared down at it, her eyes never leaving its silhouette. Slowly, it rolled over, and Lauren gasped once again in sheer terror as she saw what it was.

Lying in front of here, roughly a metre away, was a human. Its face was torn and slashed at. Deep cuts and gashes had torn away at its pale skin. The moonlight lit up everything, from the torrential bloodstains, to the sheer amount of injuries which this poor victim had. It was a man; the surviving details could show that. Lauren thought he was dead at first. He was not moving anymore. All was silent around the area, no birds sang, no wind blew. Only the silence remained, the most terrifying part of it all. Unnerved but curious, Lauren took another step forward towards the dark figure. She was inches from him, and the body had not moved at all. Suddenly, a cough erupted from the man's wheezing chest. He spluttered and choked as a tiny spurt of blood shot out from his throat. Lauren stepped back in shock suddenly, as her pulse raced once more. She could see the man's eyes rolling around slowly in their sockets. She knew that he was alive.

The bloodshot eyes turned to face her, they were horrific and scary.

"Help me," he croaked, a deep groan scraping his voice box.

153

Lauren didn't know what to do. Should she help him? What could she even do? Her mind spun hazily for a moment, before she finally decided to help the poor, injured man.

Slowly, she walked over and bent down on her knees to speak to him. She was nervous, panicking, fear in her voice and eyes.

"What happened?!" she asked uneasily.

Lauren was seriously unnerved by this man. He may be brutally injured and she needed to help him, but there was something about him which she didn't like, something suspicious.

"They will come for you," he groaned. "Those things."

"I just got chased by one now!" she responded, panicking more. "We were running. My da…" she paused on that word, and tried to hold back her tears.

"They took all of my friends. I barely escaped with my life." He looked deep into Lauren's eyes, as she could see his pain. "They will find you. They always do. Don't get comfortable that they have gone. They will come back for you. They always find you," he whispered in his weak, failing voice.

"What are they?!" replied Lauren nervously.

"Ssshhh!" he hushed her. Lauren hurriedly looked around behind her silently, just to check if there was anything there. She turned to face him once more, and he continued. "I don't know. We were simply walking through. It was a beautiful day. The sun was shining and the birds were singing. Evening came by fast. Once the siren went off we could not find our way back. We were too curious to explore the unknown areas of the forest. We soon paid the price." He was almost crying, not through pain but through sorrow.

"Look, everything's going to be okay. I'm going to get you to hospital and you're going to be alright," reassured

Lauren kindly and bravely. Her fear was still straining as she listened to the injured man's words.

The young blood stained man looked up. Slowly, he opened his bleeding lips, and carried on. "Darkness came fast. The gates were long shut. The birds stopped singing. All life here seemed to go quiet and silent. Like something had just awoken. Something evil had cast its shadow over the forest." He coughed and spluttered, as few streaks of blood spurted from his mouth. Lauren held up his back as to stop the blood from building in his throat. "Thank you," he acknowledged. "We tried to find an exit, a way out. We knew the gates were shut and we knew that there was not much hope of escaping that night. After a couple of hours we began to build a shelter."

"How many of you were there?" Lauren asked in response.

The dying man rasped. "Four, including myself. We were all on a day hike through to Peterborough for the weekend. We thought it would be a laugh, but no, we came here."

Lauren's fears were returning. She knew what was coming.

"We were building a shelter, out of leaves and sticks and branches. It was going well. Eli started to hear noises in the trees. She could sense something. None of us could hear it, we were all too preoccupied with building a resting point to…" He choked more blood up. Lauren held the upper half of his body up against her knee, blood slowly dripping onto it, turning dark blue into thick dark red stains. "…Notice anything," he sighed a long deep, wheezing sigh. "Eli just couldn't calm down, she was curious; she wanted to know what the noises were. She said they were calling her name." Lauren began to feel uneasy at this comment. "She left, out into the darkness. Jack followed her off into the trees to try and stop her." There was another moment's silence, as Lauren listened nervously. "Becky and I stayed behind and finished the shelter. The others had gone for a long time. We were starting to get worried, anxious. We

155

tried phoning them but there was no answer. They had just disappeared. We assumed they were lost at first. But then worse came." Lauren looked deep into the stranger's eyes, desperate to find out more. "Becky started to hear the voices too. Yet this time I could hear them too, like ghosts whispering in the wind, echoes and calling voices from the distance. It was terrifying. Only then, they started calling my name too. We didn't know what to do at first; we tried to shut them out, believing them to be a part of our dazed imaginations. But no, the voices were getting louder and louder, they were calling us, from out of the darkness. The night grew colder, we huddled close for warmth. That was when they came."

Lauren held the injured man to make sure he did not fall. She was very curious and afraid. "That thing?"

The man spluttered and groaned heavily. "Oh there's more than one."

"But, what do you mean?" she responded surprised.

"There's loads of them, out there, waiting, pouncing, hunting. I survived a week, but I'm afraid they'll take me soon." He looked as if he was about to cry. "They're going to come for me."

Lauren wanted to comfort him, and to give him positive thoughts, but her mind was too afraid this time. *There are more of those things!* She panicked inside her head. *They could be watching us right now! Waiting to attack!*

Suddenly, the sky rumbled with thunder. There were no stars out, only a thick screen of cloud which blinded them from any other means of light. Streaks of lightning flashed monstrously behind the clouds for a moment before another huge rumble of thunder, and torrents of rain began splashing down through the canopy and onto the damp forest floor. Lauren sighed as her head was pounded with thousands of tiny raindrops. The injured man lay facing the rain, water splashing down into his wounds.

"I've been through so much," he cried. "They took my friends. I don't know what's happened to them." He coughed loudly once more, blood spurted from his mouth onto his chest. "Run! Before they find you too."

"No," she quickly responded. "I'm taking you to find help…"

"Leave me! Save yourself. You need to get as far away from here as possible. Wherever you go they will go, they'll find you!" he choked, spluttering, before his head titled further downwards and saliva drooled from the side of his mouth. Lauren leant him back gently against the damp floor, as he lay there, and stopped breathing. He was silent, unmoving. Lauren knew he was dead.

The rain crashed down. Soil rapidly became mud. Lauren slowly stood up, and looked down at the dead man before her. She thought, standing there for a moment, taking in all that he had told her. *Voices? More of them? Always finding you?* This was very weird. She looked up into the dark cloudy sky, raindrops hammering against her fragile, tanned face. Her blonde hair was slowly becoming more and more soaked from the grim weather. She had to run, to find her family before it was too late. All of this man's friends had been taken away by those creatures whatever they were. She had to save her family, as she had an instinct in her gut, that all the other members of her family were thinking exactly the same thing.

She looked ahead. Her eyes had now fully adjusted to the eerie darkness. Evil lurked in the shadows and fear was around every corner. But she knew she could survive. She had to survive.

Chapter 21:   No-one Leaves

Jason looked around hurriedly. He opened the door quickly and entered the dimly lit office ahead. All was dark outside, as it was well into the night. One of the windows was open on a latch, which allowed a chilling breeze to come rushing through into the fairly small room. The light wind brushed against the edges of his short black hair. Jason looked up and immediately crossed over to the other side of the room and shut the window, bolting it behind him. He was scared, for one of the first times in his life, Jason was actually incredibly nervous of what he was about to do.

He walked quickly over to the corner of the room, and picked up a dark grey case from one of the shelves on the wall. He then turned to the desk and flung it open onto the old table. The case spun open, revealing the emptiness within. Jason stared down into the blankness for a moment, and then continued with his brief, silent job.

He rushed over to the shelves once more and packed all of his Playboy and Empire magazines, piling them all up and into his case. He then hurried over to a chair in a corner and pulled a large woollen jumper from the back. Before long, he had quickly packed all of his belongings and had filled his case, and slammed it tightly shut, locking it with a padlock. He looked up, worried, exhausted and sweating. He was turning red with frustration. He had to leave this place now, and never return.

Right now his nerves were getting the better of him. He couldn't let that take him down. Fear led to downfall, that was what he had been taught. He would never forget that. Yet now, he was genuinely scared. He dug his hand into his pocket and removed a photograph of himself shaking hands with General Patrick Sharnold. That was an important day to him. A day when he proved that he was not afraid, a day to remember, a day to be proud of. His training in the army had told him to never surrender, never to give up, never to let yourself down.

Jason looked sadly down at the happy photograph. *I'm sorry Sir* he thought to himself. Right now he felt alone, just like the many lives which he had condemned within Dilas Forest. Jason looked down from the corner of his eye towards the large black photo album which lay neatly upon the desk next to his case. His thoughts suddenly flashed back to the many times when he had been forced to open the cursed pages and place another horrific headline newspaper story within them. He tried not to think about such thoughts, after years of doing this; it had long ago driven Jason insane.

The door burst open suddenly from behind. Jason spun around startled to stare back at Markus and Zack, who were standing there facing him. Jason hurriedly shoved the old photograph back into his side pocket and looked up, awkwardly and shocked.

Markus looked across the room at the locked case which sat on the desk.

"What's this?" he demanded swiftly.

Jason didn't know what to say. He stared back into a pair of angry eyes, and was stunned immediately.

"Tell me!" Markus growled aggressively.

There was a long moment of silence in which Markus stared at him angrily and Zack looked over in disbelief. Finally Jason looked up at them, and replied. "I can't take it anymore guys, the guilt, the shame. It's disgusting!"

Zack looked downwards in shame, he too could feel what Jason was saying. Markus however did not. He chuckled slightly with laughter. He was a twisted man: he did not feel pain or sorrow.

"Woah, woah, woah. Are you saying that you're just gonna walk out on us like this?"

Jason looked intently back at him and nodded without saying a word.

Markus smirked grimly. "You can't just do this now. After all these years of working with this you're just gonna quit?" Markus assumed that Jason wasn't as serious as he looked, he was wrong.

"It's driving me insane Markus!" Jason said firmly back. "Look what we're doing. Look what we've done. We send helpless people into there…" he pointed out to the dark tree line of Dilas Forest. "…and just leave those who are too slow to them!"

"Jason, you know the deal…"

"No I don't!" Jason interrupted, on the verge of shouting. "Even when I first started I thought this was all some sick joke, but no. They're actually in there! One family didn't return tonight. There were seven of them, they had a young child…"

Zack was looking really uncomfortable now. He looked at Jason with saddened eyes, understanding every word. Markus was not affected. There were many things that he had seen in his life that had warped his mind. He merely looked around the room, trying to pass the time during Jason's words.

"…That policeman who came in, you knew him," Jason looked angrily at Markus. "And now he's going to come back for us. We're all going to prison because of you. And you know what?" He stared deep into Markus' cruel eyes and said coldly, "We deserve it."

"Oh, I don't think so," he replied calmly. Zack looked at him, understanding what the man meant. Jason followed a moment later. "You're both sick! Zack I thought I could trust you, but no! You're just the same as him." He threw a disgusted gesture over to Markus.

Zack now felt really bad. He liked Jason very much, yet he couldn't break away from this deal that he had gotten himself into. Jason didn't understand the entire arrangement. And he doubted he ever would. "I'm sorry man," he said gently. "But we just can't let you go."

Jason turned sharply back to Markus who was glaring with malice at him.

"I'm leaving this place, understand? I just can't take it here any longer. You can rot in jail, but I'm not." With that he turned swiftly on his heels, grabbed his grey case and turned to exit, only to come face to face with Zack, who was standing there, grimly, blocking his way out.

"I'm sorry Jason, we've known each other well for so long, but you're not leaving."

"Zack..." He was getting very irritated now. "Get out of my way."

"Oh no, Jason." Markus stood behind him. Jason turned to face him, his fear becoming rage. "You see you've gone too far into this operation. Once you know what's going on you can't quit, you can't leave. You're keeping this secret to the grave."

"And who's going to stop me?" he shot aggressively back. "They don't know, they're not going to come after me, they'll never find me, you'll never find me!"

"They know Jason." His eyes were dark and murderous. "If you leave now, and explain everything to the police, they will come for you, and tear you apart." His glare was evil, his teeth were clenched.

There was a long pause as the tension built between the three of them. Jason finally said out from the silence. "I think you're all mad. You're all going to die. They'll come for you before me. You understand? If they're going to kill anyone next, it's going to be you." Jason's stare was becoming evil too. The rage within the room was increasing rapidly. "I'm going to walk out that door now, and leave!"

Rain began to pour down outside, gushing down like tears and blood. It crashed against the roof and the windows like hail. The wind rattled against the outpost and built up a storm outside, brutal and rough. The room was becoming hotter with anger and tension. Sweat was dripping, and brains were spinning.

"Now...."

"Look mate, you're not going anywhere!" With that Markus snapped and pulled out a handgun from his pocket and pointed it dead ahead at Jason's forehead.

Everyone stared at Markus in shock and horror. Jason's face became as white as a ghost all of a sudden. He had never expected Markus to turn on him like that.

"Markus, no, don't do it," quivered Zack nervously.

Markus was staring down the aiming position. His face was livid. He would shoot if he wanted too.

"Now Markus," said Jason slowly and quietly, trembling with fear. "Please, don't do this."

"You're gonna leave and bring this whole thing down with you. I can't let you do that. You're right; they'll come for us first. And then they'll come for you, like everyone else." He gritted his teeth, burning inside.

"No, Markus. You don't need to do this!" responded Zack, his fear cautious of Markus' impending action.

Jason dropped his case to the floor with a loud bang. The lock cracked and all of his magazines and clothing spilled everywhere all over the floor.

"I didn't want it to end like this Markus," he said back nervously.

Markus clicked the trigger which loaded the gun to fire.

"No. Markus, no!" cried Zack, terrified.

"I'm sorry Jason," he breathed quietly. He looked down the gun, aiming dead into the centre of Jason's forehead. He breathed in, aimed, and fired.

Chapter 22: Crawling From the Dirt

Max was fleeing, terrified. His blood was boiling from fear and his pulse racing from the adrenaline. The moonlight shone sinisterly overhead, almost lighting up his path ahead as he ran as fast as he could through the trees and the wild forest plants. His eyes had adjusted to the dark now; he was used to the lack of light, and could easily make out a path ahead. He tried hard not to look back. *Don't look back! Don't look back! Just keep on running!* He told himself over and over again. He was not sure whether something was chasing him or not. The voices, calling from the shadows. He could not see them but they were calling his name, he could hear it clearly. Were they ghosts? Was there some kind of hostile supernatural force living within these woods? He could not tell. All he could think about now was getting away from there. Whatever they were, he knew one thing. There was more than one.

He thought he had knocked down the hooded figure he had seen, but no. It had just disappeared. As more and more thoughts confused his spinning head, he gradually became more and more afraid. Were they chasing after him? He kept on running, unsure of what to do. One of man's most accursed emotions, natural fear. It was something that was aggravating Max greatly right now.

He looked ahead, ducking and diving beneath trees and branches. Leaves and dead plants hung low from above, as he had to swerve and avoid them regularly. It was like the forest was alive, angry, all of the trees were a part of this supernatural force, and were slowly trying to take him down. Max ducked low beneath a huge dead branch which hung crookedly from above, and jumped high over a rotting log on the forest floor, as he kept on fleeing. He was breathing heavily, panting with fear and exhaustion. He had to get

163

away. Nothing could bring him down now. He gritted his teeth, trying to tolerate his pounding headache, but it wouldn't go away. There was too much rushing through his mind at the moment for him to ease the pain.

He ran and ran. Suddenly, from nowhere, a large root stuck out from the ground in front of him. Max saw it, but it was too late to stop. His mind slowed down but his legs kept on going. His two helpless feet smashed into the tree root and caused his whole tall body to come crashing down to the damp, dirt-ridden ground.

Max was dazed, as he slowly lifted his head from the mud. His headache was even worse and his vision was blurred. It took a moment for his sight to grow back to normal again, but as it did so, Max noticed that there was an even darker shape in the distance, slowly moving towards him. He could not see what it was but his fear began to increase the closer the unknown shape came. Only when Max's vision was fully restored and the form was inches from his face could he realise what it was.

Almost petrified, Max cautiously and gradually lifted his head upwards to stare face to face, through the darkness, at the hooded figure which he had encountered earlier. Its face was hidden by shadow, yet Max recognised its filthy clothing and large, dark cloak to see that it was the same thing. He ogled for a second in terror, yet no sound came out. The creature snarled back, revealing sharp, bloodstained teeth glinting in the moonlight. Saliva hung down low, almost brushing against Max's face as it fell.

There was a flash of blackness, as the figure swooped its hand down and grabbed Max by the scruff of the neck, lifting him into the air. Max couldn't breathe. The stature gripped hold of his throat tighter, squeezing the air slowly out of him. Max's glasses were slipping off as his sight was gradually becoming weaker again. All he could see was the blackness and the silhouette of the hooded thing, standing there holding him up, draining the life force out of him. It was strong, unbelievably strong, as it closed its hands around Max's neck. He was slipping into unconsciousness, he couldn't take it anymore.

Suddenly, the hulking shape let go, throwing him far back into the air, and causing Max to smash heavily into a nearby tree trunk. His head thumped hard as he slowly slumped to the ground, throbbing with pain. His glasses had flown away into the air and had landed somewhere nearby. Max could not see, his vision was blinded and blurred once again. A sudden swooping noise darted through the air, closer and closer, louder and louder. Max's sight was disorientated, yet he could just about perceive something flying rapidly towards him. He suddenly ducked swiftly as he realised it was a blade. A loud crunch of bark appeared as the sharp knife slashed deep into the tree.

Max sprawled across the floor, and hurriedly felt for his glasses. His response was quicker now, his reaction time faster. He gripped his glasses and threw them onto his face, just in time to see another blade flying through the air towards him. He ducked and swerved once again, the knife severing a few tiny hairs from the top of his head. He jumped up, constantly swerving as he looked up to see the dark silhouette a few metres away, pulling knives astonishingly fast out of his pocket and throwing them at Max. Tiny blades sliced through the air, as he dodged them all, the odd one or two cutting the very edges of his skin. He ducked down. *What is this thing?!* It was so fast, and Max could not keep dodging hurriedly for much longer. He already had many minor cuts on his arms and upper body, but that was of no concern.

Max leant over fast and grabbed a huge dead branch from the earth. He lifted it up into the air just in time as a further knife came slicing through the air towards his chest. The thick branch blocked the way just in time, as bark flew in all directions. Max then let go of the branch and threw it hard towards the dark shape ahead. The figure swerved as the branch smashed into a nearby tree trunk, and pulled out another swift blade. Diving out of the way, Max rushed for a nearby tree. Hiding behind its thick bark, he thought hurriedly about what he could possibly do. This monstrous assailant was crammed with throwing knives and if he didn't run out soon, Max could end up bleeding severely and dead.

He looked across and saw a large log sticking out from the ground, good cover. Holding his breath in, Max ran for it, a knife narrowly missing his head as he rolled forwards over and hid rapidly behind the fallen tree. The knives stopped coming. It had run out. Max was relieved for a moment. Until he looked cautiously over the log to see the figure withdrawing a long blade from within his long dark cloak.

His heart missed a beat. The being snarled and charged over to the log, smashing its blade down into the bark. It was dark and vision was limited but Max could see well enough, as he dodged the landing blade. Splinters shot everywhere, sticking into Max's skin as he rolled over, jumped up, and grabbed a nearby fallen branch for protection.

There was a moment of silence and terror, as Max stared deep into hollow bloodthirsty eyes from beneath the hood. And the creature within, glared monstrously back. Its blade glinted sharply under the moonlight, its dirt covered gloved hands wrapped tightly around it. Max stared ahead, not taking his eyes away from the thing. He too gripped tighter onto his strange weapon. This was going to end with blood.

The beast slashed forwards, running towards him and crashing it's blade down. It roared as Max quickly blocked it with his wooden branch. More bark shattered as the silver blade bludgeoned deep into the dead material. Max held on for dear life as the thing pushed down harder into his club. His weapon was not good at defending him from a sharp blade, but it was thick enough to stop it straight away.

His teeth were gritted with determination. Sweat leaked from his forehead, whilst blood dripped down from his

166

arms. All of the bark splinters and knife cuts were sinking in slowly. It was painful, yet he had to hold on. The branch swung around as the blade was flung out of it. The creature held on tightly. This was not over yet. Max lunged forwards and swung his wooden club around towards the figure's face. It ducked and swung another slash back at him. Max swerved just in time, yet the edge of the large blade just about caught the edge of his shoulder as he moved. The pain singed for a moment as Max fell. Holding on to his glasses, they were well in place now, dirty and blood streaked, Max carried on. He rolled over as the blade hit the ground next to him and splashed dirt into his face. Max spun over and jumped back up into the air again. His reaction was fast. His pulse was racing. Bring it on.

He turned around just in time to see a blade flying towards his face and blocked it with his club. His eyes were glaring with fear and rage as the creature glared menacingly back at him. The two weapons withdrew from each other once more only to lock in place again. This monster had so much energy and strength. It was never going to give up until Max was dead. He swerved out of the way once more, ducking and dodging as the same blade kept on flying constantly towards his face and limbs. Was there any way to kill this thing? He could not hold on like this forever.

The blood stains were increasing as more and more slashes penetrated his body. Max's black jacket and white t-shirt beneath were gradually becoming more and more red with blood. Max fought back. He lifted his weapon high into the air and slashed around into the creature's hand. The hit was effective, as the branch smashed into the blade, sending it flying into the air and landing several feet away in the trunk of a large nearby tree. The creature stared him in the eyes and snarled fiercely. It then lunged forwards onto Max himself. Its sheer weight was enough to bring him crashing down to the ground. It was on top of him. It's sharp teeth snapping and snarling inches from his blood stained face. The stench of its breath was horrific, like rotting flesh and disease of all kinds. Max almost vomited because of it. It was terrifying. Although the thing was right up to him, its hood and the shadows still covered its face from sight. Its eyes were red and bloodshot, sunken and evil. This thing was not normal at all.

Max held the weakening branch tighter with all his strength to stop the monstrous beast from getting to him. He couldn't let go. The creature was on top of him, snarling and using its brute force to attack this time. Its razor sharp nails gradually came closer and closer to his face like deadly knives. It raised an open hand into the air, its nails ready to strike, and brought it heavily down. Max dodged, luckily missing the sharp nailed hand by inches. It tried again, as Max skilfully dodged the other way. This was terrifying, Max didn't know what he could do.

The creature clenched and brought its fist rapidly down to smash him in the jaw. But Max was not too lucky this time, as the hard knuckles came swooping down and smashed into his skull. He spat blood from his mouth, a nerve damaged. The creature did it again, bringing its armoured fist down as fast as lightning and smashing into Max's head. He was seeing double, the pain was raging inside his head. There was nothing he could do. An increasing amount of blood spurted from the young man's face. His skull was becoming more and more damaged.

Max couldn't hold on any longer. His vision was becoming blurred again. His mind was spinning. All he could taste was blood. His strength was fading, his glasses hanging almost broken from his face. As another punch collided heavily with his skull, Max's grip on his weapon loosened. He felt his strength fail, all was fading around him. His mind collapsed. He fell into unconsciousness.

Chapter 23:   Hunting

The room was dim and eerie. The only light was from the fireplace, where a dying fire glowed its last breaths of embers and smoke before fading. Even with what little light there was in the small room, it was still enough to light up the rest of the space. It was an old lounge, with 1980s style décor which was old and crumbling. The edges of the wallpaper were tearing and falling apart with age. The furniture of ancient armchairs and rotting sofas were neat and in place, despite their dirtiness and decay. A cloud of dust floated around aimlessly in the air, as rusting pipes stuck out from huge holes which bore into the walls. The room was falling apart with age and time; no one had cleaned it or repaired it in many, many years.

Only one armchair sat facing the fire. It's brown, ancient colour glowed in the dim firelight. In the chair sat a figure, slumped and quiet, watching the last flames slowly die out in puffs of smoke.

The door opened gradually, the slow creaking noise alerting the form in the chair of the entrant's presence. The old wooden door slowly shut behind them, as they cautiously moved closer into the dimly-lit room. Shadows flickered all over the walls in all different shapes and sizes, as the figure passed in front of the fire's light rays. All of the windows in the room were boarded up with huge planks of wood, allowing no sunlight to enter but a few cracks. All was dark outside. The rain had stopped. It was well past midnight and into the early hours of the morning. All was silent outside; only the sound of crickets and birds could be heard amongst the trees. Occasionally a wolf could be heard howling up to the moon. This was a place of evil, where darkness called its home.

The figure who had just entered took a step closer to the one in the old armchair. Swiftly, the figure sitting down raised their hand into the air, commanding the other to stop. The hand was scarred and rotting. Dirt and disease gathered around the edges and long nails grew out of its disgusting skin-like claws.

"Tusk, what have you brought for me?" Its voice was rasping and monstrous, cruel and twisted.

"News," the other replied, as he stood behind the armchair speaking. "More have come. It's a family this time." His voice was malicious and cruel. "Seven of them."

There was a moment's pause, as the creature in the chair thought cruelly. "Where are they at the moment?"

"They've all scattered. I killed one myself in Rush Clearing. The others have all fled. Last time I heard, Syrak was chasing one of them and so was Shark."

Bek sat there and thought for a moment. He licked his crumbling, blood-stained lips and smiled. "Mauler caught two earlier. A young boy and girl, brother and sister I presume."

"I see," responded Tusk. "They won't return until dawn."

Bek smiled gruesomely. "Then we'll deal with the results."

Tusk nodded. Bek could sense in his mind what would happen. He had grown this way. He was a monster, and a bloodthirsty killer. Always one step ahead of everything else. He had evolved to kill anything. His breathing was cold and wheezing, as his lungs rasped for fresh air in the musty, dark room. Barely any light managed to seep in, leaving only the dying firelight to light up the surrounding area.

"One of them managed to escape last time," Tusk said cruelly once more. "A young man. Ox and I almost took him down, but he escaped again." As he spoke waves of cold, foul smelling air flew from his mouth.

"Never mind about him," hissed Bek from his armchair by the fire in front. "He will run, and we will find him. The outside world must never know about us. Hunt down all

171

that escape. We will come for them." He turned his head sideways to be more direct towards Tusk. "As for the family... find them all. Kill them if you have to. As long as we have some back here, that will be all that matters." He smiled a grim, malevolent smile, his sharp, blood-stained teeth glinting in the firelight. "What news is there on the guards at the outpost?"

"They will be back tomorrow," replied Tusk. "I've been watching their movements, their thoughts and actions. They're growing suspicious of us, worried that things are getting too out of hand."

Bek spat into the fire.

"How can they come and check on us like we're some form of animals?!" His voice was angry and enraged. "We made the rules; we put them up to the task of bringing us food to hunt; we control them! They can't throw it to us like we're dogs." He stabbed his long, jagged nails into the arm of the chair aggressively. Tusk took a small step back naturally. "We know where they all come from; they know what will happen to them if they leave. But if they come back here tomorrow like we're their slaves..." He was becoming livid with rage. "Then we'll have something waiting for them!" He smiled once more, protruding his monstrous teeth into the air.

"I don't bow down to someone whom is not my master!"

These creatures weren't normal. They had dwelt in the shadows and hunted at night for a long, long time. They were hungry. They were ready to kill.

Tusk reached behind to his back and withdrew a long shotgun from within his back plate armour. He cocked the weapon and then loaded another round into the slot.

"How many of ours are out there now?" asked Bek.

"The last I heard was that Syrak, Snake and Shark are out there at the moment. They'll be back before dawn breaks, with or without prey."

Bek breathed in and out slowly, his lungs flexing and churning as he whined and wheezed. His ribcage expanded and contracted steadily. His eyes sunk deep into his sockets. His nostril sniffed at the hot, musty air. It reeked of sweat and blood. Finally he stood up in his chair. Stretching his scarred legs, he turned to face his comrade. He was taller than Tusk by a few inches, yet this difference really affected things. They stared at each other for a moment, before a rustling noise outside echoed around the area.

"Mauler's back," snarled Tusk. He then turned around and walked out of the door, closing it behind him. Bek was now left alone in the small dark room. The only sounds outside were the rustling of feet and the humming of distant crickets in the trees. The night was his friend. He treated it like an ally. This was a time to breathe, a time to walk, a time to hunt.

The night stretched on, howling from the winds and distant wolf cries. It was like it was breathing, slowly, hauntingly. A place where many had fallen from the horrors that lurked within. The trees swayed in the wind like waving hands. Crickets chirped and birds cawed. At this time of night, the world was silent, but still alive with fear and the stench of the hunt.

Chapter 24:   Bloodstains upon Skin

The twigs, earth and soil crumbled beneath. A light breeze brushed through the trees gently as the object moved bulkily. His hair sprawled back dirty and untidy in a wavy mess of black. It was not very long, but it still trailed behind as the rest of it was moving forwards. Max's eyes snapped wide open.

At first his sight was blurry. The world above seemed to be all washed away in a haze of light. Slowly but surely, his mind adjusted to the surroundings, and as his eyes focused and his vision cleared, he suddenly realised that he was moving.

He was facing upwards, looking skyward. The vast array of tree cover loomed above him, with thin gaps of light breaking in from various places. He realised quickly that it was daytime. More importantly however, that someone, or something, was dragging him along.

Cautiously, with ease, Max straightened his mind, trying desperately to focus on the reality which was at hand, having just awoken from unconsciousness. He slowly, putting all of his strength together, pushed his head upwards to try and see what was going on. His eyes opened wide in shock as he saw what was going on.

A few feet in front of him, was the sinister hooded figure. It lumbered and pushed its way along, through the branches and the undergrowth. Over its shoulder, it carried a long rope. This travelled several feet along, before splitting into two separate lengths, tied together around Max's feet, which slowly and painfully dragged him along behind. His feet were numb and hurting, burning from being dragged along the forest floor for so long. Max looked up at the hooded assailant once more. Its cloak was not as dark as he had seen during the night before. In bare daylight, the colour came

174

out as a dirt covered, muddy brown, with gashes and tears covering the back, revealing darker shadows within. Its hood was up, covering its head. It always was. Max could hear it breathing; hear its wheezes and whines as it trudged through the wilderness of Dilas Forest, with Max dragging painfully behind.

Max didn't know what was happening. He couldn't remember anything that had happened last night. How had he got into this situation? What had happened? He was confused, fearing for his life and still trying to figure out what had actually went on.

Gradually, he remembered, as it all came flooding back to him. He remembered being chased, the hooded figure swiftly on his tail. There was a fight. The last thing that Max remembered was slipping into a distant unconsciousness.

His eyes squinted as he looked up into the light. The creature did not know that he had awoken into consciousness. He had to escape and save his family. He feared for them. What if they had been captured or killed? He tried desperately not to think about it. He had to save them. They had to get out of this nightmare now. Just when he thought it was all just a bad dream, he had awoken, and been brought back into the terror that haunted Dilas Country Park.

Max turned his head as it was dragged along. Splinters and leaf edges scratched against his skin, tearing tiny rips in his clothing. His jacket had disappeared, presumably fallen behind during the night whilst he was unconscious. All that was left was his rugged white t-shirt beneath, slowly falling apart due to nature's harshness. His eyes burned and his ears ached. He needed to find something, something to throw, something to help him escape and cut himself loose.

There was nothing. He was being dragged mercilessly along very slowly, yet there was nothing in sight which would be of any use for cutting the thick rope which sealed his legs together tightly. It hurt so much; blisters were growing by the moment, as the stiff rope pulled harder.

Max looked towards his left suddenly, to see a sharp, knife-like branch split in half and lying dangerously close to his face, as he was dragged past it. Without making a sound, and putting all of his strengths together, Max reached a weak arm out and grabbed hold of the passing stick. He then placed the sharp edge to face the rope, and started cutting. As silently as he could, Max slowly sawed the natural blade through the thick, crumbling rope. His head smashed against a rock as he was dragged, but that didn't matter. The only thing which mattered now was escaping. He had to breakaway immediately and find the family members which he could.

A few more inches through the rope he cut. The knot was now reduced to just a few straggling strings. Further and further, until finally, the rope snapped. Max suddenly halted with a quiet snapping sound. The dragging stopped. The world above stopped spinning. His eyes were allowed to focus. His brain froze.

Max turned over slowly, trying not to make a noise yet his body wanted to collapse with fear and exhaustion. The creature had not noticed yet. Instead it kept plodding on through the trees like nothing had happened. It hadn't realised that Max had freed himself, it would very soon however. Max had to escape. It was now or never.

Max turned over onto his stomach, hungry and tired. He reached out his right arm, trying to drag himself away into the undergrowth for cover. He was very weak. His mind spun, and he felt as if he was about to throw up. Trying to hold himself together and keep his strength up, Max reached out his left arm and tried to flee away into the wilderness.

The hooded figure was now far away into the trees. If it had been dragging Max along all the way through the night, its senses would have weakened greatly. Max turned over onto his side as he crawled away, his legs were still numb from the tight rope dragging him along. He could barely see the villain any more. Only a small silhouette in the distance was all that remained. He was as quiet as a mouse, crawling away desperately. The thing had not noticed him at all yet. He could do it, he could escape.

Suddenly, Max reached an arm out to grab hold of a low branch, when a sharp twig snapped beneath his body. He held his breath terrified. He did not look back. Had it noticed? Had it realised? He hoped not. He just stared down at the rough soil and earth, silent, unmoving, waiting.

Back through the trees however, through the low branches and the shades of undergrowth, Shark slowly turned his head. He rasped and breathed monstrously beneath his shadowy hood. His eyes glinted menacingly, bulging and staring hauntingly. His long coat swayed gently in the wind like some form of ghost. He turned around and looked down angrily at where his prey had escaped. Shark looked up to head height once more. Squinting his bloodthirsty eyes, he stared through the sea of brown tree trunks, sniffing the cold morning air, trying to find his victim. His eyes darted around the deceptive scenery for a moment, before finally meeting one point, dead ahead, from where he had just passed through. Lying there on the floor, in the shadows of the forest floor behind him, as still as a statue, was a young man with a white, blood-stained t-shirt. He had found his prey.

Max lay there, wondering if the thing had seen him. He had to wait for the right time to move or otherwise it would definitely find him and kill him for sure. He breathed heavily, panting like a dog. A few small leaves beneath his face fluttered slightly from the breaths being passed from his mouth to the ground.

A faint rustling noise suddenly appeared behind him. Was it the wind? He wasn't sure. The creature must have gone by now. Slowly, Max turned his head to see what the noise was.

He leapt out of his skin when he realised. Through the trees and branches, the hooded creature was sprinting towards him. Max dived rapidly out of the way, flinging himself to one side as a handful of sharp nails came flying towards his face. He managed to dodge it just in time, whacking his face against a nearby trunk as he jumped up. His question was answered. It had found him.

The monster spun around. It was daylight now; Max could see its horrific face. It was not human. Its skin was a dark grey with teeth which stuck out of its mutilated gums like daggers. Its hands were long and knarled, finger nails as sharp as blades themselves. Its eyes were red and bloodshot, anger filled the pupils and hate stared back at him. Whatever this creature was, it was livid, and it was time to take revenge.

The two opponents stood up, facing each other, waiting murderously for the other to attack. Max hurriedly reached his arm downwards and picked up a piece of dead branch which lay beside him. It was decaying and falling apart bit by bit. Sharp wooden chips stuck out at various angles, creating a weapon. It would not last very long, but enough to keep him alive.

Max lunged at the hooded creature, lifting the log into the air high and slamming it down onto the thing before him. As the wood flew through the air, the monster rapidly pulled out a blade from its cloak and slashed the wooden weapon into pieces. Max came flying down to greet the floor, shards of splinters flying into his back. The pain was rising; his body was aching with blisters and cuts.

The creature snarled a cruel, bloodthirsty growl. It grabbed Max by the scruff of his neck and lifted him slowly into the air once more. Max was in so much pain he could not fight back, as the monster wrapped its long, slimy nails around his warm, sweating neck. His eyes closed slightly, wincing as the beast growled at his terrified face. It loomed right up close, inches away from Max himself. His feet were off the ground; it was going to strangle him. Its evil, dirty eyes stared deep into Max's.

"You thought you could run from me!" it said with a monstrous, cold voice, which rasped and wheezed as its parched lips moved. It released its grip on him, and threw Max far against a thick tree with a loud crack. Max lay there at the bottom of the trunk amongst the roots, crumpled and weak, he felt as if he was dying, physically and internally. The creature walked slowly over to him, its hood never taken down. It drew right up close to the young man once more.

"No-one ever escapes from me!" Its voice was bloodthirsty and twisted with rage and hate. It grabbed Max by the scruff of the neck and threw him through the air with all of its might. Max smashed into the roots and soil of another thick tree and slumped weakly to the ground. He could not escape, this creature was too strong. Whatever paranormal muscle lurked beneath those sinister robes, it was too much for him to fight.

The monster walked over to Max's weak body through the trees. It's long coat brushing against fallen branches as it glided onwards. It was like some form of ghost, the way it moved monstrously through the trees like a supernatural being. Max had no idea what it was or what it might be. He could not think straight. His nose was bleeding. His limbs ached and bled with scratches and wounds from conflict. His brain was twisted and spinning in confusion and fear. He was very, very weak.

The hooded creature leant down closer to him. Max could feel its breath brushing coldly against his fragile cheekbones. It was inches from his face, this savage, inhumane monster. It opened its parched, grey lips to reveal a maw full of green and brown stained teeth, filed down to create sharp fangs unlike normal human teeth. Max breathed deeply into his lungs. He couldn't face this thing any longer.

The hooded creature spoke coldly, as its voice strained and its lungs wheezed.

"After all the pathetic ones who come running through these woods, you thought you could escape."

Max could smell its disgusting breath, which stank of rotting flesh and other unknown grisly contents. He tried to hold back, pushing his head backwards further as he tried to slowly slip away from the being with all his strength.

The monster carried on, its voice painful to the ears. "We haven't eaten in days." It's stuck out a long, slimy tongue and licked its dry cracked lips in hunger. "We are all growing hungry." There was a brief moment of silence, before the creature lurched back. "We need to feed!"

Max was terrified. Was this thing human? No, it couldn't be. The sight of this monstrosity was enough to drive any brave person to their insanity. It's ugliness, a dark, shadowy face, covered with scars and putrefied from nature. Max had to escape. He had to do something.

The beast stood up, wrapping its long filthy cloak around itself, sealing its face with shadow once more. Were there more of these things? Max thought to himself nervously. He had to find his family, before they did.

Max tried to lift his head up, and stared deep into the bloodthirsty eyes of the monster which stood there, looking down upon him, glaring in disgust and hunger. The two of them stared at each other for a moment, silence echoing throughout the forest around them. Shark looked down at Max once more, before speaking.

"You're just pathetic!" He suddenly lunged downwards, grabbing Max by the scruff of the neck and hurling him through the air with his barbaric strength.

Max flew through the air, blood sweeping off his cheeks as he hurtled through branches and collided heavily with a thick tree trunk. There was a loud crack, as Max splattered into the large object and sank to the floor once more. His brain felt like he was dying. He couldn't take this any more.

This creature was going to kill him. There was nothing he could do about it. He thought back to his sisters and brother, running, screaming mindlessly into the darkness of the night, not knowing what would happen during the day. He thought of his father, brave and heroic trying to save them but failing horrifically. He thought of his stepmother, what would happen to her and her daughter. A tear dripped down from his eye and merged with the blood which filled his mouth.

A new thought suddenly struck his mind. One of anger, pain, hatred, and a murderous rage. He spat blood from his mouth onto the damp forest floor. He reached a hand out and grabbed hold of a large nearby root. With his other, he pressed down deep into the floor, pushing himself upwards. Slowly, he rose up, he was going to kill. Blood would be drawn. Fresh blood.

The hooded monster stood several feet away, looking on in amusement as Max tried to draw his strength together and lift himself upwards. He stood up eventually, his knees shaking as he tried to find his balance and he tried to hold himself together. Blood dripped down from his nose as he wiped it away bravely. He stood there, turning to face his foe defiantly. They stared into each others eyes, cruelly, monstrously, vengefully. This was a war between man and monster. Only one would triumph. Only one would come out alive.

Chapter 25:   Trapped Above

The world seemed cold and grey. Even though it was broad daylight and the sun shone down heavily in the sky above, the sea of trees and undergrowth seemed dark and sinister, shadows loomed out from underneath creating eerie flashes amongst the trunks. All around was grim and quiet. Animals made noises in the distance, one or two birds occasionally made a noise from high above and a twig would snap from the pressure of some kind. But there was no joy amongst the green. The birds did not sing and the sun did not shine. Only the aftermath of the night of terror remained in all its murderous glory.

Through the trees, walking silently and cautiously was Sophie. Her eyes snapped around at every sign of movement, from a falling leaf to a squirrel leaping from tree to tree, she had her eyes wide open. They ached horrifically. All night long she had been staying awake, running and hiding from something monstrous that was chasing her. She didn't know how many there were or what they were. All she knew was that her family had scattered into the wilderness, lost and alone with those things.

Over the course of the night she had managed to scrape the bark off of a small dead branch with a piece of flint, to create a long, sharp edged blade. Through the darkness she had cautiously crept and disappeared in and out of the shadows, her heartbeat constantly pounding. She had cried and wept, but managed to put her strength together to keep going. Her eyes were bloodshot and watering. Her mouth was dry and parched. Her skin was battered and bruised. Her hands were gripped tightly around her weapon, fingers curved inwards with terror. She turned a bend around the side of a tree and gasped loudly in horror.

Before her, several metres away, hanging down low from a branch above at eye level, was a human hand. Sophie leapt back in shock and covered her mouth in disgust. She felt like she was going to be sick. The sight was horrific as Sophie tried to look back, disturbed. It just hung there, the very end of the branch's leaf extension clawing into the end of the flesh. It was pale and bloodstained. A swarm of flies hung buzzing in the air around it as it swayed gently in the wind like some form of supernatural creature.

Sophie turned on her heels rapidly and felt a wave of vomit erupt from her stomach and onto the ground before her. Using a small corner of her dirty jacket to wipe away the small remaining drops of sick from her mouth she turned around again to look upon the grisly sight. The air stunk around it. As more and more flies began to appear and feast on the tiny space of flesh, Sophie's head began to spin wildly in horror. She was terrified. At the sight of the human hand hanging from the tree branch before her, her heartbeat leapt faster by several more beats per minute. Her mind and pulse were racing. Whatever these creatures were they were hostile. No wild animal could have done this, and no human would be sick enough to do a thing like this. Sophie pulled herself together and tried to shut the terror out of her mind.

Pulling an old piece of cloth from her pocket, she wrapped it around the lower half of her face, blocking her mouth and nose from the disgusting, rotting smell of the human body part before her. Slowly and cautiously, she gulped, took a deep breath in, and began to move warily towards the disturbing sight.

Her hands quivered as she held tighter onto the sharp branch which was her weapon. Her hands were now stained with dirt and splinters of bark which dug into her soft skin. Her eyes were wide open, despite her lack of sleep. They were staring ahead, gaping open, terrified. As she drew closer to the severed hand, the flies seemed to come closer to her as she crept forward. It grew bigger and bigger from the distance decreasing between them. It was so close now that she could reach out and touch it. Sophie was scared out of her mind with what she was doing, yet she was curious. She could barely stop herself from focusing on the hand in front. Was it a trap? She did not want to find out. Yet somehow her mind was pushing her forwards. *No Sophie! Don't do it!* One side kept telling her, yet most of it was blocked out by her interest and wonder to discover what it really was there for. However savage these foes were, they wouldn't have just left something like this here.

Sophie was now deep in the heart of Dilas Forest, cold, scared and alone. She was fighting for her right to survive and find her family once again. She did not have two personalities; it was curiosity which drove her. And as she reached her right hand out to touch the severed hand, her weapon in her left hand, her heartbeat grew much faster. She reached out slowly, gently, and taking another deep breath in, touched the swaying, severed bloody hand.

Snap!

Suddenly, a tiny string connected to the hand snapped back. Sophie realised this, but it was too late. The string tore apart, releasing a trigger which flung the branch upwards. A few patches of earth flew into the air, as a sharp hook swung up from the ground, and struck deep into Sophie's lips. Sophie didn't know what was happening as she was suddenly sent flying into the air, abruptly halting to a stop several feet high off the ground.

Sophie hung there, numb for a moment. What had just happened? Everything had just flown by in a flash of dirt. It was several moments before she realised what was happening, as her eyes opened wide in terror in realisation. She was hanging in the air, metres from the ground. At first she didn't quite realise what she was hanging from, her face felt so numb. Then, suddenly the pain returned, and Sophie suddenly felt a rush of pure pain burning from the front of her mouth. She rolled her eyes down in terror immediately, to see a large, sharp, blood-stained hook sticking out from the side of her cheek.

Sophie whined immensely in pain as she suddenly lifted her arms up and started clawing desperately at the hook which dug deep into her mouth and out of the other side. The pain was soaring and burning inside her cheek as blood began to pour from her weak mouth. Her hands flailed mindlessly as she panicked and tried to remove the hook desperately as she hung from it. Her cheek was being stretched from the strain of holding her whole body up. Sophie was breathing heavily through her nose. Trying urgently to not fall into unconsciousness from shock and to try and shut out the sheer amount of pain which was tearing away at her cheek at that very moment.

She couldn't take it any longer. She was going to fall. The strong hook which dug deep into her soft cheeks was going to break away any moment, and she would fall once again, rapidly to the cold forest floor. She was in so much pain. Her eyes rolled back in her sockets with the vast amount of throbbing which she was going through. And as the blood spilt further down her chin and began to drip onto the forest floor, she knew she would fall to her death any moment now. She could not remove the hook no matter how hard she tried. She tried to look down at the eerie forest floor, even in daylight it was still a sinister, haunting place to be in. she could only see a fraction of the forest floor from where she was hanging. Her eyes rolled down so far in their sockets that it ached with pain from how far down they were stretching. The grim severed hand was still hanging on a nearby branch from where Sophie had touched it originally. She could see it there disturbingly, like some form of large, grisly spider. Her eyes were playing tricks on her as she began to loose her sanity. As just from out of the corner of her eye, she just thought she saw the bloody, dead hand twitch once or twice. She tried hard to look away.

A sudden thought clicked within a lost pocket of her mind. Her eyes flashed wide open, only not with horror or pain, but this time, with a brainwave. She was weak and her mind was spinning around in all the confusion, as her blood dripped gradually, drop by drop onto the floor, collecting in a small pile in the bottom.

Sophie thought back, hard, back to much earlier on yesterday when her father had given her a small pocket knife for her to keep for the future. The thought of her father made her tremble with fear, as a small tear began to leak from the corner of her eye. Sophie wiped the tears from her face with her right, blood-stained hand. Her clothes were now running red with the increasing stains of thick red blood, her very own. She clung onto the rope with her other hand, the skin digging in from grasping it so tightly.

She lifted her weak arm up and putting all her strength into it, reached into her left pocket. Searching around, she fumbled and rummaged amongst the clutter. She groped through sweet wrappers, a compass, and small screwed up pieces of paper, until she finally managed to find what she was looking for. Grasping her hand tightly around it, Sophie removed a small blue pocket knife from her jacket pocket. A wave of relief fuelled through her body for a moment as she held the knife up to the sunlight, as she almost felt saved. A flash of darkness passed overhead as the trees shook briefly in the wind. Sophie flashed back to reality, as the pain surged, the blood fell, the knife clasped firmly within her cold hand.

She immediately flicked open the small device to reveal a small blade from one of the openings in the pocket knife. Sophie spun her eyes around to look at the space where the hook dug deeply into her cheek. She tried desperately to focus on her objective, rather than looking at the amount of blood which was pulsating out from her cheek. Her eyes looked straight ahead. She gritted her teeth as she bit through the pain, and began to cut her way through the thin rope which held her up.

Grabbing onto the long string upwards, Sophie supported herself as she held the small knife to the thick string and was slicing away rapidly, struggling determinedly to remove the hook from her mouth. She sawed faster and faster. And as the pain surged harder, she began to slice faster too. She was half way through, she could feel the string beginning to give way, its slow creaking connection edging further and further and further apart as it began to snap.

A cry in the distance rung out. Sophie suddenly halted abruptly. Her eyes darted around. *What was that? Did someone just scream?* She had no idea. She was worried, panicking and trembling with fear. The pain stopped for a moment as her senses focused elsewhere, listening intently to hear what just happened. Suddenly, another cry erupted in the distance, only this time it was closer. Was it somebody screaming? She could not tell. She tried to look out far into the distance, deep into the forest of trees and dark, grisly green. She could see nothing. A further time the cry rang out, and Sophie could tell clearly, it was getting closer.

Someone was running this way. The noises were coming from directly ahead of her. If someone was running this way she would immediately be able to see them, and they would be able to see her. *Dad?! Lauren?! Max?! Anyone?!* she thought, screaming inside her head with anxiety. She didn't dare scream out otherwise her mouth would be torn in half by the deadly hook within it.

Sophie stared fearfully ahead into the forest air, hoping deep down inside that it was one of her family rushing in her direction. They had come to save her. They were alive!

The cry suddenly burst from ahead again, this time extremely close. She would be able to see them any moment now. She was waiting, anxiously, her heart pounding rapidly every second. And as the cry rang out a fifth time, Sophie's mouth sank downwards in terror, as she realised that what she had thought to be cries of panic, were monstrous, bloodthirsty growls. Her eyes stared unflinching at the spot ahead of her, she could not move them. Something was coming from out of the trees, coming for her.

Her eyes gawped ahead, bulging open in shock. They widened further, as suddenly, from out of the undergrowth, two monstrous shapes burst from beneath. Sophie could not see, as her eyes were spinning everywhere as the two shapes ran around her, circling her, and constantly growling menacingly, like a pair of rabid dogs. These were not dogs however. A small, slow tear trickled down the edge of Sophie's right eye, as she knew what they were. There was no family who had come to save her. No rescue team or saviour. For below her, two gruesome creatures circled her fiercely. These were not ordinary things. These were what had ambushed them back in the clearing the previous night. These were what had pounced upon her in the tree and sent her fleeing into the horrific darkness.

They were not human, no. They were too ugly, disfigured and scarred to be any kind of human. They were both of the male gender she could tell, yet their features were terrifying and a sickening sight to the eyes. Thousands of scars and bloody wounds were across their faces. Their fingers were long and bony, with thin sharp nails which thrust out from the ends like knives themselves. Their skin was dark and smudged with a combination of dirt, blood and a mixture of all different kinds of unknown, disturbing substances. Their eyes stuck right out of their skulls, terrifying, grisly and bloodthirsty, as they stared deep into Sophie's. They roared like canines, revealing rows of sharp teeth, sticking out like needles into the air above. What little hair showed on their heads was slimy, dirty and greasy from years of squalid conditions. For a moment, as Sophie was left hanging there, terrified, cold and alone, she could not move, she was frozen cold to the spot with fear.

They were circling her like sharks, she could see from out of the corner of her eyes looking down. Jumping up and biting, slashing out with their monstrous claws every few seconds. They could not reach her, yet. All the time they were jumping up savagely, hissing like snakes and biting like rabid dogs. Saliva drooled from their mouths in their hunger. These creatures were horrific.

One of them jumped up rapidly, and just managed to catch the end of Sophie's left foot before falling down again. A twitch of fear suddenly ricocheted through her body. Slowly and gradually, they were jumping higher and higher. Soon enough, they would be able to reach her, and drag her down to be savaged in the most horrific of ways.

Sophie's thoughts were revolving around inside her head. She had to make a decision, a terrifying one. She had two options. She could either cut herself free with her penknife, fall to the ground and flee as fast as she could from her deadly pursuers. Or, she could stay safe from the savage beasts which were constantly clawing at her, yet suffer an increasing amount of pain from the hook sticking out of her cheek.

Moments passed as Sophie panicked, breathed heavily and thought about what to do. The creatures beneath her were gradually jumping higher and higher in their savage hunger as Sophie tried desperately to shake them away from her poor body. Eventually, her brain clicked with a sudden jolt of realisation: she was going to escape.

Gulping with nerves and fear, Sophie held the pocket-knife firmly up to the now thin rope, and started hacking away as fast as she could. She stretched her arms, tensing her muscles, slicing hard through the ever-thinning string which was holding her painfully up in the air. Beneath her feet, the two horrific creatures were constantly jumping up and snapping savagely at her legs, they were slowly getting higher and higher as they never gave up. Sophie knew that

189

she had to free herself fast before those things got to her, and slowly mauled her hanging there.

The rope was now very thin, having been sliced through so much. The only thing that was now holding Sophie up was a tiny piece of string hanging from a branch high above her. Sophie's flesh in her cheek was straining painfully as the hook remained firmly in place. With pain trembling down through her arms and body, Sophie forcefully held the pocket-knife up once more to the remaining string, and sliced.

There was a loud crack, and a snap, a moment of pure silence, then a great whooshing sound, as Sophie plummeted rapidly towards the floor. Another loud thump echoed around through the forest air as she hit the soil and earth suddenly, trembling with bits of dirt flying in all directions as she smashed downwards. The world seemed to erupt around her as she landed hard on the cold forest floor. Her shoulders crashed into the dirt as her whole body seemed to roll around from the force rapidly. She could not see ahead of her, the force was so strong. She rolled over and over again, feeling the force of sharp objects crashing to the ground around her, narrowly missing and occasionally slashing lightly against her side. The two creatures were trying to attack her as she rolled uncontrollably across the floor, and yet she could do nothing.

Suddenly and abruptly, Sophie came to an immediate stop. She lay there silently for a moment, open sky above her. The world above was not as bright as it was the day before. It was colder, darker and more antagonistic towards her. The sky was grey, with heavy cloud cover. The sun barely shone through the thickness of it all. Everything seemed like it had suddenly died. A disturbing change from the scorching heat of yesterday's summer sun.

Sophie lay there wheezing heavily, out of breath. Her cheek still bled from the wound even though the hook had fallen away before as she had descended. Her eyes were rolling in their sockets, as for a moment, all seemed quiet and calm. Nothing was happening except the birdsong in the trees, and the distant whistling of the wind. She breathed in and out heavily. What had just happened?

The sharp crack of a nearby stick soon answered her question, as poor Sophie snapped back top reality. The faint sound of heavy, rasping breaths gradually became louder and louder, closer and closer. The birdsong died, only to be replaced with the rumbling sound of footsteps coming towards her. Sophie held her breath terrified. As she recalled the past events of the previous few minutes, a large, ugly, monstrous, terrifying face appeared overhead. Its ears were twisted and mutated, eyes like red flames bulging from their sockets, teeth like bloodstained knives being licked by a long protruding tongue from within the black hole of its maw. This was nothing like Sophie had ever seen before as she stared up in shock, completely petrified. The creature looked down hungrily over her with longing. A brief moment of silence fell between the two of them, before gradually, the second monster walked into view. Almost identical to its comrade, the newcomer stared down fiercely at the terrified Sophie Barrow.

She tried to move her eyes fearfully, desperately trying to think of a plan, yet mesmerized by the ominous, bloodthirsty stare of the two creatures above her. She rolled her eyes to the right, and saw something that just might work. Several feet away from her, lay the small bloodstained hook which she had cut herself free from. It was sharp, it was a weapon. Sophie didn't need to think twice.

The first began to lower itself downwards, crouching down very slowly to come closer to the young teenager before it. It crouched there menacingly, reaching up and brushing its long, thin cold finger down Sophie's cold, dirty skin. It ran it's fingertips through a streak of blood on her cheek and raised it to it's mouth, licking it off. These things were disgusting, monstrous and disturbing. She now knew

191

that they had acquired a taste for human blood. Were these things vampires? They couldn't be, seeing as the daylight shone down upon them. What were they? Sophie tried to crawl away, edging slowly towards the sharp hook several feet away from her. As she slowly edged away from the crouching creature, the thing only came closer and closer towards her. Both wore disturbingly cruel smiles upon their faces, revealing sharp teeth, many missing in their wide, scarred jaws. One was almost crawling as it slowly neared her, taunting her in her panic. The other, which was standing, began to edge closer towards her, its long pointed tongue out and curling around like a vile snake. There was nothing Sophie wanted more right now than to kill these things and flee to her family. The trees blew around her in the spine chilling wind. The eyes of the two savage creatures bore down into her. The terror was rising.

Sophie leapt. She flung herself suddenly across the ground towards the thick hook. At the same time as she jumped for it, the two monsters saw her plan in the blink of an eye and sprinted towards her. One of them lunged at her and grabbed her legs tightly. She yelped in pain as she was suddenly stopped in her tracks, clawing desperately for the hook, inches away from her reaching hand. The first creature held tightly onto her legs, sprawled over the floor, refusing to let go of her. Sophie pushed herself harder and harder, further and further, she had to reach the hook, she needed to. The second creature looked down at the two struggling on the floor, its comrade trying to hold on to the squirming girl. It chuckled grimly, producing a thick gleaming smile in its mutilated jaw. Instead of struggling along with the other two, it simply walked casually over to where Sophie was reaching for, and saw the hook from the trap lying there, glistening in the light. He saw the girl trying hard, struggling desperately to reach it. The creature walked over to it and picked it up sourly.

Sophie's desperate eyes began to lose all hope, as she watched the monster bend down nonchalantly and pick up the silver hook. Even as her arm followed the weapon as he picked it up, she carried on reaching forwards, in a final hope of grabbing hold of it.

There was no hope however, as the creature picked up the hook briskly, and held it dangling in front her, taunting her like an animal. It stared down at her evilly, as it waved the possible weapon two and fro like a piece of food.

"Give that to me!" groaned Sophie threateningly. She was not expecting an answer, yet she cried and longed for it savagely.

Yet suddenly, to her upmost surprise, the thing replied.

"You want this?" it rasped monstrously. Sophie halted, shocked for a moment. The creature was talking. It was almost as if it were human. "You really want this?" it said in a tone laced with sarcasm, yet its voice was wheezing and rasping, a terrifying noise to hear.

Sophie kept on reaching out; she knew it would definitely not give it to her. The thing holding tightly onto her legs was so strong it kept her forcibly rooted to the spot.

The creature chuckled perversely, its throat rising in and out horrifically. It leaned in slowly towards Sophie's ear, and whispered darkly into it,

"You listening to me? I'm gonna make you scream. You hear me? I'm gonna make you scream!"

Sophie was traumatised. Everything that had happened over the past few hours was disturbing enough to alter any mortal human's mind. What was this creature going to do to her? This hostile, savage thing. She wouldn't let it touch her any longer. She was going to get rid of it. Sophie could feel the anger rising up inside of her, boiling and thriving with hate and monstrosity. She was going to kill every last one of them in these woods. And she wasn't going to stop until every last one of them lay dead on the floor before her. She was going to save her family, and fight back against the oncoming, bloodthirsty darkness. With fear and rage building up inside her, Sophie pulled all her strength together, and lunged out for the hook.

She squirmed free just in time and threw her body weight outwards, flying a foot forwards and snatching the hook out of the creature's hand. She fell flat on her face in the dirt once more, she was free. As soon as she had rapidly recovered, she sprang to her feet, the hook grasped tightly within her blood-stained hands, anger distorted upon her savage face. The two monsters stood several feet away from her, on the other side of the small clearing. There was a moment of tension and silence, as nothing disturbed the tense atmosphere. Sophie stared menacingly into the eyes of the two creatures, who looked almost shocked and startled by Sophie's sudden escape, yet they kept their ground, and stared hungrily back, licking their lips and biting their battered, sharp teeth together.

The silence drew on for a moment, as nothing made a noise in the background. Nothing, except for the trees swaying in the wind, and the blood from the mutilated arm above in the trees, slowly dripping down drop by drop onto the cold, damp forest floor beneath.

The silence and the tension felt in the forest air lasted for a brief, terrifying moment, before finally, one of the creatures ran. It charged at Sophie barbarically, raising its bloody claws into the air, nails as long as knives, and sliced down savagely towards Sophie. She ducked just in time to see a handful of razor sharp claws come flying down upon her and just manage to catch the very edge of her t-shirt. The edge of one nail slit through and cut a tiny piece of her skin, leaving a bright red mark. It stung for a moment as Sophie winced briefly in pain, before ignoring it altogether and stabbing the hook down into the thing's eye. She was enraged, and experienced a sudden monstrous thirst for power as she felt the small sharp hook come crashing down into the bloodshot eye of the first creature. It whined in pain, grasping at its wounded eye repeatedly, before falling to the floor screaming, clutching its gashed face.

Sophie flung herself around to face the other who rapidly came charging monstrously towards her with the brute force of a bull. It came in a flash of brown and grey and smashed into her, sending Sophie flying back painfully into a large tree trunk. She gritted her teeth angrily as she fought off the pain and tried to climb up. As she stood up, the creature lashed out again, slashing a handful of knife sharp nails into the tree towards her. She ducked rapidly, breathing heavily as she fell back down again, only to swing round and up and to her feet, before punching the hideous monster straight in the face. She lashed out with her fists, smashing her right arm into the face of the creature before it had time to react. Its face was knocked to the side suddenly. Sophie could not believe she had just done that. She was no expert in martial arts or fighting, yet what she had just done was something really unearthly.

The creature spat blood from its mouth before rising up again to face her slowly, its expression twisted into one of anger, a dark terrifying rage which traumatised Sophie to the darkest parts of her bones. It punched her back, smashing her to the ground with its rage. Its partner may have been knocked down, yet one on its own was still as deadly as two. Sophie plunged to the ground. Her strength was fading and her body was weakening. She leapt to her feet and ducked just as another fist came flying down to greet her face. She ducked and swerved luckily, as more and more claws came slashing towards her face. This creature was firing away; it was like some other race of supernatural being. Sophie swung her left leg around and smashed it heavily into the right leg of the thing before her. It fell to the floor suddenly, it was weakened. She had to act now.

Without thinking, Sophie ran hurriedly over to the other dying creature on the floor, and quickly swiped the bloody hook from its eye. It reeled in pain and whined loudly as she did so, before crawling back up into a ball again. Blood sprayed of from the silver and red hook as she flung it around with her to face the monster, soaking all the nearby plants in a torrent of blood and pus.

Her eyes burned like fire. She was going to kill. The creature stood up slowly, and cautiously. It looked at her, its eyes wide open in what looked like a mixture of fascination and anger. It was a terrifying being, sinister and deadly. Its face was hideous and scarred, like some kind of orc creature. Sophie raised her weapon in her hands, positioned defensively, and lashed out.

She ran full on, angrily and scared to the bone by the horrific being. She raised her hook into the air and brought it down forcefully towards it. The creature leapt back, dodging the weapon entirely and avoiding it. She swung again and again, desperate to kill this savage beast. It dodged another attack, then paused as she recoiled, looked at her creepily for a moment, then rapidly slashed at her with its claws. It missed, but only just. The edges of Sophie's chin began to bleed slowly as she realised that the very tips of the monsters claws had grazed her chin too deep.

She coughed and spluttered weakly. The monster took a few steps back lazily, looked at her amused and laughed horribly.

"Pathetic!" it said in its sinister, bloodthirsty voice. It slashed out at her again. Sophie was weak, yet she was still wide awake and well aware of what was happening around her.

She jumped back in shock, just managing to keep herself on her feet. It slashed out again, its barbaric razor sharp nails just missing her dirt covered face. Sophie ducked and sprung backwards as the creature was gradually pushing her away from the brightness of the clearing and into the darkness and tree cover of the undergrowth.

Sophie tried to wipe the blood from her face whilst desperately trying to avoid the hideous monster before her from tearing her apart. She had already defeated one, but yet still its comrade was attacking her bloodthirstily. She held the hook firmly in her hand; she had to strike as soon as possible. Clenching it tightly within her fist, Sophie dodged another swing of its arms, and slashed back with her own. She flung the hook high into the air with her hand and brought it swiftly down upon the monster's skull with clenched teeth and an anger of full brute force.

There was a loud crack, followed by a brief moment of silence. The creature stood there still, as if stunned. The large silver bloody hook stuck out brutally from its head, its spike lodged deep into the thing's forehead. Sophie gasped in a mixture of shock and relief. Had she killed it? She didn't know. It just stood there like a confused animal. She had no idea what was going on. Its eyes were focused straight ahead, staring, pupils bulging. Its mouth gaped open wide, as a thick drool of saliva dribbled down from its wide maw.

Sophie inched a few steps back, slowly moving further and further away uneasily. It was dying. She had killed it. Sophie let out a long sigh of relief, as she slouched down. A gargling sound erupted from the creature's throat as blood drooled out. It then slowly sunk to its knees and fell to the floor, dead.

Sophie let out an even greater sigh of relief, she had killed it, it was dead at last. She was still traumatised however, still terrified by the surroundings and happenings of the last few hours. All night she had been wandering the woodlands, tired, afraid, alone. It had been the most disturbing climax of her life so far, and she knew it was not over yet. She had defeated two of them, yet she knew that there were much more than two of them in the vast world of Dilas Forest. She knew that there were more coming, elsewhere, fighting the rest of her scattered family. More would come, but for now, two were slain. Or so she thought.

A hand suddenly burst from the ground and snapped at Sophie's ankle, grabbing it tightly and clenching its fist around it menacingly. Sophie leapt out of her skin and reeled back in terror as she rapidly spun around to see what it was.

The thing, the creature which she had just killed, was still alive, breathing, looking up at her and grabbing her ankle. It rasped wheezing, letting out a gust of foul air from its rotting lungs. Sophie screamed in fright, exploding the sound around the entire area of the forest. The monster groaned and whined, grasping at her foot with all its surviving strength. Sophie wriggled and squirmed, desperate to try and break free. It pulled harder and harder on her leg, rasping louder and louder like a sick animal. The hook still stuck out from its dirty, blood-stained forehead like a knife.

Sophie pulled at her leg, trying to wrench it out from the hold of the creature on the ground. Finally, she managed to tear her ankle away from its grasp, leap to her feet, and run. She fled wildly and almost blindly into the tree cover. It was daylight now as the light rays from above lit up the forest clearly. It was easier to see than the previous night, yet even so, the forest was like a monster itself, dragging innocent minds into its dark and unearthly trap.

Sophie ran and ran. She began to splutter and wheeze, yet even so, she still fled terrified for her very life. The trees flashed past her in bolts of light and colour. They stretched high above her like monstrous giants, reaching out for her with their long twisting branches. It seemed the whole world was against her now. She was well and truly, on her own.

Far from behind, the wounded creature gathered its remaining strength and flung itself upwards. It stood up fully, focusing its deep black pupils into the surrounding shadows which flickered around it, searching for its prey. Its eyes flashed past a certain point, as it glared menacingly, and set off. It was on her tail.

She kept on running, through branches which cut her face and roots which tripped her over, she kept on going strong.

She could see it gradually approaching behind her, closer and closer. It had the speed of a wolf, and the agility of an eagle. It was so close now, yet she daren't look behind her. She knew it would only slow her down.

It was so close now. She could start to hear the approaching breathing of it getting louder and louder. Suddenly, she tripped and fell, her face falling flat into the damp mud once more. She spun herself around like a bolt of lightning, as she saw the creature feet away from her, advancing, licking its savage lips. It slowed down, walking towards her a steady pace. Its eyes gleaming like fresh blood against the dark light and shadows of the surrounding world. Sophie tried to crawl backwards, yet she could not move. She was paralysed with fear and petrified to the bone.

The creature smiled angrily and cruelly. Blood stains leaked out from the hook and gash in its forehead, as it revealed a maw full of sharp, fanged teeth.

"You can't run from me!" it growled viciously, its voice disturbing to hear. It rasped loud and clear, like its vocal chords were slowly rotting over time.

Sophie pushed her arm back and tried to crawl away, the earth was damp and wet. She slowly began to crawl backwards and away from this horrible nightmare. Yet as she moved away terrified, the thing only came closer and closer towards her. It bent down closer to her, ripping the hook from its forehead, as a trickle of blood spat out from the savage wound. It raised the hook towards Sophie's face and said cruelly,

"I'm gonna make you scream. You hear me!" It bent down closer, "I'm gonna make you scream!" it whispered bloodthirstily into her small fragile ears.

Sophie couldn't breathe. This creature was going to do horrible things to her, unspeakable, disturbing things. She couldn't escape, not this time. Her eyes stayed wide open, her lungs breathed heavily in anxiety.

199

The creature was suddenly flung back, as a loud bang erupted from the air and a torrent of blood showered the area. The monster was suddenly flung through the air and landed several feet away, smashing into a nearby tree. Sophie couldn't move. What had just happened? The creature lay there metres away from her, a large bullet hole in its shoulder. It lay there quietly, slumped at the bottom of the tree, flinching every few moments. Sophie rapidly spun around in the dirt, to see something which she never would have imagined. For standing there boldly, with a face exhibiting anger and rage, a small pistol in hand, was Lauren.

She stood there, a position of utter fury and monstrosity. She pointed the gun down at the severely wounded creature. Her gun never moved, neither did her line of sight. Her whole body was torn and blood-stained. Her hair was rough and dirty, whilst her clothes were cut and ripped. Looking down in rage upon the dying creature, her eyes focusing directly upon it, she spoke with a voice angelic to hear.

"You stay away from her!" she placed her hand over the trigger, and fired once more.

Chapter 26: Freaks

Max stood there, facing the savage hooded monster which stood before him. Several metres away, on the other side of one of the many small clearings in Dilas Forest, was Shark, one of the murderous, bloodthirsty creatures which had terrorised him and his family over the past few hours. All through the night Max had been fleeing and fighting, until he had finally fallen into the hands of this vile beast. Now he had a small dead branch in his hand as a weapon. He was going to slay this creature. It wouldn't survive.

Shark stood there on the other side staring cruelly back at him in the disturbing moment of tension. It licked its lips hungrily and clenched its sharp nailed, skinny hands together in and out, ready to fight. Any moment now they would engage in combat, a savage, brutal combat.

Max clenched the branch tightly in his hands and ran suddenly, a face distorted with hate and pure rage. He raised the weapon high into the air to strike. As he ran towards Shark, the creature pulled out a blade from its coat pocket and slashed it into the branch. Max's weapon was thick and therefore was not immediately shattered in half by the strong iron blade. Splinters came flying out in all directions and dug deep into both of the opponents flesh. Yet still they kept on going. Max withdrew his weapon from the locked combat and struck out again with force. Turning around, he smashed his branch into the creature's leg. Shark flew back brutally, falling to his feet with sheer force and hitting the ground violently. Max ran over to him, fists clenched tightly around the weapon and brought it down sharply. Shark dodged and spun around and away from the splintering branch. It rolled around, jumped off the side of a nearby trunk and leapt to its feet suddenly. This creature was fast, and Max knew that well by now.

It picked up its blade quickly and threw it across the clearing towards Max's face. He saw it coming luckily and dodged his head out of the way just in time to see a sharp iron short sword come flying rapidly past his face, brushing and snipping off the very edges of a few hairs on the side of his head. Max breathed in and out like a bolt of lightning. Shark dashed past him, darting across the clearing like a fox. It picked up its blade sticking out from the ground and raised it once more on guard. Max was panting, out of breath, but still alive. He raised his weapon like a club and ran towards Shark ferociously. Bringing the club down sharply, the creature quickly rolled around and under his arm, slashing its blade out and cutting into Max's side. Max groaned and squealed in pain. The left side of his body was bleeding. Blood was slowly appearing onto his once pure white t-shirt. He bent over wheezing and spluttering. He could not let this creature kill him.

Putting all of his surviving energy from what he had left together, Max spun around, stood up, tears now beginning to flood from his eyes, he held his branch out in front of his face defensively and murderously. He could feel it inside of him. The pain which was driving him was converting him. Max himself was beginning to turn into a monster. He was turning into one of them. He was letting his anger thrive; he was allowing himself to turn into the beast which he was trying to kill. He shut out all of his conscience. He gritted his battered teeth, and growled fiercely at the monster before him.

Max ran towards it, blood flying from his slashed skin as he charged. He was bitter with rage and hate. He raised the club up high, splinters falling like rain as he flung it skywards. He clenched his teeth and brought it down rapidly upon the creatures head. Shark yelped in pain like a wounded dog. It fell to the floor dazed for a moment. The sudden jolt from the blow of the weapon was too fast, it couldn't have avoided it.

Shark was livid. It grasped its hand tightly around its cold blade and stood up. Its foe was steaming with rage, as Max smashed the branch over its back over and over again, denting deep wounds into its cold grey, bloodstained skin. Shark ignored these constant attacks. He too was monstrously angered by the young man's sudden attacks. It continued to stand up, whilst Max was constantly smashing blow after blow into its back. Shark ignored them all.

Max delivered one final blow into the back of the hooded creature, before it finally stood up fully in response. There was a moment of silence, as Max stared back into the thing's cruel bloodshot eyes. He stopped attacking with shock. The ominous glare of this creature was disturbing and horrifying.

Shark stared back at Max, before he scrunched his face up into an expression of fury and slashed out at Max's belly with his blade. Max was flung back. The sudden strike of the blade slashed slightly into his belly and cut into the edge of his skin. He flew back rapidly to come back to back with a nearby tree trunk. He rasped, as blood gargled in his mouth. He was weak and felt like he was dying, but he was still there, alive and vengeful. He slowly placed his hand down towards his stomach, and felt the bloody wound. He looked up into the sky, tears forming in his eyes, as one fell down his cheek. The thought of his family screaming in pain and terror flashed before his eyes, as a sudden jolt struck him. This was what he was fighting for, to save his family. Max blinked several times, watching the creature slowly walk towards him, its heavy feet smashing into the ground, causing it to tremble and shake.

Max spat the blood from his mouth, and coughed several times. He was fighting back. Dust and earth began to fly up and hit him in the face as the monster neared him. Max reached his right hand out slowly, pushing all of his surviving strength together at last, and grabbed hold of a long sharp piece of wood. Blood splattered the new weapon from his wounded hands. He looked up in anger and wrath at the oncoming storm, and jumped up fiercely.

He flung the spike around in his hand rapidly, slashing it towards Shark, who leapt back. Max slashed out again, back and forwards with his weapon, desperate to kill the thing. Shark was fast. It ducked and dived like some form of ghost. Occasionally one of the attacks would hit it, yet to no good use. He still survived, and as Max continued savagely to attack the deformed creature, he could not bring it down.

Max was growing bitter and increasingly bloodthirsty with rage. His attacks became more brutal and his speed and agility began to slowly increase. He held the sharp, splinter covered branch firmly within his hands, and lunged once more. This time he was fast and menacing. Shark leapt back to dodge it, but it was too late. Max jumped up and struck the spike deep into the creature's chest.

There was a moment of pure silence, as the disgusting monster stood there, its face covered by the shadows of its filth covered hood. Max could not see its face clearly, but he could just make out some of the tiny details. It was in shock. Its gaping bloodshot eyes were sticking out from their sockets in horror, as a long chain of drool slowly protruded from within its mouth and crawled downwards towards its knees.

It suddenly gasped horrifically and sank to its knees. The deadly spike wedged in its chest, blood stains gradually increasing around the area on its filthy ageing clothes. Max looked down upon the dying creature and said coldly,

"Stay down." His voice was monstrous and vicious. He had become like that. From all of the pain that he had endured, from all of the horrors which had fought, he was slowly becoming as savage as his very foe. His heart was becoming cold and cruel.

Shark said nothing back. It merely knelt there on its knees drooling and staring dead ahead in the shock of the sharp weapon sticking out of its chest. Max looked down upon the thing and grimaced, disgusted by it. He stood there patiently, waiting almost gleefully for it to die.

Suddenly, the creature stopped. The trail of drool fell. Its mouth shut abruptly. Max's focus suddenly flashed immediately back to the thing on the floor, which was now staring disturbingly back at him. Max reeled back in horror as the monster stared savagely at him. Suddenly, it let out a monstrous roar, echoing throughout the surrounding forest. Max leapt back in terror, as the creature stuck out its huge fangs and sharp teeth.

Slowly, as Max edged further and further away, the hooded beast stood up, and, placing a thin bony hand to its chest, removed the sharp spike. A short gust of blood poured out, but only for a second.

Shark stood there, eyes widened, staring bloodthirstily at Max. It was not dead. It was very much alive. Max stared back, thoughts ringing around terrifyingly inside his head. *Why won't you just die!* The thought echoed throughout his head like a raging storm. He thought he had killed the thing, but no. It was still alive. It would never die. And now, it was going to kill him.

Shark suddenly leapt towards Max, flinging its whole body into the air, and bringing its force down swiftly upon him. Max was hit. He came flying down to the worm-eaten earth by the full force of the creature. It landed brutally on top of him, causing him to splutter and cough as his insides felt as if they were about to come flying out. The creature held the blade up and started trying to slash it down towards Max. He writhed and thrashed about, desperately holding on to the edge of the spike to stop it from plunging into him. The tension was growing strong. Max didn't know how much longer he could take of holding it. The creature looked down menacingly upon him. It snarled and groaned, screaming horrific screams and cries into his face, which deafened him and blinded him from the saliva which spat out rapidly from the thing's mouth. Max squirmed, desperately trying to stay alive. The spike was gradually getting closer and closer to his heart. He breathed heavily in and out. His muscles contracted back and forth vigorously, putting all his strength and energy into keeping that thing away from him.

Max pushed and pushed, gaining more control as he pushed further and further into it. The creature too was becoming weak with strength. He could do it. Harder and harder he pushed, his muscles were tensing beyond all reason. Finally, Max reacted back suddenly, and shoved the monster away from him. It rolled over violently and fell into the corner of the small clearing. Max seized the moment and leapt to his feet. He grabbed the severely damaged spike and ran towards the wounded creature. As he charged towards it, Shark saw him and jumped up, leaping out of the way rapidly like a wolf.

Max brought the spike down into thin air, turning his head around quickly to see where the thing had jumped away too. It looked back and turned around to face him. Max gritted his teeth, desperately trying to stay awake and alert. The thing began to circle him. It groaned and creaked from deep noises within its throat. Max circled opposite it, never taking his eyes away from it.

Shark jumped suddenly, throwing itself towards Max, who rolled out of the way just in time, as the thing's large silver blade came crashing down to the muddy earth beside him. He dodged swiftly out of the way, removing his feet from the path of the blade.

Shark stood up to its feet, growling like a savage wolf. This thing really was an animal. It bit and snarled viciously as it stood to its feet, Max staying several feet away. The two of them eyed each other cruelly, waiting for the other to attack first.

Suddenly, there came a sudden ringing sound from across the clearing. Both their heads suddenly turned curiously. Max's mouth abruptly gaped open in shock as he realised

206

what the odd ringing sound was. The two beings, one normal and one monstrous stared in surprise and shock at the object which lay ringing and vibrating upon the ground several feet away. There was a moment of silence as the two enemies stared in confusion and horror, at Max's phone, which was lying there amongst the dirt.

Max breathed in and out with stress and panic. It must have slipped out of his pocket whilst he was fighting. He looked closely down at the number ringing. Shark was eyeing the phone too. Its face gradually grew more and more twisted with greed and ruthlessness. It couldn't let Max answer it. No-one could know where its next victim was. Max stared down at the lone phone and read the one word written in tiny letters upon the front screen, 'Lauren'.

Max dived for the phone, falling face first into the dirt and earth. Shark, filled with hunger and fury, leapt after him. Max's glasses fell from his face. He quickly realised they were missing and snapped around to put them back on again. They were dirty and grimy, yet he could still see through them. Shark lunged towards him. A thin grey hand lashed out at the helpless young man and grabbed him around the scruff of the neck. Max was pulled aside. He choked and spluttered with shock, rasping for air, as he was savagely turned over, the creature snarling heavily down on top of him. Max stared into its eyes and saw the pure bloodthirsty rage which was driving it on. The phone kept on ringing. Max looked over at from the corner of his eye. He had to get to it. He had to get help. He reached an arm out as far as he could, yet the hideous monster remained on top of him, pinning him down and growling into his face.

He reached out further, and further. He had to reach it, somehow. He stretched and stretched. His left arm reached out as far as it could go, whilst his right was stuck up, desperately trying to keep the creature from tearing his face off with its razor sharp claws. He just managed to turn his head, as the phone kept on ringing. He had to reach it as fast as he could. He could not let Lauren go away. She may still be alive, and if so he needed to help her, or more importantly, she needed to help him.

Max's vision kept on darting back and forward. From the monster to his phone, his eyes kept on moving around. He had to focus upon the two at the same time; it was the only way which he could survive.

Suddenly, Max noticed something from out of the very corner of his eye, something which he would never have noticed before. Something strange, something useful. Sticking out of the creatures' grime-covered belt, surrounded by its dirt-ridden clothing rags and cloak, was its long blade. Max's eyes widened in realisation. He had an idea. He did not know why the monster was not using its bloody weapon, he had not a clue. All he was concerned about was that he was going to use it.

He drove his hand away from the reach of the phone, and instead towards the blade which was in reach. He hoped with all his might that the thing did not suddenly notice, and drive the blade back into him. Slowly and cautiously, he reached up towards the weapon. The thing had not noticed, all it cared about right now was killing Max, and with its hands waving around towards his face, it seemed that was going to come very soon unless he did something.

Up Max's left hand slowly rose, waiting like a snake for the moment to seize the blade suddenly from its hold. He was almost there, just a little further, it hadn't noticed. *Please! Please!* Max begged inside his head.

Suddenly, the time came. He grabbed the sword from its holster, withdrew it rapidly and plunged it deep into the creature's right shoulder blade. Shark rasped and roared in pain, shrieking deep into the cold morning air as blood slowly poured from out of its wounded shoulder. Its hands suddenly let go of Max's upper body, as it clutched its shoulder in pain. Max sprung free of its grasp and pushed it aside as he rolled over and out of the way. Shark was crying

208

out in pain and anger. It was mad and savage with rage, yet it could not fight back since its shoulder ached horrifically. Max did not know where exactly he had hit it, but it must have been a crucial ligament in his shoulder for it to be in that much pain. It turned around and stared at Max lividly, who was sprawled across the floor having suddenly rolled away from the thing. It was kneeling down on both knees; one hand clutching its wound, the other grabbed hold of the blade suddenly, and twisted it out from within. The sword was ripped out of its wound, a few spurts of blood flowing out from the injury. He stared at the human enraged, and rushed towards him. Max's eyes widened in horror, as the creature came crawling towards him fast, its vicious blade at the ready, ready to butcher him into pieces.

Max crawled backwards, the creature was almost on top of him again. Closer and closer it came, as Max crawled edging away from it backwards. He had no weapon, nothing. He didn't know what to do. The creature came closer and closer, it was almost at him. It was a few feet away from him. It raised its blade high, about to strike. Max had nothing to fight back with. The only thing he had left was his body. Shark growled in rage, about to tear him in two. Max couldn't do anything else; he was drawn into a sudden, urgent last resort. He crawled back rapidly, and raised his leg, and flung it forwards, smashing his foot into the creature's heavily battered face.

There was a sudden crack, as what felt like a wave shook through the ground. Tremors rung like spiders up Max's leg from the force. He looked down in shock at what he had just done. The thing knelt there for a brief moment, before falling over to the ground, lifeless, dead, a trickle of blood drooping down from its nose.

Max wheezed in and out, his throat was gasping for air. He choked and spluttered as he turned away slowly from the dead creature, rolling over and reaching out for the ringing phone. He sighed a deep sigh of relief as he tried to relax, yet couldn't. He lifted the phone into sight and sat up, weak, yet still going. He looked down at the front screen which read 'Incoming Call – Lauren'.

Max quickly lifted the phone lid and placed the phone to his ear and spoke rapidly into it.

"Lauren? Hello? Lauren?" he almost bellowed into the phone with fear.

"Max? Oh Max! You're alright!" came the happy, tearful reply from the other end.

"Are you alright?" Max said nervously, "are you hurt? Where are you?!" He spoke very fast, terrified for his younger sister.

"I'm okay. I've got Sophie with me. We're alright. Sophie's cheek has been badly wounded but apart from that we're okay, for now..."

"Sophie? Is she alright? What happened to her?!"

"She fell into one of..." She paused, frightened, and looked around briefly. "...Their traps."

Max gasped in shock. "Oh My God! Sophie!" he exclaimed in astonishment.

"Her cheek is badly bleeding. I've put some cloth around it, but it won't stop. She's okay for now, but if gets worse then..." She couldn't carry on. She almost felt like she was about to burst into tears.

Max didn't know what to say. He was terrified and worried for his sisters. He couldn't think straight. He needed to calm them down.

"Look, everything's going to be alright. I'm going to find you, understand? Try and find the edge of the woods, they're bound to be somewhere nearby; we've been in here for so long."

"Max?" Lauren was starting to cry. Tears were welling in her eyes. "What are those things?!" she said traumatised.

Max was frozen in thought and horror. He didn't know what they were. He didn't know how many of them there were. He didn't know where they came from. All he knew was that there were horrific creatures lurking in Dilas Forest, and they were hunting the Barrow family mercilessly. "I don't know Lauren." He removed his glasses and wiped a tear from his eye. "I really don't know. But I know that as long as we are talking, we are exposed to them. They might be able to hear us right now, so that's why we need to stay calm and find each other as soon as possible." He was so scared, yet he remained brave and took control of the situation.

"They took dad and Eve." She was really starting to cry, Max could hear her panicking in tears.

Max froze suddenly. They had killed his father and step mum. He felt a cold icy wave ripple through his wounded body, a wave of shock passed through him as he realised what had happened. He did not speak back, even though he could hear the constant 'Max?' 'Max!' coming from the other end, he could not answer back he was so scared. A moment of eerie, deadly silence passed as Max tried to shake the horror of the news away. He began to cry gently, tears welling in his eyes. He could not control it, his darkest nightmare had actually happened. The world seemed to fade into blackness around him slowly.

Max gritted his teeth, and stayed with it. He had to take responsibility now. He shook away the aching sadness in side of him, and pushed it away. He was depressed and terrified to the bone, yet he had to act now, and become the hero, and save his sisters and whichever surviving members of his family that were still out there. His thoughts flashed to Sean and Sarah, helpless and alone. He closed his eyes briefly and opened them, tears beginning to fall down his bruised, bloodstained cheeks. He picked up the phone once again and spoke firmly into it.

"Lauren? It's okay. Calm down. Everything is going to be alright. Keep Sophie with you, avoid the clearings, stay well out of sight, hide amongst the undergrowth. Don't let them see you! Understand?!" He was now fierce, determined and

211

vengeful. He wanted to kill. A dark lust had awoke from within him as he felt the seeds of vengeance arising swiftly.

"Yes," cried Lauren from the other end. "What about you? Are you okay?!"

Max brushed his left hand across his bloodstained stomach and bleeding skin. He hesitated for a moment. "I'm fine. Yeah, I'm fine. Don't worry about me."

"Max? You sound hurt," came Lauren's worried response.

"No I'm serious, don't worry about me," He began to speak quieter. "Just keep going alright. Everything's going to be just fine, you understand me? Just find an exit to the woods and wait for me. I'm coming for you girls, I'm coming for you!"

Lauren sniffed inwards, holding her tears back. "Okay. We're not leaving without you though. And..." she paused suddenly.

"Lauren? Lauren?!" Max became extremely worried.

Finally, a reply came back. "One of them is coming Max! It's here!" she said quietly yet shrieking under her breath.

"Hide! Hide now!" he answered back, trying not to bellow too loudly.

"It's coming Max! It's coming for us!" she was terrified more than ever; Max could feel it in her breath and her speech.

"Lauren? Hide! Quickly!" he urged back down the line.

"I need to go. It'll only give away that you're still around too."

"I'm coming for you Lauren! You understand me? I'm coming to save you!" he said hurriedly and determinedly.

"I know," she replied quietly and fearfully. "Good luck Max. Don't let them find you too." And with that, there came a quiet bleeping sound, and the phone line cut dead.

Max looked down at the cold, damp ground. All went quiet and dark around him. They were in trouble; they might not even make it out. Max felt sadness rushing through him, his dad and step mum were dead, the rest of his family were wandering the wilderness helplessly with those things following them on their tail. That sadness was suddenly filled with anger, a monstrous rage which burned through his soul and lurched outwards almost uncontrollably. He stood up livid, and smashed his phone into the ground with a sudden brutal force. He looked up into the cold, grey sky, and bellowed at the very top of his lungs.

"YOU'RE ALL FREAKS!"

Chapter 27:   Hatred's Knife

Lauren shut her phone lid down and quickly crawled into the small space where Sophie was hiding, wiping the tears from her watering eyes. She was sitting there, her back up against the thick trunk, as silent as the grave. Lauren crawled in next to her and hugged her tightly.

"Everything's going to be okay, you understand? Everything's going to be okay," whispered Lauren fearfully into her younger sister's ear.

Sophie looked terrified back at her older sister. She tried desperately not to speak for her cheek bled severely and the wound stung when she moved her mouth at all. She held the ragged cloth over it gently, occasionally pressing down harder to allow the blood to soak in. She wiped a small tear from her eye, and tried to bear with the pain of everything that was going on around her.

Lauren sat beside her. Huddled closely together amongst an array of leaves and thin branches, the two of them waited silently, holding their breaths in, as slowly and gradually, the echoing sound of footsteps came closer, and closer. Sophie breathed in hard, preventing herself from even moving a muscle when their follower came into sight. Lauren held Sophie's hand tightly. This was the most scared she had ever been in her entire life, and it was showing severely.

The footsteps started off quietly, like a tiny mouse scrambling away. Gradually they grew louder and louder. Lauren bit hard and Sophie held her breath for as long as she possibly could. Suddenly, the bushes and plants several metres before them parted aside, and a horrific creature stepped out from the undergrowth. It was disturbing; its skin was grey and scarred. It was thin and pale. Its bones stuck out from its extremely thin skin. Its teeth stuck out like knives and its eyes bulged outwards, bloodshot and

214

staring ahead, cruelly and malevolently. It was a terrifying sight to see, as the two girls hid there, silent and unflinching, barely feet away from it.

Lauren recognised it in an instance. It was the one which had chased them from the clearly. It was the one which had killed her father. She blinked several times, trying to hide back the tears from the thought of it. As did Sophie, gently moving her hand from her wound cloth to wipe away her tears. The tension was strong. Neither of them had any idea how long they could hold on.

The creature looked around swiftly, its eyes scanning the trees and bushes in search for any sign of life. It sniffed the air, flaring its huge nostrils to try and pick up a scent. It kept on looking around, focusing its pupils on every tiny detail.

Lauren and Sophie lay there, quietly in the undergrowth, not making a sound. It was like they weren't even there. The thing turned its head and suddenly stared straight at them, glaring menacingly. Sophie jumped and flinched slightly in her position from the shock, but she did not move greatly, and tried her best to remain calm.

Lauren stared back at the creature through the maze of brown and green leaves. She was confused, and scared. Had it seen them? It was staring right at them, but had it actually noticed them?

It continued to stare at the bush, as if curious, as if it had noticed something. A sudden terrifying thought struck Lauren's mind. *It's going to come in here! It's going to find us!* She held her sister's hand tighter and held her breath, desperately trying to shake the horrific thought away.

The thing continued to stare at them. It stared straight into Sophie's eyes, yet it still didn't seem to notice them. *Maybe it's waiting for something* thought Sophie. It wasn't coming for them at all. It was merely just standing there, several feet away, staring like a dog into the haze of leaves and branches. They waited several long moments, hiding in wait in the shadows. Sophie's pulse was racing. She had already fought off two of these things, but this one was different. It was skinnier and smaller, yet it had a presence about it that was much more nerve-racking than the other two. They were all monstrous creatures. No-one knew what they were or where they had come from. It was terrifying. They had just descended from out of nowhere and terrorised the Barrow family all night, and even the next day. They weren't going to stop. Sophie and Lauren both knew that. They weren't going to stop until every last one of their family was dead.

The thing ahead suddenly stopped. It turned its head slowly, and began to slowly walk away into the woodlands once more, and out of sight. Sophie and Lauren both passed long sighs of relief and exhaustion. The thing was still nearby, and so they remained as quiet as possible.

Sophie's head remained where it was as still as a statue, as she whispered to her older sister.

"Lauren? Do you think it's gone?"

A bleeping sound erupted suddenly from Lauren's pocket. Her face flashed as pale as a ghost. It was her phone. The sound rang loudly out into the trees and air above. Lauren scrambled immediately, desperate to find her ringing phone. She had to shut it up now!

Sophie had also turned ashen. The thing, wherever it may be, would have clearly heard that. Lauren ripped her phone out from a pile of other objects in her pocket and turned it off as quickly as her fingers could. She held the phone tightly within her palm, hoping that it wouldn't go off again. She breathed in and out panicking. She stared around out into the open forest, flashing her eyes back and forwards to see where that thing was.

Many long metres away amongst the trees, the thin, grey skinned monster flashed its head around rapidly. It had heard something. Something back where it thought it had seen something before. Like a bolt of lightning, it sprinted viciously on all fours, back to the sound of the noise.

216

Lauren turned to face Sophie, whose eyes were welling with tears suddenly.

"It's okay Sophie," she mouthed silently towards her sister. "Just don't panic..." She froze immediately in terror. Her eyes fixed straight ahead in pure fear. The footsteps began to increase in volume once again. Suddenly, the savage creature burst from the undergrowth opposite them.

Lauren held her hand over her mouth to prevent herself from screaming. The thing before them growled fiercely. Its teeth looked like a wolf's, and it eyes were livid with hunger and rage. It crawled on all fours into an open space, before standing up onto two legs and snarling, looking around the area, to see where the noise had come from. The two girls lay silently in the undergrowth directly ahead of it, looking up at it in fear and terror. Neither of them made sound. Neither of them moved a muscle. They just lay there, against the trunk, hoping that it would go away.

Lauren's eyes squinted in determination. She lifted her right hand slowly and reached it down into her pocket and slowly, edging bit by bit, withdrew the penknife which Sophie had given her moment ago from her previous encounter. Without making a sound, she withdrew the bloody, sharp, silver knife, and waited.

Suddenly, Sophie slipped. Her leg could not stand the pressure of holding back any longer and slipped sideways out amongst the dirt outside of the undergrowth. She gasped in shock and quickly withdrew it, dirt flying upwards rapidly as she did so. Lauren flashed her eyes towards her worriedly and back. The creature snapped around, its head seeing the foot disappear into the bush again. Its eyes widened in hunger and rage. It had seen its prey.

Lauren held the knife sturdy in her hands, as all of a sudden, the monster lunged into the undergrowth where they were hiding. Sophie screamed as a dark blurred shape crashed into view. Leaves and branches smashed against them as the thing clawed its way towards them. The creature

217

growled and snarled fiercely as Lauren and Sophie edged
further and further away in desperation. Sophie frantically
tried to keep the bloody cloth against her cheek as Lauren
constantly kicked the thing in the face to hold it back many
times. It reached forward with its long grey skinny arms,
grasping and wrenching at feet and ankles like a drowning
man. Its mouth was wide open, snapping like a shark as it
crawled faster and faster into the enclosed area. Lauren tried
to hold herself back from stabbing it in the face. *Not now!
Wait for it!* She knew she had to wait for just the right
moment before she could strike back, wait until it was well
and truly trapped. They were both struggling desperately as
the thing moved closer and closer towards them. Its eyes
were livid and bloodshot, staring at them in what looked like
sheer hunger and fury.

Sophie kicked it in the face hard, but it simply ignored the
pain and roared its loud eerie scream and carried on
crawling rapidly in amongst the undergrowth. Lauren
couldn't take it anymore. She tried to hold herself back, but
she just couldn't. Lauren lifted the knife into the air and
struck it down hard into the creature's forehead. The knife
collided viciously with the grey skin and slashed deep down
into the thing's forehead. It suddenly stopped dead in its
tracks, and writhed in pain monstrously. It screamed in
agony as Lauren still held hold of the knife, blood emerging
from within. It struggled, desperately trying to break free,
yet it couldn't.

Lauren could feel the hate rising inside of her.

"You think you can come here and terrorise us?!" She
twisted the knife inside its head, blood seeping out and
causing the creature to scream vilely in pain. "You think you
can tear my family away from me?!" She twisted it again,
more blood emerging as the creature screamed louder. "You
think you can kill my dad and not expect me not to come
back and kill you?!" She drove the knife downwards as the

grey skinny thing writhed in sheer agony, blood now dripping down its face.

"You little freak! I'm gonna find my family, and I'm gonna kill all of you!" She was on the very verge of shouting; she gritted her teeth, ignored the thing's blood, and drove the blade harder down into the creature's head. It squealed one last time in pain, before Lauren pushed it over into the mud and dirt. It fell down and collapsed there silently, dead.

Lauren waited for a moment before withdrawing the knife and wiping it clean on her jacket. She looked up and around at the surrounding forest, which was silent, except for faint birdsong, and the leaves shaking in the wind.

Sophie stared at her, in amazement and shock. She held the dirty cloth still to her cheek as her eyes scanned the dead monster up and down. It lay there, grey skinned, pale, unflinching, lifeless. Lauren had killed it.

Lauren's eyes squinted in determination. She could feel the hate rising within her. Her pulse was racing, her heartbeat pounding like a caged animal. This was the second creature which she had killed this morning, and she had a dark, twisted feeling that it wasn't going to be the last. She looked up and around into the chilly air. Nothing had seen her; the forest surrounding the two girls was silent and sinister.

She then turned around to look at her pale sister, who was now dripping red with blood.

"Come on," she said gently, "let's get out of here now."

Chapter 28: Death Before Dishonour

Markus sat quietly on a small chair in the corner of a dark room in the outpost. The shutters on the windows were closed and boarded up. Little light managed to break through. Markus's face was facing downwards into the darkness, the tiny gaps of light lighting up the smallest of details on his stern face. His eyes were focused straight ahead in thought. In a few moments, he and Zack would leave the outpost for what might be the last time, to take revenge on the things which had caused them so much pain.

He remembered back many years before, to when it all began, when the fear first started, when the evil first came. He lifted up a dark black t-shirt from a pile of clothing on the floor beside him. He lifted it up and down over his head. His vision never strayed from the one place in the dark dusty corner. Three words in the form of tattoos were emblazoned upon the back of his shoulders, 'Death Before Dishonour'. His thoughts sank to a lower level, that phrase had died inside of him a long time ago, along with most of his sane mind. Over the past few years he had become a more monstrous and twisted person at every waking moment. Every time he had mercilessly sent a group of innocent bypassing civilians out into Dilas Forest to be slaughtered like cattle, he had become a lesser being. He was a monster by now, and Markus himself knew that. He knew that he had become one a long time ago, and was never going to change.

His mind flashed back to when it all started. As he put more and more of his clothing layers on, as the pile of clothes on the floor beside him decreased gradually one by one, his mind sank deeper and deeper into his disturbing past.

It was six years ago and Markus was walking home from work one night. He had previously come home from fighting in conflict issues abroad. After many years of training and fighting out in the hostile environments, he had now come home, home to his wife, his family, and his beloved world which he adored so much. Now, he worked as a security guard along the outpost borders of Dilas National Park. He had done his duty serving in the army, and now it was his time to devote the rest of his life to something greater, his passion for wildlife and the environment. Markus was a peaceful man back then. He had a good interest in the wonders of the natural world.

There had been a team back then, when he had first started, there were environmental scientists and tourist guides. Markus merely worked there as security, a protection for the border areas of the park. Every night, he would run a quick search through the woods and retire home to his glorious house and family in the city of Cambridge.

Occasionally, when Markus was doing his usual nightly checks, he would see something, something strange, like a larger figure pass through the trees briefly, something that wasn't part of the natural wildlife. He would stop and stare for a moment, wondering what it was, before assuming it was his tiredness or his eyes playing tricks on him that was the reason. He would pass on home ignoring the matter. The forest was spooky, especially at night. There was a mysterious air to it, like something was constantly watching you. Markus had learnt to ignore this, and merely carried on with his job. The forest was beautiful to his eyes, every last element to it. Yet now the beauty was long dead. It had died before his eyes a long, long time ago.

Markus was walking home from work on a fine summers evening, the sky was a beautiful orange as the setting sun glowed luminously. He walked up to his front drive, slipped the keys from his pocket, and opened the front door. The door handle was warm, very warm, as if someone had

221

recently entered. Markus thought to himself. *Susie must have just come back from the office late tonight.* He ignored the matter and stepped into his front hallway. His house was normal, as it usually was. Nothing had changed, everything was neatly in place as his wife Susie liked to keep it.

"Honey, I'm home!" he shouted out into the house, shutting the door firmly behind him, the lock clicking into place loudly. He walked forwards, hearing no reply at all. The house was silent and eerie. The only light came from the dim lamps on the hall table and the streetlamps outside. The house was quiet, too quiet.

Markus took several steps forward into his house.

"Come on guys, where are you all?" he called out loudly, trying to catch someone's attention. Yet still, no reply answered. He took another few steps forward and looked left into the kitchen. It was completely dark with no sound emerging from it. No one was there. He took another few steps forward and looked right into the dining room. Again, all was dark and quiet, no one was in there. Markus was becoming slightly worried now. Where could his family be? They should all be at home. No one had arranged anything about going out that evening.

He looked around, and suddenly heard a faint sound, a distant muffled sound came from straight ahead. He looked up and saw that the living room door was open, slightly ajar, a tiny gap in the door leading through into darkness.

"Honey?" he asked ahead toward the living room, but no one replied. "Honey? Kids? Are you in there?"

Still no one replied.

Markus was becoming even more anxious now. Something wasn't right here. Something was very, very wrong. He took a few more steps closer towards the living room. Every step his pulse grew faster and faster. He was feet away from it now and there was still no reply. The darkness of the room beyond seemed more intimidating now, more strange and eerie. He was now inches away from the door handle. He was extremely worried, something was in the room beyond, and he hoped deep down inside that it was his family. He stepped back, took a long deep breath inwards, and pushed the door open.

All was quiet inside. The darkness came towards him as he faced the dark room. The window curtains were still open, allowing some light to reach inwards. Markus scanned his eyes around the dark room.

"Hello? Is anyone there?" His voice echoed out into the silent, dark living room.

A sudden muffling sound echoed around the room once again. The same sound that he had heard out in the hallway moments before. He breathed in and out slowly, trying to calm himself down. *It's okay Markus, they're just going to surprise you that's all* he told himself inside his head. He looked over to the side of the wall and saw the light switch. Breathing in and out one last time for reassurance, Markus reached his arm across and flicked down the light switch.

The light was blinding at first, Markus couldn't see a thing. The blackness was suddenly drowned out by the sudden golden glow from above. Quickly, his eyes adjusted to the light, and as he looked on into the living room, his pulse shuddered and shook violently.

On the far side of the living room, cowering in fear and horror in the corner of the room, were his wife and two kids, beaten, gagged and tied up together. Markus' face was immediately twisted into shock and terror as he realised what was going on. He was about to rush over immediately and help them, before he suddenly realised that there was something else. Something else was standing there in the room with them. Above the terrified, traumatised faces of his family, was a figure, several feet away, staring at Markus. It was the most disturbing thing he had ever seen in his entire life. Its face was covered in scars and its eyes were staring and bloodshot. Its teeth stuck out like blades amongst its ripped up gums. Its skin was dirty, foul and repulsive. A stench hung over it, it smelt of corpses, blood, and disease. It looked straight into Markus' eyes, as he stared, terrified back. This thing had come for him, and him only.

When it spoke, its voice was old and rasping, straining its lungs to talk. It knew that Markus was a security guard for Dilas Forest. It knew that he worked there and watched over it daily. What the creature in his living room told Markus that night disturbed him in the most terrifying of ways, he almost lost his very sanity.

The monster was one of several, each one of them living amongst the darkness of the forest, emerging by night to feed on anything they could find, bark, animals, even the last stragglers who were lost amongst the woods and had not reached the entrance in time. This was the first time that they had risen up from the darkness to confront the outside world. It spoke of terrible things, things which man had forgotten long ago. It wanted Markus and his crew to guard them, to watch over them and lead helpless stragglers in to them... as food.

The thought rung out in Markus's head over and over again.

"And if you ever mention a word about us, the police, the outside world, anyone... we will come for you, and we'll tear you all apart!"

The thought still disturbed him to this day. The team started to go missing from then on, the scientists, the workers, everyone. Markus was the only one who knew about these disappearances, and yet he could do nothing. The creatures knew, they knew everything. Whenever a police member would come investigating into the forest to learn more about the disappearances, they would find out, they would track them down, and they would kill them just like the so many others whose lives had been taken.

Gradually, people began to find out. A young man named Zack who had been working for the forest for a long time encountered one of these things, and he too endured the same pain which Markus had gone through. More and more of the security team found out one by one, many cowered away and were consumed by the fury of these monsters which dwelled in the darkness. No one knew what they were, no one.

Eventually, a young man named Jason joined the team, he was inquisitive and quiet, yet once he found out his mind went completely insane just like the rest of them. After a while he couldn't take the pain of sending so many innocent people to their deaths. He too tried to flee, so Markus had spared him, from falling to a worse death from those beings.

Many joined, and as many fled to insanity and to their deaths. The creatures couldn't let anyone know about them. Whenever anyone fled to tell the authorities, they would track them down, one by one, and kill them without mercy.

Markus held on. His family were being cared for under supervision in a mental health ward, obviously being traumatised after the nightmarish event from before, yet still, they were alive. They were his family, and he wouldn't let anything happen to them. Those creatures wouldn't lay a single hand on them, ever again.

The door opened slowly into the dark room, as the shadowy figure of Zack stood silently in the doorway for a moment. After a second of silence, Markus put on his final piece of clothing, his dark black protection pad, and turned around to face his last comrade.

"Are you ready to go?" asked Zack patiently.

There was a moment's pause as Markus sat there quietly as the past few minutes of his distant dark memories flashed before his eyes. Markus turned to the young man, and said softly. "Yes. Let's go."

He stood up, his huge muscular body glinting in the few rays of light which escaped through to the dark mysterious room. Zack saw him stand up and left the doorway to go and prepare for the mission. He had not done this before, or anything like this, but this was his turn to exact revenge upon the monsters which had terrorised his family.

Markus walked over to the door and closed the large dusty wooden frame behind him. He sighed deeply as he closed the door tightly, knocking the knob into place. He then turned on his heels and proceeded into the next room. The outpost where they worked and waited was small, yet big enough to hide many large things. Markus walked into a separate room and over to a large crate, which read 'LAST' in large stencilled letters on the closed lid. Markus looked at the sign for a moment before squinting in determination, and opening the large box.

What lay inside was unbelievable. The interior of the secret crate was lined with rows upon rows of large matt black weapons. From the largest of snipers to the tiniest of pistols, this crate contained all of Markus' weaponry which he had slowly been collecting over the past years, counting down to the exact moment when he would exact his revenge on this very day. The wait was over, it was show time.

Markus reached his hands into the crate and removed a small pistol, a shotgun, a silver knife, and a large semi-automatic carbine. He had four weapons which he was taking, into the eternal darkness of Dilas Forest.

The doorway to the next room opened, and Zack stood there once again, waiting for his superior's command. Markus turned around to his old friend, the one who had survived the torment all these years, a carbine in his hand. He loaded the ammo into place.

"Come on Zack, We're getting out of here."

The two of them opened the door to the exit, and out into the chilling morning air. The light was bright, yet there was no glaring sun outside for warmth, no happiness amongst the woodland region which they stood. Zack walked over to the large black truck and flung a small crate full of weaponry into the back. Markus followed in suit, bringing his weaponry out and flinging the bulk of it into the open back of the truck. Zack then walked over to the side door and opened the door to the driver's seat.

"Hang on!" Markus said loudly as Zack was about to enter the car. "I'll drive. It's going to be a long, bumpy ride." He then turned his body and walked over to where Zack was standing. Zack in turn merely nodded in agreement and walked over to the other side of the car. He opened the passenger seat, and entered the large sturdy truck. Both doors closed in unison. Markus slotted the keys into place and turned the engine on and revved it. He stared ahead, squinting in fortitude. His expression was fierce and mysterious. He was not going to fail.

"Ermm... Markus, ermm... Are you ready?" asked Zack quietly from the seat opposite. He was quiet, not just because of fear, but also because he was naturally like that. He was even quieter than Jason when he had been around. He did his part, and saved his family.

Markus looked over at him suddenly, snapping back to reality.

"Sorry. Let's get going. They'll still be back at District Four at the moment if I'm right. The last of them should be clearing from the woods. Let's go." With that he placed his hands firmly around the steering wheel, and accelerated. The large old vehicle suddenly started forwards, and began to drive on, turning off away from the beaming rays of light, and into the shaded darkness of Dilas Forest.

Zack thought to himself grimly as Markus drove the truck on towards the entrance to the huge forest itself. After the many years which he had worked with the team at the Dilas entrance outpost they never spoke about District Four. It was forbidden amongst their conversations. No one ever mentioned it; no one ever dared to speak of it. It was a place where the foundation of this evil had all started. That was where it started. That was where it was going to end.

Zack gulped inwards in nervousness. Markus looked over to him briefly whilst driving.

"Are you scared?"

Zack looked back hurriedly for a moment, before quickly focusing upon the path again in front. "Oh, me? Well, ermm, no not really." He sighed shamefully. "Just a little."

Markus glanced over at him for a split second. "You shouldn't feel fear. When I was fighting in the war in Afghanistan, we would teach ourselves to fear no evil. We would rather die before being cowards." Zack kept looking at him back and forth whilst he was talking. "That thought died inside me a long time ago. Now it has suddenly resurfaced. We fight now for our families, for what we were fighting for all along. Remember that Zack. Remember that, and you will stay human. Fall away from that thought, and you will fall deep into insanity and mindless rage. We are higher than them, remember that, we are higher than what we are fighting ourselves."

Zack stared at Markus for several long seconds.

"Thank you Markus." He gulped nervously. "I am not afraid of them. Are you?"

Markus sighed thoughtfully as he steered and drove ever deeper into the wilderness of the blood wreaked forest.

"Zack my old friend, I will embrace death whenever my time may come."

Chapter 29: Broken, Torn, Alone, But Not Down

Sophie walked on and on through the blistering pain which she was suffering. The steep hill before her seemed to go on forever. She couldn't take it anymore, she had to rest. Sophie collapsed suddenly onto the vast muddy bank. Lauren approached swiftly behind her to aid her.

"Come on," she urged. "We need to carry on," she said gently, as to not alarm her younger sister.

"I can't go on," Sophie moaned constantly, struggling to lift even her arms.

"Come on," fired back Lauren. "I'll carry you up the hill. Then we can rest."

Sophie was struggling severely under the amount of pain she was going through. She closed her eyes, almost letting herself fall into Lauren's arms.

Lauren breathed in and out, assessing the situation. She flexed her fingers, and placed them underneath her sibling, using all her strength upon her and pulling Sophie up. She struggled for a moment as her body adjusted to the sudden burst of extra weight, before her muscles became used to the burden, and tensed.

"It hurts, so much," Sophie said. She could barely speak she was so weak.

"It's alright Sophie. Don't die on me now," Lauren replied back. She knew her sister would survive, yet still she worried and cared for her safety. "We're almost there. Just try and relax, the pain won't last forever," she said comfortingly.

Sophie closed her eyes for a moment. She wished she could relax so much and let all of her pain and sorrow flow away from her. Yet because of all the chaos she had been

229

through over the past twenty four hours, this was too much to bear. Her mind couldn't take it anymore.

Lauren hauled them up the hill slowly, her sister hanging in her arms. She was not strong, but this was a moment of dire emergency. She couldn't do anything else. The hill seemed to go on forever before her. As she struggled desperately up it, Lauren could feel her muscle strength weakening step by step. She gritted her teeth, trying to cope with it. Sophie was not particularly heavy; but this was just too much for Lauren to bear. It felt like she was heaving an ever growing bag of weights up the hill as her strength weakened second by second. Yet she was a survivor, and had to carry on.

Up and up the steep hill she climbed further and further, ascending into the morning light above. Her feet dug deeper into the damp soil and sweat dripped down from her forehead. Her hands were dirty and wet with sweat. She could see the top of the hill in sight. It was gradually getting closer and closer, just as her strength was growing weaker and weaker. She almost could not take her sister any longer. Closer and closer the top of the steep hill came into sight. There was no path to lead them up, nothing. It was all down to her legs, with Sophie lying weakly in her arms.

"Come on Sophie. We're almost there!" she clenched her teeth together, pushing the last remaining fragments of her power into carrying her sister up the hill.

There was a sudden burst of air, as Sophie fell from her older sister's arms and rolled across the ground. She was at the top of the hill. They had made it.

Lauren scrambled over the top using her arms to pull her up, as she dragged her weak body over the ledge and onto the damp earth where her sister lay panting like a dog. She clambered over the top of the damp ledge slowly and sat her back upright against a tree. She breathed in and out; her arm muscles were weak, as were her legs from the long hike up the hill carrying her sister. She was absolutely shattered, yet she knew that they had to keep on moving soon. They could not stay put for long. Those things would be hunting them. The more they stopped the more they were vulnerable. Lauren lifted her head up into the sky and caught air into her lungs rapidly.

Sophie, who was lying next to her leaning against the thick old tree trunk at the top of the hill, rolled over and opened her eyes. She fought back the last surviving remnants of the pain, and sat up next to her older sister. She sighed in and out sorrowfully.

"Last night. What happened to you?" she asked worriedly.

There was a pause, and a moment's hesitation, as Lauren tried to fight back what tears were starting to well, and remember the memories of last night's horror.

"I was with dad and Max. We spent ages wandering around, trying to find even the slightest thing to what could be a path. But we found nothing, absolutely nothing." She paused for a moment, breathing heavily in and out.

"It's okay," Sophie said gently back. "Carry on."

"Max decided to stray away from us. He thought the only way for us to be in with any chance of finding a path would be to split up. He ran away into the darkness. I know he's alive, but I haven't seen him since, and I just hope he's okay now..." The end of her sentence cut short, as she buried her head in her hands, tears starting up again. Sophie put her arm around her sister, comforting her. "Dad and I carried on. We kept on searching. It was cold and dark, we could barely see a thing, our torchlight was so weak." She paused for a second, breathing gently. "It must have been around nine o' clock... We heard noises, horrible noises, it was like something was eating, loudly and disgustingly... We crept quietly around to where the noise was coming from. And then suddenly, there was this thing, this... creature. It was out in a small clearing, eating on this old piece of meat. We had no idea what it was. It looked human, yet it couldn't be. No, it was too monstrous and horrific to be human..." She

231

shuddered at the thought, wiping the tears from her watering eyes. "It saw us! Dad and I, we ran for our lives as it was chasing us through the woods like a wolf..." She stopped suddenly, crying deeply.

"It's okay Lauren. I'm here," comforted Sophie gently. "What happened? Please tell me," she urged kindly in a gentle manner.

There was a moment of pure silence, as the background noise of the forest echoed around them eerily.

"Dad fell over," Lauren finally continued. "He stumbled and fell. I stopped to go back for him but he urged me to keep on going, he screamed at me to carry on... so I left. I ran through the woods and into the constant darkness. My torch fell from my hand in panic. I was left alone... in the dark... that was the last time I saw him." She buried her head in her hands and cried sorrowfully. She looked up after a moment of silence. "I kept on going, running constantly into the forest. I found someone... I thought it was one of them at first, but it wasn't... it was a survivor. He had been fleeing for a week from these things. I learnt so much more about them. He didn't know what they were, but they were hostile, and they wouldn't stop until they killed every last one of us." Sophie was repulsed at the sound of this. "He couldn't last any longer. He died in front of me. I didn't know what to do. I took his pistol which he had in his backpack. I ran throughout the rest of the night, avoiding everything I could until eventually I found you. It was so good to see you again." She leaned over and hugged Sophie tightly. "That thing that was chasing you, I killed it, shot it dead right in front of you. I was angry. I wanted to kill them all. Those were the last of the rounds in that gun. I had to drop it since it would only weigh us down." She looked at Sophie sorrowfully, wiping the last of her tears from her dirty face. She had to stand it now. She had to be brave and carry on.

Sophie sat beside her, looking at her defeated sister, tears beginning to come to her eyes now. She felt like she almost couldn't breathe. Her father was dead. She would never see him again. She wiped the tears from her cheek. She began to speak to Lauren.

"Last night, Eve, Sean, Sarah and I were waiting in the clearing for you to come back for us. We began to hear noises, and the constant feeling that something was watching us from a distance. Suddenly, when I felt I couldn't take it anymore, something burst from the undergrowth. It was horrible. This thing, it was huge and towered over us. We couldn't see well in the dark, but this thing was still monstrous. We could see its eyes glowing in the darkness. They were angry and enraged. I ran into the woods, fleeing for my life..." She too was now beginning to cry, as Lauren began to wipe away her tears and listen to her story. "...I couldn't see a thing I had no torch. I don't know what happened to the others but I haven't seen them since. Everybody ran, all I could hear was the constant screaming and the image of that thing chasing after me inside my head. I had to find a place to hide. I saw the tree nearest to me and climbed further and further. Eventually I found the top, and stayed there silently for a moment." She hesitated. "I thought I was safe up there, but no. There were more of those things. There was another. It jumped out of nowhere and knocked me down. I fell, smashing my face into every branch that passed by as I fell." She rubbed the right side of her face in pain, feeling every last cut and scratch. "I fell to the ground, badly hurting my back. The creature came down after me. I could see it coming closer and closer, I just couldn't do anything I was too weak. It bent over me." She began to shake as she recalled the memories. "It leant down over me. I could see the red glare in its eyes. It was horrible! I put what strength I had left and smashed my already weak legs into the thing's legs. The agony was too much. I jumped up and ran for my life. The thing chased me.

233

Through the trees I ran with that creature constantly on my tail. I leapt into the nearest bush and hid there for a long moment as the creature passed. When it was gone I stood up, I picked up a dead branch as a weapon. I wanted to pursue that thing, I wanted to kill it! But I didn't. I couldn't. I spent the rest of the night wandering, avoiding everything. I stuck to the shadows and stayed there. All night I was awake, searching for any of you." She paused for a moment, trying to relax but knowing she couldn't. "By the time morning came I could see so much better. I fell into one of their traps, I was lifted into the air. It cut through my skin!" she pointed aggressively towards her sore cheek wound. "Two of them rushed out from the undergrowth after me. I was in so much pain! I eventually managed to cut myself free and fought the two things off." She hesitated. "I don't know how I did it though. I'm no karate expert. I can't fight for my life. I guess it was just... anger, which drove me on." Lauren looked back at her in shock and horror as Sophie told her story courageously. "I just managed to take down one before the other came savagely after me. I was weak and my cheek hurt so much! I ran through the woods. I thought I was going to die... until I found you." Sophie looked back at her sister thankfully. "You killed that thing. You killed it Lauren."

Lauren put her hand on her sister's shoulder, and spoke gently. "I know Sophie. It's okay now. I've got you, and I'm never leaving you again. As long as we stick together, that's how we keep our faith, that's how we survive. If we have hope and trust in each other, we will get out of this in the end. We're going to keep on going, find the others, and get out of here right now!" she said, her teeth firmly together in forcefulness.

Sophie looked up at her sister, wiping her tears away. She trusted her sister completely. The fact that she had found her was unbelievable and life saving. She looked warmly into her sister's eyes, and followed her every word.

Lauren stood up, and held out her hand to Sophie, who looked up at her before taking it, lifting herself into the air. They hugged each other kindly. They had each other to support, and they would stay together, until this was all over.

Lauren looked firmly at her sister and said determinedly, "Let's go." She then turned away, and started heading on ahead. The trees started to clear in front of her, daylight was breaking through. She could see the other side. The forest was clearing, the end was near.

Sophie could see it too. Beyond the trees, through the many great trunks which rooted in the way of view, there was a thick ray of light, which passed between the gaps in the trees and undergrowth. She started to follow her sister, as she wandered further and further away from her. Eventually she broke into a short run and caught up.

"Hey Lauren, wait!" she called out quietly as she approached.

Lauren smiled as she saw her sister approaching as Sophie smiled back. The severe wound on her cheek was gradually healing, the blood had now stopped bleeding, with little more than a few stains left.

"Come on," called Lauren back. "We're almost there."

The light gradually became lighter and lighter as they walked on. Both of them were very weak and worn out, but the sight of fresh new light breaking in from behind the sea of trees was enough to drive them on.

"The sun, I can see it at last," appreciated Sophie longingly. "It's been so long since I saw sunlight, rather than covered by tree canopies."

"Yeah I know," responded Lauren. "Fresh air, freedom! This place drives you insane after a while. All that silence. With those things after you. People would go mad in there after a long time. We've got to get as far away from here as we possibly can... What the?!" she suddenly exclaimed loudly.

235

Sophie looked ahead fully and saw what had shocked her sister. Her jaw gaped open widely, as she saw what it was. They had exited the forest and were now standing on the top of a large bank facing down over the countryside. But something was there. Something in between them and their escape. Something that shouldn't be there, that couldn't be there. The two girls stood there for a moment, their mouths wide open in shock, as they realised what it was.

Chapter 30: The Terrifying Truth

His eyes snapped open sharply. The world seemed bright and blinding all around him at first. But gradually, his eyes adjusted to the settings as he saw where he really was. At first his vision was just a blur, but then it slowly faded back into focus, and eventually into reality once again. His mind was spinning with confusion. He felt like he was almost going to be sick. He leant over rapidly, moments after he awoke, and opened his mouth to vomit onto the floor. Nothing came out, he was not throwing up. He lifted his head back up again and groaned in a moment's agony. He then opened his eyes fully, trying to find out where he was. His eyes then suddenly widened rapidly as, for the first time, Sean Barrow realised where he was.

The room was dim and cold, the only light came from a small fading light bulb on the disgusting, dirty ceiling, which lit up the rest of the eerie, foul, slime infected room. It appeared to be what might be a cellar, its cold stone walls indicated. There was barely anything in the room as he looked around desperately in horror. He looked down, realising that he was tied tightly to a small old wooden chair in the centre of the room. He groaned in pain as he eagerly struggled to break free. But it was no use. The rope was tied too tightly around him and the chair. He had no escape.

The room was almost completely empty, making the dirt covered stone walls stick out in colour and depth even more. He looked around to his right and saw Sarah, enclosed in a small animal cage on one side of the room. As he awoke from unconsciousness more and more, his hearing gradually became more and more acute, and as it improved better, he could hear that his younger step sister was well awake, and crying helplessly at the back of the claustrophobic cage.

237

"Sarah? ... Sarah!" he called out, desperate to grab her attention.

Luckily, she heard his calls, and looked around quickly to see him tied there awake.

"Sean! Sean! What's going on?! Where's Mummy?!" she called out loudly, tears gushing from her sweet young eyes.

"Sarah?" he asked back, breathing in and out heavily, desperately trying to calm himself down. "What's going on? Where are we? How long have you been awake?"

These questions were being fired at Sarah hurriedly; she couldn't understand as they were too fast. Her mind was confused, upset, and scared.

"I don't know!" she replied helplessly. "Where are we Sean?! Where are we?! I want to go home!" she pleaded back at him.

"I don't know Sarah! I really don't know!" he said back angrily in confusion. He wriggled around harder, trying to break free, but it was still to no use. He breathed in and out stressed, thinking dramatically of what he could do.

He thought deeply. "Sarah? What happened last night?"

The young girl looked over at him in tears, she did not respond at first. Then finally, she replied back.

"There was a monster."

Silence followed, as Sean thought harder. Something had happened to make them get there. Something had taken them, captured them from the woods. It was the creatures. He didn't know what they were or how many of them there were, but now they had captured them. They were trapped.

Sean groaned in anger loudly and lurched forwards in his chair. The ropes dug deep into his chest, pulling back like a cold hand dragging him down. He spat wretchedly onto the floor. It was all happening. Yesterday, when he and Max had been talking they had felt this fear. They were nervous, uneasy, and felt the strange eeriness of the forest around them. Sean remembered back to the night before, when that thing had leapt out upon them from the darkness and sent

238

them fleeing blindly into the darkness. He had taken Sarah, he had hidden. They thought they were safe, but he was wrong. That was when he had found out that there was more than one of them. That was when he had realised that this was only the beginning. He took a long breath, and gritted his teeth at the thought of what he had gotten them into, and what was going to happen next.

He didn't know how many of family were still out there. What had happened to them? He was completely oblivious to everything that had happened since last night. He closed his eyes and muttered rapidly under his breath, hoping for some kind of saviour.

"Sean?" asked Sarah quietly from the cage. "Someone's coming."

Sean looked over in surprise. "What?"

Suddenly, the door burst open, dust flying everywhere in all directions, a loud banging sound erupting as the dirty old door slammed suddenly into the wall. Sean coughed and spluttered for a moment as the dust settled. Slowly, once it had all died down, he opened his eyes, to see the most disturbing thing he had ever seen.

Standing in the doorway, amongst the sea of dust and dirt, was a figure, mostly covered by shadow, yet the scariest, most disgusting details were lit up by what little light escaped through to the area. It was a male figure, he could tell from the physique. It was tall and muscular. Its clothes were torn, ripped and ragged, they clung to his body and through them the countless number of scars and gashes in its dark, greasy skin were visible. Its skin itself was covered in dried mud and dirt which looked like it had been gathering all over it for a long, long time. Its ears were crooked and bent as they stuck out at odd angles, one of them, a huge chink missing from the lower half. Its nose was broken and almost completely crushed inwards; with two large nostrils sunken into its face like gashes. It eyes were cold, bloodthirsty, and staring into Sean's own. It stood there for a long eerie moment of complete silence, as it gawked down at the tied up teenager in the chair.

Sean stared up at the horrific monster for several long moments. His mouth was open, as if about to scream, yet he couldn't. He was petrified to the bone with fear. The thing stared back, a look of hunger burning in its eyes. The silence lasted on and on, until finally, Sarah screamed.

She let out a sudden cry of terror and crawled into the corner of the small cage.

"Sean?! Sean?!" she wailed in fear.

Sean didn't reply, he was too scared to even blink. The creature looked over at Sarah as she screamed and snarled menacingly in her direction suddenly, a dollop of drool slithered down from its mouth and collected on the dirt covered floor in a small puddle. Its head then snapped around to Sean suddenly once again, its eyes glaring cruelly. It ground its teeth fiercely, and began to step into the room on its two feet, gradually walking closer and closer into the dimly lit cellar. It walked three large steps into the space, and stopped. This one was new. It was one which none of the Barrow family had encountered so far in their night and morning of terror.

It stood there for a moment, as Sean began to gargle. He was trying to speak yet no words escaped his parched petrified lips. The tall terrifying monster stood over him, its shadow covering Sean completely. Slowly, it leaned down into the light, inches from Sean's face, and said coldly and sourly,

"Hello Sean." Its voice was hoarse and wheezing. Its nostrils were flaring horrifically as it spoke.

Sean reeled back in terror suddenly. The silence was broken and he was petrified no longer. He almost fell straight off the back of his chair in fright. How did this thing, whatever it was, know his name?

"H...h...how do y...you...kn...kn...know my...n...n...name?" he asked back, shaking with anxiety.

240

The creature smiled a cruel evil smile, revealing a jaw full of sharp broken teeth which stuck out at different angles from its gums.

"I know everyone's name. You, and all the rest of your pathetic little family."

Sean could not find words to talk back. He was terrified beyond belief. What was this thing and what had it done with his family?

"My f...f...family?" he asked back queasily.

"Oh yes," it replied fiercely. "Your sister was the first to wake up here, but I thought I'd wait until you were awake too. We wouldn't want her to miss anything, would we?" its voice was cold and merciless. This thing had no heart, or if it did, it died a long time ago.

"Where are the r...r...rest of my f...f...family?" he stuttered worriedly.

"Oh I haven't seen them yet, but I'm sure they'll show up sooner or later... and when they come... we'll be waiting for them." It grinned cruelly, walking away from Sean only to turn around and face him once more.

Sean merely looked back at him in fear. There was nothing he could do.

"Don't you go near them! Don't you lay a single hand on them!" He tried to lunge out and punch the thing before him but his chair held him down and prevented him from attacking.

The creature snarled cruelly, growling once more at its prey fiercely, at Sean this time. It slowly walked towards the boy again, until it was inches from his face.

"Last night, you and your family got yourselves lost in these woods. We hunted you down but still you managed to slip away." It was growling as it spoke, its tone cold and vile. "We killed your step mum, and your father, and soon you'll be next Sean. You'll be next!"

It growled once more, opening its bloodstained maw wide. Sean sat there horrified at what he had just heard. His dad was dead! As was his step mum. He felt like he was almost going to be sick. He leant forward and choked, facing downwards, as the creature walked away slowly. Sarah was crying. Her pale face was as white as a ghost. Tears streamed down her little cheeks. The creature heard this, and slowly turned its deformed head to face her. It flared its nostrils fiercely, and started to walk closer and closer towards the small cage on the floor where Sarah was enclosed.

It knelt down to look in through the bars towards her. Sarah stopped crying as she immediately realised that the thing was staring down at her. Her eyes widened in terror as she froze, petrified. The creature licked its lips savagely. Its eyes widened too, only this time, in hunger.

"I haven't eaten in so long," it said slowly and cruelly. Its voice was quiet, yet almost chanting and taunting. "And I think you'll do nicely first."

"Don't you touch her!" spat Sean angrily from the centre of the room, sweat flowing from his forehead rapidly. "You lay one finger on her and I'll tear you apart, you freak!" He lunged forwards in his chair again, straining at the ropes, desperately trying to break free.

The tall creature turned its focus away from Sarah, and slowly turned its head and attention towards Sean, who sat there, pulsating with rage and fear. It stood up, and began to walk, once again, towards the helpless teenager.

"You're gonna do that are you Sean? Are you?" it asked sarcastically and cruelly. "Are you gonna come after me and tear me apart with your bare hands?"

Sean spat on the floor at his feet. "I'll take my chances."

The monster smirked menacingly. "You don't know what I've heard. I've heard a hundred voices screaming those very words at me and I still carried on. I've heard so much of it. I'm sick and tired of this world. I'm sick and tired of everything, even from the start. You think we are freaks? You don't even know the half of it!" it hissed monstrously.

"We all had lives once. We weren't all monsters living in the darkness. We had lives, we were normal..." it hesitated for a long eerie moment. "...back then... We were human."

Sean was repulsed at the very sound of what he had just heard. They were human! These creatures, these horrific monsters which had terrorised them in so many disturbing ways; these things, which had killed his father and step mum, were human! He couldn't believe what he was hearing. He couldn't understand. What was going on? He felt like he was about to throw up.

"No... You're not human. You're monsters, animals!"

"I was not one of them back then," it continued. "I lived far away, from any of this. Far from the woods and the countryside. I lived in civilisation, with a family, and friends, and a life to live!" He paused again for a moment, eyes bulging out of their sockets.

"They lived here once, many years ago, in this village, on the far side of Dilas Forest. They were a family, a hermit family. They lived on the outskirts of the village, staying away, and never communicating with the rest of the village inhabitants. No one really knew much about them at all. They were isolated, quiet, and as silent as the grave. A small house at the top of the hill was where they lived, all alone, by themselves." He pointed out to a boarded up window behind Sean, where narrow streaks of light just managed to break through.

Sean could not see where he was pointing too, but he presumed that somewhere out amongst the wilderness in that direction, there was the house which he had just mentioned.

"People used to say all kinds of rumours about them. Some said they were murderers, thieves, some even said that they were cannibals. No one understood them, so no one really knew what was truth and what wasn't. One night, a little girl from the village went missing. After days of searching her body was found several nights later in a ditch at the far end of the village. No one knew who had done it, so they blamed the only ones which they believed could be responsible: the family from the house on the hill.

"That night, a mob gathered in the centre of the village, they brandished their weapons and they lit their burning torches. They gathered en masse and charged towards the house on the hill. The villagers burnt the house to the ground that night. Most of the family managed to escape, except for one, a young boy, who was horrifically burnt alive whilst trying to escape the burning house.

"The family fled, terrified into the darkness of Dilas Forest, blindly following each other deep into the heart of the woods where no one could find them.

"They were gone for weeks, surviving in the forest, feeding off whatever food they could find. They had nowhere else to go, so they lived in the forest, thriving there, like animals for months upon months. Over that period of time they lost their sanity slowly and steadily. Whatever was human inside them died long ago in the darkness of Dilas Forest. Their minds were warped, their appearance changed. These people were no longer human; they were now bloodthirsty, crazed monsters. And they were going to take revenge upon the village which made them that way.

"Many months passed and the village on the far side of Dilas Forest remained peaceful and ordinary, life went on as usual for all the villagers. Until one day, on one cold winter evening, the darkness lurched out for them. The crazed and monstrous forms of the once human family came charging out of the forest and into the town below. They slaughtered... everyone. They devoured the village. Tore everyone apart, not a single person survived. No one escaped to tell the tale of those things. The creatures came biting back, and consumed every last villager. They burnt the town to the ground as the villagers had once burned their home. The village was theirs now. They were the only ones alive. They would dwell there, once again, in their new, blood soaked isolated world."

Sean sat there, gradually becoming more and more disturbed by this horrific story. The monsters, all of those things which had terrorised and chased them through the woods last night, the ones which had killed his father and step mother, were humans. They were the family which had been chased into the forest that night and transformed into vicious bloodthirsty monsters over time. His pulse was racing in nervousness. These things would never stop. They were driven by revenge and hate only. They would hunt down and kill every human who knew who they were until they were all gone, and no one else knew about them once more. He thought worriedly of his family, and what had happened to those which had survived. He closed his eyes, praying dearly for their safety.

"It was many years ago, when I was on my way home from holiday with my family, when my story began," rasped on the horrifically deformed man. "November 1987. My name was Benjamin Tiers back then. I was normal, I looked like everyone else that was human." He lifted his long nailed hand and brushed it against one side of his brutally scarred face. "I had just returned home from visiting my parents in Manchester with my wife and young son. He looked just like you, his name was Thomas. He was my world, they both were.

"Outside was raining and wet and cold. The roads had become slippery. And as I drove around one corner, the car skidded slightly and smashed into another car. The two cars crashed into each other. My family were killed in an instant.

"I just managed to survive, yet my face was scarred and battered from the crash. The driver of the other car had survived too. He was a student, young and selfish. He had been drinking recently, and combined with the weather upon the road, he was one of the causes of the crash.

245

"He leapt out of the car rapidly, but he could not walk in a straight line because he was too drunk. I hated him so much. He was the reason why my life was now over. We were both alone, in the middle of the countryside, with no one around for miles upon miles. There was nowhere to run, nowhere to hide, and no one to save him.

"I couldn't take it anymore. My family, my world, was dead. I felt the hate rising inside of me. I couldn't hold myself back any longer. I lunged for him, blinded by rage; I grabbed his throat and killed him in an instant.

"I couldn't believe what I had just done. I had killed a person. After a few moments of panicking and fear, I placed his lifeless body back into the car, and made it look like he too had been killed in the accident. The rain was hard and heavy upon my bloodstained skin. I was covered in injuries. Dismissing what I had just done, I fled to the nearest hospital, the feeling of raging anger never leaving my mind." He kept staring deep into Sean's eyes, unnerving him, disturbing him. Sean stared helplessly back; the man's eyes were haunting and hypnotic in the darkest of ways.

"A year later, four of my friends decided to take me on a hiking trip, to take me away from my past troubled experience," he continued. "You have never lost family like I did. I was still in the most horrific pain I had ever experienced."

"You killed two of my family last night and are still trying to kill the others, you monster!" Sean bellowed in the man's face. He spat into his eyes and tried to lunge forward in his chair to attack him. But it was no use. The ropes held him down tightly to the chair, he could never break free. The monster wiped the spit from its face slowly in anger. It raised its clawed hand high into the air and slashed it down across Sean's face. Sean cried out in pain as the sharp nails scraped the edge of his skin. A few of the cuts began to bleed slowly. He looked up at the thing once more, tears beginning to well in his eyes.

246

Slowly, the creature bent down, and continued his savage story.

"We travelled for hours amongst the trees and never-ending undergrowth of Dilas Forest, the thought of my dead family never leaving my mind. We didn't know about the dead village on the very far side of the forest. It was an isolated housing community that no one knew much about and no one ever would.

"We carried on. The sun was getting to me, it was irritating and frustrating. My mind was weak and blinded by sorrow and anger. And as the day passed on, we never stopped going, I began to think darker and darker thoughts, and cultivated the hate within me.

"It was October sixteenth 1988. That was the day I went insane. I hated the world. My family were dead. My friends had dragged me into isolation to drive me mad. I killed them, all four of them. That was the last straw. I had ruined my life in every aspect and sense. I slaughtered them like cattle, and fled into the wilderness."

"You really are a monster. You killed your friends because your family had been accidentally killed a year before. What's wrong with you?!" fired Sean aggressively. The psycho raised his hand once more in threat, then lowered it as Sean cowered his face in fear.

"I lived in the darkness of Dilas Forest for years, living off whatever I could find. I could not return to civilisation. I would be hunted myself for what I had done, and what I had become."

"And that's why you're like this. A freak, a monster, a psychopath. You hunt innocent people just passing by and slaughter them like animals. I'm gonna kill you!" Sean threw viciously at the man.

He sneered in the young teenager's face and spat at him violently. "Not before I kill you first... I didn't know about the creatures which lived on the other side of the forest yet.

247

I was still new to this scavenging life. I was young. My mind had only just warped. I was still alone.

"I began to hear noises in the trees, something supernatural, something out of the ordinary. The noises began to grow in number and volume over the days as they flew by. There was something there, something was watching me, something was hunting me.

"After two weeks of being lost in the wilderness I was attacked by a creature. It was so monstrous and menacing, I could give it no name. Without warning, the beast attacked me and I had to fight it to survive, then I finally killed it. Another day passed as I wondered what that thing was, before another attacked me. Instead of killing it this time, I let it flee off to find its leader, trying to learn more about what these monsters were. I thought they were aliens at first, demons, ghouls, all sorts, but no. It was only when I faced their leader that I found out the real horrifying truth about them.

"I found their leader in the centre of their little 'nest' and fought him until I killed him. Then they looked up to me. I was their leader now, their ally. I was respected and feared by the rest of their disturbing society which knew about my arrival. Fortunately, all those who did know about us, we were able to track them down and slaughter them before they told anyone else."

Sean was still staring at him in absolute horror from what he was hearing. He could not believe his ears. Half of him was blinded by hate; the other was blinded by pain, sorrow and fear.

"I was no longer Benjamin, I was no longer human. I lost that long ago...My name is Bek now." He looked deep into Sean's eyes, who saw his dark and disturbed soul. This thing was human, but not anymore. It was now a monstrous abomination of nature. It had devolved in life, and was now nothing but a psychopath and a freak consumed by nature's madness.

"A few years later, a group of environmental workers set up a nature reserve here. This was good. It would bring, tourists, travellers... food. When the security guards patrolled the borders we warned them of us, and of the consequences if they stopped bringing us fresh victims to feed upon. All of them were under our command, and it was all because of me." Its eyes flared like fire, it was crazed and berserk beyond imagining. Sean was becoming more and more haunted by the minute, strapped down and forcibly fed this news from this monster. "Whenever travellers would pass by, we would wait for them; a siren system was set up to stop people from becoming too suspicious. Only those foolish enough to fall behind after the siren was set off would become our prey, as you and your pathetic family have become."

Sean stared up at him savagely; his eyes were now flaring with rage as he held back from struggling and attacking the creature.

"You twisted freak! You're all human and yet you kill humans for food. You monster! If you lay a single hand on my family, I'm gonna come after you and I'm gonna kill you all. Every last one of you!" he bellowed out of his mouth frantically. He wouldn't let that thing kill his family. They were his world, his adoration. A sudden thought struck his mind. How many of those things were there?

He knew that the group consisted of Bek and the other mutated family but he did not know how many of them there were. How many could he or any of his family take on? These creatures were brutal killers, they had trained themselves in combat for years, and Sean was inexperienced and hopeless in fighting.

Bek stared down at him cruelly.

"Oh believe me Sean. We're gonna be the ones tearing you apart." He whispered disturbingly into his ear. "Out here, the darkness never ends. There's constantly a deafening scream ringing in your ears. And it's not long before you realise that the forest has turned against you. It was always against you, and it always will be."

Sean sniffed, holding the tears and the urge to shout out. He could do this, he told himself over and over again inside his head. He could do this. Him and Sarah would get out of there alive.

Bek slowly turned his back away from the angry teenager and the crying girl. He didn't care. He had lost his sanity a long time ago. He walked away from the two children, looking around at them one last time; he squinted murderously, and slammed the door shut behind him. The room was dark and grim. The lights above flashed momentarily, before eventually switching off, leaving the two of them in complete darkness. The world became cold around them, everything was plunged into blackness.

Chapter 31: District Four

Max staggered on through the sea of tall green trees and fields of undergrowth scattered everywhere. He wheezed like a panting dog on a hot summer's day. But there was no summer here. The morning air was cold and chilling, as gusts of wind screamed through the trees like wraiths haunting his presence. He looked up and around, expecting to see one of the creatures leap suddenly from a nearby tree, but no, the woods were silent, sinister, and mysterious. He gripped the bloodstained branch weapon firmly in his hand, which was covered in dirt, grime, blood and sweat from the last thirteen hours. He gritted his teeth in fear and rage. They were emotions which were constantly flowing through him, as the search for his family continued without rest. He knew his two sisters were alive; he had heard their voices and wished them the best of luck and prayed for their safety as he thought of them. His mind now drifted towards Sean and Sarah, as he hoped they were alright, he prayed for their safety too, begging for them to be still alive amongst the chaos and bloodshed.

He could see daylight ahead. The trees were parting as the sunlight shone through, gradually getting clearer and clearer as he moved forwards. After a few moments of realising what it was, Max began to break into a run, moving faster and faster towards what appeared to be the end of the forest. He was almost there.

Suddenly, the last few trees flashed past him, as a cool breeze greeted his hot face and new sunlight bathed across his tattered body. He breathed in and out gently, catching the new waves of wind and the refreshment of clean air. His eyes remained shut. Trying to relax his body for however long he could for just a few short moments of peace.

The moment passed quickly, his freedom was over. He opened his eyes widely, bringing himself back to reality. His eyes darted across the new landscape, confused for a moment as he wondered what it was. His mind suddenly broadened in thought as he slowly realised where he now was. His eyes darted back and forth across the surrounding area. The forest had ended, and as the trees parted to make way to the surrounding countryside, Max was standing there, looking out over what appeared to be the deserted ruins of a small village.

Max looked around, shocked, confused. He could not believe his eyes. Many houses stretched out in front of him, not big enough to be a town, yet there must have been at least forty houses in sight. It was a small village, but every house was crumbling, in ruins. The rooftops were blackened with ash and dirt. Some had caved inwards, with huge holes in all of them; some had even completely collapsed inwards. They were crumbling and decaying. The whole village had been burned and charred. There must have been a fire of some sort. He had had no idea that there even was any form of civilisation right on the other side of Dilas Forest. His jaw gaped open in surprise, this was really weird.

He slid down the bank of the steep hill which separated the tree line from the houses. The grass and earth were dead. And as he stepped down the hillside slowly, dead soil and dust crumbled and scattered beneath his dirty worn out feet, and parted in front of him. He still held the battered branch firmly within his grasp. Something was wrong here, very wrong.

His eyes were squinted in suspicion. He was very much awake, very afraid, very angry, and very conscious of everything around him. He could hear the slightest whistles in the chilling morning wind, and the faintest bird song in the distance. There was no life around here, nothing. Not a single bird in the sky, not a single noise but the quietly screaming wind. Tiny bits of dead plants rolled across what appeared to be a small road which lead into the village. Not a single human being was in sight, no sign of life, nothing. The village seemed to be completely deserted. But from what Max had learnt from over the course of the night and the morning, in Dilas Forest, nothing was what it seemed.

He slid down to the very bottom of the hillside. Looking around at the outskirts where the first of the ruined houses lay, he breathed deeply in and out again, grasping his weapon firmly within his hands, he began to walk towards the start of the road ahead, into the midst of the mass of deserted houses.

He walked on, eventually joining the road whilst constantly looking all around and over his shoulder. His pulse was racing, terrified. His nerves were getting to him, affecting him greatly. He was constantly alert as he walked. The road led on and on, past more and more ruined houses. Dust and dead plants rolled out in front of him as the cold shrieking wind howled all around him. He looked around at the houses for many long moments whilst walking before finally realising something; the age of the houses.

They all looked very old, yet their style was quite recent. The decoration of the outside was dated back to the 1980s. This was very strange, as Max realised more and more about what was happening as he travelled on. This was an old village, which had suffered and been abandoned due to a fire sometime in the 1980s. He looked around at a door, which lay slightly ajar to his left. Looking suspiciously out towards the silent door, Max decided that he should try and discover more about what had happened. He may even find his family here somewhere. He made a decision in the blink of an eye, he was going inside.

Max turned his head, looking all around him, scared, he began to walk over to the door of the nearby house. Holding his slashed at branch within his palm, raising it at the ready, Max reached the door, and pushed it open slightly with his fist.

He half expected something to jump out at him, but no. Nothing happened. The whole house before him seemed as quiet and ghostly as the rest of the abandoned neighbourhood. Max looked deep inside into the dark eerie house. Breathing rapidly with fear, he pushed the door open further, and walked slowly into the first room.

As he entered, the door slammed shut behind him immediately, the strong wind blasting it closed. Max flashed around, ready for anything. But nothing was there, nothing was ever there. He turned around once more looking on into the dark ruined house before him. All was silent, all was sinister.

The windows were all smashed, as if some kind of a fight had broken out in the house, and resulted in chaos. The kitchen before him was smashed apart. A table lay broken into pieces in the centre of the room. The furniture, the sink, the dish washer, everything, was blackened with ash and dust covered, as well as being battered and dented by some kind of brutal force. But what was worst was the smell. The whole room reeked of rotting flesh, and the stench of blood haunted the area. Max looked over to see blood stains splattered all over the remains of the shattered glass in the window frames. He looked down at his tattered and injured body. It wasn't just him that stank of blood in this house.

This was disgusting. Max kept on looking around in all different angles, extremely nervous. This wasn't right, none of it was right. He looked around once more into the burnt, bloodstained kitchen, before deciding to pass through, and continue through to explore the house further.

He walked over to the door on the far side of the first room, which lead through to another room, the living room. This too was mysteriously burnt and charred throughout, the reeking stench of blood constantly hanging round in the air. Max walked through the living room, past the destroyed remains of sofas and armchairs, until he found another door

254

which lead back out into the hallway. He looked around, whipping around occasionally at the slightest of movement. Most of these only turned out to be the scurrying of rats behind him. Tiny animals which fled from him in the darkness, yet there was absolutely no sign whatsoever of other life. Due to the foul stink of flesh and blood, he had a dark and horrific feeling that it was more than just the fire which had destroyed the town. The creatures from the forest had been here too, and the result, had most likely ended disturbingly. Max felt a shiver of fear flow down the back of his spine. If a whole town had fallen to these creatures then how could he even last to make it out alive in the end? He held his weapon firmly, gripping and squeezing it tightly, ready for the slightest movement of an ambush. He knew he was in the middle of a trap.

He looked ahead to see a closed door beneath the stairs, which presumably led down to the cellar of the house. He breathed in and out nervously, shaking with fear yet eager to discover more. He stepped forward and opened the door.

The cellar was dark below. The light from outside lit up the first few stairs, before after the fifth step, the rest descended into the darkness. Max gulped. Looking over, he saw a light switch on the wall. Flicking the trigger down, he turned on the bright lights into the cellar, and saw beyond.

The light was flashing, dim, on and off, but it still showed the way down. Max took a foot down onto the first step. Hearing it creak he immediately removed it. The walls leading down were blackened with ash as well as the stairs. Max knew that the house was slowly falling apart. He knew he had to be careful.

He replaced his foot back onto the first step gently. It creaked again loudly, but Max did not press down hard. He slowly placed the other one down on the step after that, gradually moving down the dimly lit wooden staircase into the cellar. He could feel the hairs rising on the back of his neck, his pulse racing inside of him. After a few moments of slowly descending with fear, the lights clicked fully on, revealing the whole of the large cold room at the bottom of the stairs.

The room beneath the house was large and spacious. Its walls were covered with ash and dirt along with the rest of the house which was slowly falling apart. Several different objects lay scattered around the room. In one corner was a table, covered with all kinds of sadistic weapons, including axes, sickles, and long blades. All of them were covered in dust and staining, from presumably being forgotten for many years down in the dark. In another corner was a rack of clothes, all hung up eerily like figures themselves. Moths and other insects had eaten away at the edges, leaving holes of all sizes on every item of hanging clothing. In the middle of the room, directly opposite the staircase, was a fridge. Its edges were burnt and charred but certain areas seemed white and unaffected. This was peculiar. Max thought suspiciously for a moment. Finally, he came to a decision, and moved forward to open the fridge door, listening silently for a moment; he paused, before gripping the blackened handle and throwing the door open.

Max stared inside to see what the contents were, blinded for a moment by the sudden green light and the disgusting stench of strong rotting flesh reaching his nose. He stumbled back in shock suddenly, and dropped his jaw in horror at the sight.

Inside the open fridge, amidst the swarm of flies and flashing green light, were piles and piles, of human meat. Max almost felt like he was going to be sick. He reeled back in disgust and revolt, before coughing loudly, spraying the floor with saliva. Pieces of arms and legs lay stacked up in place on the five shelves within the fridge. Blood was stained all over the interior sides of the walls. A jar of eye balls stared horrifically back at him. A skull cleaved of flesh sat on the middle shelf, its jaw broken apart.

Max fell back onto the floor and threw up in front of the fridge. Even when he wasn't looking at it the thought of the fridge full of human limbs remained fixed in his mind, an image that wouldn't go away. He vomited intensely and lay on his hands and knees spluttering for a moment. He coughed violently for a few seconds, before jumping up and slamming the door of the fridge shut in horror. The creatures ate humans: there was no denying it now. The body in the hole last night, the fridge full of human limbs. He was next on the menu, and he knew that he and his family were in grave danger unless they got out of there, fast.

The lights flashed on and off once again, constantly hovering between activation and shut-down for a few seconds. Behind the traumatised young man, as the lights flashed on and off, something was standing there watching him. It stared hauntingly at him for a moment, before vanishing completely.

Max turned around to face the table of savage weapons. He dropped the stick down onto the floor and replaced it by picking up a large blade. He then turned immediately on his heels and fled up the stairs. They cracked and shattered behind him as he ran in terror. He was putting so much pressure on them he didn't care anymore. The only thing that he cared about right now was getting out of the cellar. He sprinted up the last few steps and slammed the door to the cellar shut behind him.

He stood there silently for a moment, resting his back against the burnt wooden door, holding it shut at the same time. A terrifying feeling had engulfed him whilst he had been down there. Something was watching him. The desire to sprint as fast as he could up the last few stairs was urged by the fact that he could sense something else down there. One of those things, watching him, waiting for him. Max knew it all along. He was walking deeper and deeper into their trap. But he knew he had to go on. His family were in this town somewhere, he could sense that too. Gripping the blade within his palm, he moved away from the closed door and continued.

He approached the back door of the house and passed cautiously out into the open once more. The town was cold, isolated, and eerie. The wind shrieked around him, and shutters on windows high above in the small streets creaked open and shut again menacingly. This was the one of the scariest moments Max had ever felt in his entire life. The whole town was watching him. The whole town was closing in on him.

Max walked down the street, before shortly walking over and into another house. The door was wide open, its front window smashed. Whatever had happened to destroy this small village, it had happened a very long time ago.

He cautiously looked around at the house, as it opened up before him. Just like the other house which he had been in before, it was large, crumbling, and deadly quiet. Max was breathing nervously. The blade felt cold within his hands, as he held the handle tightly. He began to walk forward, into the shadows of the house. The decaying wood snapped and creaked around him as he walked. He tried to remain as silent as the grave for his own sake.

Max walked slowly down the hall. Along the walls axes and other savage weapons hung on hooks, like decoration plates in a house, only this time, it was a murderous collection. There was something inside the house; he could sense it in his bones.

He could see a door up ahead. It was open and light was cascading out from the cracks. A light was on inside, someone, or something was in that room. He carried on walking down the long sinister corridor. The windows up ahead were either shattered into pieces or boarded up with large planks of wood, blotting out the sunlight from outside. He could still see the light from the other end of the corridor. It was calling him forward. Max raised the blade into the air in a defensive position. If anything jumped out at him, he would be ready for it.

As he approached the door, his pulse raced faster and faster. He could feel the hairs on the back of his neck constantly upright, never going down. He began to hear breathing, loud breathing. It was only faint at first, Max did not know whether it was human or not, it could be one of his family, or one of those things. But then he began to hear it clearer, and as he approached the door, the breathing became rasping and violent; he could hear the voice wheezing and choking as it inhaled and exhaled. It sounded just like the one he had fought out in the forest. He gripped the blade handle tighter, gritting his teeth to bear with the sudden surge of anger within him.

He was now inches away from the door. The breathing was loud and monstrous. Max was going to kill it; he was going to rid the world of one more of those freaks. Slowly and gently, Max pushed the door open inch by inch, as quiet as a mouse. He held the blade ready, about to strike.

As the door was gently pushed further and further, the room came more and more into sight. The lights were on, hanging from a small chandelier on the ceiling, they swayed back and forth in the wind. The door did not creak or make any noise, as Max was deathly silent. The room was fairly small, old, and burnt like the rest of the village. In front of the empty fire was a large antique armchair, with pieces ripped off leaving the fluffy interior sticking out at all different odd angles. Max looked into the room from the now open door frame. Over the top of the armchair, he could see the very top of a bald, scarred and filthy head. There was something in the room, and it was one of those things.

Max could feel a surge of anger and power rising inside of him. The urge to kill was building up again. He raised the blade high into the air, ready to bring it down hard upon the creature's ugly head. It just sat there silently, not doing anything except breathing its horrible disturbing growl. Max was about to strike down, any moment now.

Suddenly, a thought popped into the back of his mind. When he killed the thing, it would scream. And when it screamed, it would call for help. He needed to find his siblings now before a whole horde of the monsters were fast on his tail. Max was fighting the urge to kill. He could feel the anger writhing like an animal inside him. He couldn't kill it. He had to save instead. Revenge would come on swift wings. He fought off the rage and lowered the blade. His lust for vengeance was over; the only thing he could focus on now was finding the others. Max turned around silently and crept out of the door. As he walked down the corridor heading for the outside world, he could feel something coming off his chest. He had avoided falling into temptation, and it felt uplifting. But it was not over yet. He was trapped in an isolated village full of monstrous creatures. There was no escape yet.

Max walked hurriedly but silently out into the open. He held his blade close to him, in case anything jumped out at the most unpredictable of moments. He looked around, staring into the wilderness trying to find anything which could lead to some form of hope. He walked to the edge of the street, the road crumbling and torn apart, and saw something. Ninety degrees to his left, several hundred yards away, was a fountain. *That must be the centre of town.* He thought to himself. He knew the road had to lead somewhere. Immediately he started hurrying towards it, walking swiftly closer and closer. A dark shadow flashed behind him suddenly, but Max didn't notice. He had no idea that they were actually watching his every action, stalking his every move.

Max walked past an old red car, its bonnet smashed in at the front and all its windows shattered. The whole vehicle had been utterly destroyed. Max knew that when the creatures had first come they must have driven the small

260

village into absolute terror. He was surprised that no one had ever spoken of it. He only lived roughly a two hour drive away from Dilas Country Park and he had no idea whatsoever that there was an entirely hidden village beyond the forest itself. He had not seen it in the news or anywhere. It was like the world had completely forgotten all about the small place. No one knew, or no one even cared.

Max turned a large bend around the corner of the street to face a big ancient fountain in the centre of the village. A sign on the corner read 'Dilas Village Town Centre', marked with a crack down the middle and several streaks of rust.

The fountain was very old. The stone work was a deep grey with weeds growing all over it. It was easy to tell that it had not been tended to for many years. It featured a statue in the centre of a soldier, standing grand and noble; its face blotted out from where the rock had worn away and disintegrated. The water had all completely disappeared from the bottom, the pumps broken; the water may have even all been drunk. Nothing remained except an old statue surrounded by a wall, slowly falling apart over time.

An old bicycle lay smashed by the edge of the fountain, its wheel bent and its handle skewered. Every so often, the front wheel swayed gently to and fro in the shrieking wind. As Max walked on, more and more cars seemed to emerge, the deeper he got into the almost abandoned village. Each of them smashed inwards and shattered like broken toys. Max walked around, past the bike, and began to walk on deeper into the village, terrified by what else he might find.

A loud bang erupted suddenly out of nowhere, as a large shotgun blast soared past Max, missing him by centimetres and smashing heavily into the edge of the fountain. The bike shattered into pieces, bits of it flying everywhere in all directions. The strong stone smashed from the force of the shot. Max leapt around in fright just in time to see one of the creatures standing high above in a broken window looking down menacingly. It was snarling, an evil glint in its

261

eyes. It was holding a large shotgun in its hands; and was pointing it directly at Max.

Max jumped out of the way. He rolled over and ducked, hiding behind one of the many cars in sight. One of the sharp pieces of statue flew away from the explosion and hit Max straight in the ankle. He groaned loudly in pain and winced, gritting his teeth as he slowly pulled it out of his leg.

The monster in the house nearby pulled its shotgun away from the window. Its name was Tusk, and it wasn't going to stop at him just yet. It ran past window after window, until finally it reached the final one along in the destroyed bedroom. It placed its gun along the edge, holding it firmly, and looked out at the injured Max.

Max saw it out of the corner of his eye just in time to see the figure emerge in the window frame and raise its gun again. Max ran, keeping hold of his blade. He fled, escaping from behind the car just as the shotgun blast fired down and smashed the car into pieces. Max ran behind the fountain and hid there. Tusk snarled. He had hunted humans like this many times before, but this one was fast. It ran off into the house, into the shadows, and out of sight.

Max breathed in and out rapidly. He was panting like a dog. The cold wind wrapped around him, but his body was keeping him warm, all of the adrenaline and terror that was flowing through him. He looked around rapidly, desperately trying to see where the thing was. But he couldn't see it, he had no idea. The creature had completely disappeared from out of sight. Max's head snapped around, looking from door to door, window to window. It could appear from any one of those. He was trapped. Maybe it had gone for help. He still did not know. All he knew was that he had to move fast, and now was the time to act.

Max crawled onto all fours and began to edge away from the fountain, as quietly as he could. The silence was broken suddenly by a loud shotgun blast as Tusk emerged behind him from the door to one of the many houses. Max burst into a sprint on the ground, kicking away at the sand and dirt which flew up in clouds of dust behind him. He crawled rapidly towards one of the houses. Tusk chased after him, one of his arms was injured, which was why he could not aim accurately. But this did not stop him from giving chase. The creature roared, drool flying everywhere as the savage beast charged down the abandoned road after the innocent young man.

Max stood up, believing his speed would lie in his amount of movement, and ran on two feet once again. He ran up a short flight of steps and into a nearby house, the shotgun blast from behind blowing the lock off for him, and allowing him to run through the house. He collided with the door, smashing into it and falling through the weak rotting wood. He ignored the splinters and kept on going. Hearing the beast approaching he leapt to his feet and ran. Sprinting through the house, Tusk was constantly reloading and firing through the walls at him. Max ran through a living room, jumping over tattered sofas and ancient armchairs, bullet holes constantly appearing in the wall behind him as he ran. The creature could sense where he was, and if he slowed down now, it would kill him.

Flinging himself out through the glass of the back door, his glasses flew from his face amongst the thousands of sharp pieces; he grabbed them from the sea of glass and pushed them back onto his face. He ignored the many cuts which grazed into his skin and kept on running as fast as he could.

Tusk ran through the living room behind him, smashing through the door, breaking all the weak wood and bursting out to where Max was fleeing, firing aimlessly in hope of hitting his next victim.

Max sprinted through the back garden of the house, tripping over a sandpit and knocking over a dusty old see-saw, the terrible monster constantly chasing after him, crazed for fresh blood. He leapt over the garden fence, and out onto the street. Out onto the road he ran, sprinting past smashed up cars and great piles of rubble. He spat blood from his mouth as he ran. He could see another house on the far side of the road, he was heading for it. Closer and closer he got, maybe he could almost escape his pursuer. He was metres away from the dark old house ahead. He was almost at the flight of stairs leading up to the door. He ran on and on, until suddenly, from out of the darkness of the open door in front, from out of the shadows, stepped the most monstrous thing Max had ever seen.

It lumbered out of the door, two enormous feet stamping on the ground below. The ground trembled as the thing stepped forward. It hulked and towered over him like some form of giant. It was colossal. It was bald, the last of its hair falling away into its huge skull. Its eyes were huge and gleaming, as they stared down at Max horrifically. Its hands were large, almost like great clubs, along with razor sharp nails which could easily tear his flesh from his bones. This was the biggest and most bestial creature which Max had ever seen.

It roared suddenly, a huge gust of wind blasting Max back off the edge of the front steps with force. The smell of rotting flesh gusted back into Max's face as he fell flat onto his back. The noise was deafening, as it stormed Max's weak ears. Its name was Ox, and it was the largest and most savage out of all the twisted and mutated humans which had destroyed and devoured the small community of Dilas Village many years ago.

Max fell, and, stunned, only lifted his head up once the deafening roar had stopped. He lay weak on the ground with shock, looking up into the doorway where the beast was standing there, staring evilly down at him with its huge great bloodshot eyes. Max gulped for a moment as a second of silence echoed around them for a very brief moment. Tusk, who had been chasing Max monstrously from behind had stopped, several metres away, and was standing there, shotgun in hand, watching as his towering brother Ox stood there, looking down in hunger and realisation at their next prey.

Max looked up from the cold concrete floor at the hulking creature.

"Oh God no!" he said quietly, terrified. The monster looked down at him fiercely. It stared cruelly into his eyes for a brief terrifying moment, realising that he was an imposter. He then roared another monstrous, deafening roar, which blew Max's head down to the ground from the force once again, and began to walk heavily down the stone steps towards him. He was metres away from Max. The young man looked up, pushing his glasses back up his nose; he looked up at the huge beast which was hulking slowly towards him. Max's jaw dropped open, petrified. When the creature was merely inches away from him and looking down, about to smash him into the ground, Max jumped up.

He shook away his fear and leapt to his feet. Springing onto his feet, the nineteen year old ran as fast as he could towards another open house on the opposite side of the street. Tusk snarled fiercely and raised his long shotgun ready to fire.

Max ran and ran, panicking and almost completely out of breath, but he was still going. He could see a door wide open shaking in the wind. The front of it had been blasted apart by round after round of bullets. He could feel the ground shaking violently as Ox pounded viciously after him along the abandoned street. A shotgun fire erupted from behind as the front window of the house ahead shattered into a mass of smashed concrete and wood. Max gulped as he fled, he knew that if he was going to get there, he had to get there fast.

Chased and shot at, Max sprinted up the front steps and rolled through the blasted front door, narrowly dodging another blast from Tusk's gun. He hurried through into the living room, hearing the loud smash behind him as Ox brought the front door straight off its hinges as it chased him into the ruined house.

Max darted through the living room, throwing old pieces of furniture in his wake behind him to slow the creature down. But it was to no avail. Max flung a small wooden chair behind him, only to hear it smash into pieces as Ox brought his huge clubbed fist down upon its weak legs. Max ran on through to the kitchen, opening the door rapidly and slamming it shut behind him. He fumbled around in the cold charred kitchen, searching around for something to defend himself with. He had dropped the blade in shock when the monstrous creature had first appeared. There was an erupting crash, as Ox charged through the once closed kitchen door, slamming it down flat on the floor. Max spun around, gargling in shock roughly two metres away as he had nothing to defend himself with. Ox grunted a loud snorting noise through his clogged nostrils, as if waiting for Max to run ahead.

Max spun his head around to a shelf to see a pile of ash covered plates on a cupboard up high. He hurriedly grabbed the stack and threw the first at the brute's large bald head. It hit the creature with such force that it smashed into pieces, leaving the already scarred and twisted face with one extra. Ox roared, shaking the whole house in his wake. His expression broke into one of anger and pure fury as he began to charge livid with rage towards the helpless Max. Max gulped in fear before turning on his heels and sprinting as fast as he could through the mess of the untidy, cluttered kitchen before him. As the giant monster charged through the room after him, Max continued to spin around every second or two to throw a plate fast and violently at the huge cannibal. The creature growled viciously, ignoring every single plate which crashed over his head, every new wound which appeared on his face. He had learnt to shake away the pain. That was how he had grown to be, a fearless, indestructible creature. The only thing he thought for, was killing and feeding.

Max ran through into what appeared to be a dining room. A table lay smashed in the centre of the room along with candlesticks and drawers full of burnt cutlery. He ran up and crawled hurriedly over the broken table, Ox bursting into the room shortly after. *Won't this thing ever die?!* he asked himself, panicking and desperately trying to find a way out, a chance to escape. He spat blood from his mouth and held his almost broken glasses to his battered face.

Max picked up a chair and threw it across the room at the towering monster. Ox caught the flying chair and crushed it to dust within his iron strong fingers. Advancing further, Max needed a fast escape before he was cornered.

He looked over across the room and saw another doorway. He could not see what lay beyond but had to take a chance. Max ran as fast as his legs could carry him over to the door and hurried inside. The moment he was into the room he turned on his heels and slammed the door firmly shut behind him. Turning around, he saw that he was in an office. A desk lay in one corner with a couple of bookcases and filing cabinets. Max ran over to the other side and pulled the desk across with all his might. His muscles strained painfully as he pulled the heavy desk as fast as he could across the room to block the doorway. He managed to do it just in time. Once he had finished he began tearing pictures and all kinds of random objects from all corners of the room in a desperate attempt to block the other side from the huge muscled creature breaking through.

He grabbed an iron cane from the side of the desk and raised it ready in front of the door, waiting for the monster to start breaking through his set up line of defence.

To Max's sheer surprise and almost shock, there was complete and utter silence. The whole house was silent. Max's jaw slowly dropped further and further in dismay, his ears attentive, waiting and listening. Nothing could be heard.

The only thing which he could hear was the faint tweeting of birds singing outside in the distance. The strong smell of decaying flesh was always hanging in the air, yet he did not pay attention to that right now. He was standing there, weapon in hand, waiting for something to happen.

Suddenly, Max began to hear something. A faint, but sudden, drumming sound in the distance, beyond the barricaded door. It sounded almost like something running up steps. It carried on around and heading upwards. Max could hear where the noise was coming from and followed with his eyes to the position of the distant noise. It was gradually growing louder and louder. The distant footsteps were coming closer and closer towards him. But they were not in the next room, he could tell, they were too distant and muffled to be next door in the remains of the smashed up dining room. They were somewhere else, somewhere close, somewhere near him.

Max suddenly heard them coming from above him. He looked up in terror as he suddenly realised that the creature was...

The ceiling collapsed before him suddenly, sending him sprawling back towards the pile of objects blocking the door. The middle of the ceiling of the medium sized room completely caved in onto the once empty floor space below. Max choked and spluttered amongst the rubble and dirt as the dust came flying up to meet his lungs. He closed his eyes for a moment to stop the dust from flooding into his eyes. When he opened them again, tears beginning to swelter, he saw that the thick haze of dust which was forming where the ceiling had collapsed had almost completely cleared now. And standing in its wake, livid with rage, eyes burning red with hate, was Ox. It growled savagely like a wolf and charged in a flash of light towards Max.

Before he could even move, the huge creature grabbed the young man by the scruff of the neck and hurled him backwards with such force through the window behind.

268

Max wined in pain as he was thrown through an already shattered sheet of glass, the remains shattering even further. He fell to the floor rapidly out into cold morning air. His arms were bleeding with scratches and wounds from the glass. He gritted his teeth, trying to ignore the pain. The whole window frame smashed behind him, as a few metres away, Ox came blasting through the back of the house, destroying everything in his monstrous wake. Max breathed deeply in and out rapidly, panicking. How could he kill this thing?

He spat blood from his mouth onto the floor and picked up his glasses which had fallen from his face again. Flinging them back onto his nose bridge, Max sprung up painfully and ran on. He could see something up ahead. Was it an exit out of this nightmare? The only thing he could see from his position was a sudden drop in the ground. A hill, an escape route. He focused his eyes directly upon the point ahead, knowing he had to get there. Max ran as fast as his weak legs could carry him. The drop was getting closer and closer. He could see the edge well in sight. He sprinted up to the edge, and halted immediately, stopping suddenly as he reached the end, swaying on his legs as he was about to fall to his death.

The drop below was no small hill. The village itself had been built on the very edge of a small crater in the ground. The earth crumbled and fell away beneath his feet as Max stepped backwards hurriedly. He looked out across at the crater to see the other side far in the distance. His hopes suddenly fell like a ton of bricks. There was no way he could possibly escape across the crater. He looked around the edges, searching for any signs of a bridge or any way across and out. But no, there was nothing, the rest of the crater was blocked by the houses built right on the edge.

Max looked out into the distance beyond the crater. Miles and miles of isolated countryside spread on into the distance. Not a single house was in sight, not a single road or any sign of life. The devastated village was well and truly isolated.

Max spun around rapidly as he heard footsteps swiftly approaching. He turned around to see an axe come flying in a flash towards his face. His reaction was fast as he ducked just in time. Ox was standing right over him, having picked up an axe somewhere; he was now attacking the innocent human more and more viciously. Max rolled over across the ground, luckily avoiding Ox's blade by inches as it came crashing down second after second. He leapt up and dashed back towards the village. There was no way out. The only escape was to go back once again, through the danger. He wheezed heavily, choking on his own blood inside his mouth. He could feel the brute's heavy steps clunking behind him, shaking the ground, as he ran. The thing was on his tail. He had to get rid of it.

Taking a sharp dramatic right, Max turned off into a nearby house, kicking open the door and bursting through into the house with force. He ran up the stairs straight in front of him, step after step falling beneath as he sprinted up them like a bolt of lightning. When he reached the top of the stairs he halted suddenly and snapped around to look down. Ox stood there at the bottom of the stairs, just standing there in the broken doorway, as if waiting for something. Max leant against the banister and the wall, his arms out either side, supporting his weak and injured body for a moment.

Ox stood there completely silent, it's strange grunting and roaring sounds had stopped. Instead all Max could hear was complete silence. This was strange. He stayed awake, aware that anything could happen at any unnerving moment. The huge monster suddenly opened its maw wide; its gaping jaws falling down and down, the sides of its mouth were slit to create more room for its mouth to open up even further. A sound finally emerged, into the most deafening roar Max had ever heard. The whole house shook from the erupting booming noise. Max went flying back from the force of the sound waves pounding up the stairs towards him. With a final crash, the staircase itself collapsed, leaving a pile of rubble in its wake. Ox closed his gaping maw, and ran around the corner out of sight. Max let out a sigh of relief. The giant ogre-like monster had gone for now, but Max knew that it would shortly be back, ambushing him from the darkness ahead.

Max turned around slowly, clutching his side, covering a huge gash which the thing had sliced into him. His arms were covered in cuts and wounds in his skin. He was becoming weaker and weaker by the minute. He turned right and crawled along the charred remains of an upstairs corridor. As he walked along it slowly, he looked down to see burnt remains of photographs which had once hung on the walls. There were people, happy and innocent as they seemed. They were smiling, waving at the camera. These were the villagers before the creatures had come and slaughtered everyone. There were families, landlords, merry men and all kinds of Cambridgeshire country people in eighties clothing. Since the attack, Dilas Village must have been completely forgotten by everyone. No one came to help them, no one even cared. The village had rotted away in the dust and the dried blood. Burnt, and decaying, with the creatures waiting constantly amongst the forest, waiting bloodthirstily for innocent civilians to come, wander and lose the way, to be dragged off into their hole of hunger.

Max walked down the corridor limping, clutching his wounds, and thinking about what might have happened before any of this was destroyed and burnt to ruin. He lumbered on, bleeding in all various places over his body. He reached a window, its glass shattered into a thousand tiny pieces on the floor, allowing the cold air to come rushing in furiously. He stared outside, his vision blurring for a moment because of his dazzled, confused brain. When his eyes focused, he was forced to duck down below the

271

window pane rapidly, as a huge shotgun blast came shooting in through the empty window pane. Out in the street, looking fiercely up at the ruined house, was Tusk, standing with his weapon, and shooting at Max's position.

Max gritted his teeth and handled the surging pain that was slowly killing him. He rolled over onto his hands and knees and began to crawl as fast as he could towards the end of the upstairs corridor. The murderous creature outside slit another load of ammunition into place. Looking up at the dark house once more, he closed one eye and looked down the sight of the double barrel and, sensing Max's presence as he crawled on, fired another shot at the house.

The shot hit the stone walls and dented deeply into it. Max, who was fleeing hurriedly across the floor, felt the whole house shake from the blast. Outside, realising that his shot was not succeeding, Tusk loaded another load of ammunition, and prepared to fire.

Max was panicking severely. He raced across the cold burnt floor within the house, almost at the other side. Another blast smashed through the remains of the window frame, crashing through to the wall on the other side, missing Max's head by inches. He had to get out of there now.

In the grim haunted street outside, Tusk snarled, spitting drool onto the floor. He threw the shotgun to the ground, completely out of ammunition. Grinning a bloodthirsty, evil grin, showing the rows of jagged green and grey teeth, Tusk clenched his long twisted fingers, realising that the young man was still inside the house. He roared a loud monstrous roar into the night's air, and ran towards the front door of the house.

On the other side of the blackened village, Syrak, the female in the group of savage monsters which had attacked Sophie the night before in the forest, looked up from a dark and flesh reeking corridor. She looked up into the sky.

272

Hearing the roar of her companion, she too opened her large maw, and roared horrifically.

Ox, which had retreated from the fight and chase, but was not down, had grabbed a large scythe from a disturbing and ghostly cellar. Hearing his brother's roar, he too looked up into the dark grey cloudy sky, and roared his lungs out.

Mauler, the large monster which had captured Sean and Sarah the previous night, looked up from the remains of a children's bedroom. He looked around the room rapidly. Hearing his brother's roar, he looked up into the darkened sky, and roared monstrously.

Bek, the leader of the pack of animalistic savages, the one who had tormented Sean and his younger step sister in the most terrifying and traumatising of ways, looked up from his den in the remains of a collapsed cellar. He tore the piece of meat from his mouth having heard the monstrous roar of his companion. He spat the half eaten flesh from his mouth, chewing the last remaining parts; then he threw it down to the ground. The call of the twisted being came flooding in from outside like a gust of wind. He knew from this that something was happening. Max had arrived. He leapt to his feet and sprinted out of cellar into the daylight.

All four of the mutated savage humans ran almost mindlessly from their lairs. All of them had heard the call of Tusk, and were rushing towards his position. All of them were hungry, insane and merciless. All of them were coming for Max.

Chapter 32: Salvation

Sean sat in complete darkness in the small, cold cellar. He could hear the faint sobs of Sarah in the blackness to his side. Many times he had tried to comfort her as best as he could. But it was no use. They were trapped, alone and helpless, waiting for death in a chilling cage.

"Sarah. Stay with me Sarah," he said, trying to be comforting to her cries. "Just listen to me. We're going to be fine, you understand me? We're going to be fine. Max is going to come and get us okay? We're going to be saved. You just remember that. We're going to be saved." He gulped inwards, trying to be brave. He knew that little hope was possible.

Suddenly, the deafening sound of roars erupted from outside. He had no idea how many of them were out there. Whether there were three or a hundred. Bek had only mentioned that there was more than one. There was the twisted, mutated family which had slaughtered the people of the village... and Bek himself, the ring leader, the one which had been driven insane and murdered his friends savagely. He was the most demented of them all, driven on by a never ending hunger and lust for revenge upon all others.

The roars echoed on for a long moment. Both Sean and Sarah looked up towards the ceiling from where the disturbing noise was coming from above. He took a deep breath in fear. He did not know what was going to happen. He prayed inside his head as the roars raged on around them outside. This was the most terrified that Sean had ever been in his entire life.

Suddenly, the light from outside flickered violently for a split second. Sean caught a glimpse of it from out of the corner of his eye. He spun his head rapidly around to see what was going on. The light from the hallway outside flickered between shadows and brightness for a moment. The roars outside had stopped, coming to a sudden halt. The light flickered again. It was a cold dark moment of confusion before Sean realised what was actually going on. Something was coming, and it was heading towards the room.

The flickers were shadows passing in front of the light as the unknown figure passed down the corridor. Sean began to hear footsteps clanking down upon the cold stone floors outside. His pulse began to race again. He could tell from the distant footsteps coming closer and closer that there was not just one of them, there was more.

Sean really began to panic. Bek had come back, with more of them. They were coming to take them. This was the end.

Sarah's crying came to a stop, as she too heard the emerging footsteps and stared in horror up at the door and flickering shadows from her small cage on the floor.

"Sarah?" whispered Sean, turning towards her to try and be comforting. "It's alright. Just don't panic. Everything is going to be okay." He spoke to her rapidly, the words sprawling out of his mouth in fear as the footsteps came closer and closer. "Sarah. Listen to me! We're going to be okay, you understand?! We're going to be okay!" He was almost at the verge of shouting now, desperately trying to get the message into the young girl's head.

For a brief second, everything stopped dead. There was not sound which could be heard except the loud clunking of footsteps, and the cold, frightened breathing of the two children, and the things outside. Sean stared ahead, expecting the door to come creaking open slowly and reveal the terrors beyond.

Soon enough, it did. The door creaked on its hinges and slowly drifted open, being pushed eerily from the other side. The door swung open fully, leaving a blast of light rushing to meet Sean's terrified face. Two blackened figures stood in the doorway, their hands by their sides, towering menacingly. One of them reached out to the side of the door to flick on a light switch. As it did so, Sean could see a long bony hand produce from the darkness, fingernails long and coiling like talons. The hand carried on, the light switch was flicked down, and Sean saw what lay beyond.

Standing in the doorway, a cold air hanging over them, and the stench of decaying flesh creeping over them, were two of the large group of savage once human creatures which haunted the forest. They were both the same height, and almost looked identical in most of their original features, meaning that they could possibly be twins. One of them had an eye which was swollen up with blood and dried flesh, like something had been stabbed and torn from it not too long ago. The other had multiple large wounds in its shoulders, bandaged together by dirty old rags which had been scraped from whatever it could find.

The two of them looked down at the young boy tied tightly to the chair in the middle of the dim cellar room. They recognised him immediately from his features. His sister had been the one which had lost them their eye and shoulder muscle. They were hungry, bloodthirsty, and eager for a slow revenge.

One of them ran up to Sean and grabbed him by the scruff of the neck, its many pelts waving and swaying from the force and momentum of the rush. "You little twerp!" it spat violently in his face. It then growled savagely.

The other one, its shoulder broken and painful, looked down into the cage at Sarah, who was beginning to weep strongly once again.

"With all of the others mauling your freak of a brother outside, no one is left to guard you. Leaving us, down here, with you!" it said menacingly and cruel, walking slowly over to the small cage like some form of mutated ghost.

"Your sister was the one who tore out my eye. Now I'm gonna tear out yours!" spat the other one, throwing Sean's head to one side as he choked and spluttered from having

276

the creature wrap its hand tightly around his throat. It began to step back, fingers stretching.

"I'm so hungry, and you'll do just nicely," the other one said to the little girl. It stepped towards her closer, tears welling in her sobbing eyes. It licked its lips and snarled disturbingly.

The one-eyed creature immediately turned and threw a filthy look towards its brother. "Back off. She's mine!" it growled. The thing ran over to its brother and started attacking him viciously.

"She... is... mine!" the other cried, struggling to wrestle the other one off of him. He punched him in the face, sending it flying off to the other side of the room. Sean merely watched as the two mutants struggled and fought savagely.

But One-eye wasn't going to give up for nothing. He leapt to his feet, spitting blood onto the floor. Gritting the remains of his sharp teeth, he roared and flung himself on top of the other. One-arm saw the other one coming just in time and flung his dead arm into the air, smashing it into One-eye's face as he jumped onto his back. The two of them struggled and wrestled violently for several long moments, neither of them refusing to back down. They were like animals fighting over food. It was disgusting. What had become of these people? Sean thought as he could not take his eyes away from the fighting creatures. The villagers had made them that way, burning down their home and sending them fleeing into the woods. The family had been driven mad from being lost in the wilderness for so long. This was what made what they were like now. It was other humans which had made these things.

One-eye raised his long sharp claws into the air, and brought them down violently onto his brother's head. One-arm stood there dazed for a second, his eyes staring into the wall, into oblivion. A second passed as One-eye stepped back, wiping the blood from his face. One-arm fell to the floor, dead. A trickle of blood drooled out from the claw marks in his battered skull.

Sean looked up in shock and terror at the monstrous thing in front of him. One of them was dead, but the other was going to take his sister. The beast looked down at the little girl in the cage, its prize.

"Don't you touch her! Don't you lay a finger on her!" he shouted at the creature.

One-eye merely looked around at the teenager, ignoring the constant shouts and bellows.

"Patience Sean." it hissed sinisterly. "You'll be next!" it growled at him, bearing its fanged teeth.

Sean looked up in terror. There was nothing he could do. The rope around him was too tight. Blood from the monster's hand and his own sweat dripped rapidly down his face. He couldn't do anything.

One-eye moved closer and closer towards Sarah. It reached out a long thin bony hand towards the bars, when suddenly...

The door burst open, smashing into the wall behind, and leaving a huge gaping dent amongst the dirt. One-eye spun around from where he was standing. Sean and Sarah looked up, bewildered, not realising what had just happened.

The dust parted in the air, as the shadows disappeared, everything came into sight. From out of the dim light and shadows of the corridor, Lauren and Sophie emerged.

One-eye roared viciously at the sight of imposters. He turned around and began to charge towards the two girls. When he was inches away from them, Lauren reached into her back pocket, and pulled out a large knife. As the creature charged towards her, she positioned the knife and stabbed it into the monster's head. The thing paused, coming to an abrupt halt as the knife struck deep into its forehead.

"Stay... away... from...my... family!" she bellowed into One-eye's face, slashing the knife in and out. She was murderous, deadly and aggressive. Lauren had now become a killing machine. She would stop at nothing to get her family back to safety. She drove the thin blade in and out of One-eye's head psychopathically. She was almost going completely insane from this sudden rage. With one final slash, she withdrew the blade back from the creature's head, allowing it to fall to the floor, silently, lifeless.

Sean stared up at his younger sister Sophie and older sister Lauren who had come to save him, tears welling in his eyes with happiness. They were saved. Sophie immediately ran over to behind Sean's chair to help untie him. When the ropes finally slipped off, she turned around and gave him a huge warming hug. Lauren stood a few metres away, slightly shocked and astonished by what she had just done. Sean ran over to her and gave her a thankful hug, embracing his older sister tightly as she hugged him back.

Sophie ran over to where Sarah was in the cage. She withdrew a sharp unfurled clip from her pocket and began to start hacking her way through the lock on the cage hurriedly.

Lauren looked down at her younger brother.

"Thank God you're safe," she said happily, hugging him once more.

"You too," he responded back. "I was so scared."

"I know, I know," she said calmly back to him. "We all were. It's okay, it's okay."

The lock finally broke free, releasing the crying Sarah from her cage and sending her running into Sophie's arms. "There there. Ssssh. It's alright, it's alright," Sophie said almost whispering, comfortingly towards her younger step sister.

The four of them closed in together, all facing each other warmly.

"Come on," ordered Lauren. "Let's get out of here." With that, they all turned and hurriedly left the cold dark room. Sean turned around at the last moment, shutting the door behind him, making it look that at first glance that they hadn't escaped. He slammed the door shut in hurry and panic, leaving the empty cellar in total darkness once more.

Chapter 33:   Bring On The Horde

Max crawled towards the edge of the corridor as fast as his injured and weakening body could carry him. He breathed in and out over and over hurriedly, panicking and out of breath. He heard the large shotgun come crashing down to the ground outside, the great bang clashing against the dusty concrete pavement. The creature erupted into a loud deafening roar, filling Max's ears with a ghastly, monstrous sound. It was the most horrendous noise he had ever heard. He covered his ears quickly, desperately trying to block out the horrific sound. When the roar had stopped, Max removed his hands from his ears and looked around above him from the corner of the charred corridor from where he was taking refuge.

He listened out, a moment of silence echoing throughout the ruined village. All was quiet, with birdsong and the gentle wind, until suddenly, from the far side of the ruins, another roar responded back. He sat up a little, trying to listen closely to what he thought he heard. Another roar erupted also in response to the second. What was happening? They were all contacting each other, like a war cry, like a...

Max suddenly paused in his tracks as he was about to stand up. He realised what was happening. The one which was just attacking him was calling the others. It would only be a matter of moments before many more came rushing from all sides of the village to come and kill him. Max remained silent and ducked down. Slowly, he moved over to the window frame, and peered over to see what was on the other side. The very top of his head just slipped over the edge to look over.

Outside, in the middle of the street, Tusk, was nowhere to be seen. Max looked around the area, into windows and

281

around corners, the strange creature was nowhere to be seen. This was weird, very weird, one moment it had been giving serious chase, the next, it had suddenly stopped.

A crash suddenly broke out from one of the downstairs rooms. Max shot back from the window in answer to his question. The thing was in the house. Staying away from the corner of the corridor to the landing, Max stood up, hiding behind the edge of the crumbling old wall. He took a deep breath out, trying to relax, but it was no good. He was too scared. In a matter of moments, the house would be swarming with creatures, all after him.

Max picked up a large shard of glass from the remnants of one of the shattered window panes. Gripping it tightly in his hand for security until he was almost bleeding from it, Max slowly crept towards the edge of the wall which met the landing area. He could not see around the corner, only the occasional cracking or destroying of objects as Tusk was getting closer and closer towards him. Little did he know, that Tusk was right around the corner, sneaking sinisterly up the weak and rotting staircase.

Tusk breathed heavily, his nostrils flaring back and forth like a machine. He walked, slowly and cautiously up the stairs, his claws sharp and curved at the ready like eagle's talons. He was going to find the young man, and take him out once and for all.

The final step creaked as the beast reached the top of the staircase. It could sense Max's presence, hiding behind the edge of the wall leading onto the upstairs corridor. He raised his hand high, about to lunge and strike. Max, who was hiding around the corner, could feel the creature's presence feet away from him. He held the glass fracture ready, waiting for it.

Tusk jumped forward, reaching its inhuman hand around forcefully and rapidly flaying it around the corner. Max ducked, just in time, as the monster flung its long nails around and dented the walls deeply. Max ducked beneath it, flung the glass knife around and struck it deep into Tusk's leg. The creature roared terrifyingly in pain and anger, removing its hand from the wall to meet the other, holding onto its wounded leg. Max rolled away to the side and ran into the next room along.

He ran inside hurriedly, desperately searching for something to fight with or an escape route.

The room turned out to be the remains of a child's bedroom. The walls had been burnt and charred but the rest of the room had been surprisingly recreated. A broken crib lay on one side; eerie, haunting dolls lay in rows on the many shelves on the walls. A muffled scrunching sound suddenly broke out from the other side of the room. Max spun around in shock, only to see nothing there. He frowned in surprise. The noise broke out again, only this time, Max heard where it was coming from.

Slowly and suspiciously, Max began to walk around to where he heard the noise. It started off as a faint crackling noise, then the muffling became louder and louder gradually as he approached. Max walked around the room, past the old battered crib, to see, behind the broken structure, a small child playing with one of the many creepy dolls.

Max reeled back in horror at the disturbing sight. He gasped loudly in shock. At that, the little girl looked up to see what had entered its room. But this was no ordinary little girl. Her face was as scarred and twisted as all the other monsters in the forest and village. Her mouth was wide and gaping open, drool spitting forth. Her eyes were wide and beady. She almost looked like one of the little dolls she was playing with, their faces equally burnt and scarred from the horrors they had endured. She was one of them, one of the very first creatures to consume the village in hunger.

She opened her mouth wide, exposing a mouth full of sharp and broken teeth. She screamed excruciatingly at the top of her lungs.

"DADDY!"

283

The sound was more deafening and mind destroying than any of the other roars which Max had heard so far. He was almost completely thrown back by shrieking sound. He staggered back, covering his ears in pain. He almost fell back into the shelves of hundreds of different dolls of all different shapes and sizes.

Tusk ripped the shard of glass out of his leg with force out on the landing. He roared in anger, blood trailing from his leg and drool from his mouth. He stood up fully, and burst into the next room suddenly.

The door flung open, almost completely flying off its hinges. Max fled back in terror as Tusk lunged into the room. There was nowhere he could go, no escape routes except from the door which was blocked by the terrifying brute. He spun round and saw a window, closed, but clear. Without thinking, Max ran as fast as he could to the opposite end of the room. He flung himself through the air, and straight through the glass window.

It shattered spectacularly into a million tiny shards around him as he soared through the air. The world around him seemed to slow down for a split second. A blinding light, and a pitch ringing in his ears. After that split second passed, he returned back to reality, and saw the ground approaching rapidly.

Max fell head first into a skip at the bottom of the house directly down from the window. There was a loud crash and a sudden moment of blackness, as all went dark around him. Max flashed his eyes open, rubbing his eyes to clear the dust particles erupting from his sudden landing. To his sheer relief, he had landed in an old rusting skip, on top of an old moth-eaten mattress. It had presumably been thrown away long ago, yet it still had a strong, soft foundation, which had luckily saved his fall, and even his life. He breathed outwards, having held his breath whilst falling. He coughed and choked from the dust in the air for a second, before rubbing his eyes again, and standing up to look around.

The street around him seemed quiet and deserted. Not a single creature was in sight. He looked up as the last tiny fragments of glass fell from the broken window above. Tusk's roars had stopped as he had hit the bottom. The room above seemed deserted and lifeless. Max gulped in realisation and fear. He knew that the monstrous beast was rapidly on its route towards him. He had to move fast, before it found him again.

As Max jumped energetically out of the skip and the rotting rubbish and rubble, he saw one of the creatures come bursting forth from around the corner. The street was wide and open, as the new monster came from many metres away, sprinting on its hind legs with raw power and speed.

The creature's name was Mauler. It was fairly tall with gigantic muscles and dark clothing which it had taken from one of the previous guards which had been killed in the forest for desertion. It was the same one which had captured Sean and Sarah, and had taken them down to the cold dark cellar of one of the many houses with Tusk to be mentally tortured and disturbed. Max did not know this, as the dark clothed creature came rushing towards him, but he would soon find out.

Turning around hurriedly, Max reached back into the faded yellow skip, and pulled out a huge iron bar from the remains of the rubble. He held in out firmly in front of him, and screamed out as he charged viciously towards the monster.

"Where's my family?!" he bellowed at the top of his lungs as he sprinted, bar held high.

He reached contact range with Mauler, and swung the heavy metal tube around, smashing brutally into the thing's legs. Mauler screamed in agony as he was flung to the ground from the barbaric force. Max stood over the top of him, holding the sharp edge of the metal bar to the monster's throat.

"You sick freak!" he spat in the creature's face. He lifted the bar up high into the air whilst the thing was still weak, and smacked it down into the creatures head, knocking it out, unconscious.

Max walked backwards, away, slowly, getting to grips with what he had just done. He had not killed it, but it would not disturb him again, for now. He stepped back to look around and jumped back in horror as he saw what was approaching.

From the street ahead of him, about four hundred yards away from him, stood two more of the gruesome beings in the middle of the road. One was tall, muscular and bald, like a giant. It was already wounded slightly, with several injuries on the top of its bald head. It was Ox, the massive thing which had chased him through the house earlier, and tore the stairs apart with his bloodthirsty deafening roar.

The other, was as tall as Max himself, bald as well, with green fading skin like some kind of orc creature. Its name was Bek, the leader, the most insane of them all, the one which had mentally tortured Sean and slaughtered his friends through pure insanity. This being was the most twisted and monstrous creature out of all the ones which stalked the woodlands by night. Why? Because it was the most human.

The two of them stood there ahead of him like cowboys in an abandoned western town, grimacing at the young injured man before them in the opposite street. As Max stared back, he knew that this was where it was all going to end. On the blood filled streets of Dilas Village. Only one side was getting out of this alive.

Ox burst into a run, picking up more and more speed as he came closer and closer, the towering creature charging at Max, nearing ever closer the second. Without thinking where to go, Max turned on his heels and fled, jumping over the body of the fallen Mauler. Running down the wide open street, he ran like a deer, fleeing for his life.

Suddenly, he took a sharp right into a garden, leaping over a fence. The chase was on. Ox soon came thundering after, smashing through the weak rotting fence completely, breaking the remaining white and brown wood into dust, which shattered around him like glass.

Max fled up to the front steps. He raised his leg hurriedly and forcibly smashed down the front door. The hard wooden frame creaked for a split second on its hinges, before falling to the ground heavily, dust flying from the crevices. Max leapt through the swirling mist of dust in the air. He barged through into the ruined house, desperately fleeing the monstrous creature lumbering after him. He was almost in the same position as he was before, in a house, with the biggest of all the twisted mutated humans which haunted the place. Now he just had to find a way of getting rid of it once more.

He jumped over a sofa and into a living room. Turning around and halting momentarily, the second the beast emerged into the room, Max picked up a lamp from a side table and hurled it viciously towards the Ox's face. The frame shattered into pieces over the huge bald skull, causing a few more tiny scratches to join the many countless scars and dents in the brute's head. The lamp smashed, but the effect was to no use. Ox's head was merely shunted to one side from the force. He then slowly bent his neck back into shape, and snarled louder and louder savagely at its next victim.

Max stared back into the creature's menacing blood-shot eyes. He was truly petrified for a long moment, before coming to his senses, and running rapidly away as the beast pounded after him through the ruins.

Max found a flight of stairs which led to the upstairs region of the house. He ran up them immediately, hoping that the huge thing would not chase after him as it did before. He reached the top of the landing and spun around suddenly to see where the monster was.

Ox burst around the corner after the young man. He looked up the flight of stairs to see the tall, dark haired man panting, holding his glasses onto his face to prevent them from slipping due to the blood and sweat on his face.

Ox knew that he had trouble reaching the top of staircases. He could bring them down to rubble from bellowing the very air out of his lungs, but climbing up them with his heavy muscle and weight was a challenge too far for him. He was so hungry though. He could smell Max's scent, his fear, his blood. He could not resist the hunger and rage any longer. Gritting his large broken teeth, Ox ran forward, and charged without stopping, as fast as his legs could carry him, up the flight of stairs towards Max.

Max looked down for a split second as the huge man lumbered up the stairs two at a time. He turned on his heels and fled, terrified by the fact that the creature was actually chasing after him up the stairs this time. He ran along the corridor, flinging himself past the already crumbling banisters. He tripped and would have surely fallen down had he lost his balance altogether. The area of banister which he had reached smashed and crumbled beneath him as he tripped and he clouted his hand into it. It shattered into pieces and fell down, landing heavily on the already blackened floor. Max swayed for what felt like a long terrifying moment, before luckily regaining his balance and fleeing on ahead. Ox had reached the top of the landing and was now chasing the young man, thundering down the rotting upstairs corridor.

Max wheezed and panted as he ran. He arrived at a room and flung himself inside. Once in, he spun around and slammed the door shut. He pushed his back up against the door to try and hold the thing back for as long as he could.

Suddenly, like a bolt of lightning, a fist came crashing through the door. Wood flew everywhere as the monster's vast hand came soaring through, inches from Max's face. He looked to the side suddenly in shock, before ducking out the way as the fist came plummeting through the weak door once more. Max was fairly strong and was able to hold it back, but not for long. A sudden blow of weight hammered against the door from the other side as Ox bashed and bashed inwards constantly. The door almost flew off its hinges from the force, almost breaking Max's back from the huge dent inwards.

Max was panicking more and more. He snapped his head around to see a crow bar lying a few feet away from him in what appeared to be a tool cupboard. Max extended his legs out, trying to reach as far as he could stretch whilst trying to hold the door back from the constant heavy blows. Max reached and reached, stretching his legs to their very limit. He kept on reaching. He did not know how much longer he could hold on for.

With one final stretch, Max managed to wrap his legs around the long silver crow bar and pulled it back to his arms. He picked it up and, still holding the door from blasting back, wedged the crowbar into the crack at the bottom of the door. He then let go, making sure that everything was secure one last time, then he fled back to the other side of the room.

He ran over to a shelf on the other side of the fairly small room and grabbed a drill from on top of it. Revving the drill to make sure that it was still functioning, Max looked over at the door where Ox had nearly torn his way through completely. Looking down at the drill quickly, he started it up. It was time to end this nightmare. Right here.

Chapter 34:   Again We Shall Rise

The large, dented black truck drove on through the last stretch of trees. Sunlight was beginning to become visible up ahead. Outlines of grim grey cloud came shimmering through the trees like a form of ghostly presence. The world beyond the forest seemed just as grim and haunting as it was within.

As Markus drove the truck on, the light from outside hit him suddenly as the truck drove around a bend in the rough muddy woodland road. They had travelled for the last twenty minutes to reach the other side of the forest, without stopping. Throughout the entire time, both Markus and his companion Zack had been travelling in tense silence. Neither of them talked nor uttered an entire syllable within the length of the journey. Only the faint distant sound of branches rustling in the wind and birds singing eerily had reached their ears.

Both of them were afraid. At first it had come like an infection, a flu which could be taken care of over time. But now it had become unstoppable and completely natural. They were entering hostile territory for what may be the last time, in a final attempt to fight back, for revenge, for their families, for a last desperate attempt for glory and hope before death. They had been traitors the whole time that they had worked under the operation of keeping the bloodthirsty mutated cannibals a secret, just to keep their families alive.

They knew their plans by now. Both Markus and Zack knew exactly where they would all be; back in the ruined, scorched remains of what once was Dilas Village. When daylight ruled supreme the creatures would return to their home on the very far side of the forest, hiding away from the rest of civilisation. This was to avoid awareness of their presence. If too many people went missing it would arouse suspicion immediately. It was only when darkness overtook the ocean of trees and undergrowth, when the creatures would enter Dilas Forest, and hunt for food. Anything they could find they consumed in their anger and mindless hunger; animals, leftovers, even the last humans to fail to reach the exit on time.

That was where the guards entered play. They would limit the time slot within the woods so that anyone who was foolish enough or weak enough to fall behind once the siren rung would be left behind, and most likely, never be seen again. They were savages, monsters, murderers. Not just the creatures from beyond... but the guards themselves too.

The truck pulled over to one side on the edge of the hill looking down over the dead village. Markus parked it, and slowly, put his hand onto the small hand gun on his belt. He looked over at Zack, who looked back at him, eyes determined yet evidently showing his fear.

"Are you ready?" he asked the young man patiently.

Zack hesitated for a moment before answering. "Y... yes." his lips trembled.

"Just remember," said Markus gently, "It's your family you're fighting for. When you're out there, killing them, just think of your family, and what you'll return to once this is all over."

Zack looked upset for a moment. He looked from the ruins outside down the hill to his old friend and companion beside him.

"Thank you sir. But what if there is no return? What if this all ends here, right now? What if we fail?!" His eyes were now saddened and bulging in their sockets.

Markus looked down trying to think for a second.

"Trust me Zack. Out of all the years I've known you, when have I ever let you down?"

Zack too looked concerned for a moment. Markus may have once been a horrible cruel man, but now, on the eve of their last stand, he was being kind to him. He was polite and patient. When Zack came to think about it he couldn't think of a good reason when Markus had actually let him down. "No sir. We'll win sir, we will win."

"That's more like it." He smiled kindly. Markus looked down the bank at the remains of the charred village below. One of the creatures suddenly emerged from a building far into the distance. It rounded the end of the street and disappeared from view, running like a bolt of lightning. Markus scowled at the sight of the thing. It must have been chasing a deer or some other animal which strayed into the village. He had no idea that Max was down there, fighting for his life from many other creatures which were constantly on his tail.

Markus looked over at Zack again.

"Okay. We'll get everything prepared before we set off down the hill. I'll grab the spare equipment in the bag in the back..."

Suddenly, a huge object smashed with an almighty impact onto the bonnet of the truck. The whole car shook from the force; almost lifting it from the ground it was so violent. Both Markus and Zack slammed forward, crashing their heads into the front of the car brutally. After a few seconds of dark spiralling silence, Markus slowly lifted his bruised and bleeding head from the steering wheel. He looked through one eye at the object which had suddenly hit them. He stared at it for a moment, before realising in shock, that it was a large rusty silver spear.

"Go! Go! Go!" he bellowed immediately. He lifted his entire front body up and spun around to shake Zack over and over again. When the young man finally awoke in shock Markus shook him again with force, shouting constantly in his ear. Go! Go! Move!"

Realising that they were under attack, Zack shot up out of his seat and flung the door open, then he rolled out of the car as to not be seen. Once he was on the ground, he crawled over to the rear end of the car to remove the weapon bags. Markus followed in suit from the other side. Meeting him in the middle, the two of them reached out to grab their weapons. This was war.

Markus grabbed a large shotgun whilst Zack reached out to firmly hold onto a carbine rifle. The two of them crouched down hurriedly. One of the creatures had seen them, and was heading as fast as the wind in their direction.

Zack shot around to one side of the truck. He removed a round of bullets from a pouch at his side into the gun and loaded it up, preparing to fire. Markus ran around to the other side, preparing to run down the hill quickly into combat. Once he had loaded his weapon ready, he shouted across the top of the vehicle over to Zack. "Zack! Are you ready?!"

There was a moment of silence as Zack tried to calm himself down from panicking too much. "Yeah. Ready when you are." He clicked the gun into place. They were about to descend.

"Ok!" yelled the commanding soldier back. "On my count of three! One..." He took out a picture of his family from his pocket. "Two..." He stared at it warmly and sadly for a second, before tucking it back into his front pocket and holding his gun up ready. "Three!" he bellowed at the top of his booming lungs.

Zack leapt to his feet and began to sprint down the enormous hill ahead of him. Markus jumped up also, as the two last standing guards began their final attempt to fight back. As Zack ran rapidly down the dried untidy grass bank, a monstrous face appeared over the horizon of the slope to greet him frighteningly. It was Mauler, awoken from the smack in the face previously given by Max; therefore he was now more savage and livid than ever. Zack held his carbine to his shoulder. He aimed and fired twice towards the monstrous beast. The two bullets struck deep into either shoulder of the black armoured creature. It fell back

293

suddenly, almost tumbling down the hill from the brutal force. But Zack wasn't going to wait till it was down, no. Zack was going to fight this thing to the end.

He darted down the hill and lunged at the creature, flying into it and knocking it to the ground. The two of them fell and rolled over the side of the huge bank as they were propelled through the dirt and dust, arms and legs flying in all directions from the launch of sudden brutal contact.

Markus saw the two struggling together, but he did not join the combat. He knew that Zack could easily fend for himself for now. He himself was searching for one thing only amongst the ruins of Dilas Village... Bek. He was not normally one for revenge himself. But this was the mutated freak which had haunted him and his family all those years. He was the one who had wasted Markus' life and terrified his family into hiding. Markus had not seen his family in so long. It would be his greatest desire to launch a bullet into the back of the thing's scarred and twisted skull.

Markus ran down to reach the bottom of the hill. His eyes darted around. From the brawl between the beast and his companion to an eerily swinging tavern sign his eyes flashed like a wolf's. He ran over to the charred crumbling inn, the door already kicked down off its hinges. He stepped inside. Sniffing the air like some kind of animal, he could pick up the creature's scent. Bek had been here before, and somewhere in the blackened ruins, he was still here.

Markus ignored the sounds of cries and roars from outside. He was here to kill their leader, not to help his friend with what he could already conquer. He stepped over a burnt piece of wood, which crumbled from the wind produced by the passing foot. At the slightest noise Markus would leap around and raise his shotgun in defence. But nothing was there, nothing except the squeaking of rats, and the cry of distant crows outside.

The quiver of wind swept upstairs as Markus reached a flight of stairs. He could see upstairs the remains of a curtain blowing from something which had passed a moment ago. He could recognise anywhere the distinct reeking smell of Bek from the moment it had stepped foot into his house. He knew it was here. He could smell its wake in the cold air.

Markus ran up the stairs hurriedly but silently, stepping carefully for fear of any broken or ancient steps. He was not like Max; he knew the area well and knew exactly what was going on. When he reached the upstairs landing he halted, looking left and right. Anything could jump out at him at any moment. He was as silent as the grave, turning left and continuing onwards. He carried on along the corridor, passing a few more closed doors until he reached another flight of stairs. There were only five steps, which appeared to lead up to another room above. The door lay open by just a crack, the wind blowing through from the other side. The smell of his prey lingered in the breeze. Bek was there, right on the other side.

Slowly and steadily, Markus raised his shotgun at the ready in front of him. He passed stealthily up the stairs, approaching the door. It was inches away from him. He could feel the wind brushing against his face. Breathing in and out for a final time whilst keeping the gun raised in preparation, Markus kicked the door open, to see the horror which lay in the room beyond.

On the other side of the door, at the far back of the crumbling, burnt, large room, was Bek. The thing was larger than life to Markus' eyes. It had been many years since they had last seen each other face to face. Markus looked up and down at the brutal monster as he cautiously and slowly entered the room. Not much of him had changed. More scars gashed into his visible skin. His eyes were much more bloodshot and savage. His skin was darker and covered in grease, sweat, filth and blood. He was still the most monstrous and horrific creature out of the lot. He stared at Markus for a long, uncanny moment, as Markus stood several feet away on the other side. Gun raised, teeth clenched, trigger ready, pulse racing.

"Hello Markus," he greeted him, the voice the same rasping sound which it had been years ago.

"Four years since I've last seen your ugly face." He clenched his hands around the gun tighter, his index finger waiting ready on the trigger.

"Oh very funny," he grinned evilly. "I knew you were going to come crawling back. Ever since you sent two of them to us about a year ago, we all knew that you would come back eventually sooner or later. And so you did. You and, what's the name of that other little scum of yours?" he sneered cruelly.

"You don't need to know his name!" He bit down hard into his lip to prevent himself from letting out all his rage at once. Not just yet.

"The only things which are scum are you. You and your disgusting swarm of freaks!"

"Ah." Bek began to pace back and forward slowly and gently in a small area, looking back and forth from Markus and the black ash floor. "The coward speaks back. Tell me, when we first came into your existence, did you fight back?" He was sarcastic and mocking, twisting and playing on the guard's mind.

"I wasn't a coward!" He raised the gun to its peak and took a further step closer to the monster in the room. He would not miss. "I was only trying to save my family from you finding them. They've been traumatised. Traumatised, are you listening?!" He was almost at the point of bellowing. "I've waited so long for this moment right now so that I can come and take you down like I should have done six years ago!"

Bek stood there for a moment in thought, staring down the barrel of the matt black shotgun. "You've been good to us Markus. You've led people to us. You've managed to keep the media and police off our trail for so long. A cop

296

came to you the other night didn't he? We heard his car approaching. We knew. We always know. Good job we took care of him, before he contacted others and informed them of our existence. You told them of us, and our plans with the humans which may come to us so weakly. He made the mistake which all the others have always made. He didn't kill you. They never do. This is how we take care of our enemies. He chuckled cruelly. "Out here there's no law Markus. Its only kill or be killed."

These words were like poison to Markus' ears. He couldn't take it anymore. All the horrific suffering which he had endured throughout his entire time serving the revolting cannibals had been a living nightmare from which there had been no escape.

"Violence isn't the answer." He held the gun firmly. "I've killed innocent lives because of you. I've killed humans. Ones I've known, ones I've cared for because I didn't want them to fall to you. One I had to kill just last night. He was young, innocent. I shot him dead to the ground and it was all because of you!" He was straining to say this, tears welling in his eyes and rage constantly growing.

"Your commitment has been appreciated greatly," Bek smiled, revealing a row of twisted, crooked teeth.

Markus responded by walking a step closer to the disgusting creature. "I wasn't doing it for you. If you thought I was sending innocent civilians to their deaths because of you then you couldn't be more wrong. My family were destroyed because of you. Now it is our turn to fight back." He looked around towards the back of the room. There was only one thing which was separating this room from the next. It was a Japanese based design of a thin screen of wood and reeds with rays of light breaking through.

The tall creature smiled sadistically. It stopped on the spot and looked up to face Markus, its whole body facing him.

"Yes. Indeed you have come back. Welcome back to our world Markus. We've haunted you, your family, and fed upon normal passers by. You say you've waited so long for this moment. Come on then. Unleash your anger. Bring it on." He snarled savagely, the animal inside him returning.

Markus stared down at the ground in a last moment of thought, his eyes sinking like sunset. He then looked up and opened his eyes to stare menacingly back at the twisted thing.

"You're right," he sighed. "I've been waiting for this for so long. Like you said... bring it on...!"

Markus fired the shotgun, blasting a round deep into the side of his foe. He then leapt through the air, launching himself off the ground in a burst of sudden uncontrollable rage, and flying towards his surprised enemy. He crashed straight into Bek, smashing his weapon forcefully into his chest. The two of them went flying backwards, breaking through the wooden barrier, splinters flying everywhere, and colliding heavily with the cold floor on the other side.

Bek leapt up, enraged by Markus' quick actions and the wound in his side. He attacked. He stood up fully on his hind feet and pushed Markus off him. Markus rolled over and crawled back, never taking his eyes away from the creature which was standing feet away from him, claws stretched out, nails sharp like knives. Markus stood up. His gun was lying on the floor several feet away from him, well out of arms reach. The two of them stared cruelly at each other for a second, a never ending hatred writhing inside each of them.

Bek ran, sprinting towards Markus, claws reaching out to strike. Markus dodged, ducking underneath the raised hand and slamming himself into Bek's side. Bek coughed as he was thrown back slightly, before striking out again, flailing his hands in all directions, desperate to try and kill the resisting guard. Markus was ducking and diving in response, avoiding the constant claw attacks which were raining down upon him. An arm came crashing down unexpectedly into his side, it was too late to dodge this time. Markus struck out his left arm, slamming into the dirty, rotten arm and holding it back with all his strength. Bek was very strong, the horrors of living in the wild and nature had developed him that way. He was more animal than man nowadays.

Markus didn't know how much longer he could hold on for. The arm pressed down into him, gradually pushing him further and further down to the floor again. Markus knew that if he could not find a way to fight back now then Bek would force him to the ground and seize the advantage.

Markus pushed back as hard as he possibly could. When he had forced Bek's arm back to a certain point he quickly dived out of the way, releasing his grip, and rolled over to leap up and smack Bek in the face. Bek fell back from the force, before lunging again at Markus. Markus dived towards the mutant, wrestling him to the ground and punching him over and over again. Bek lurched both his arms up violently and wrapped them around Markus' neck. He crushed them inwards, choking the guard as Markus attempted to choke him back. They rolled over on the floor surging, both of them at their upmost extremity of strength.

Bek finally took one hand away from his enemy's neck and slashed him across the face. Markus fell back, clutching his face. He wiped a couple of fingers against his left cheek, as he looked down at them, he could see that blood had been drawn. Bek leapt up and jumped on Markus whilst he was distracted, slashing at him over and over again like some kind of rapid machine. Markus was swerving his head back and forth, desperately trying to avoid being hit. Bek raised his claws high, and sent them flying down towards Markus' face. Just at the last moment, Markus dodged, sending the sharp fist of nails crashing through the weak floorboards and becoming stuck rigidly within them. Bek snarled aggressively as he hurriedly tried to remove his trapped hand. Markus saw the opportunity and seized it. He pulled his two feet up and kicked back angrily, sending the ugly monster flying back through the air to hit the wall violently.

Bek smashed into the hard stone wall and fell downwards, ash smearing all over his back as he hit the floor. Markus stood up fully and walked over to the injured Bek lying propped up against the wall. When he reached him, he knelt down beside him, grabbed the scruff of his neck, and stood up to look down over him. Staring savagely into his eyes, he spoke coldly.

"You separated my family from me, you killed innocent people, you forced me to kill innocent people. What kind of monster are you?!" He punched Bek violently in the face as he lunged outwards.

"You said they always fail to kill me, those who come searching after us. No one is going to kill me. Instead, I'm going to end all this, and kill you and all the others along with it. Everything will end today!" He punched the creature hard in the face once more. He then let go of the thing, leaving it slumped up, brutally injured against the wall.

Standing up fully, Markus began to walk over to pick up his shotgun. As he was half way across the room, Bek gritted his teeth and clenched his fists in anger. He suddenly leapt to his feet and roared loudly, deafening every living life form nearby for a split second. Markus jumped around in shock, but it was too late. Bek sprinted towards him and smashed his hard fist into the side of his head. Markus fell to the floor, he felt like he was almost about to be sick for a moment.

As he was lying weakly on all fours, Bek walked around him and picked up his gun. Looking one last time into Markus' eyes, Bek smashed the butt of the gun into the back of his head. Markus hovered there for a second, his eyes swirling into the distance, before falling to the cold black floor, unconscious.

Bek looked down at the silent, unflinching man with cruelty and rage swelling in his eyes like fire. He said three words, darkly down to his prey.

"No one kills me!"

Chapter 35:   Take To the Grave

Sophie slipped her head around the corner of the corridor, nothing was in sight. The rest of the corridor seemed long and dark, endless and sinister. She immediately turned around to face her siblings.

"Ok. The coast is all clear." She was panting slightly as her nerves were starting to show again.

Lauren then addressed the other three, speaking quietly as to not be noticed.

"Alright then. Be as quiet as possible. We'll all go together up to the doorway at the end. Something was bound to have heard the noise so we need to get out of here as soon as possible. Everyone okay?"

The others were all silent, and very afraid. They nodded once in understanding, before Sean poked his head around the corner and began to silently sneak around. Lauren picked Sarah up and looked around every few seconds frequently checking that no one was sneaking up behind them.

When Sean had vanished around the corner Sophie followed in pursuit, looking at Lauren to check whether she was alright. Sophie turned around the bend and began to creep stealthily along the dimly lit cellar corridor.

Lauren could feel blood on her hands. She had killed three living organisms in the day so far. These were sadistic horrific monsters which had killed her father and step-mum, but she was no murderer. She was a simple young woman from Cambridge. She had survived this long. It was only a matter of time before they were trapped in the isolated little village with those things coming for them.

As she turned the bend to follow Sophie and Sean in a group, she could hear the distant roars and shrieks of the creatures outside. She had no idea what they were, but to her ears, they seemed to be growing louder and louder.

Sean had almost reached the end of the corridor; the door grew nearer and nearer as he approached the end. He turned around hurriedly as he reached the door.

"Guys. Are you alright?" he whispered down the dark corridor. Sophie was just coming up behind him, followed by Lauren carrying Sarah in her arms. The two of them nodded back in response, not even mouthing a word.

Sean turned around slowly, looking down along the dim corridor which they had just come from, checking just in case anything was actually coming at them from behind. He then turned to face the doorknob. It shone with a bronze reflection from the light hitting it. He reached out his hand, slowly and gently. He had no idea what was on the other side. As his soft bloodstained skin touched the round spherical shape, he grasped it hard, and turned swiftly. He rapidly turned the knob and swung the door open slowly.

Nothing lay in the area beyond.

He turned around to face the others. "It's okay. The coast is clear."

The others all breathed out in relief. But it was not over yet. They were not out of the building yet. Sean looked back around. The room beyond seemed wider and much vaster than the cellar where they had been held. The edges were piled up with rubbish and clutter. A huge range of random objects and pieces were all thrown wildly into corners, forming a room full of waste objects.

"Wow. Look at all this stuff," gawped Sean, almost gasping in surprise.

"Do they ever use any of this?" said Sophie in response quietly.

"Well, judging by the fact that it's all down here I highly doubt it." He kicked a small car battery into one of the piles. "This is all their waste. When they first took the town this is where they dumped all their junk."

"Sshh!" whispered Sophie. "Not so loud. They're still outside."

Sean looked at her in apology and realisation. He then turned around to face the mindless heaps of rubbish once again.

"Come on guys. We have to keep going," ushered Lauren from behind.

The other two then immediately began to walk on, avoiding and carefully treading through the disordered litter all over the floor.

As they were passing through, Lauren suddenly stopped. Something amongst one of the piles of rubbish had caught her eye.

"Lauren?" said Sarah softly. "What's happening?"

Lauren hesitated, saying nothing for a moment. "Nothing sweetie. Nothing." She never removed her eyes from the thing which she had seen. Finally she looked across at Sophie and Sean, who were standing several feet away, watching her in confusion. "You run along to Sophie. Sophie take care of her for now." She let her younger step sister down, who ran along to where Sophie was standing. She picked her up and hugged her tightly for comfort.

Lauren turned back once more towards what she had seen. Leaning inwards, she looked closer to see if it really was what she thought. To her upmost surprise, it was. Sitting there, amongst the rubble of broken mechanical objects and rusting metal, was a set of explosives. They were covered in dust and dirt, but they were still there, as clear as daylight.

"Lauren come on! We have to go!" Sean pleaded from the other side of the room. He looked up towards the hatch above which allowed light to enter the room. A shadow flickered past for a split second, as something walked past outside. "They're coming!"

"Ok, just... one... second." Lauren reached further, even stepping out onto the pile to try and grab the explosives.

Her foot sunk down into a small pit of rusty nails as she reached out. She was almost there, just a little bit further. She stretched her arm out as far as it could go.

"We won't even need those," said Sophie, covering Sarah's terrified face with her shoulder.

Lauren stretched her fingers out and grabbed the set of explosives, just managing to keep her balance and not falling into the pile and hurting herself. Turning to Sophie, she threw the red box a few inches into the air and caught them again with both hands. "You never know what might happen."

There was a moment of silence, except from the dripping of water from a burst pipe, before Sean finally broke the silence. "Well, I'm getting out of here. I don't know about you but..." His sentence was cut short as he trailed off into murmurs and began to head towards the stairs at the other side of the room.

Lauren and Sophie glanced at each other before heading on in pursuit. They left the room and started their ascent, up the dim cold stairs on the other side, just as another shadow flickered past the small window of dim light in the middle of the ceiling.

Sean ran up the last few stairs to open the door. He was so desperate to escape and find a way out.

"Sean wait! Slow down!" called Lauren from further down. "There might be..."

But it was too late. Sean had reached the top and opened the door, only by just a few inches at a time, but he was still opening it. A gust of wind blew down from outside as the sudden rays of light soared down the stairs into the dark and dingy cellar. They had reached the open air. They were out. Lauren and Sophie ran up the stairs to join him, still holding tightly onto Sarah. The light at the top was blinding at first. Gradually, their eyes adjusted to it, and they could see again.

The door opened up to reveal a cold charred isolated street, not a single living organism lay in sight. The four of them stood there in the frame of the door, looking out and the grim scene.

"This is the town?" asked Sean quietly in surprise and shock.

There was a moment of silence, before Sophie finally broke it. "This is Dilas Village. The same place you said those things burnt down and slaughtered all the towns folk years ago."

Sean looked around, almost puzzled. The wind blew eerily, chilling them now that they were out in the open. It almost seemed like it was screaming, a living organism of its own. The town had a sinister atmosphere along with being haunted by many disturbing things. They were being lured more and more into the place's deadly trap.

Suddenly, Tusk appeared on the other side of the street.

"Quick, everyone down!" Lauren whispered loudly as they saw him. The rest of them all quickly hid around the corner of the doorway entrance. Peering their heads out, they watched as the gruesome creature ran.

He was running in the opposite direction and therefore did not see them. He ran down the road, a huge scythe carried in his hand. He ran towards a huge house right at the end of the road. Approaching the door, he lifted his foot up and kicked the door inwards off its hinges. The tall creature then disappeared into the shadows of the house beyond.

Little did they know that Max was in that very house, fighting for his life against a huge bull sized monster and another soon to be joining it. When Tusk had roared, sounding the alarm, four of the other bloodthirsty creatures had been lured to the source of fresh prey. Tusk had then retreated to another house further down in the village to grab his preferred weapon, a huge deadly scythe. He had used a shotgun when Max had first appeared, but he was also a murderous demon in close combat. And now, this was his turn to use this.

The four civilians poked their heads around the corner, following the mutated monster into the house with their eyes. Sean then slipped around the edge of the building into the chilling fresh air outside, soon followed by Sophie, Lauren and Sarah.

"This doesn't make sense," whispered Sean, turning face the rest of them on the open pavement. "Someone else must be here. That's why they're not all focusing on us. That's why that one ran into the house just now, because they're chasing somebody else." They all began to move across the pavement, sticking close to the wall, edging further and further towards the corner at the end of the deserted street.

Sophie and Lauren both looked at each other in shock. "Max!" they both realised together. Sophie moved swiftly as if about to run over to the old house ahead. Lauren quickly put her hand out to stop her.

"We've got to save him!" she cried desperately.

"No. We can't, not just yet," responded Lauren. "We came into this to save each other rather than cause our deaths. If we go running in there empty handed and join in the fight we're only going to kill ourselves faster. We've got to wait, find a way out of this first, find help!"

"But there is no help!" cried Sophie back at her. "Can't you see?! This place is completely isolated. There's no help coming. We tried calling everyone last night, the police, relatives, friends. This village is so isolated that there's not one chance of getting a signal! You've got those explosives! Now use them. We can't let him die in there!"

Lauren looked up into one of the windows of the mighty house on the other side of the street. She could see shadows moving about. One of a tall thin man moving about, dodging attacks from another huge creature in there with him. She could tell immediately it was Max.

"He'll be fine for now, so long as he keeps fighting. He is strong, and agile. I need to use these for something else,

307

which you'll soon find out." She hesitated, looking down at the ground and wiping away a tear from her eye and speaking quietly in shame and fear. "But I really hope he's okay." She looked up once again at the shadows fighting wildly amongst the darkness. They would save him, when they had the chance. They would save him.

Sean began to walk on in disgust, picking up his pace yet uncertain of how they could save their brother. Sophie tore away from Lauren's grasp, wiping the tears from her eyes, and followed Sean.

All of a sudden, a dark shape flashed around the corner. It stopped dead in the middle of the wide cross roads, feet away from the Barrow group. All four of them suddenly halted in their steps with a jolt of fear. Lauren quickly held her hand over Sarah's mouth to stop her from screaming and squeezed her other hand tightly. The creature slowly turned around, its face gradually coming into view. It was a long, haunting moment of standing there frozen before the thing finally saw them. It faced them evilly in the middle of the street, eyes glaring like burning embers.

It was Syrak, the bloodthirsty savage female of the cannibalistic group. Sophie recognised her in an instant as the one which had ambushed her in the tree and chased her through the forest. Her long hair flowed dirty and grimy. It was like it had never been cut or washed in years. A stench of rotting flesh and decaying life surrounded the creature. Anyone could smell it from a mile away. Syrak stared in murderous wrath at the group of survivors as they stared horrified back.

"Sophie, Sean," whispered Lauren loudly as to grab their attention, still frozen, not a single muscle below her neck moving. "When I say run, run."

The two of them nodded, never taking their eyes away from the thing in front of them.

"Goodbye guys. I love you all, and don't you ever forget that."

"What do you mean?!" Sophie whispered in confusion back.

"Try to survive. Get out of this place and as far away as possible. I love you. I always have." Lauren gently let go of Sarah's hand. She looked up in fright towards her as Lauren whispered "Ssh," very quietly as not to alarm her. No one knew what she meant at all. It was only Lauren who knew what she was going to do. She had almost completely given up hope, but now, she had found what may be the only possible answer for their escape, however it may end.

Syrak sniffed the air, to check that they were actually live prey rather than her eyes playing tricks on her. Lauren drew her hand deep into her pocket and removed the roll of explosives. She began to slowly unravel them, breathing quietly and extremely nervously at the same time.

Suddenly, Syrak roared her loud deafening shriek. It was more of a wail than a roar, a high pitch bellow as a sign of attack.

"Run!" shouted Lauren. At that precise moment, the four of them scattered. Sarah ran into Sophie's arms as she picked her up and fled backwards. Sean turned on his heels and ran far to his right, sprinting immediately for a place to hide. Lauren finished unravelling the explosives just as she shouted for them to flee. She fled backwards, turning around frantically and began to head towards a large group of houses straight ahead of her.

Syrak, unable to decide which one to follow, decided to chase the eldest, the tallest girl who was fleeing directly ahead of her. It was time to feed. Syrak sprung back her legs and gave chase. She pounded along the weak, charred ground like a leopard chasing an antelope. She was fast, livid and hungry. There was no stopping a mutated creature like this. Only the smartest and the fittest survived.

Chapter 36:   The Burning

Zack threw Mauler off him. The huge creature flew from
the front of the young guard and smashed through the
window of a nearby house. The glass shattered into millions
of tiny shards, flying everywhere in all directions. The
monster disappeared into the dark shadows of the room,
and completely vanished from sight. Zack jumped up, his
black armour now covered in red blood, both that of his
own and that of his enemy. He wiped a hand down his
scratched face, wiping the blood and sweat away. Looking
around, he grabbed his pistol which he had dropped during
the fight. He seized it swiftly and looked around, ducking
behind a nearby wall. He was weak and injured, yet still full
of energy and the desire for revenge. He wasn't going to
stop just here.

Mauler ran out of the front door of the house. His eyes
snapped from left to right, ready to kill his victim. Scanning
the area, he saw a young teenage girl run into a house a few
streets away, his sister Syrak chasing rapidly in pursuit. The
woman was carrying a set of explosive devices in her hand.
Mauler snarled viciously. He clenched his fists in anger. He
would not return to fight the pathetic rebel guard. Instead
he had found a new victim, one which was weaker and
appeared more satisfying. Building his strength back up and
picking tiny shards of glass from his skin, the bleeding,
enraged Mauler began to sprint, through the streets and
alleys, across the village itself, towards the already pursued
Lauren.

Zack, hiding around the corner did not see the
bloodthirsty brute race past him. He was clutching a wound
at his side, wiping the blood away with a piece of ragged
cloth. Earlier on, Mauler had stabbed him through the
shoulder with a large shard of broken glass. Zack cringed

310

from the unbearable pain. He looked up, throwing away the cloth to the ground. He would not back down now. He could not back down now. He grabbed his gun from the floor and reloaded it with bullets in a pouch on his belt, never taking his eyes off the surrounding houses. He thought hard about where Markus had disappeared to. He was the one who had motivated him and given him the courage to fight; he was the one who had been driven insane and only wanted to inflict revenge upon the twisted creature which had caused him so much pain over the years. He looked up, and saw something in the distance. Several streets away, through the morning mist and rusting cars, he saw a figure. He raised his gun at first, expecting to see a murderous being come running through the streets towards him. Instead, the dark shape stayed where it was. Zack was surprised. *What is that?* he thought confused. The morning air was bright and his vision was slightly weaker from his injury in the truck. He stared at it for several long seconds, before finally realising what it was, and jumped to his feet in shock. The shadowed figure wasn't one of the creatures. It was a man strapped down to a chair. It was Markus.

Zack began to run, at first starting off as a slow jog but as things became clearer he gradually ran faster and faster. He was sprinting down the street, passing house after house desperate to reach his trapped companion.

Markus' eyes flashed open suddenly. Bright rays of light hit his weak eyes, almost blinding him. After a few seconds, his eyes adjusted to the light, he was able to see again. He did not know how long he had been unconscious for. All he remembered was fighting his arch enemy Bek, and falling down, weak, unable to stand, after a blow to the back of the skull.

He tried to wriggle free, but suddenly noticed in utter terror, that both his arms were tied behind his back, a thick rope held him down. He squeezed his muscles, he tried to

311

rip the bonds apart with his brute strength but it was no use. He was well and truly tied to the old, blackened chair.

He looked around him, as a haze of burnt wood and brickwork filled his vision. It was not long before he realised that he was tied to a chair, and out in the open streets of Dilas Village. The cold wind blew around him, chilling him to the bone. But he could deal with that, he had trained himself to become as hard as steel, a guard, a soldier focused on what he was fighting for. Right now he had to figure out a way out, and fast before the monsters returned. He tried wriggling free once again; squirming and biting down into his lip from the force he was trying to break through the rope with.

Suddenly, a great dark shadow passed over the ground in front of him. Markus looked up in a flash, to see Bek, standing menacingly over him, a large liquid container in one hand.

"You freak! You twisted little freak!" Markus bellowed into his face. "When I get out I'm gonna kill you all!"

Bek merely stared down at the helpless guard and smiled cruelly. "You won't be getting out of there soon Markus, believe me! You won't be getting out of there at all." He tipped the container over and began to pour the warm liquid down over Markus' body. He coughed, choked and spluttered as the liquid cascaded down over him like a shower. Some went into his mouth, he soon spat it out in disgust.

"What is this stuff?!" he cried repulsed.

"Gasoline," the creature responded casually. "You've helped us out for years Markus, so now I think it's time we put you out of your misery." He finished pouring out the gasoline and threw the container far away to the side of the road. Slowly, he pulled out a lighter from his pocket.

"Wait! No! Benjamin don't do this!" Markus pleaded dearly for his life.

312

Bek looked up suddenly, completely freezing for a moment. Maybe Markus had gotten something through. The mentioning of his real name might have brought some sense to him. Markus actually thought that Benjamin had returned.

Bek looked down at the lighter, his eyes passionate and meaningful, as if in deep thought. He then looked back up to face the bound and still struggling guard.

"Goodbye Markus." He smiled grimly, a cruel, evil smile, and dropped the lighter.

There was a moment of total silence. Not a bird sung, not a branch creaked. For a split second which flashed before his eyes, the lighter spun round and round falling through the air, to land in the puddle of spilt gasoline on the floor. In a flash of light and the blink of an eye, Markus burst into flames. The fire soared up, starting a metre away from him and spreading rapidly like lightning, in a split second Markus was completely engulfed in fire. The once dark armoured guard was now a burning body of flickering yellow and orange flames.

He did not feel it at first, but after a long second, Markus' petrified frozen face transformed into screaming agony, as a raging constant pain erupted all over him. The flames hit him in a flash. From the moment that Bek had dropped the lighter from out of his hands, Markus knew there was no hope. He sat in the chair struggling and screaming constantly without rest from the fire which was burning him alive slowly. He cried out, a loud, deafening, blood-curdling scream, out into the cold morning air.

Bek stepped back, staring for a moment at the helpless dying guard.

"You can't stop us," he muttered sinisterly to himself as he watched the man struggle and shake about screaming in the chair. "No one can." He was drunk on power. His rage never ended. His hate would never die away. He turned around and began to head towards the centre of the village, leaving Markus to die alone. Tusk emerged from a house to the side of the road, angered and sweating from the adrenaline rushing through his veins. He stared cruelly at the dying guard, and waited for a moment, before heading on past the edge of the crater.

Suddenly, the unexpected happened. The rope which was tying Markus tightly to the ground burnt away and disintegrated amongst the flames. Markus put the last surviving elements of his strength together, and broke free. He ripped his arms away from the burning pile of wood as the rope vanished. He stood up, fire still engulfing his body. He looked around, the skin around his eyes burning away. A final rage filled them. He was going to complete his revenge before he died. Nothing would stop him.

He turned around, lifting his weak body bravely, putting everything he had left into it. The flaming man turned around, and saw, not too far away, Tusk, standing near the edge of the crater. He may not kill Bek, but he would take one of them down with him. Seeing his target in sight directly ahead of him, Markus lurched forward.

Ashes flaked off behind him as he ran, charging forward, vengeance burning in his eyes as the rest of his body blackened. He was metres away from Tusk; it still hadn't noticed him yet.

Zack came running towards the end of the road. He saw his friend burning, charging towards the savage being far into the distance. Towards him, the repugnant Bek approached slowly. He was not concerned by Zack's appearance. To him, he was just another pathetic victim to be taken care of. Zack didn't care what lay in his way. He had to save his companion, and fast.

Markus charged indestructibly towards Tusk, his skin now as black as ash from head to toe, the fire still covering him entirely. With one final attack, Markus jumped. He lunged through the air, flying powerfully towards Tusk. The mutated human looked around right at the last moment.

314

Turning its head at the sign of noise, its mouth dropped open in utter shock and terror. Markus flew through the air, a burning ball of fire flaring in his wake. He smashed heavily into Tusk and brought the two of them crashing down over the edge of the cliff together.

Zack saw his friend collide violently with the creature and disappear over the edge. His face suddenly collapsed in resentment and sorrow.

"Markus! No!" He screamed at the top of his lungs, the whole village shaking from it. He ran suddenly, charging forwards towards Bek in a mindless assault to avenge his old friend's death. He held his handgun high and fired bullet after bullet at the monstrous leader. Bek was flung backwards slightly, a bullet hitting him hard and suddenly in the left shoulder. He growled, picking himself up and ignoring the pain. He had taught himself to ignore the pain. He was a killing machine. Bek gritted his teeth, bearing with the pain.

He began to charge forwards, feeling the burning inside of him too. He ran faster and faster towards Zack. Zack too came sprinting mindlessly towards his enemy, firing shot after shot in a final desperate attempt to kill Bek. Two more bullets hit Bek hard, one in the same shoulder and the other scraping his side. Zack did not care about aiming anymore. All that he cared for was dying slowly, and as he fired blindly, his soul drifted further and further away from him.

Bek withdrew a large blade from his war torn belt. He held it firmly in his right hand. Another pest to kill, was all that he thought about as he ran chaotically, partly wounded, towards Zack. The two of them were ten feet apart, decreasing rapidly by the second.

Finally, the two of them collided. Bek held his rough sharp blade tight and smashed into Zack, stabbing the blade through his stomach and driving it right through and out the other side. Zack stood there silently for a moment. He coughed and choked, as a trickle of blood came pouring out of his mouth and fell down to the floor. He stared emptily ahead, his eyes gazing into the horizon. He was almost resting against Bek's blade as it stuck right through his armour and himself.

Bek withdrew the blade, quickly slicing it out again, and watching ruthlessly as Zack perished slowly. The young man suddenly fell to the floor, his pulse slowing down more and more. He rolled over onto his back, looking up into the light for the last time as his brain slowly died. He thought of his family, his companions, and all that he had died for. Bek spat onto the floor with disgust at him, before turning around and walking away to find Max. He breathed his last final breath, as on the desolate streets of Dilas Village, Zack Caleb closed his eyes, and whispered his final words to his dead wife. "I'm coming home Tara."

Chapter 37:   Become Like You!

The door burst open, shards of burnt wood and copper flying everywhere. Max ducked rapidly as tiny pieces scraped past his body, some slashing into his skin and leaving large blistering splinters. He cringed, never taking his eyes away from the now shattered door frame. Ox burst into the room. His huge hulking presence covered the shelves of rusty tools with shadow. He towered over Max, slowly advancing more and more into the room.

Max revved up the drill, pressing the button down harder and harder until the swirling blade was now spinning at maximum speed.

Suddenly, Ox ran. He charged towards the young man in what little space there was. When he was barely feet away from him, Max jumped. He leapt into the air, raising the drill in his right hand, and brought it down deep into the creature's large thick skull. He grabbed hold of the thing's thick neck and held onto it tightly as the beast swung around, desperately trying to shake Max off as he attempted to drill the blade deeper and deeper into his head. Max clung like a barnacle to Ox's back, swinging round and round, still never letting go. He stabbed the drill down and down again, aiming for a clear strike. Ox was becoming more and more enraged by the second. He had to shake this pest off his back. If his own prey gained the advantage over him then this would lead to his downfall.

Max clenched his fist tightly around the drill. With one final attack, he stabbed the drill down, through the top of Ox's head, and deep down into his skull. Ox flung Max off himself, he came flying off and landed heavily against the wall. He slumped down slowly and weakly, watching as the enormous creature died.

Ox swayed around for a moment. The drill stuck out of the top of his head, blood pulsating slowly out of it. His eyes rolled around into the back of his skull, before finally, he collapsed to the ground, the whole house rumbling from the wake of it. A shock wave rippled across the burnt stone floor, slapping Max hard in the face from the impact of the dead monster. He breathed out a long, wheezing sigh of relief, covering a wound in his shoulder with his already bloodstained hands. He scrambled up to his feet and looked around. It was not over yet.

Far on the other side of town, Lauren fled into a group of houses. She sprinted through a doorway which opened up into a large courtyard. Empty horse stables and farming storage facilities lay on either side, surrounding her. This was presumably once the small local farm of the village. She twisted around, her eyes passing every door and window in the courtyard until she was staring in horror and exhaustion back at the doorway from which she had came. She gripped the explosives tightly within her hands. It was now that she knew she had to act.

The doorway lay open behind her, the remains of two broken and charred wooden doors swung open slowly, gently creaking in the chill morning wind. Lauren stared out at the doorway. She stood there in the centre of the courtyard, her eyes wide open, her pulse racing like lightning. Immediately she set to work. Laying the explosives down on the ground, she unwound the wire and unravelled it out along the ground in front of her. A long twisting curling wire circled around, connecting a large central button with a large box full of TNT. She clenched the button tightly within her hands. And finally, she made her last prayers for her family's safety, waiting for the end.

Suddenly, from out of the shadows, around the corner, came Syrak. Her long black hair waved around in the wind and with the speed she was running at. Her eyes were red with bloodshot. Her maw was gaping open, revealing a mouth full of sharp twisted teeth and mutated gums. When she ran she screamed a horrific ear splitting wail into the air, alerting all others to their presence as she sprinted towards her prey.

Lauren stood up fully in the centre of the courtyard, completely in the sight of the oncoming monster. Another creature suddenly flashed around the corner. Lauren's face was torn between surprise and content. Another had fallen into her trap. This would make things a lot easier for the others. Mauler too came running savagely towards her, saliva drooling from his mouth in hunger, his black armour glistening with blood.

They were ten metres away from her, getting closer and closer. She could see the hunger and anger burning in their eyes now they were that close. She held her thumb over the button, preparing to make her final act on this world. Syrak screamed monstrously as Mauler roared horrifically, sprinting closer and closer.

Only a few blocks away from the farm courtyard, Sean heard the roars from his hiding place. Slowly, he stood up and began to move out from behind the old grimy wall.

"Sean! No! Don't go out there!" hissed Sophie loudly, holding Sarah back at the same time.

Sean ignored her however, and continued to walk on slowly outside. He peered his head around the wall, looking in the direction from which the roars had come from. They were coming from the same place which Lauren had been running towards. Suddenly, he realised what was going on. He understood what Lauren was going to do.

"Lauren!" he bellowed loudly, a wave of shock passing through him.

Lauren held her finger a centimetre away from the button, ready to press when exactly the right moment came. "You've killed my dad, my step mum, you've terrorised my family, you've wounded all of us, you've mentally scarred my brother!" she howled. The two mutated humans were a metre away from her, about to enter contact. It was now or never. With her last defiant breath, Lauren shouted at the top of her lungs into their faces.

"You won't eat me!" With that, she slammed her finger down onto the large red button.

There was a loud bang and a surge of white and yellow light. A huge explosion erupted skywards around the courtyard. The fuse sparked down the wire and set off the explosives. A wave of energy shot through the air as soon as the explosion went off. It blasted through the entire village, knocking Sean, Sophie, Sarah and Max to their feet as it pulsed across the collection of ruined buildings. When the explosion finally died away, all that was left was the blackened, charred ash remaining. The courtyard was completely burnt to the ground. The stone foundations had crumbled completely. Nothing had survived.

Sean watched the explosion from his view far away, his mouth gaping open in utter terror. Sophie covered Sarah's eyes as she began to cry. All three of them could not believe what had just happened.

Max fell through the window, jumping through the shattered glass frame and falling for a second before landing heavily on the ground below. He was bleeding from head to toe, a night and morning full of injuries that were excruciatingly painful, but he had still survived, he still kept on going bravely.

He turned a bend, walking on. He had heard the explosion from a distance, and feared that it had involved anyone from his family. He had no idea that Lauren had sacrificed herself to save the others. As he moved on around the corner, still holding his wounded left shoulder, he saw something, something in the distance. Something moving closer and closer towards him. It was the same shape as the figure which had been moving slowly towards him through the trees the previous night before he had fallen into the pit. It was another of the twisted humans heading to kill him. *Don't these things ever stop coming!* he groaned to himself inside his head. But this was no ordinary creature. This was Bek, the leader, the master, the unstoppable one which led them all. It came closer and closer towards him, a long blade grasped within its hand and eyes burning black and red.

Max picked up the axe which Tusk had dropped earlier. He began to walk, ready to kill another one to end this horrific trail of events. On the far side of the road ahead, Bek began to speed up too. The two of them continued to walk faster towards each other. It was as if they knew each other and were going to embrace, but they were not. Whether it was fear, anger or impatience, something was drawing these two towards each other. As they approached each other the anxiety of conflict grew. The tension was rising. This would mark the end of it all. Only one would survive.

"Well well well, Max Barrow," said Bek cruelly as they met in the middle of the street. "Finally a pleasure to meet you." He began to circle Max, who stood still, yet never took his eyes away from the creature.

"Who are you?" Max spat out angrily.

"Who am I?" Bek almost chuckled evilly. "They used to call me Benjamin, when I lived among society, before I lost everything. Before I lost it all."

"I don't care what you've lost. Where's my family?!" Max said back, livid with rage, just managing to hold back from attacking.

"Oh your family are fine. They managed to escape earlier on this morning. But I don't care about them any longer. I only wanted you. The one who dared to fight back first. All the others fell, ever since we started preying upon them, they've all fallen one by one. But you, you seem to still be alive. Now I wonder why that is." He was voice was rasping and painful to listen to. His tone was cruel and malicious.

"It's called surviving. You and your scum have taken my dad from me. And now you're going to pay for it all!"

"We're all human Max; survival is a part of nature. Some just have more potential at it than others, let's just say."

Max walked back a few steps and held his axe up defensively. "I don't need to know who you really are or why you're here. I'm going to save my family and kill every last one of you!"

Bek smiled sinisterly. "I'd like to see you try. You've come all this way now I'm going to take you down. Just like your father. So weak and pathe..."

Max couldn't take it anymore. He raised his axe and ran. Sprinting forward, he slammed his axe downwards. Bek dodged swiftly just as the weapon struck out. He moved backwards, lifting his own blade and bringing it down to hit Max's axe. The weapon came flying out of Max's hand and spun around to the ground, spinning away and stopping several metres away from them. Max didn't run to grab it. Instead he rapidly spun around and punched Bek hard in the face with his clenched fist. Bek fell backwards slightly, choking. He then ignored the pain and gritted his teeth in aggression once more. Max took the opportunity.

He ran, running over to the spot, he leant down and grabbed his axe. The two of them ran together once more, meeting in the middle and slamming their blades into one another. There was a loud clanging sound as axe met knife. They withdrew and slashed out again, trying to find different angles to kill each other. The metal clashed again and again, as each opponent deflected the oncoming weapon. Bek kicked, sending Max flying backwards. But still he didn't let go of his axe. Bek's blade sliced against his other arm as he fell backwards. He cringed in pain, clutching his shoulder for a moment. He lifted himself back up again; just as a fearsome Bek came sprinting towards him. Max jumped up and swung his axe around to knock Bek sideways. The blade just caught the edge of a small plate of armour, denting it badly but not wounding him.

Bek fell to the floor suddenly, becoming more and more brutal as the fight went on. Max ran over and raised his axe high to kill. He screamed as he lifted his weapon, rage filling him in the presence of conflict. He slammed his axe downwards, just as Bek rolled over and out of the way, missing his face by inches. The blade smashed into the weak ground. Dust flew up, covering both men for a split second. Max struggled hurriedly, desperate to rip the weapon out of the ground before Bek stabbed him back. Bek leapt to his feet, and almost pierced Max through the side, but Max finally managed to remove his blade from the ground and deflect the dirt and blood covered blade back.

The two blades clashed once more as the duel raged on. This time, Max kicked Bek in the legs, swinging his leg around and slamming into Bek's. He fell backwards, stumbling for a moment before picking himself up again. The mist began to gather around them from the chilling morning air. Bek kicked and punched outwards, throwing his large blade aside and pulling out two large knuckledusters and placing them around his fists. Blades stuck out of them like razor sharp claws. Max dodged and deflected as fist after fist came flying towards him. He dodged them all. Occasionally one would just manage to scrape into his already scratched skin. Suddenly, Bek pulled out a razor from his armour and slashed it out across Max's face. Max fell to the floor in agonizing pain. He choked and groaned in agony. Lifting his battered and bleeding hand to his face, he felt across it, and discovered in sheer horror, that Bek had sliced it across the side of his lower jaw. The razor blade had torn straight through skin and flesh, and now left his teeth exposed amongst the rest of his cut skin. He crawled away. He was becoming weaker and weaker by the moment. He reached for the fallen axe, putting what very little strength he had left into fighting back.

Standing up bravely and very weakly, Max pulled out the pocket knife from his pocket and threw it straight towards the horrific mutant. Bek dodged to the side, but just a little too late. The edge of the small silver blade scraped into his shoulder plate and stuck there rigidly. Bek turned his head around to remove the knife, when suddenly Max came charging back. He swung his axe around and slashed into the large creature, sending him flying and knocking him down to the ground.

Bek lay on the floor struggling and coughing as he lay there injured. A huge streak of blood gashed across his chest through his clothes and armour. He looked up into the sky to see Max suddenly appear overhead, looking down at him menacingly.

"I'm going to end this now!" said Max defiantly.

Bek chuckled disturbingly, even as he lay there weak and bleeding.

"What are laughing about?!" Max spat back defensively.

"You're becoming one of us!" he grinned savagely. "That rage you felt. That sudden burst of anger. That is what made all of us. Hatred can make you do twisted things. It can even drive you insane."

"No!" Max responded bitterly and shocked. "I'll never become like you!"

"Just wait Max. Time will deform you like this!" he coughed and wheezed, dying slowly. "Before long, you will have mutated so much, you won't even feel the pain, or love or sorrow any longer. Only hate will live inside of you!"

"No!" he shouted back, clenching the axe tightly. "I'll never become like you! I have too much to fight for. Too much to care for and treasure to die like a freak! I've done horrible things, I've murdered, over the past night and day. But now it's all going to end. My hate will never triumph over what I really am. It never will!"

"Yes!" Bek barked back, growling like an animal. "You will fall like the rest of us!"

"NO!" he screamed into the mutant's face. "I'M NOT LIKE YOU!" With that, he swung the axe high into the air and brought it crashing down heavily into the man's face.

There was a moment of silence as Max watched in horror as the axe stuck out of the creature. Its eyes flew open wide and its mouth ajar. It lay there unflinching, unmoving, lifeless. He had killed him. He had killed the last of them, the last of the terrifying creatures which had tormented so many, and consumed the lives of so many more. Bek was gone. They were all gone.

Max stood up fully and unclenched his still shaking hands. He breathed out a deep long sigh of relief. He looked up high into the grey misty sky, just as the clouds were clearing, and the beautiful sun began to shine down upon him once more. It was like he had been liberated. He was free.

He pushed his breaking glasses fully back onto his face, looking around for others. On the other side of the street, a door creaked open, but instead of a terrifying beast emerging, it was the friendliest sight he had seen all day. Sean, Sophie and Sarah all emerged from the ruined house opposite him. Their faces were covered with tears, but they were happy. Happy to have escaped alive. Happy to see his face again.

Max, with outstretched arms, welcomed the sight of the others dearly. The three of them ran forward. Through sweat, blood and tears they had triumphed. They had lost so many and fallen down so much, but in the end, they were together once more.

In the middle of the blackened and charred ruins of Dilas Village, the four surviving members of the Barrow family stood there, lost, cold and wounded, but... together.

Chapter 34: The House of Wolves

"And so my story ends," said Max. "I lost my dad, my sister and my step mum to those things. And now I've gone and endangered you now Mr Wilson." He stared across at the shocked and bewildered reporter, who had sat there, listening intently throughout the entire time in the small dark room.

"Wow... Mr Barrow. You story was very, very interesting." He blinked a few times in shock, finding the story fascinating and curious. "Thank you very much for your time." He rubbed the bridge of his nose between his eyes and thought, concentrating for a moment. "I shall look deeper into this. Read into past newspaper articles, look into disappearances around Dilas Forest. I'm sure the police have already looked into this."

Max gritted his teeth. The slashed part of his jaw that revealed his broken teeth moved apart slightly. Mr Wilson cringed whenever that happened. The story had severely scared him. "My sister and brother have gone to live with my mum now, whilst my step sister remains in hospital. I have not heard back from any of the police yet. Not even one," said Max mercilessly. He started to head towards the door, standing up and opening it. A gust of fresh cool air greeted his face soothingly. Max walked out of the door and started heading down the corridor towards the light of the exit at the far end. Mr Wilson followed him hurriedly in pursuit, grabbing his tape recorder and documents in folders and walked quickly up to his leaving subject.

"But... that must mean that there are more of them! In Dilas Forest!" He said quickly walking alongside Max down the corridor.

"I do not know how many there were Mr Wilson," came the serious response. "We were all caged horrifically within the house of wolves. The constant screaming, bleeding and never ending darkness. There was no peace or silence or anything there. Only death and chaos remained. At first I thought that we had defeated all of them. But now when I have had no contact from the police in days I've been beginning to fear that some of them may have survived. I cannot confirm anything. I have given you my story. My family and I are safe and secure under watch."

They reached the door as Max opened it and exited out into the street. The sky was dark above as night had reached them. The bright street lamps shone down from above, illuminating the pavement where they were standing below.

Max turned to Mr Wilson once more. "Now it is just a question of your own safety."

"Safety?" Mr Wilson replied in worry.

"Once they know that you have learnt of them they will come for you Mr Wilson. They know everything, they understand everything. Even if at least one of them survives it will come for you without rest!"

A large black car pulled up outside the building, turning around the corner and stopping immediately in front of them. Max opened the door of the car, stepped inside and closed it shut once again. The window rolled down as Max's deformed face looked out at the confused reporter for the final time. "They will come for you Mr Wilson. They are like locusts, never resting and swarming like wild animals. Run, hide, do whatever you can. They will come for you." With that, the large black car pulled out and drove off around the corner and out of sight.

Mr Wilson stood there under the lamp light for a few moments, watching the car drive away until it was completely out of sight. He looked down to the ground, thinking deeply about what Max Barrow had just said. Had any of them really survived? Were they really coming after him now that he knew of their existence? He stood there thinking about it for a moment.

327

Finally, he shrugged his shoulders and pulled out his car keys from his pocket, beginning to walk. He strolled across the street and over to his car. He had found the story of a lifetime. He was the only reporter to interview the Dilas Forest survivor Max Barrow, and most likely the last. He smiled to himself happily and contently. He unlocked his vehicle, opened the door, sat down and started up the engine, then sighed deeply. The car was on and he was ready to go.

Suddenly, a loud creak thudded from above. Mr Wilson shot his head up rapidly in horror. The thud was soon followed by the eerie, echoing, terrifying sound on the roof of the car, of 'Clunk. Clunk. Clunk!'

THE END

The author and publisher would like to thank the
following people for pre-ordering this book, and
supporting its publication.

Max Bottomley
Rob Byrne
David Cattermole
Tom Coode
Mike Cook
Jack Fryer
James Gaule
Tracey Hallett
Adina Halpern
Saul Halpern
Phillippa Law
Dalia Matthews
Mark Norman
Bernice Onegi
Anthony Radjenovic
Catherine Radjenovic
Garry Rigden
Laurence Routledge
Virginia Routledge
Amy Rubin
Jennifer Rubin
Carol Silver
Edward Smyth
Nick Waite
Clare Williams
Emerald Young

For teenage readers, from
www.hirstpublishing.com

All Aliens Like Burgers
By Ruth Wheeler

Young, polite and intelligent Tom Bowler has barely ever ventured out of the small English town where he grew up. So when he applies for a job in a fast food restaurant at a "local" service station during his gap year he is rather surprised to discover that the vacancy is in fact based on Truxxe, a planetoid stationed between local galaxies Triangulum and Andromeda. Hes surprised further still to find himself becoming friends with a purple alien and that he has strange feelings for his android supervisor, Miss Lola. Tom soon discovers that Truxxe has many hidden secrets - just what makes it so special? And why is its terrain so rich and varied that it can be used for fuelling such a diverse variety of intergalactic spacecraft? What are the Glorbian space pirate brothers Schlomm and Hannond plotting? And just what is it that they put in those burgers?

For teenage readers, from
www.hirstpublishing.com

**One Night Under Castle Moor
By Mark Leyland**

A spooky adventure for 12-14 year-old readers

The Martens have to be the coolest craziest bunch of kids ever. Steve
is new in town, the friends he's made here are all Martens and he's
desperate to join. But first they've set him a test, to spend the night
in a kind of stone cellar up on the moors - and he's not that wild
about tight places. Luckily hard-girl Sophie volunteers to keep him
company, but they find out too late about the Curse of Doom Castle.
The story is that a knight was once left to starve to death in that
cellar and he's supposed to return every year, at midnight on the
day he died, to take revenge on anyone he finds there. And guess
what day it is!

Another fast-moving scare from the award-winning author of Slate
Mountain.

**Georgie Jones...
and you thought your family was weird!
By Nicky Gregory**

An exciting adventure for 10-13 year-olds

The last thing that Georgie Jones wanted was to have to spend her Christmas Day with Dan Parsons - unknown entity from school. However, when Dan gets sucked into a 'loophole' transporting him to the land of Molitovia, Georgie is quick to follow! How could she possibly have known that her arrival in this strange land was far from coincidence? In fact, if what they said was true, it was not only her birthright to be here - it was her destiny! But should she really believe that she was one of them? They all seemed to have their own reasons for wanting her there and the only person Georgie had to help her try and make sense of it all was Dan, who was not exactly taking the situation very seriously! Georgie had a lot to learn - and most of it about her own family!

From our 'Fresh Talent' range, for teenage readers, from www.hirstpublishing.com

Silk Rain
By Lucy Wood

A tantalising tale of revenge, love, deceit and murder, Silk Rain will have you hooked from the first page. When Eve Sileos life is turned upside down, she puts her faith in the only person she has left; Vaile Chevalier, a charming vampire. The problem is that Eve only met her vampire companion on the night her life was changed forever, so it will take time to get to know him and unravel his vampyrrhic secrets. Will she like what she finds? Can a werewolf and a vampire ever fall in love? While Eve is still getting to know Vaile and trying to piece her life together a handsome man comes into her life and he, like her, is a Werewolf. The two instantly take to each other, but will this be just the simple eternal love triangle? More evil is at work than anybody had ever imagined, and Eve is caught in a struggle of demonic forces threatening her and those she loves.

Would you like to publish your book? www.hirstpublishing.com

At one thirty-three in the afternoon, on the second Wednesday in May, something happened which was to change Robert Handle's life forever. At the time, he did not realise it would be a change for the better. Rob is man who has reached his forties without achieving anything at all. To his mother's dismay, he has dug himself into a rut so deep it will take more than a shovel to dig him out. It will take someone...or something, very special. Paddytum is the funny, poignant and heart-warming story of one man and his bear.

Also from www.hirstpublishing.com

Vanitas
By Matthew Waterhouse

When you wish upon a star...?

Your dreams come true...? They did, at any rate, for Florinda
Quenby, though not in the way she had planned. When she flew
out to Hollywood to become a movie star, she could not imagine
the terrible struggles ahead of her, from riches back to rags, or
that fame and wealth would finally come from an entirely different
quarter, her fantastical soup factory in Harlem modelled on the
Taj Mahal... Once she was famous, she became one of New
York's grandest hostesses and one of America's most beloved
celebrities. Her parties for the Christmas season in her huge, gold-
lined apartment overlooking Central park were an unmissable part
of Manhattan's social calendar. Those parties grew wilder and
wilder every year, until finally she decided to throw one last party,
designed to top all the others... This is a tale of ambition and
wealth and fame and vanity. This is Florinda's incredible story.

Also from www.hirstpublishing.com

Back to Nature
By Sam Bossino and Nigel Terry

Neil is bored. His two best friends are a broken hearted workaholic
and a man who would rather Hoover than have a night on the town.
Neil has a wife, two kids and a never decreasing mortgage but what
he really wants is a holiday. A chance to get right away from it all, to
bring Steve out of his depression and Adam out of his marigolds.

It's his belief that they have all been emasculated and what they need
is a week in the wild, camping and cooking with their closest friends.
A week of beers, bugs and yes, ok, the occasional conversation about
boobs. That's all it will take, just one week away from work, from
women, from whining children and that one little problem Neil hasn't
been able to tell anyone else about.

Now all he has to do is convince the other two. But Neil isn't going
to take no for an answer, not this time, because Neil needs this
holiday more than either of them. He knows that the only thing that's
going to bring them all back to life is a real boys-own adventure and
thats exactly what he's going to give them - because whether they
admit it or not, everyone has a reason to want to get Back To Nature.